WORTHLESS: DIVIDED KINGDOM BOOK 1

Caught between debt and desire, she battles to reclaim her freedom.

Grace Williams

Amazon

Copyright © 2024 Grace Williams

All rights reserved

The characters and events portrayed in this book are fictitious. Any similarity to real persons, living or dead, is coincidental and not intended by the author.

No part of this book may be reproduced, or stored in a retrieval system, or transmitted in any form or by any means, electronic, mechanical, photocopying, recording, or otherwise, without express written permission of the publisher.

Cover design by: M Waqas Fiverr

FOREWORD

To all my readers:
For those who cherish the joy of escaping into a story, thank you for joining Elodie on this journey. Sit back, relax, and enjoy the adventure!

Cimmerian Mountain Range
Mount Karayan
Mountain Pass
War Zone
Dark Forest
The Void
Northfield
Newgate City
Wolf Creek
West Road
Silver Marshes
Jade Valley
Port
Cliffs End
South Sea
Calithiel
Dragon Isle

PROLOGUE

Screams permeate the air. The smell of burning flesh, wood, and buildings infuses my senses. I can taste the acrid smoke flooding every space, causing my mouth to dry and throat to constrict, forcing a violent cough to rack through my lungs.

Thunder sounds in the background, and the sounds of growls, snarls, and roaring animals roam the street. Alarms and sirens follow the destruction. I shout with a dry, scratchy throat, but my voice is weak, thread-like. Tears blur my vision, my hands grasping ahead unable to find any purchase.

My room? Is this my room? Stumbling over debris, the heat around me intensifies. I know I need to get to safety. Griff. I need Griff. Falling into what I believe to be a bed, I frantically search for my teddy. I want my mum, crying harder I try to call for help, "Mum? Mum please!" Tears burn hot dirty tracks down my face.

Jumping as agonising male screams and fighting can be heard downstairs, then the sound cuts off abruptly. Rounding the corner, a rancid smell fills my nostrils, making me gag and choke, the sound of an animal slurping and sucking a sloppy meal makes me pause. Vomit rose into my mouth. Peering through the thick smoke- black hair long and matted with liquid - a strong hand with a sword - Dad's sword that he keeps on display above the mantelpiece? Those delicate hands lift me from the floor, cradling me in her arms, the smell of smoke, blood but underlying vanilla and…cookies? … Mum!

Comfort allows me to breathe deeper, burying my face into the familiar warmth of my mother. "I'm sorry, little one, I'm so, so sorry, tears fall from her eyes leaving tracks in the ash covering her face, we love you, firecracker, please remember you are loved." Excruciating pain erupts in my chest, red hot fire burns a path deep in my heart- it stutters, beating out of rhythm. I can't draw breath, my eyes widen in surprise, my mother's face contorted with effort, skin glowing with a bright light as tears run down her face mixing with blood.

Darkness, pain, quiet. I gasp as the recurring nightmare of the night I lost both my parents in the rebel invasion pulls me from a restless sleep, as a 15-year-old orphan, I'm expected to comfort myself, there is no one here to offer up pleasantries, soothing cuddles or words.

Tiptoeing through the cold, dark dormitory, I head to the water table, pouring a glass of water and drinking deeply. Wiping the sweat from my damp brow, the cool night sends chills across my arms.

I have lived here amongst other children for three years, working and training daily. Although I'm not sure what we are training for, this is no mainstream school. We rise early for conditioning and weapons training and then we have languages (we are taught several, therefore I'm fluent in at least three different tongues!), dance, etiquette - to include diplomacy; race and skills and the usual accounting and finances, a strange mix for an orphan!

Looking around the quiet dorm I share with five other girls my age, the bland room shows little of our personalities, not that we have our own money or are given anything to call our own. I pad back to the narrow cot with its scratchy cool blanket in an attempt to grab a few more hours of sleep, the recurring nightmare visits most nights, meaning I have grown accustomed to functioning on little sleep.

"Hey, pisttttt Ellie, you awake?" Lucca calls from the corridor, his room is close to mine, so I often wake him.

Silently I run to the door, slipping out into the cool night, smiling at the one friend I seem to have kept in this place. "Hey Lucca"

"The dream again?" He cocks his head not offering a hug or making a big deal out of the nightmare at my request, he knows me well!

"I'm fine," I say, crossing my arms, uncomfortable with his attention.

"Wanna see if we can steal some honey for our porridge tomorrow?" He wiggles his eyebrows in mischief. Before I can agree, he grabs my arm, pulling me along the hall to the darkened stairwell, holding a finger to his lips, a plea for silence. Not that I need to be told, the punishment for sneaking around at this hour would be the lockup (they need us unmarked, so at least physical "punishments" are out.... but psychological punishments are not).

Entering the kitchen, Lucca draws out an unlocking kit (another handy skill we are taught) and starts work on picking the locks of one cupboard.

"Shit... ouch," sucking his finger into his mouth with a few choice curses. "I can never get the hang of this," he frowns, handing the little tools back to me.

Kneeling, I make short work of the lock with a smug smile. "Easy when you know how!"

"Yeah, yeah, that's why you will not be forced into the type of work yours truly will," indicating himself with a grimace.

"What do you mean? I thought we could request a job at the same place, maybe waiting staff? Or the bar?"

"Ellie, come on, open your eyes, love! Surely you have seen Electric Eden and the older ones over 18?"

A sick dread flutters in my gut, I do know, but I choose to live in a blissful bubble where I will never have to give my body to anyone, especially paying customers.

Reaching into the cupboard, I pull out a pack of biscuits.

"Here, take some and put them back. If we take the pack, we will be found out, so it's best to take a little." I shrug with a small smile. "You keep your strength up."

Lucca does so without argument. Nice food is in short supply in this place, and gods, he needs it more than I do. At 16, he is growing fast, along with the intense training sessions he has to undertake, so we are all aesthetically pleasing to the eye.

"Come on, we better head back," he says, kissing my forehead like a brother to his kid sister. He pulls me to my feet, and we head back to start another day like any other.

CHAPTER 1

6 YEARS LATER
Elodie

Fate is a devious bitch, a cow bag who likes to create chaos with us mere life forms for her entertainment!

Only, I'm not laughing. I get the distinct impression I'm not one of her favourite toys, or maybe I am, and that's why my life has never run smoothly.

In the 21 years I have lived in this god-forsaken realm, I can't remember a time when I felt truly happy or had free will to do as I please! Ha! Choice is a luxury long forgotten in this place. I work and keep my worthless head down. Those who rock the boat end up in much worse conditions than me.

A feathered brown head nudges my hand, ending my morbid reflection. Green cat-like eyes peer up at me!

"Pumpkin.. hey, cutie," I say, smooching kisses and ruffling his feathers, narrowly missing the snapping razor-sharp beak at his protests.

Pumpkin is a half hawk... half... God knows. Beast, with a large hawk-like brown and white head, with a large, hooked beak, and body like a wolf? No! A large cat? Or maybe those paws are some other four-legged predator?

He needs to grow into himself. He is more like a gangly puppy. Then his tails.... plural, as in two big bushy fox-like tails.

He comes and goes as he pleases, often popping out of nowhere when I least expect him, but always when I seem to need him. Warmth spreads through my chest as I look at my feathered friend. Running my fingers through his soft feathers, down into the fur at the nape of his neck, a deep purr rumbling in his chest.

We found each other a year back when I was hiding from a particularly insistent, hungry, and hunting vamp who forgot I was not on the menu. Pumpkin, the little lifesaver, took a liking to said vamp's eyes, which gave me the opportunity to end the vamp with a crystal stake to the chest- so naturally, I gave shelter and food to the little bundle of fluff.

The rest, as they say, is history. We are like a dynamic duo or peanut butter and jelly—completely different but perfect together.

Little did I know that tiny fluff ball, which was half dead in the back of a piss-smelling alley, would grow and keep growing.

"Starlight... Starlight, for fuck's sake... Elodie, if you don't get your ass ready and on stage in one minute, I swear..." A deep growl follows his words as he pauses running a hand down his face in frustration, standing behind me.

"You'll what? Make my life hell?!" I look up at the towering tank of a male, Hank, in the mirror I'm sitting in front of.

He sighs. "Just get ready, Elodie and the bloody bird goes, or he's my lunch."

"Oh Hank, no, please," I mock gasp, bringing my hand dramatically to my chest!

The eye roll directed my way would win awards. I drop my hand to pick up my dark purple lipstick, slowly running it over my plump lips, keeping my gaze soft and full of sex as I stare at the man behind me. I know how I look. It's the only reason I'm on stage and not on the lower levels. I bring in and entertain the punters in a different way.

My eyes skim down his huge chest, catching a glimpse of black swirling tattoos decorating his neck. His arms are crossed, barely contained by his crisp white short-sleeved shirt. My breath hitches. Hank is breathtakingly handsome, and his presence always makes my heart do little backflips.

My eyes flick back up to meet his heated stare and my lips kick up into a knowing smirk. Entrapped in my gaze, his tongue licking along his lower lip.

"Like what you see, Hank?" I purr seductively.

Clearing his throat, his eyes flashing dangerously. With a slight shake of his head, one hand running over his head massaging his neck, a movement he always makes when we have our little moments like these.

"You will be the death of me. Elodie," he says, running his hand over his hair, which has been pulled back into a dirty blonde top knot. "Now get ready and on stage." He spins on his heels and storms away to his next charge.

"What, no, please?" I chuckle at his retreating back.

"Two minutes," he barks from across the room, not pausing in his stride.

Hank and I have a strange work relationship. He's well

over six feet and built like a warrior. Dark tattoos span his left arm and up his neck, and scripture coats his left pec. And yes, we shared a steamy kiss pressed up hard against the wall many moons ago, but he now has this professional. *"I don't sleep with Trixie's merchandise,"* rule, so now we just share heated, flustered moments.

Standing, I flick my dark, blue-tinged hair that descends down my back, over my shoulders and stare at my reflection. Seeing not Elodie but "STARLIGHT," my stage name, given to me by Hank.

Probably due to my pale, almost pearlescent skin that glitters slightly under the light. Obviously, from my fae fairy descent, or who knows? I'm an orphan and know little of my heritage. The few memories I have of my parents are hazy and fraught with trauma.

A black and blue leather basque with matching French knickers cling to my body- my income - my survival.

In the suburbs of Newgate City, if you have little funds or choice, or you are an orphan (like me) of the war, you have few choices;
- Learn to fight - army
- Learn to serve - noble or royal servant
- Learn to be on your back or knees.

Fuck, anyway, someone is willing to pay for it! I, on the other hand, can pretty much carry out all three of those choices rolled into one - you see, orphans can be bought, sorry, adopted as long as they are cared for, and by cared for I mean given the basics in life and forced into any role their owner (sorry carer) deems fit. I was kept, fed and watered, and even given an education, then given a "different" type of education, all of which cost money - that money I have to work off, and have been working off said debt for the last five years as a dancer and waitress.

My keeper, Beatrix, or Trixie, as she is affectionately known, puts me to work on the stage to entice clients, and then it's the bar or waitressing in the VIP section.

I seduce, dance, escort and listen, gaining information. That is my role within her establishment. No one ever suspects the strange little orphan fae with little to no magic, and information is a huge currency in this world.

I steady my turmoil. Angry me is not a good look on stage, especially if I threaten the punters. I lace up my patent black leather thigh-high boots and head towards the first of my twenty-minute stints, performing for my supper. I descend into the pits of my mind, switching off all emotions to separate my work from the real me.

CHAPTER 2

Elodie

After performing and then working the room serving drinks for several hours, my feet were seriously killing me. The sweat stuck to my skin starting to cool, leaving my skin clammy as I walked towards the heavy black velvet curtained area at the back of the darkened club floor. The section roped off for staff and some VIP customers.

Music still pounds from the speakers, and as the lights dim, our top dancer takes to the stage—Vanessa, a stunning wolf shifter with long black and silver hair and striking mixed blue and green eyes. She was Trixie's profit maker and prized possession reaching the perfect height and curves in all the right places.

I slipped between the curtains, nodding to Dane, the wolf shifter guard on the door,

"Elodie, hey Ellie, over here," a bouncing, waving Lucca calls. His full-on grin lights up his face, laughing as we do a little dance-off towards each other. The dark bronze male dances rumba style towards me, stripped to the waist, wearing his signature leather pants and biker boots, abs leading into a sharp V, disappearing under his waistline.

He threw his strong arms around me in a bear hug, lifted me from my feet, spun me around, and caused genuine laughter to spill from my lips.

"Put me down, you loon!" I giggle, kissing him on the cheek and playfully swatting his chest.

"Drink?" he asks, placing me back down carefully, and indicating the bar.

"Gods ...yes, I'm dead on my feet," I say, flopping down into the booth with him and a few others already sitting drinking cocktails.

The atmosphere is starting to buzz with laughter and excited chatter. Now is the time we get the chance to unwind and forget the night. Some people's nights aren't just dancing and avoiding pushy customers and roaming hands. Some of Trixie's purchases are here to deliver any sort of pleasure, and nothing is off the menu in this establishment ... for the right price.

Tosca and Zara, two gorgeous elf dancers also owned by Trixie, are draped across one another and will need to move to another room pretty soon.

Relationships are strongly advised against or forbidden for most of us, so a quick fuck and heavy petting is all we can get away with when the need takes us. That is if you can be bothered after a night full of sex for sale.

"One spicy nipple and a long gnome for little Miss Sparkle."

Lucca smiles as he hands me the strongest cocktail and shot in the whole bloody realm, with a flourished bow and pouted air kiss!

"Am I playing catch up?" I question as I down the spicy nipple and grimace at the bitter burn of liquid sliding down, hitting my empty stomach, which I will regret come morning, I'm sure.

"Yes, you are," he quickly downs his own shot. "You know I have spent the night with the troll," he shudders, and we all stop and pray to the gods, "and I must erase the last four hours." He grabs another shot from the tray and downs it quickly. The flamboyance can't fully hide the disgust and pain hidden deep behind the laughter.

I take his hand and kiss his knuckles. "One day, I promise, we will be free."

He nods, bear-hugging me with one arm. Lucca spends at least once a week "entertaining" Patricia, and yes, she is a toweringly tall half-troll and as broad as a bull, but she pays well, and her favourite is poor Lucca.

The drugs he has to take to perform always leave him ill the next day, therefore he will have tomorrow off to rest and recover.

I laugh and sip my drink, knowing these rare and brief nights cost us all in more than one way. Everything we "take" is added to our debt, meaning most never pay back Trixie for her kindness and education and fail to be free... ever.

A few hours later, Lucca and I stumble drunkenly up the stone steps of a large building five minutes down the street from Electrix Eden.

'The dorms,' as they're called. I run a hand down my tired face, the baggy sweatpants and tank top doing little to keep me warm as we take in the gloomy residential space. Most of Trixie's staff, especially those still paying off their debts, live within these grey stone walls.

The building is three stories high, with the ground floor allocated for communal activities, a dining room with two basic meals provided daily, a dance theatre for practice, classrooms, and the physician (Trixie wants us healthy and protected).

My room is on the second floor in the right wing, while Lucca, being male, is in the left wing. Kissing Lucca on the cheek, I say goodnight and head right at the top of the staircase while he heads left.... It's 3 a.m., and breakfast is served between 10:30 and 11:30 a.m., so I have a few hours to get some sleep.

"Oh... babe," Lucca shouts, jogging back along the corridor. I pause and turn to look at him,

"yeah?"

"Hank said you have a meeting with Trixie at 1 p.m. tomorrow at her office. I'm sorry, it totally slipped my mind," Lucca apologises.

"Shit," I mutter as I open my door, why would she want to see me? Worry knits in my stomach, and I'm regretting drinking the night away with my friend.

CHAPTER 3

Elodie

It's early afternoon, and I sit on a vintage green leather sofa outside Trixie's office on the upper levels at Electric Eden, hands sweaty. My mind grasps at different reasons for me to be sitting here: Is this the time I'm forced to change my role? Is my dancing no longer attractive enough to keep me on my feet?

Becoming increasingly jittery, I stare at the broody, angry man sharing the room with me. Hank stands with his back pushed against the open door of the waiting area, his arms folded across his chest, and his jaw clenched.

"You are making me nervous, Hank," I snap as I look over to his rigid posture.

His eyes flick to me, and dark fury burns in them, jaw ticking as he rolls his lips as if stopping himself from responding.

The office door opens, stealing my attention and a man in a black and gold over-the-top damask three-piece suit strides out, pausing. His face brightens, and his eyes roam over me, a predatory leer glaring too long over my chest. A trickle of fear seeps into my skin. Something about this man makes me want to turn tail and run as far away as possible. I sense Hank shifting, readying for action, an enraged sneer fixing on the gentleman before me, which only makes the knot of worry in my gut churn more.

His shark-like smile sets my heart rate soaring. A warning growl resounds around the small waiting area, and the man sends a brief unaffected look Hank's way.

"Perfect," he states as he nods to Hank, then leaves at a brisk pace.

Before I can fathom what the hell is going on, I'm summoned.

"Elodie," a voice purrs, "please come in."

Beatrix Rossi is wealth personified. She is kitted out in designer clothes and is immaculate. There was a time when I envied this woman and even wanted to be her protege until I understood all that she stood for and the lives of the people she controls. Now I feel nothing but contempt and anger toward the woman who controls my worthless life.

She is sitting behind a large desk made from an old oak tree, polished and varnished.

"Darling, please sit. I have some very exciting news for you," she beams at me.

I sit but know better than to interrupt, clutching my hands together in my lap, palms sweaty. My breathing is slightly shallow as the tension builds. We are alone in the room, and the sounds of employees setting up for tonight are the only noise.

"So," she starts, "I suppose you saw the fine gentleman that just left, yes?" she pauses, and I nod. Her lips are pulled wide in a fake saccharine smile, and the twinkle in her eyes betrays her obvious excitement. Experience states she has some sort of lucrative deal lined up.

Dread begins to pool in my stomach. I recall the feel of the man's eyes raking over my body. I swallow the rising nausea, keeping my face blank of the churning emotions, trying not to jump to conclusions.

"Well, he requires a special kind of talent," she continues.

My face falls, and my heart begins to pound. I knew I was on borrowed time before I was forced into whoring. I'm no virgin, but so far, sex has been my own choice, not that of a paying customer.

Bursting into laughter, Trixie dabs at her eyes and sips at her vodka martini while she regains her composure.

"You should see your face. It is not what you think," Trixie ploughs on, finding my inner turmoil amusing.

"I need a girl that can walk into the King's palace and fade into the background and do what you do," waving a manicured hand with talon-like false nails.

I frown, not fully understanding.

"A girl that is pretty and can go under the radar... who is not powerful magically." She stands and begins to pace back and forth behind her desk, pinching her chin in thought. "But a charmer, a seductress, someone the King will like but not suspect or pay a lot of attention to, in the way of a threat, that is. Someone who will be able to entertain and work as a serving girl and listen! Then, of course, report."

She stops, and her shrewd, sharp eyes lock onto mine. She raises one perfectly manicured eyebrow at me, seeing my confusion and unease. A flicker of irritation rolls at her tight lips.

"Do you understand, girl?" she demands in a bark, all evidence of that smile gone, nothing but the harsh businesswoman left with it.

"Do you want me to sleep with that man?" My brain is not following Trixie's words, and I am too panicked at the thought of that lecherous man.

"What? No." She stops in front of me with a scowl, "Did you listen girl?"

"So, you want me to spy? On the King?" I stammer.

"Oh, so crass," she huffs. "Gather information–"

"The same king," I continue cutting her off. "That has had people executed for stroking his prized unicorn stallion or for gaining too much magic? Or fucking breathing in his direction... he killed the old king." My voice rises, all these stories are rumours but rumours come from somewhere, don't they?

Trixie smiles, amused at my rant, and walks over to her computer. She types for a few minutes, leaving panic riding my senses, then turns the screen to face me. Her head inclined towards the screen with a smug, satisfied smirk, she waits.

"Do you know what this is, Elodie?"

I look at the spreadsheet in front of me. It's full of columns and figures—large figures, transactions, purchases, earnings—the smallest amounts.

I have been educated in finance, so I recognise 'the books' for what it is - 127 Miss Whitlock heading the title.

"This is the money it has cost me," Trixie points a red-tipped index finger at several columns on the screen and then to herself. "To educate, clothe, feed, and generally care for you," she points her finger at me, "This figure here is what you have so far earned and paid back with your work at the club, and this, my dear, is what you still owe."

My eyes widen as I take in the sum she has indicated, and I quickly do the maths. It will take me at least a decade to pay her back! Ten fucking years at my current rates of pay, and that's if I don't need any extras like medical support (that costs extra and is deducted) or buy something I need, I'm truly at her mercy.

The flush of utter worthlessness surrounds me. No one is looking out for me. If I died, I may have a few people saying farewell, but I would not be missed! A smug smile graces her red lips.

"The work you do currently is not highly profitable, unless you are willing to specialise in other areas?" she asked, raising a questioning eyebrow, that smug smile back on her harsh face.

"However, Lord Hamlington is willing to pay a very fair fee for the right candidate... in fact," she pauses for effect, "it would double your current wage and," she draws out the word, "as an incentive, any useful information will receive a bonus," she smiles, knowing this is not really a choice. "You could be out of here in a few years, standing on your own two feet, if you play this right, young lady."

She knows the draw of freedom and escape. A flicker of hope ignited after years of dreaming of my future when I was a teenager which had stopped after a year or two working at Eden. Five years... shit, five years! I could do anything, have anything, but a burning unease makes itself present.

"Do I have to sleep with anyone?" I question again, the line I vowed not to cross becoming blurry in the hopes of getting my own life back in just five years. Flutters of hope take flight. No, I squash that hope like a bug under my foot, I learnt that trick many years ago. She laughs at my expression.

"Only if you need to, darling. You do know it's often the easiest way to gain information!" letting out a raucous laugh at my disgusted expression. Not in my life! I'm not fucking some prick just to get a few years shaved off my debt. That line solidifies now I know it's not a requisite.

"Look," she starts, "take tonight to think about the offer. At the end of your shift, pack your bag and meet me here, but keep your mouth shut. This is not to be shared." She snarls the last bit, "I don't need to remind you of our king's brutality... Go. You are dismissed. I have work to do."

Standing on my legs like a deer on ice, I leave her office.

"Fuck," I exhale, a small sense of relief soothing over my shoulders. Hank looks even angrier, blocking my exit with his broad frame.

"Say no," he growls, outrage boring into my soul.

"Pardon?"

Hank always has my back, never showing many emotions, and certainly not this level of fury. Storming towards me, closing the space between us, he bends so his face is inches from mine. His fury is palpable, and I raise my hands to place them on his chest to try and give me some resemblance of control. My breath catches in fear of his dominance.

"I said.. tell her fucking no." He pushes the words out in a harsh, low bark.

"Hank? I could be out of here in five years, maybe less.... I could actually have a normal future," I stress, pleading with him to see reason. Unlike me, he chose this employment and can walk away at the drop of a hat. He grabs me by the arm and roughly drags me from the waiting area and down the corridor. I stumble to keep up.

"Hey Hank, what the actual fuck? You're hurting me!" I try to pull out of his grip, but his fury has me locked down tight. Opening a door to what looks like a storage cupboard, he throws me in, slamming the door behind us. He places one hand on the closed door with his back to me, panting hard, fists clenched, banging the door in frustration, making me jump in fear and the thick wooden door splinter.

"The palace is a viper's nest, Starlight ... you would be caught up in all that shit," he sighs heavily. "And what of Maddison? She loves you like a sister. Would you leave her behind on her own? The kid has no one." The hurt of his words makes me pause, thinking of the young girl who follows me around like a big sister, guilty of my own selfishness, so used to being alone and having no one to consider, no family. That is until Hank, Lucca then Maddie came along. But if I can get out, I can help with her debt, too, and hopefully get Maddie out sooner.

A new hope surges through me. I can endure anything to help the sweet, brave young girl who has yet to finish her education and begin work.

"It's what I was trained to do! That's why I have managed to keep off my back, Hank," I respond, my own anger rising. "As for Maddie, I will see her every other weekend. She has you, too!" Moving cautiously closer, "Look at me, Hank," I plead.

He turns, and deep worry is etched across his face. His eyes look like he has just lost someone, and horror shines from them. I reel at the intensity from him.

"I can't fucking protect you there, Ellie… please," he closes the distance between us and takes my face between his two hands. For a moment, I think he may close the distance between us and kiss me, but he holds himself back.

"Please don't go," the anguish in his voice surprises me, one thumb caressing my cheek.

"Hank, there is no future for me if I have to spend the next ten to fifteen years working here. You have seen what happens when ladies lose their looks in this place. I will NEVER get out. I will be stuck here whoring my wrinkled old pussy out to feed myself and never experience…" I cut myself off. What, love? Family? Adventure? Shit, I don't even know what I would want if I was free. I have never let myself dream that far into the future. Not many do make it 'out'.

"Please don't do this," he whispers softly. I have never seen this side of Hank, and emotion begins to burn behind my eyes. I can't look at the intensity on his face anymore. Anguish pulls at his brow, and his shoulders slump in defeat.

"Hank, we can never be anything. You know that, right?" I question, shocking me as much as him, but our friendly banter and easy stoic friendship is something I want to keep, and crossing that line could lose the one friendship I can rely on. In a better setting, in different circumstances, we could have become something more.

Hank jerks back like I have slapped him. The cold fury returns, his walls slamming back into place, deep brown eyes darkening.

"If you go into that palace, you will not come back out. That's the fucking choice you are making... you're choosing not to have a life at all," he clenches his fist and grinds his jaw in an attempt to stop himself. With a withering look, he turns, grasping the handle, ready to open the door. With a last look at me over his shoulder, he sighs.

"Looks like this will be goodbye, good luck Elodie... you will fucking need it," and with that, he leaves me standing dumbstruck in the storage room.

CHAPTER 4

Hank

Adrenaline drives through me, my pulse thumping in my ears as I storm back toward the street, people steering clear throwing weary looks my way, sensing the volatile nature of my beast. Why the hell would she choose this? I can't protect her there and she will be eaten alive by the vultures of the palace, she has no experience with those types of people, panic rising at the thought of her hurt or worse, my thoughts whirl, trying to figure a way to protect her without exposing the truth, it's no accident I work for Trixie, and I'm not tied to her in the same way as Elodie is.

I need to put a stop to this and fast. If she takes this opportunity, and I can see the appeal, my hand will be forced. Keeping my distance all these years was always hard. Painfully watching, unable to intervene.

Nerves stab at my gut at the up-and-coming change of finally putting myself out there to her and the world. I pull out my phone and, with a deep breath, dial.

"Hank darling, what's wrong? Please don't tell me there has been another..." she pauses, "incident at Eden?"

"It's about Elodie," I start.

"Don't, Hank," she snaps, all fake smile and banter gone in an instant. "Don't let any more words come out of your mouth."

Beatrix Rossi is a calculated cold-blooded and ruthless businesswoman, her heart dried to a husk long before I crossed her path, Pleading to her better side is all but futile.

"Why her? I question, "You know she will not last five gods-forsaken seconds at the palace. Choose someone else."

"Careful Hank, anyone would think you had a thing for my sexy little spy," she chuckles, a pause as she sips a drink, the ice clinking in the glass. I grip the phone tighter in my hand, frustration and anger coursing through my veins. My heart pounds as I feel my control slipping... fuck Hank, *get control, get fucking control*. I chant to myself, rage pumping and my muscles tensing.

"Anyway, Hank, you are my employee, and she is my property... at least until her education is paid off." Trixie laughs as she knows very few people ever achieve such a goal.

"Choose someone else," I say, taking a deep controlled breath. "Please," I beg, voice quiet, my mind a whirlwind storm.

Beatrix sighs, "Look, she has been personally requested for her skills. I don't have a choice, Hank. Do you think I want to risk an asset like her?" Anger rushes through me again.

"She is not your fucking belonging! A coat you can loan out without a care!" I fume, but silence drifts down the line, Beatrix refusing to rise to my rants, "Will you allow her the choice to stay?"

"No." Blunt, No room for argument. The reply was exactly what I expected:

"When will she go?" I demand.

"Tomorrow, you can't stop this Hank." The line goes dead leaving me standing frozen with panic and failure running deep through my blood leaving me with nothing but pointless guilt and longing to turn back the hands of time, I have failed her.

CHAPTER 5

Elodie

Standing once again in the waiting area of Trixie's office she slowly turns to me, her eyes roaming from my chunky boots, tight black jeans up over my neon orange crop top and high ponytail. Her eyebrows raise.

"That is what you chose to represent yourself?" She waves a manicured hand, and a look of disgust travels up and down my body. "To Lord Hamlington? To The Palace?"

"What?" I frown. "I have limited money and limited possessions." Due to the fact that I don't get paid, I speak in my head, not out loud of course.

She pushes a button on her table. "Bring in the items please Julia, it's a good job I am organised then, isn't it." she smiles at me, not a warm smile but one created by a shark toying with its prey. Hank walks in carrying a large suitcase, which he drops at my feet. He does not look at me but turns and stands by the door back ramrod straight. Trixie grunts in annoyance at the huge shifter. Confusion crosses my face as I look at the case now deposited at my feet. Tilting my head with one cocked eyebrow, looking to Trixie for an explanation.

"I took the liberty of packing a suitable wardrobe and tools you will need while you're at the palace, you will also be given a uniform and all necessities."

"Oh, is this extra to pay off?" I question. The suitcase is huge and I worry about the added debt this will cost me.

"Of course, darling, nothing in this life is free," she laughs as she walks to me, placing her hands on my shoulders, her made-up face mimicking a maternal softness that ultimately she fails at. "Now be careful, do what you have been trained to do, and if you fuck anyone, protect yourself." a shiver of disgust runs through me at the thought. "And Elodie, if you get caught, you don't know me. Do not bring trouble to my door.... or people close to you may find themselves injured in a freak accident!"

My eyes snap up to hers. Is she threatening my friends? I glance back at Hank. No emotion shows on his face, but his eyes darken, and his fingers twitch at his sides, the only indication of his fury.

Out front a car waits, Hank places my suitcase into the trunk with a slam as he approaches me.

"Here, take this." he hands me a sheath with an onyx dagger, the hilt decorated with intricate runes and small semi-precious stones inside. "Keep it on you at all times" his eyes lock with mine. "Promise me," he demands as he thrusts the dagger into my hands, closing his hands around mine and pushing them towards my chest. I stare at our entwined hands and the beautifully crafted, rare as rocking horse shit weapon.

"It's beautiful," I gasp. "It must have cost a fortune, Hank. I can't accept this!"

"It was a gift given to me many years past and served

me well. I want you to have it," he inhales deeply, closing his eyes, but not before I catch the flash of worry in them. "It may well save your life," he leans down, pulling me into his huge arms, his lips pressing against my head as if he is trying to remember every inch of me. Is this truly goodbye?

"Hank, you big softie." I giggle to try and lighten the mood. This feels like more between us than an easy, comfortable friendship, although the hug is a little out of the ordinary. Not that I'm complaining.

The driver comes around the car and opens the door with a pointed look, that's my hint I need to get moving. With a quick kiss on his cheek, I climb into the back seat. The driver shuts my door, and we are off towards the city. Hank's stone gaze follows the car until we are out of sight. A pang of loss aches in my chest.

CHAPTER 6

Elodie

Celestial Palace is huge. The driveway travels for several miles of rolling landscaped meadows. Large oak trees line either side of a smooth road. This is the only large green space within the city. Past the palace boundaries are streets and streets of houses, shops, restaurants and businesses. The hustle and bustle draw my attention, excitement buzzing in my veins. Topiary gardens with intricate swirls, loops and steepled bushes connect extravagant water features that span as far as the eye can see. We travel down vast, colourful parterres separated by central water avenues leading to a beautiful fountain of an imposing kneeling man with curling horns sprouting from his head. I gaze at the detailed craftsmanship in awe as an imposing creamy sandstone building appears over the horizon. A second larger circular fountain sat in front, the sculpture rising from the water depicts a battle scene with a rising golden angel.

The road forks to the left and we drive away from the main entrance of the palace for another quarter mile before we travel around the less ostentatious back entrance, yet these servant quarters are still miles better than the dorms I grew up in! I climb out of the car and grab my suitcase and bags.

The courtyard is beautifully crafted with large arched

windows lining the walls of the building with highly decorated wooden doors, staff rush about their various tasks - the whole place is bustling with an infectious energy and I can't hide the smile pulling at my mouth.

"Don't just stand there gawking, girl," a stern voice snaps me out of my trance. Follow me, we have been expecting you." She is an elderly woman with greying blonde hair pulled back into a tight bun. She is dressed in a formal white shirt, red and gold waistcoat, and pencil skirt. Marching through a door down a dark corridor, her comfortable pumps stride away at a brisk pace, leaving no space for questions.

Grabbing my things, I hurry after her. Everything is huge. I have never seen such grandeur even in these servant quarters every surface is detailed or engraved! An attractive shifter stands before a set of double doors. His short blonde curly hair is neatly styled, and he's in the court's uniform of black trousers, shirt and tailored jacket. He could easily be on the front of billboards throughout the Kingdom advertising sex or something! His face is set into a solemn expression, we pause in front of him, attention solely on Ms Anderson.

"Mr Roberts, take Miss Whitlock to her chambers and show her the ropes." The woman flicks her hand towards the doors, handing me a stack of documents addressed to me.

"Read this before tomorrow. I expect perfection from day one," she says, looking my way with a sneer on her lips. "Be in the kitchen tomorrow morning at six am... do not be late." Irritation mars my expression, but I make the effort to crush the rebel within.

Smiling sweetly, performing a perfect curtsy, I state,

"Certainly, Ms. Anderson."

With her parting instructions, she walks away without a backward glance. I have dealt with people like her all my life. I know how to play the game. It's just finding the will to play it.

"Don't mind her. She just needs a good seeing to." I look to the guard, rolling my eyes at the matron's attitude.

"Takes her frustrations out on anyone who is gorgeous" he looks me up and down with a bright smile. "She is going to make your life hell", he laughs, and it lights up his whole face. Extending his hand, he introduces himself,

"Alfie Roberts, footman and guard for His Majesty King Barrett The Brave, and definitely your next boyfriend." He kisses the back of my hand, giving me a sexy wink.

I smile, my insides fluttering like a teenage girl and my cheeks warming. *Get a hold of yourself, Elodie. Don't fall for the first stranger who smiles at you!* Ugh, it's been too long.

"Here, let me help you with that, and I will show you around." He takes my case and pushes through the double doors using the hand scanner to the left.

"You will have your prints taken tomorrow so you can access the living quarters and areas you will work within. Security is pretty high in this place, and your whereabouts are monitored 'everywhere' except…" He wiggles his eyebrows, "in the dorms, so you have some privacy." He winks and runs his tongue over his lower lip, looking me up and down.

A faint cringe makes me shudder. He's a little full-on but friendly enough. I'm not sure how to react. At the club, I would give a noncommittal backhanded compliment and deflect the attention; here, I'm unsure of myself.

Pulling up my big girl pants, I fall back onto my years of training. Time to turn up the sass.

"Are you flirting with me, Alfie Roberts?" I smile, putting my hand on one hip, kicking it out to emphasise my round ass, "on my first day," I gasp in horror. He laughs, throwing his head back.

"Yes, Miss Whitlock," he cocks his head in question. "First name ravishing, I am," he purrs slowly.

"Elodie! Please, Elodie Whitlock, it's lovely to meet you, Mr Roberts."

"My friends call me Alfie. So call me Alfie, only my mother or that bag Miss Anderson calls me by my full name." He pauses, looking me over. "Anyway, this corridor runs the length of the left wing. It's split into smaller residential areas, each with three to six rooms, all en-suite, and each area has its own communal kitchen and living space to relax in. There is a gym and library at the end downstairs." He points to the far end where crowds of people are hustling about. "This is you: residential C. You will be sharing with three other girls. I'm just over in ressy F." He knocks on the door, and a petite redhead with sharp features answers, smiling straight up at Alfie.

"Hey, what do I owe this pleasure?!"

"Jenny, this is your new roomie Elodie"

Jenny gushes. "Oh, how exciting, come in please I will show you the spare room. Esta is on evening duties, so she will not be back until late, and Sasha is never in!"

Alfie brings my case inside and wraps a huge arm around my waist pulling me to his side.

"I will let you settle in then come and find you later" he kisses my cheek goodbye. "See ya, Jen. Look after my girl." he laughs.

"Ha, Alfie Roberts is laying a claim to the hot new girl!" Jenny smiles, shaking her head.

"Should I be worried there?" I question once he has left the room, as I take in the space of our dorm.

"What? With Alfie, no, he is dreamy, isn't he?" She walks towards a cream-coloured door by passing a living area with two large sofas placed around a coffee table, indicating a boring wood door, "this is you, just place your palm here and push your magical signature through, and no one else can enter." I do as she instructs and open the door.

"I'm making some food if you're hungry. Why don't you get unpacked and meet me in the kitchen," she says with a bright smile as she leaves me to my own devices.

My room is clean and decorated in neutral tones with a bed, desk, wardrobe and en-suite with a shower. I unpack the suitcase Trixie gave me and gasp at the range of clothing, skin-tight jeans, silk shirts, tank tops, short dresses, ball gowns! ...lingerie what the actual fuck?! It's like Trixie packed items for any situation and, of course, my tools, lock picks, my daggers, items I have trained with but never really had to use at Electric Eden.

Peeling a floorboard up under the bed, I place my 'tools' in the hidden compartment, pushing the little magic I have into a basic deterrent spell.

I step out to the kitchen to see Jenny has a pasta dish on the go, which smells amazing. My mouth waters as my stomach makes itself known.

"Wow, you're some cook," I laugh, inhaling the heavenly scent.

"Tsk, this is basic at best. Come on, sit. I'm just dishing up." We sit in silence while I devour her food. "Jeeze, girl, slow down before you choke," Jenny laughs. "It's like you have never eaten before." Her eyes widen as she watches my manners fly out the window.

"I forgot to eat this morning. I was too nervous." I slow down and take a drink of water, giving her my full attention. "What do you do here, Jenny?"

"Oh, I'm mainly serving, so my shifts rota either early mornings or evenings." Esta is the same but is often pulled into evening drinks and entertainment. Sasha is a chambermaid for the higher-ups, so she is always up early." Taking a fork full of pasta, she pauses to chew before pointing it my way. " Do you know what you will be doing?"

"Not sure, I think I'm serving, but I suppose I will find out tomorrow. I have to meet Ms Anderson before six in the kitchen."

A knock sounds at our door, grabbing our attention. Alfie's voice sings songs through, "Where is my girl? Has she settled in yet?" I giggle, rolling my eyes, and jump up to open the door. His bright, smouldering eyes sparkle as he takes me in, pulling me into a hug and kissing me straight on the lips with a peck that lasts a second too long to be friendly. Saundering in, he grabs my fork, shuffling pasta into his mouth. Those lips are dreamy, and the way his body flexes beneath his shirt makes me stare a little too much.

"So I thought I could crash here tonight and make sure you receive the best well-cum. Hopefully, several times." he purrs seductively. I feel a blush creeping into my cheeks and laugh.

"No, I'm not some hussy that will drop to her knees at the first cute guys to cross her path-"

"So you think I'm cute?" he smirks, cutting me off.

Jenny scoffs, "Alfie, everyone thinks you're cute until they realise what a man whore you are."

"Me a man whore?!" He gasps in horror. "Do not listen to this wretch. She is just jealous. I have not ridden her ass into next week, and instead, she has to rely on her own hand.... Which is a poor substitute, I might add."

"Still, thank you for the welcome, Alfie Robert's, but this lady will have to decline your offer. For now," I smirk.

"For now." He nods in agreement, fingers holding his chin in contemplation.

"Then I will leave you to sleep" he stands, kissing my cheek, lingering to whisper into my ear, "Sweet dreams, Miss Whitlock."

Flustered, I stare, trying to calm my hormones… shit day one, and I'm being played like a bloody fiddle. Jenny giggles as she clears the dishes.

"Alfie Robert's always gets what he wants, girl. Be careful. Some of the noble women have their eyes on him too and can make life difficult for us mere servant girls." With a tight smile, I help her clean up and excuse myself for the night.

CHAPTER 7

Elodie

Miss Anderson bombards me with her strict instructions on the morning service, how to act, how not to act blah blah blah. I spent my youth in classes perfecting my manners, so this is nothing new to me. She has eight of us lined up in crisp palace uniforms - my role this morning is to pour the morning coffee. I watch the lords and ladies of the court waiting for a signal that someone wants a top-up... it's boring, and I stifle a yawn. Sleep did not come easily last night, and I'm feeling the full effects now. Sandpaper-drooping eyelids, fuzzy head, it's taking all my effort to keep the serene mask in place. The Lord (Lord Hamlington if I'm correctly informed from the barrage of information in my welcome pack), I saw leaving Trixie's office a few days ago, sits close to another imposing officer to my left. The man is huge with a short military-style haircut decked out in a green camouflage combat uniform. His eyes flick to mine, and he jerks his head - coffee, my cue. Moving slowly to his side I pour with my eyes downcast. I straighten to walk away, but hands grab my waist and ass, holding me in place. I freeze in shock, unsure of how to act in this new setting.

"Now, Captain, this is a nice piece of ass," the lord from Trixie's holds onto me, his grip more of a warning than sexual, and surely to leave a mark. Hank's dagger at my thigh warms against my skin and my fingers twitch with restraint. Biting down on my anger takes some effort. Smiling, I gently try to peel his palms off me.

"Good morning, sir," I say with a nod. Captain Thomas Carter looks my way, assessing, silent, his eyes narrowing, and I drop my eyes, realising my stance. A lifetime of standing your ground showing no weakness has been ingrained in me. Fighting off amorous punters is second nature, but here at the motherfucking palace! Do not square up to the captain of the guards. Shit, Elodie, get the hell out of here... politely.

My mental pep talk does the trick! Giving a small courtesy I return to my place, raucous laughter follows me as Lord Hamlington maliciously smirks in my direction, he has plans for me I just know it, disquiet cement in my gut Hank was right I'm so out of my depth here. I'm a small fish in a huge shark-infested ocean swimming against the current. Breakfast passes with no other incidents and I'm sent to another hall to wait on the ladies of the court. My sole job is to run around after their needs— great! I ponder to spoilt upper fae what could possibly go wrong?!

Four high-fae females sit around a table gossiping in the most luxurious gardens I have ever seen, bright blooming flowers arranged into structured beds around winding paths that are beautifully maintained, the fragrant air stimulating me as I take large deep breaths and relax into my work I stand alongside Esta, a young brunette human servant, I know we share a room, but I'm yet to speak with her, we both allow our minds to wander as we wait to serve.

"You there, girl." A stunning elf clicks her fingers at me. "Grab the tray of treats and the wine. We ladies want to have some fun!"

The statement is an instruction, not a request: no response bar moving to do as she demands is required. Gathering the tray overflowing with tiny, delicate sweet treats, I make my way to the table, listening for anything the Lord may find useful. Yet, I have not been given any instructions as yet.

"You are new. What is your name?" the woman asked with a friendly smile, taking me by surprise with her direct question.

"Erm..." My eyes flick around the room, unsure of the protocol, catching Esta's wide-eyed and worried stare. Instantly, I know this is a trap, and I'm the new target of this woman's games.

"Wow, is that difficult for you to understand?" Laughter follows her mocking. "W H A T I S Y O U R N A M E?" She stresses slowly as if speaking to an imbecile. Holding my temper, I reply with a clear, confident tone, no hint of the fear that is gnawing at my insides.

"Miss Elodie Whitlock," I reply, lowering my head with a curtsy, the picture of elegance and demure.

"Are you a whore?" she questions while taking a small cake and popping it into her mouth. "You have that look about you," she sniggers, as do the other three beautiful women at the table. A moment of shock widens my eyes, but I push the indignant resentment, keeping my face a solemn mask.

"No," I incline my head with a sweet smile. "My body is my own; I simply serve food and drinks." Trying to keep the sneer off my face, I reach for the wine to begin filling their glasses. "Would you like me to have Ms. Anderson arrange someone for your taste?"

"I beg your pardon?" The smile is gone along with the friendly voice, "Do you hear that, ladies this one thinks she can speak with her betters," she snarls, leaning in. "Do you think you are above spreading your legs?" She grabs my wrist hard in a vice-like grip, and in a flash, her teeth sink in, drawing blood filling her mouth. Pain blooms through my wrist as I cry out in shock, my blood welling to the surface.

Grabbing a knife from the table, I twist my body, taking her arm, twisting it behind her back driving her head to the table with my elbow. Blood pours from my wound, soaking into the bright white lining; pulling the knife flush with her creamy, slender neck, I hop onto her back and knees, pressing down hard; she gasps in pain, gritting her teeth in fury. I hear the ladies gasp and begin to scream for the guards… day fucking one and drama, fuck Elodie, you idiot! At Electric Eden, I always had Hank on hand to defend me, keep the clients in line and protect me. Here in the palace, I am on my own, unsure of what is deemed acceptable. However, I am sure biting the staff is not. Lowering my head, whispering into my new problem ear.

"Do not underestimate me, and DO NOT lay your filthy hands on me again." I straighten pulling my uniform down, placing a white napkin over my wrist, throwing the butter knife to the table with a clatter, and walk back to the far wall where Esta is standing wide-eyed in terror and shock. Back ramrod straight and face devoid of emotion I stand, Blood trickling down my fingertips to drip on the floor.

Several guards rush in and stop to assess the apparent danger. The woman's eyes narrow in anger,

"See ladies, the gutter tramp has to resort to violence. I tasted nothing but rot in her blood, not an ounce of power in her" she stands, addressing the guards, "That…" she points an elegant finger at me, "attacked me. Make sure she is escorted to Lord Hamlington and punished accordingly" turning to her shocked friends she smirks "all dogs can be taught. It just takes the right sort of education. I am sure Lord Hamlington can deliver." The smile she sends my way makes my stomach knot, and my neck flushes with anger.

Fear claws up my throat making swallowing hard as my pulse throbs in my neck. One guard grabs me roughly dragging me along without a word, looking up at him I gasp, "Alfie?" I plead, he avoids my eyes, continuing to drag me roughly through the garden and into the corridors of the palace. I rush to keep up with his long strides, a glimmer of hope that all will be okay.

For several long silent minutes, I'm dragged via my upper arm through long busy corridors, eyes snap our way and words are gossiped behind hands. Finally, he shoves me through a small door into a small windowless office with a bland desk and grey sofa to one side. Stumbling away from Alfie I spin, arms windmilling for balance, to face him, shocked at the look of utter rage and disbelief, I pause and straighten.

"What the actual fuck, Elodie, one bloody day, and

you're making enemies with Lady Serena Carter… you know who she is?" I stay quiet, knowing better than to interrupt "She is the King's cousin," he fumes at me, throwing his jacket open with one hand and running his hand through his curly blonde locks; he is packing knives and two guns across his torso. Wow, he did not look so lethal last night! Distracted but not forgetting what that bitch did to me.

"She fucking bit me!" I shout, throwing my wrist under his nose. He grabs my wrist, looking at the puncture wounds from her elongated canines.

"So? If Lady Carter wants you to perform a chicken dance while only wearing titty tassels and a thong, then you bloody well do as you're told… you DON'T pull a knife to her throat!" he exhales heavily, "I mean, who even does that?"

Throwing my wrist back at me with a snarl, pacing away from me before turning back,

"I hear Lord Hamlington already has you marked this morning, so all he needs is an excuse to touch you or punish you! And now he has it" Alfie rants, his face turning pink in anger inches from my own. Breathing, he pulls upright, rubbing his palm down his face with a sigh.

"Take a seat and take that look off your face. Your only way out of this is to act like you're sorry." He stops, canting his head to one side, listening before he adopts a more formal guard position by the wall.

Seconds later, I hear footsteps and a booming voice sound from along the corridor.

"Where is she?" In strides Lord Hamlington. His white tailored silk jacket with silver embroidery across the lapels is open showing a large, broad chest through to an open white shirt, his long black hair is groomed to perfection, dark eyes light up upon seeing who waits for him, his full lips kick up into a nasty grin.

He is a beautiful man, chiselled jaw, and a muscular frame but malice is evident in his features. His appearance draws you in only to show his true poison underneath. My stomach twists with nerves. Something about this man screams at me to run, his presence dangerous and fraught with animosity.

"Miss Whitlock, apologies we have not formally met. I'm Lord Hamlington." He extends his hand out towards me; Alfie takes a step back and morphs into the background with a blank expression. Rising to my feet, I take the lord's palm in mine in a brief handshake; his large hands squeeze to the point of pain and hold on. "Ah, she tasted you," he laughs. "You must be a threat, Lady Carter hates competition of any kind. And now, you have put me in an awkward position." His shark-like grin making me shift and look to the floor, the warning moments before from Alfie has me more on edge, following his advice, I try to smooth out the tension in my face.

"I'm sorry I let my temper get the better of me. I'm not used to dealing with such esteemed people," I begin to ramble, but he stops me with a raised hand.

"No." He waits. Silence follows, sweating as my throat dries out forcing me to lick my lips nervously, his eyes tracking the movement. This man pays me to be here and the look in his eyes is anything but professional. With my heart pounding a thick fear clogging my senses I question softly.

"What do you want from me?" I watch the way his eyes travel over my body lingering on my cleavage, disgust and panic sending my heart rate soaring. This is the man who now owns my worthless shell.

"BOY, LEAVE!" he commands; Alfie's eyes flick with concern, then he leaves, closing the door without a word; I feel the first surges of adrenaline, Alfie's warning swimming in my head. Hamlington steps closer. His fingers run down the side of my cheek softly before he takes my chin roughly in his hand, tilting my face up to meet his as he moves in even closer, the cruel lust shining over his face. He gets off on my fear and his power. I summon all my strength to hold his stare to stop the fear that runs through my body from showing. I have little power; he can have me killed right here, and no one would care or have enough influence to make waves for someone to notice.

"I saw you dance, Miss Whitlock, back at Eden. You're intoxicating, an exquisite female." lowering his face to mine, inhaling deeply, "All I could think of was having you on your knees doing as I bade," he grinned with vicious intent. "However, your owner insisted you have other skills that would be more useful to me, and I do find myself in the market for information," he drops my face and pushes me back with force onto the small sofa. "You," he pauses. "May, however, have just put a spanner in the works with your barbaric act."

I hold my breath and bite my cheek to stop me from opening my mouth again. Clenching my hands to my sides to stop the trembling.

"But to answer your question, I need to know everything that is happening in this court so I need you not to make waves and drama with the King's cousin but keep that pretty little head of yours down and get me the information I need."

"What makes you think I can get close to these people fetching coffees and serving cake stood by a wall?" Now there is space between us. I relax slightly, feeling the stirrings of my rage once more.

"Use your supposed skill I'm paying you handsomely, or rather, I'm paying your boss handsomely for." Laughing, he looks at my chest. "STAND and give me a proper look at my purchase," he barks; I struggle to hold back the snarl. My skin crawls where I can feel his eyes, but with my still racing heart in my chest, I stand and gracefully turn. I hate the fact I'm turning my back on this predator. My whole instincts are screaming at me to keep him in sight.

Grabbing a fist full of my hair, he pulled my back flush with him... he moved so quickly I did not even react. With his body pressed to mine, I can feel his arousal pressed against my back. Pain shoots up my scalp, my pulse throbbing in my neck. Lord Hamlington's hand aggressively grabs my boob, squeezing hard.

"Get me information, Miss Whitlock, or I WILL take my payments in other ways" Biting my neck hard enough to bruise, he turns me and lands an almost tender kiss on my lips; frozen in terror, I don't move, nausea rises, and I swallow. Tears pool at the threat.

"A list of nobles will be sent to you this evening. You will be serving drinks. Dress up, use your skills," he gestures to my whole body. "And find out what is happening within this palace." With a second gentle, almost tender kiss to my forehead, he rearranged himself, moving behind his desk.

Too shocked to move, I stand in the quiet, stifling office, a lone tear running down my face. What have I done? Hank was right.

"You may leave little one." I jolt turning and rushing from the office not realising how long I stood frozen, showing that predator my weakness in plain sight.

CHAPTER 8

Elodie

I stand in the empty corridor for several minutes, only startled out of my stupor by the grandfather clock chiming.

"shit!" I jump. I'm due for cleaning duties this afternoon and need to make haste. Approaching Esta by the storage cupboard, smiling with a small wave.

"Hi, Sorry I got held up. What is the routine here?" Observing my flustered state but choosing to ignore, Esta chuckles with a bright smile and indicates the room beside us.

"Simply dust, polish and tidy each of the rooms along this wing, it's done daily so it's not hard work" Esta looked me dead in the eyes, a frown lining her brow, before dropping her gaze worrying her hands around a cloth.

"Are you ok? just I have never seen anyone stand their ground with the nobles, let alone bloody lady Carter!" She huffs a laugh and stares at her feet, pink dusting her round cheeks. "It was pretty awesome, but Carter and her tribe of bitches will make you their new target."

"Yeah, I figured as much. Maybe I need to work on my temper." I re-tie my long blue-tinged black hair in a messy bun and grab the cleaning supplies we will need.

"Should we do this?"

"Let's." her face lights up in a genuine smile, and I start to think today may just get better. "We share an apartment, you know, sorry I was busy last night, so did not get a chance to properly introduce myself." her hand is thrust towards me "Esta… human servant and general dogs body," she says, laughing and taking her hand to shake I reply,

"Elodie… indentured servant here to pay off my education."

"Ah, there are worse ways in which to pay off that sort of debt, oops sorry," Esta blushes again, gaze downcast.

"It's fine. I have seen that side of things far too close for comfort."

We walk as we chatter easily. Esta is a short, petite human with soft, long brown hair and brown doe eyes. She looks demure and innocent, and she has an open, honest, and happy face. We get to work on a large library, working at opposite ends while still talking aimlessly. The room is stunning, with wooden panels lining the walls that open out to a huge stained glass window that casts the room in splendid notes of colour. The bookshelves span several rows with dark oak desks between them. I run the duster along the spines of the books, revelling in the wealth and knowledge on display.

"I would love to sit and study some of these books. They are amazing," I called across the room to Esta. "There is one here on past wars and lands of the ruling families!"

Excitement tingles at my fingertips, itching to explore, I have always loved the written word and losing myself in a book that takes me away from the horrors of my own life.

"God don't let them ever see you sat reading! You will be sent to clean out their chamber pots as punishment."

A shock jolts up my fingers as I brush a green and gold tome. I gasp, I try to pull away, but my body does not respond. I pull again, dropping my feather duster and using my other hand for leverage; what the hell is going on? Electricity immobilising me, power rushes up my arm heating my blood, the power slithers around my torso, trying to wrap me in a blanket of heat, stirring sensation pools and I feel the panic ebbing away, replaced by a sense of comfort, my breath slowing, head lolling to one side stretching my neck as the power engulfs me, this feels so right I was meant to have this! All of this, it should be mine!

A dull ache begins to pound in my temples, memories of that night and the pain. The pain, I scream, the pain increases... my mother's face laced with concern, panic,

"Elodie darling please listen! You can't show your true self. I have to do this. I'm sorry, I love you, we love you, and you will always be loved."

Agonising pain rebounds through me, still unable to move. Heat sizzles over me, burning, screaming.

"Elodie, drop it" A blunt object slams down on my forearm, severing the connection. The heat drops away my blood, taking on an icy chill as shock has me collapsing to the floor, the pain slipping away along with the memory. What did my mother say? Love?

Sorrow for the loss of a life I could have had sinks into my heart, panting, unable to breathe around the pain and loss made afresh, my vision blurs as unshed tears well.

"Are you ok? What the Gods was that? You have a bloody knack for getting into trouble" worry lines Esta's whole body as she helps me to my feet, "I'm going to have to watch your every step. These books are full of old magic, never touch them," she says, placing both arms on my shoulders to steady me.

"It's a bit late for that advice Esta!" I muse dusting off my uniform. "I think this room is done." Esta nods quickly,

"Ha!! Definitely. Come on… next room!"

CHAPTER 9

Elodie

The apartment is quiet as I take a short break, too shocked to really process today's events, deciding to make the girls some food I get to work in the kitchen. I have never been much of a cook; instead, I rely on the basic canteen meals provided by Beatrix.

Ok, where to start? The cupboards are packed with ingredients, herbs, spices, dried pasta, tins and cartons, the fridge is equally well stocked, I have never seen so much variety of food and drinks.

"Shit, what to cook?" I mumble to myself, dragging some meat from the fridge -"Burgers! I can't go wrong with that surely?"

Reading the instructions, which seem simple enough, I set the oven and throw the meat patties in while I grab some bits to make a salad (that's got to be safe?) I spend time creating perfectly sliced tomatoes, cucumbers and leaves. Adding all the veggies I can locate into a bowl,

"What's this?" A green, tree-like bunch sits in the fridge, so that is thrown in, too! I set the table for three along with an ice bucket with wine (one or two glasses will not hurt). The smell in the kitchen sets my stomach rumbling, and I smile at my achievement. Placing the salad concoction and buns onto the table, I stand back to admire my work. I feel a sense of pride at such a simple task.

A knock sounds at the doors as steam starts to seep from the oven. I run to the door to find Alfie in casual wear, looking like a fae model, his blonde floppy hair set to a just fucked perfect style!

"Hey gorgeous," he smiles as he moves in closer, his strong arms sneaking around my waist as he lowers his lips to my ear to whisper, "You look so scrumptious, I could eat you and forever be satisfied" I sink into his embrace enjoying the closeness of a hot body and the desire flowing through me, it's been a long while since I was held and that small ache of wanting to belong never really disappears.

"God, Elodie, I can smell you," he purrs as his lips graze lower down my neck. With a pause, he shouts,

"Fuck what's that smoke?" He dashes into the kitchen, turns the oven off and draws out the charcoal lumps of what used to be burgers! Black smoke billows into the kitchen, following him. I cough through the hazy kitchen and stare at my absolute failure at a meal.

"Ah, shit," I curse "I was making food for everyone. You know, as a hi, I'm Elodie, and I can pull my weight around here and be an asset and perfect flatmate," I state sarcastically with a huff and a pout; Alfie bursts into hysterical laughter and throws the burnt-to-a-crisp meat patties into the bin before taking in our surroundings.

"What's that? he questions, pointing to my salad bowl.

"A salad, you know, to go with the burgers." I shrug,

downplaying my disappointment in myself. Seeing my demeanour, he grabs me into a hug and kisses my temple like I'm an adorable puppy or child who needs loving guidance.

"This is not a traditional salad, but I'm sure it will work, come on let's see what else you have to go with it."

"Thank you, Alfie. I have never had to cook before," I admit sheepishly, fidgeting awkwardly.

The heated stare he gives me has excitement running down to my core. A smirk graces his lips, and he senses my desire for him, in two-step he has me pinned back against the table, his lips meet mine in a kiss full of lust, lips hard against mine, moaning into his mouth, heat runs between us as his hand runs up my thigh hitching my knee over his hips putting his large length closer to my core,

"God, you're a wet baby girl," his voice thick, his need to devour me growing. I need this man closer. My hands tear at his Tee, pulling it over his head as our kiss breaks for a second, our hooded eyes locking before our lips crash in desperation. Moving my skirt up, Alfie's fingers graze my core, running through my wetness; a deep growl builds in his throat, lifting me onto the table and pushing my non-traditional salad to the floor with a crash. His hands rip the top of my uniform, pulling my bra so his mouth can find my erect nipples sucking and nipping with his teeth sending shock waves directly to my wet entrance, making me gasp loudly.

"Shit, shit, sorry," a small voice filled with embarrassment shrieks from the apartment door;

scurrying feet follow, and a crash as Jenny falls over the small coffee table in the living room.

Alfie growls in frustration.

"Fuck off Jenny," his mouth heading back to my breasts. Sitting up and using both hands

"Alfie, stop, please," I giggle as I try to push him off me, pulling my top up to gain some dignity!

"I'm hiding here, guys. Either take it to the bedroom or stop! I don't want to see this," Jenny cries from behind the sofa.

Without a word, Alfie carries me down the corridor, holding my hand over the door scanner and kicking my room door open without breaking his stride. Our lips collide again as Alfie spins us so my back is flush hard against the now closed door, my legs wrapping around his slim waist, his hard abs tense under the strain of holding me prisoner.

My need to consume him now increases. I want to feel him inside me, a keen desperation for the release building.

"Alfie fuck me now," I demand, my hand moving over his erection.

Growling he spins and deposits me onto my narrow bed so I bounce gently.

"Take it all off." His heated gaze roams my body as he pants.

Slowly, I remove my shirt and slide my skirt off my hips and down my legs, leaving me exposed in only my soaked knickers and skewered bra.

"All of it. I want to see all of you." I do as he commands. A fresh wetness floods me; Alfie's nostrils flare as he scents my arousal, his fist clenching with restraint. It's been a long ass time since I allowed myself to be intimate with another, the excitement building knowing this man will not be whoring tonight to earn his keep, and this is pure sex at its best! Smirking, I purr,

"Your turn, I want to come all over your cock"

Alfie snaps, pulling his clothes from his body before diving on top of me and thrusting into me without any ceremony. A slight sting pulses through me before my body relaxes, bodies colliding at a furious pace. Alfie's mouth never leaves my body; pleasure builds, tightening through my stomach, panting.

"Fuck... more," I cling on, my body on the brink. I gasp as a powerful thrust sends me over the edge pleasure rippling through me leaving me boneless and panting, he pauses letting me ride out my orgasm, my muscles spasming around his cock, gently kissing my neck, he slides from my body,

"You ready, baby girl?" He flips me over, grabbing my hips and pulling me onto my knees before slamming back into the hilt, "that ass" he spanks my cheek hard making me clench around his cock, "Fuck! You're gorgeous and so fucking tight," he hisses as he pounds me into the mattress, swelling further before stilling and emptying into me with a satisfied grunt.

We fall flat to the bed panting through our excretion, sweat coating our naked skin, kissing softly as our passion cools.

"Well, that escalated quickly, "I blush. I'm not usually that person who does this sort of thing."

"What? Enjoy fucking the brains out of the hot wolf shifter that only crossed your path two days ago?"

"Stop seriously, I'm sorry," I stammer,

"No!" He cuts me off. "No, Elodie don't you dare apologise for what we have just shared; I like you; you're gorgeous and after what I witnessed today, fierce as fuck! And believe me, that was the biggest turn-on!"

Jumping up he grabs his trousers, checking his watch before opening the door,

"Look, I have to run, but… I'm taking you out all day Sunday, so don't make plans!" His smile is infectious and adorable but I'm left wondering why he is up and running so quickly.

CHAPTER 10

Hank

It's been two weeks since I watched Elodie walk away from me into the world I swore I would never return to. I vowed to avoid the repulsive and toxic environment that seems to bring the worst out of people. Now, I may have to step back in to protect her.

This need to be near her, to protect and guide her, I don't fully comprehend, my beast rising and unsettled at a distance between us; I can't gain peace guarding the employee of Electric Eden, knowing she is under the employment of that sadist. I have seen girls leave his apartments carried straight to hospital beds with compensation for their time. Any undesirable actions pay off and are forgotten in an instant.

Rage boils my blood as I reflect. What have I done? The past is fast approaching, and I'm not ready. Picturing Elodie's sultry features, swollen and bruised from his attention.

I grab a beer from the fridge to gulp down, trying unsuccessfully to cool the rising tide of anger. A crash sounds from my living room, and I pinch the bridge of my nose. To top it off, Pumpkin, her infuriating pet, keeps popping up in my apartment, following me around like a lost puppy. He sneaks towards me, dragging a tangled lamp that he's obviously knocked over. Hence, the crash.

"Hey kin," I sigh, lowering my hand while he rubs his head against it. "You miss her too eh?" Ruffling his thick feathers. "Pizza?" Pumpkin drops his chest in a play bow like an overgrown dog, with his tails wagging in excitement. "Okay, okay," I grunt, grabbing my phone. "Pizza it is then?"

A squawk and a bounce is his response, Causing further destruction to my mediocre apartment.

Half an hour later, we sit eating the best damn pizzas in the whole of Newgate. My third beer slides down my throat, and a warm buzz fills my body. With the T.V flickering in the background, some drama playing out on the screen unacknowledged, I feel my eyes drifting closed, edging me towards the oblivion I crave, failure and regret sour in my mouth.

"Hank... Hank big human lliissssssten," a voice sounds in my semi-conscious mind.

"Yeah," I think, confused at this strange dream, mind foggy with the pull of sweeter dreams and places to be.

"Go to the palace, protect, your mission," the broken, childlike voice continues.

What? Confusion pulls my brows down, but I drift into a sleep filled with strange images of mythical creatures and Elodie's face. Her sarcastic, mocking smile as we banter at work morphs into the sweet, soft smile that actually reaches her eyes, the one she gives out so infrequently. The prophecy from long ago spilt through my unconscious mind:

When the final dawn is shrouded in shadow,

WORTHLESS

*Blood will fall to change the Fates.
Before there is peace and power.
From royal veins magic will bloom, in the
hands of Kin, ancient power will ignite.
A princess' gift, passed through the veil,
shall breathe life into the forgotten pearl.
Unseelie and Seelie, divided no more.
Together, they will halt the storm.
The price of failure is steep: the very
essence of magic shall forever sleep.
Look to the darker pearl with bonded wings.*

CHAPTER 11

Elodie

The ballroom is lit with a spiralling crystal chandelier hanging from high vaulted ceilings, giving the large room a romantic feel. Priceless artworks and statutes catch your eyes in an atrocious sign of power and wealth. The items in this room would feed and educate every single child under Trixie's so-called care until adulthood.

The high class of the court is present in all their fine, expensive glory. One outfit would pay off my debts to Trixie, and the jewels these women wear would keep me fed and housed for the rest of my life. Mixing with the anger already travelling in my veins, a thick disgust is beginning to churn, changing my judgement of the people of this palace who rule this realm.

Dressed in a floor-length black plunging cocktail gown that hugs my curves and emphasises my breasts and pale silver skin, I offer drinks and compliments to the guests, listening to gossip and conversations, but most people here have little interest in politics or anything that would be of interest to Lord Hamlington. The few power-hungry nobles that stand out whisper in close circles; the King's name frequent their lips often, I listen, and I record before sending his way weekly.

Two weeks have passed in this routine: Get up,

serve breakfast to the General and Lord Hamlington... basically all the high ranking nobles. Once, the King even graced us with his presence for all of a minute. I watch as they posture and circle him, all false smiles and promises while bitching and moaning behind each other's back.

Then my day turns from boring to super frustrating as I carry out any duties Miss Anderson requests while biting my tongue and refraining from punching the wrinkled old cow in the face! Luckily, my sanity is saved by a rest break where I eat and chew the fat of the day, catching up with Esta, Jenny and Sasha: the latter if she graces us with her presence and detaches herself from her man!

Evening service follows, probably the most similar role to Eden. Conversing and entertaining people while serving the room comes second nature after years under Trixie's employment. Many evenings, there is some altercation to fan the gossip flames and bring a little excitement to the monotonous day-to-day activities at the palace. Falling into bed alone each day, all energy zapped from my cells, I tumble into a dreamless sleep and wake feeling like a hamster in a very shiny wheel.

This evening, so far, I have managed to avoid both the King's cousin and Lord Hamlington.

That luck has run out tonight.

"Shit." He's here. Walking in like a man who is used to the room bowing to his every need. The man prick of the hour, Lord Hamlington, shaking hands and kissing cheeks as he works the room. I have nothing to report, barring minor gossip of people having affairs or ill thoughts about the King, the same as last week. His threat is never far from my mind. I have heard the rumours about how he likes his women, and I don't want to gain that sort of attention from him.

"Elodie sweetcheeks, come, come and entertain us with your wit and beauty," Jade, the court jester, for want of a better word, calls me over to his table. He has a group of men and women crying with laughter, and they are well on their way to a hangover tomorrow! Sliding to perch on the table next to him, I bend, kissing his cheek. He pinches my ass as his face lights up mischievously, spinning an illusion of a mini dancer, the resemblance to me is staggering in his hand.

"We want to play a game," he looks from his creation to me, and I know tonight is about to get messy, the table giggles in anticipation.

"Oh, no, no, no, your games," I air quote with my fingers, "always get me into trouble, Jade"

"Yes, I know, but this will be hilarious," he sulks, giving me puppy dog wide peepers, fluttering his eyelashes, evaporating the illusion and resting his hands on the table and leaning forward.

"Please, this night needs spicing up, Ellie," Jupiter, a high-fae owl shifter encourages.

Across the room, I feel Hamlington watching me. He is surrounded by nobles trying to gain favour, all hanging on his every word. I shiver, revulsion prickling my skin.

"What do you have in mind?" Jade pulls out a small

velvety pouch and swings. Jupiter gasps,

"Is that La fee verte?"

"It is the finest La fee verte, 100% pure and guaranteed to liven up this party," Jade suggestively waggles his eyebrows. I can see this party becoming raucous very quickly! La fee verte is a stimulating aphrodisiac and overall increases endorphins, enjoyed at a certain type of party (Electric Eden, for example), and the royal palace is NOT one of those parties! Jade continues,

"Let's play a little game of hide-and-seek. If you are found, you take a sip of your drink infused with this." He swings the pouch and locks eyes with the table. "Each time you're caught, you have to cause a scene! Who's in? Or are you all craven?" He gasps with his hands on his cheeks.

I lift my drink, angling it towards him, "Let the games begin!" It's been so long since I let my hair down, and this could be the easiest way of sneaking out of work and away from prying my eyes.

Benny, a wolf shifter, is the first to be found. Jumping onto a table, he begins to sing a crass drunkard song that is not appropriate for a royal court. We all move around the room to hide from him, and the antics escalate, sliding towards the King's Dias (who currently is not in attendance). I watch as Benny locates Jade behind a statue of a mermaid... a pretty obvious place to hide, and I can tell he is keen to get everyone in the mood for more fun! They drink, then kiss deeply and unashamedly, causing several members of the court to stare in horror before they dash off to hide again! I creep under the table covered by a crisp tablecloth and runners in royal colours; just being here could send me straight to the basement prisons, so I doubt anyone will come looking.

I sit for what feels like half an hour, watching as Jade finds and grabs Jupiter next from her spot and see them both down their drinks "Ohhh," my eyes widen as I see Jade stripping to the waist and encouraging several ladies to dance in the open space between dining tables their body's close and hands roaming, they have the rooms full attention. Still, I hide, sipping my drink absentmindedly and thinking I could hide here all night and avoid Lord Ham.. hock little cock, I giggle, ham hock little cock!!!! I giggle again, this time letting out a laugh loudly, and my hands fly to my mouth! Oh gods I have drunk my wine, alllllll of my wine substance and all!

My mind tapers off as I repeat a sing-song of Ham hock little cock, my smile widening. The room falls silent as a guard announces a new arrival.

"His Majesty King Barrett the Brave ruler and protector of the Kingdom!"

Everyone in the room claps as the King and General Martinez aka The Raven (deadly protector and a very dangerous person), enter the room and walk through the crowd towards the Dias- "fuck, fuck, fuck" I can't move, now, I will be seen but if I stay here and I am seen, shit I bury my head in my hand but a hysterical laugh bubbles up my throat. Peeking through the tablecloth, I watch in indecision.

King Barrett dominates the room, standing over six

feet and sporting a lean, toned, and athletic body built from years of fighting. This male lion shifter has golden blonde floppy but neatly styled hair, golden-flecked emerald green striking eyes, and a square jaw with a dazzling infectious smile. Fine lines dust his eyes when he smiles, but he is full of lethal grace... and he is heading my way.

Every fibre of my body tingles, and every feeling intensifies as the drug begins to take effect. With a swoon, I watch the gorgeous man prowl towards me, breathing a little harder and brewing reckless energy within. I see this man most days at a distance, but my role bids me to avoid contact or even stare as a serving girl would be punished. But now I can really look at his prowess.

Turning my attention to his General: The Raven, he, on the other hand, has little warmth. He has dark, brooding, almost purple eyes lined with silver, a square jaw covered with a cropped goatee, and is shorter than the King but not by much. His muscular, athletic frame is covered in battle leathers, and his hair is shaved on one side, with the top longer and pulled back. His slightly pointed ears show his high elf status.

Warmth rushes to my lady bits, and I rub my thighs together to create a little more friction - gods, those two men are gorgeous. My heartbeat increases, and a vision of myself naked between both hot bodies, strong fingers exploring mine, flash in my mind, calloused, strong hands demanding my attention, sharp canines grazing my neck. Slipping my hand between my legs, I gasp at my own touch, a soft moan leaving me as I sink into a drug-induced fantasy!

the King sits, and I'm dragged from my fantasy. I'm face to crotch with the fucking king, Man spreading his legs wide, and I can't go anywhere.

The Raven stays standing, posture stiff. From beneath the table, I can't see anything now but the strong thighs … heat flutters down my core… I'm in trouble.

CHAPTER 12
The Raven

Pheromones and the scent of arousal assaults my senses. I stay standing by my King rather than take a seat, my eyes scan the room, and several groups of people are halfway towards an orgy. Typically, the illusionist, Jade, is at the centre of it all, but that scent? It's potent, fresh, and so close, my cock twitches, and I grind my jaw tight, eyes narrowing, inhaling my nostrils flare… so close.

A soft exhale catches my hearing from under the table. Instantly, I dive under, grabbing the culprit, dragging a fae female out from the table; before she has a chance to draw a breath, I have her pinned face down over the table with her arms behind her back.

the King stands watching the action with a detached air, eyebrows raised and a smirk. His nostrils flare at the scents of her, and the lion beneath makes itself known.

A quick search of the female turns up a fatal-looking onyx dagger, slamming it down on the table. I lower myself over her to snarl in her ear.

"Explain." I smell another hit of lust from her, gods is she turned on?" With a chuckle, she pushes her hips back into my crotch.

"Sir, you seem to have me in the best position. Please don't keep a lady waiting."

the King roars with laughter, as my cock hardens against her round ass.

"General, let the girl up before you become the entertainment for this evening.. not that that would be a bad thing!"

I drag her standing, "Do you make a habit of hiding under the King's table?" I demand, "I have seen you at breakfast, NAME?" She sways, drunk, and her pupils are dark with lust. Is she high?

"Miss Elodie Whit..cocks oppps ha! Sorry Whit-lock, not cock, I mean, I was pretty close to your."

She stops herself, dropping into a dramatic bow towards the King, then stumbles, on instinct my hands hold her steady on her waist, shoving her against the table facing both myself and the King. She gasps, her hands move to my chest, eyes following the contours of my jacket, lust filling her face, taking her lower full lip between her teeth. A gentle blush rises over her cheeks as she unashamedly devours us with her eyes.

"Fuck," she whispers, "imagine the fun we could have." Both her hands fly up to cover her mouth as she stares in horror. Stepping back to create space, removing her hands, I ask again.

"Explain what you were doing under the King's Dias, Miss Whitlock?"

"Your majesty, may I explain?" Jade, a noble known for his sexual engagements, staggers towards the Dias in nothing but his tailored trousers. Without waiting for consent, he rambles on.

"You see, I suggested we play a simple game of hide-and-seek with a twist to liven up this party. Poor Ellie just happens to choose the best dam hiding place." He laughs loudly, clapping and saluting Elodie with a flourished bow! Before he falls into a table, spilling drinks and apologising, he attempts and fails to repair the damage.

The man is high as a bloody kite. Narrowing my eyes, I study her closely her soft, full lips sit in a sexy pout, and her skin shimmers. Looking passed the facade, her muscles are tone and she is balanced like a fighter despite being drunk and high, her eyes are sharp taking in the room and the dagger—— a perfect assassin: unease flows through me dousing any lust, leaving her face I scan, eyes flickering over the people of the room.

Lord Hamlington: relaxed, sitting lounging on a soft sofa with two other nobles, his tell tail tick and jaw grind is the only emotion that escapes his face. He knows her, and the slight anger behind his eyes is directed at her... why?

"Sounds like the start of a good evening, Miss Whitlock. I'm sorry I arrived so late in the evening!" the King laughs

"And the dagger?" I growl at the King, my anger at the blatant disregard for his safety over a pretty face.

"A lady needs a little protection in this place, General, a prick for a prick if you like" She throws the King a sexy wink, palms the dagger, and slowly slides it under her gown back onto her shimmering thigh. the King's eyes follow the motion and he licks his bottom lip, rational thoughts flying out the window as this woman captures him.

A strange anger rises at the King's response. Can he not see the lethal weapon I see? Reaching out to grab her arm and disarm her once again, she slips past my attack with a well-executed twirl, blowing a kiss my way—well trained, too?

Gritting my jaw the burn of rage building.

"General, allow the girl to take a seat next to me, you," he points to Jade. "Bring us some wine and join us," the King is hooked with one flash of flesh. My blood heats: invading her space I hold her captive,

"What of Lord Hamlington?" There it is... the slight widening of her eyes, the flare of her nostrils, but she squashes the fear quickly,

"Who? She questions, tilting her head before lifting her glass and sitting down next to the King, dismissing me. Pulse ticking at my temple I move to stand directly behind her and the King, she will not succeed on my watch. I vow to find out everything I can on this temptress and destroy her.

CHAPTER 13

Elodie

His stare never left the profile of my face, the intensity crawling down my spine. I sit outwardly relaxed, laughing and joking with the King and Jade, ignoring the stoic giant towering behind me.

"So Elodie, tell me what's the most scandalous situation Jade's antics have gotten you into." the King smiles while taking another drink. I get the impression he rarely lets his guard down to relax in this manner.

"Well, as of today, I would say." I tap my chin and pretend to think, "kneeling under a table with my face inches from the King's cock!" We howl in hysterics, the booze and drugs helping us along!

"That will be a hard one to beat... no pun intended!" We laugh, and the King wraps one arm around my shoulders and pulls me in tight. "You are a breath of fresh air," he chuckles, his wide smile lighting up his gorgeous features.

I find myself relaxing into his touch as he wraps one arm around me, pulling me flush with his body, my hands instinctively holding his biceps in a cliche girl fan move, a sense of trust and comfort I never find with anyone surrounding me. Is it the drugs? Or the shots Jade is encouraging us to consume. The General shifts a step closer, fist clenched.

"Ah," the King looks up, his grip loosening around my shoulder. "My guard obviously feels I'm too familiar." His eyes snap to The Raven, his smile dissolving, the bubble bursting.

"It's been a pleasure to share your company," he says, standing. the King nods his farewell. "Elodie, Jade," without a backward glance, we are dismissed, and he leaves the ballroom, his shoulders tensing with each step, the relaxed, playful king is gone. A touch of sadness lines his shoulders. The void he leaves behind has me aching to cross the room and demand more time.

For the first time in forever, I want to get to know a male I'm attracted to, not just on the surface but also in the real thoughts, pains, and joys they harbour.

"I'm watching you, assassin, tell your Lord he will have to try a little harder than throwing a sexy palace whore under the table."

I jump, realising that The Raven has watched me pine after the King; with that remark, the General smirks and follows his king. Heat rises up my neck; it takes all my composure to remain seated next to Jade and not tear a new one in that stuck-up prick's arse. How dare he.

The shame at how close he sees me, I may not be a whore, but I am under Lord Hamlingtons employment to gather information including from the King. My thoughts were broken by Jade.

"Wow, that was fun. We will be the talk of the court, the two minxes who entertained the King all evening," he paused, taking a breath while fanning himself dramatically. He is hot, with a capital H! And I'm sure he liked you, Ellie. I have never seen him so relaxed or talk with one person for more than a few sentences. You could be the next queen of the realm." Jades's face takes on a faraway look as he enters a daydream, grabbing my shoulders, forcing me to face him.

"Please remember me as your friend!"

"Ohh, if the General has his way, I will be locked up before dawn." I remove his hands gently. "On that note, my friend, I'm going to head to bed." Reaching over, I give Jade a kiss on his cheek, making my way towards the double door. Every pair of eyes in the room follow, people sharing whispers and several looks of loathing, the fight for power in their eyes seeking me out as a new target. Saying good night to Jupiter, I move past the many occupied tables; Hamlington catches my eye and nods with a smirk. A rush of fear shoots to my core, and I quickly avoid his gaze.

Outside in the corridor, I pause to catch my breath. Gods, Elodie, you're playing with fire - three powerful men that could take my life all have their eyes on me.

A shuffle along the quiet corridor snaps my attention. Scanning every nook slowly catching my breath, I see nothing. Adrenaline surges through me, my skin itching with awareness, feeling a presence - mind alert. I push from the wall and begin walking towards my apartment. The oppressive feeling stays with me, as if someone or something is watching my every step, closing in. Choosing not to ignore my instinct, quickening my pace, I round the corner and see the doors to the residential wings, my heart pounds, and a thick, oily sensation glides over my shoulders, the dark presence drawing closer, bursting through the door at almost a run I slam my palm against my apartment door and push through. It's quiet, so I dive for my room and enter; before I can take a breath, a huge mass crashes into me, taking me to the hard floor. Pain runs up my back, stealing my breath.

"squawk," I pause in my hunt for my dagger as the realisation hits home.

"Pumpkin, oh," flinging my arms around his furry neck, I hug him close, burying my face into the soft fur as tears glisten. Overwhelmed with emotion, I hold on tight to my friend. Weeks have passed with me in a constant state of tension, always watching my back, sneaking about, and trying to avoid the few enemies I have already made.

"Oh, Pumpkin how I have missed your fluffy floo little whittle facey face," I coo.

"El? You in?" Jenny calls from the living area, halting my smooches. Wiping my eyes, I head out with Pumpkin at my feet,

"Now, Jenny don't–" I'm cut off with a scream, "freak out," I sigh.

"What in the gods damned realm is that? Is it dangerous?" Jenny moves behind the sofa to the furthest point in our small apartment, crabbing the first object that comes to hand... A remote! Brandishing it like a sword! I ruffle his head.

"This is my friend Pumpkin... Pumpkin, meet Jenny: he's very friendly, well to me he is!"

"Hey, nice to meet you. Please don't eat me!! " Pumpkin slowly rises from a crouched position, moving one step at a time towards us. Pumpkin moves closer, his head snapping at an angle like he is trying to read her intelligence, clearly assessing my roommate.

"You know we aren't allowed pets. They will cage him if he is seen." Jenny nervously lifts her hand as Pumpkin pushes his head into her "Ohh, you are soft! Wow, you are beautiful."

Pumpkin purrs at the compliments and plops his huge frame onto the sofa, curling up and tucking his beak under his paw, and we mere mortals are forgotten in aid of sleep.

"I don't know how he got in. He was staying with a friend back home, so I better check in." Grabbing my device, I messaged Hank.

Elodie
Hey big guy...
Just wanted to check in on Pumpkin?
And you, of course!!!
El X

I wait, but nothing.

"He may be at work or busy, Kin can just stay here for now if that's ok?"

"Well, I'm not going to argue with that. I mean, is he

like a griffin or a falcon?"

"Possibly a Griffin, but then he has those odd tails and no wings. I don't even know how he moves around; he just pops up when I least expect it!"

Jenny runs to her room, "Wait, wait." She rushes around excitedly. "I may have a book on endangered rare creatures." She pulls out a dark purple hardback book with engraved mythical creature across the cover, she settles at the kitchen unit and begins paging through the book,

"I'm sure we will get a clue from this. It was a gift from my mother when I was younger and obsessed with finding an all-powerful artefact or familiar that gives you protection and power," she laughs. "And here I am serving the noblest of the realm six days per week!"

Excitement bubbles. Will we get answers to this strange creature that seems to follow me around? Brewing a cup of herbal tea, I watch as she reads and concentrates, brow furrowed, stopping at certain pages and flitting back and forth.

"I don't think he's a griffin, but could he be your familiar?" Jenny sips her tea while still reading, eyes flicking and scanning the text.

"I'm not a witch, though, I thought familiars were small animals attendants of witches, I'm fae and have very little magic!"

Grabbing another biscuit as Jenny shakes her head,

"No, they are spirit guides sent via Salem... Hel... or by fate, look here," looking at where she points. "They can take any form, usually based on the person's past or needs, they help protect and guide an individual," she pauses, turning her attention to me,

"Elodie, he's got to be your spirit guide. Why else would he keep popping up? How did he get into the palace with all the wards and staff around?"

I read the passage Jenny points out:

A familiar, where typically gifted to witches as a spirit guide is not restricted to magical users but rather a person in need is chosen.

It is unknown where familliars come from or what their true form is, but they can shapeshift and choose how to appear to their selected master. Once a familiar or spirit guide chooses its master, it will create an unbreakable bond. It is unclear how this bond is secured fully, but sources suggest a merging of magics by both parties; once the bond is fully formed, both master and spirit will protect one another until death.

Through the soul connection, power will be increased and shared, strengthening both parties, enhancing existing magical signatures and skills. Power levels are thought to alter as the bond develops, and communication may include telepathy and dreamwalking. Teleportation and powers of illusions have also been documented in very rare cases. The last familiar recorded was back in the time of the two realms where both the Seelie and Unseelie courts practised strong elemental and witch magics.

Laughing, I close the book with an eye roll,

"No one has seen a familiar in hundreds of years. Gods,

are the separate courts even recognised now? He is just a fluffy hawk, a cat beast that likes me 'cause I saved his life, and he saved mine!"

"Seeeee!" Jenny wags her finger, eyes wide. "You saved each other already."

Laughing, I pick up my tea, "It's time we both get some rest. I spent the evening with the King and his General on the" With a dramatic flare. I flick my hair over one shoulder and, with a backward glance at my friend, "Dias."

"What the Helllll, Elodie, get back here! Explain"

"Night, Jenny!" I call, dashing to my room, leaving a disgruntled roommate chasing after me. I head to bed feeling lighter, recalling the words from the book. Could Pumpkin really be my familiar? Dismissing the idea, the days of powerful magic and mythical creatures have long since passed. He is simply a mutated cat… hawk, a fox thing, I think.

CHAPTER 14

The King

"A pretty face! For goodness sake Barrett, she was under YOUR fucking table with an onyx dagger."

My general, Alexander, fumes at me, "Where does a serving girl get a deadly dagger like that? fuck I would struggle to get my hands on one of those."

"She is not an assassin, Alexander." I sigh for the hundredth time, running my hand through my hair as I change from my tux. Riled at his tone, anyone else would have felt my wrath by now. He is my trusted friend, more like a brother. I have known Alexander from childhood, fought by his side, loved and lost together, and we understand one another. Alexander is probably my only true friend.

"She is the perfect assassin," he stresses, throwing up his hands. "Beautiful, witty, toned and strong. Why would anyone suspect a poor little fae with no magic, certainly not the King… Your thinking with your cock first," he continues to shout, sparks dancing along his arms and hands as his agitation builds.

"Careful, Alex, you are speaking with your king," my anger starts to rise as I realise he may have a point, but the girl was fun and not trying to gain something from me. She was just unapologetically normal and up for a laugh! Refreshing in my day to day life as king.

"Tell me, Alexander, as a friend, when was the last time you saw me relax or genuinely smile?" I point towards the war table set with a map of the Calithiel realm, armies dotted throughout the borders, and piles of papers flung across the desk. The weight of war and uncertainty of the realm add more tension to my body daily.

Sleep is plagued with anxiety-filled nightmares of what-ifs and possible plans. The Shade army fights along our northern territories, emerging from the Jade alder forest, attacking villages, and pillaging supplies. All attempts at negotiations have failed, and we don't even know what they seek.

Currently, they are too weak for a full-scale war, and our informants state that the Demon Prince, Osiris, is not the main driving force behind the attacks, as we first thought.

"Anyway, you think she is beautiful?" I wink at him and watch as his posture stiffens, and his barriers slam over his features, "Ha! You could smell her, couldn't you? That hot lust, I wonder what she was thinking of." I wiggle my eyebrows at one of my oldest friends, not admitting to myself that my own desire had risen in response to the alluring woman. No one has held my attention for a very long time, a select few see to my needs on a basic level, there is no conversation or getting to know one another just sex, on some level my subconscious feels a little guilty for the treatment of these women even though I have always been honest in my intentions.

"Well, she practically had her head in your crotch," he mutters dryly. "Can we move on? I will keep tabs on her, and you just stay away. I don't like this" I'm not willing to let Alex off that easily, the mirth at making him uncomfortable too easily!

"Look at this footage," he says, bringing up my laptop and keying in the required codes. A few minutes of scrolling I burst into laughter, wiping my eyes as I freeze frame to where Alex has her bent over the table with pure lust and excitement over her face. A twitch in my trousers lets my own desires be known. The girl is stunning with a lethal look to her, I find myself staring once again at the freeze frame. Alexander is mortified!

"Ha, ha, ha," I laugh, snorting the drink I have just taken to my lip. Alexander grabs a neat drink from the cabinet and drinks deeply.

"The enemy is advancing closer to central Newgate, and attacks are becoming more violent. We need to stay one step ahead." and there it is, back to fucking reality closing the laptop and sighing heavily.

"Where are our armies now?"

"Two attacks came from the Jade Forest on the border of the Shades mountain. They managed to take the 3rd battalion by surprise. We took heavy losses." Alexander stands and moves the large lion figure to the North of the realm. "The 2nd battalion sent high fae magic users to set up warning systems, wards and traps, but it's more like closing the gate after the horse has bolted. If we send more infantry to the Jade Forest, it leaves the wastelands vulnerable, giving them easier access to close in on Northfield and then the city itself." We stare at the map, visualising the army and their locations. "I am worried we are spreading our resources too thinly; it's impossible to defend the whole mountain range. There are too many inaccessible areas."

I exhale, deeply exhausted. Pinching the bridge of my nose as another headache builds, pouring another drink,

"Do we need more fighters? A new strategy?" The jovial mood from this evening has disappeared. We are winning this war, but only by the skin of our teeth. Being king sucks ass - I fought my way with the rebellion to overthrow the old tyrant king, forcing him to advocate the throne and sending him to his death. Making me the new, very young king. Especially for fae who live longer lives than humans. I thought that would be the end of any conflict, a time of peace allowing us to build a fairer new realm. How wrong was I? We had a few years of relative peace. Then strange attacks began on villages to the North near the Norrvyn Mountains.

Reports of Unseelie organised armies marching in and destroying towns and villages. Strong magic users are often considered Unseelie in nature. They all follow the demon Prince Osiris, or that is what we believe. We are not sure of his end goal, and all attempts to contact him and begin a discussion have failed. Fae usually don't identify as two separate courts. We have not done so for decades, Gods over a hundred years, but the soldiers of the Shade army are typical Unseelie. So we have been fighting an increasing war, unsure of our enemy or their intentions.

The demon Prince and Shades live a mysterious life.

"Call the war council together for daybreak tomorrow. I want clear plans put into place; I will not let this Kingdom fall to another tyrant."

CHAPTER 15

Elodie

With no word from Hank or his whereabouts, I ready myself for breakfast service worrying about the lack of response. Pumpkin slept on my bed all night and is a bundle of energy this morning bouncing about stealing food from my two housemates, who are smitten by the huge ball of fluff.

"So much for me being your chosen one, kin! Here you are cheating on me with these two over a little bit of food." Pumpkin squawks at me but turns his attention back to Esta and Jenny, who both lavish the creature with snacks and cuddles, cooing and air kissing. A knock at the door has me moving. A squire hands me a sealed envelope with a bow and leaves. The paper tingles in my hands, reading my signature, allowing me to open it.

Miss Whitlock
1pm my office
Lord Hamlington

When I open the message, my heart plummets. Simple words, but potentially terrifying consequences, the letter heats in my hands, the words dissolving, leaving a blank page.

"El… Elllloodie!!"

"What? Sorry Jenny?" I question.

"I said, Who was that at the door? God's, you're a million miles away!" Eyeing the page in my hand, she hands over a fresh cup of coffee. Smiling, I hissed through my teeth.

"I have been summoned. I probably messed up again, and that dragon, Miss Anderson, wants to punish me with extra duties, or I will be warned off the King." I roll my eyes.

"Yes, what the hell happened there? I was on room service all night, so I missed all the fun by the sounds of it," Jenny pouts, plonking a butt cheek on the back of the sofa. Pumpkin nuzzles my hand, letting out several clicks and purrs while he begins to wrap himself around my legs like an oversized house cat!

"She got high as a kite and snuck under the King's Dias," Esta calls, plaiting her long brown hair into a complicated braid. Jenny's eye swung between me and Esta. "Then when the Raven grabbed her from behind and pinned her to the table, he is hot, by the way! He looked like he would devour you whole," she shivered, exaggerating a film star swoon.

"Wait, what? Back up a second, *the* Raven, as in General Martinez, had you bent over the table?" Jenny's brows furrowed in confusion, as I cringe at the reminder of last night's actions and his hard erection pressed against my butt!

"Yeah, then she proceeded to back her pert little ass into his crotch. He was definitely hard for her, too!" Esta shrieks "I have never seen that man so ruffled!"

They both burst into laughter. Heat pinks my cheeks, and an unwelcome spike of lust fills my knickers. Storming to the kitchen, I grab a slice of toast and make to leave.

"I have to get going. I'm serving bitch face today, so I can't be late," I say, dashing to the door, I stop to give Pumpkin a big squeeze and smooch.

"Wait, we are not done here, Miss Whitlock. I want all the juicy gossip, girl!" Jenny dives around the sofa in an attempt to block the door, but she falls flat on her face over thin air. Pumpkin clicks his beak in her direction and ruffles his feathers.

Huh? Maybe he has powers, after all? Shrugging, I run! "Esta, you coming?"

CHAPTER 16

Elodie

Lady Serena Carter gracefully enters the breakfast room with two equally beautiful high fae nobles, all holding an air of importance as they take their seats, waiting for the staff to scurry around, ensuring their every whim is upheld.

Annoyed, I barely hide the sneer of disgust at the display.

"I hear the King is after a taste of gutter trash," Lady Carter talks overly loud to the women with her, making sure I hear, as well as all the staff and people present. "He is bored and will take anything that is offered up. Did you see the blatant way that-" she pauses, cutting a glare my way, curling her lips. "Apparently it... threw itself all over the King and his general - high on La Fee Verte." She fake whispers behind her raised hand, gave another gasp, and then continued the conversation.

"I heard she pleasured both under the Dias first, then allowed them to share every orifice later that night." The third continues their words, sending shame and indignation through to my core.

"the King is concerned that he may have caught the pox and is heading to the medics first thing. I will be surprised if it does not get locked up for infecting our king."

My stance stiffens as I feel eyes shift my way, judging my actions without evidence or even facts. I know this will spread like wildfire across the palace, and I will be forever known as the King's whore. Rising above the gossip, I keep my gaze forward as if I could not give a shit while inside, fury seethes.

Lady Carter summons a page as she makes her request. His eyes flick my way and drop quickly. He nods and rushes from the room, avoiding eye contact as his face burns bright pink in embarrassment. Unease surges within my chest. I continue with my duties, trying to ignore the clawing disquiet.

"Gutter rat, come here and bring the coffee," she says.

Ignoring the degrading name with my head held high and a sardonic smile, I exaggerate the sway of my hips. Only jealous, petty women would slut shame an individual,

"My Lady, it would be my honour to serve you," I say, filling my gaze with sex. "With all your needs."

She pulls back like I slapped her in the pie hole, pink warming her cheeks. I lean closer to pour her damned coffee, my breasts brushing her shoulder gently. Her body tenses, an audible hitch to her breath. Smiling, I pull back with a nod.

"Ah," she sees the page is back, the boy scuttles towards her with a silver-topped covered serving dish. "I hear the best way to rid the world of pox is through a good iron-rich diet."

As I move back to allow the page through, Lady Carter

stands to take the bowl. The fact that she lowered herself to hold a serving dish sends further warning bells ringing. Lowering my head and shoulders, being as small as possible, I begin to sneak away.

"Stop, you," looking around the room in the hopes she means another of her prey, I freeze. With two long strides, Lady Carter upends the full bowl and contents over my head. The smell hits me first, death, blood, rotten meat. I gag as the foul mixture of visceral intestinal remains soaks into my clothes. Cold seeps into my skin, turning my stomach as I try not to react. Sniggers flowing around the room.

Lady Carter dismisses me, turning her back on me as if I'm nothing but the trash she keeps referring to.

"Clean that mess up. Oh, and I will be ensuring Ms Anderson docks a week's pay for fraternising above your station. If you want to be a whore, get paid for it. At least, then you would be able to buy a nice gown rather than that piece of rubbish that barely covered your skin last night." The nobles all stand, each taking their coffee mugs and throwing them over me.

Humiliation curdles in my gut. A week's pay docked for nothing. I wanted to keep a small portion back this month to buy some second-hand clothes for Maddison's birthday. Eighty percent of my earnings go directly to Trixie, leaving me with very little.

Indignation runs through me, but I need that money. How dare a woman who has never once gone without, deem that a fair punishment for what? Doing my job?

Swallowing my pride.

"Please, please." I almost sob before Lady Carter moves from the room. A wicked smile turns to me.

"I'm sorry, did someone hear something? I could have sworn," she pauses as if waiting.

"Please don't take my wage, it's important," I beg in a small voice, sorrow overwhelming me as I think of missing Maddie's birthday.

"What could be so important that you would beg, and in such a poor fashion, at least pretend you mean it?" The nobles lean closer with rabid malice smirks.

"I think she should beg on her knees," another noble sneers.

"Well?" Lady Carter waits "beg on your knees!" With arms stretched spinning gracefully like a dancer. "Let it be known that I, Lady Serena Carter, am a fair and just person. This degenerate needs to learn her place so I will give her the opportunity to repent"

With a look of triumph, she waits. I drop my head, the strength leaving my limbs. I lower to my knees, kneeling in the entrails at my feet, defeat etched on my face. How do I fight this woman?

"Please," I begin.

"Oh, no, no, no, state your full name and title. Gutter rat, worthless whore, et cetera." That word burns, and my anger rises on a tidal wave, unable to hold back the force of it rushing through me.

"I'm no whore, worthless gutter rat in your eyes, but no whore," I hiss, my breathing turning rapid as I try to control my temper. Attacking her a second time will see me behind bars, reminding me of the bigger picture and the sweet wolfish face that lights up whenever I'm near and who adores me like a big sister. I only receive every other weekend off to visit now. I can't fuck this up!

"No? I beg to differ, 'Estella de Luz', is that not your whore name? Excuse me, your," she makes quotation marks with her fingers, "stage name!"

Shock runs through me. Shit, no one is to know I'm an owned servant. If Lord Hamlington knows she has outed me, he will be furious. Panic courses into my chest, the shock evident on my face.

"Why don't you dance for us? In fact, you have far too many clothes on, take it off her"

She indicates to two male guards that have flanked the noble ladies. They pin my arms within seconds and tear my uniform down the front, exposing my underwear, stained brown with blood and entrails.

Snarling and tugging aimlessly, I try to escape their grip, directing my heel into the shin of the guard behind me, but he laughs at my pathetic attempt at defending myself. They continue to strip me of my pencil skirt, exposing my flesh streaked with red and brown blood beneath.

"Do not fucking touch me!" I scream as true panic overtakes my senses, robbing me of all the defence training that Hank drilled into me back at Eden. But this feels real, not just the odd overkeen drunk punter but real hate and malice. An elbow connects with my temple, blurring my vision. The three women's eyes light with wickedness and power over me.

"Hold her still. Let's remove some of that cumbersome coal-like hair." A sharp pain slices across my scalp as Carter roughly hacks huge chunks of my hair on one side. They are getting bolder, and the viciousness is escalating. I know if I don't get out of here soon, I will lose more than my hair.

Twirling her hand, air magic pushes over my mouth, halting my screams and forcing me to drag ragged breaths through my nose, thrashing against my tormentors. Panic clouds my mind, knowing my actions are useless against these people and magic. Breathing through the panic and fear, trying to clear my mind to allow rational thought. I focus on all the lessons spent sparing with Hank or Lucca back at Eden looking for a plan, a way out of this situation.

"Out now," Lady Carter bellows at the gawking servants still remaining, and they vacate the room quickly as my chest heaves, held between the two guards. Blood trickling down my body.

"If you need the money that much, why don't I pay for these guards to have a ride? They will not mind a little mess. It may even be a turn on. How about it, boys, would you like to sample the infamous Estella de luz of Electric Eden?"

Excitement and desire are evident in the guards now, one palming his crotch while the man behind me presses me against him tighter, and I feel his hardening bulge up my back, bringing a sickening fear. Groping one breast hard, bringing his mouth to bite deep into my flesh, groaning with need.

Move Elodie or pay the fucking price for your inactivity, I'm no whore, and I will not be defiled by some letch. Slamming my head back, I smash the guard's nose, pain ricocheting through the back of my scalp, spinning from his grip to take up a knife, which I hurl at the chest of the second guard- it lodges in his pec not deep enough to kill, thanks to it being a butter knife, but enough to stop his forward movement. Chaos ensues - now's my chance, I run.

Shoving through the noble women, throwing hard punches and running like mad in my underwear, covered in blood and guts with half my gorgeous hair hacked off, tears of frustration and anger clear paths through the blood down my cheeks. I sprint away, not daring to look back, drawing in oxygen through my nose, choking on the sobs, unable to release my still gagged mouth.

CHAPTER 17

Hank

Stoically, I observe the new recruits, who are sectioned into four quadrants depending on their rough abilities.

Predator shifters are soldiers who can turn into their animal fighting forms, such as wolves, lions, or bears.

Aerial Fae- those that can fly, often shifting into birds or sprouting wings.

Seelie Fae- elves- many holding elemental magic, although few elves and Fae truly hold strong magic.

Unseelie Fae, the smallest section, housing only a handful of orcs or half-bloods.

They look untrained wiry, and shit fucking scared.

Perfect, my father was the Seelie king's general hundreds of years ago. He moulded me in his image. He lived and breathed for the battle, the power, the respect and glory. On the other hand, I loathe the attention and responsibility for another's life.

Sighing, running a hand down my face, I acknowledge the captain beside me. "These are to be ready when?"

"They are to be deployed in six weeks to the outer perimeters to continue patrols and further training, and then the main front six weeks after that, if they make it that far." Captain Thomas Carter scrutinises the recruits as they break up for morning drills. "It's good to have you back amongst the military. The Lord knows we need someone of your skills, and the King values your intel."

I nod noncommittally. The only reason I'm here is for her. The dream and sense of urgency to protect her are overwhelming. In the eight days I have been here, I've yet to cross her path. I feel an ache in my chest, along with a pressing need to find her and protect her, Gods! My inner beast is insistent, wanting to hunt her down and destroy any who cross the petite fae that haunts my dreams.

I analyse the device in my hands: a Calithiel map showing our armies' locations and numbers. The imposing Norrvyn mountain range stood North, showing the known Shade army barracks.

The military units have so many unplugged gaps that I am not sure how we are winning this war against the Shades, least of all the low-level magic users employed at the front.

"Let's head inside. I want to take a look at the recruit's profiles and allocate training units that will strengthen their abilities. Follow me." Captain Thomas Carter heads for the left wing of the palace, which is kept primarily for staff and military officers. The cool morning air caresses my bare arms with a soft glow, warming my cheeks as the sun starts to rise above the protective outer walls. It's still early, and I feel my hunger increase as we walk past the kitchens and the delicious aromas carrying our way.

The extra training and sparring causing a surge in appetite and muscle mass already. My shifted form will be huge in a few more weeks with this level of calories! I hitch a half smile letting my mind replay the hungry look Elodie often threw my way when she thought I was not looking.

Entering close to the kitchen, I call to a page to bring breakfast for myself and the captain. I may as well make the most of the food on offer if I have to suffer the toxic palace nobles on a daily basis.

Agitation quickens my pace, my beast demanding action to a threat I cannot see. I scan the long corridor, looking for the threat, but seeing nothing. Pausing, nostrils flaring, scenting the air, still finding nothing? I am confused at the stirring emotions within. My beast is still uneasy pushing its way to the surface. Inhaling and closing my eyes, I push back to remain in control.

"Are you feeling okay, Sergeant? You look ready to take on the whole war effort single-handedly. Are you… under control?" Carter side-eyes me with a look of worry, taking a step away, giving me space. Am I that unstable? My muscles tremble with the effort to stay humanoid.

Few people know my shifted form. I am rare as rocking horse shit, probably one of only a handful of males left. My species has been kept as top secret most of my adult life. Those who do know have either seen or felt the wrath of my viscous brutality.

Put it one way - you want me on your side!

"I'm fine, just agitated. I'm not some young pup about to explode," I smirk, but judging by his face, I'm not sure if he is convinced. I am not sure even I'm convinced.

The smell of terror saturates the air, followed by the sound of pounding feet, as if sensing the same. The aptain draws a wicked-looking dagger in one hand, undoing his safety catch over his handgun. I prepare my stance, eyes focused on the corner. I have no need for a weapon; my shifted form is restless and preparing for a fight.

A dishevelled woman sprints around the corner, looking behind her in a state of panic. The smell of blood, fear and sweat drenches her. In nothing but blood-soaked underwear, she skids to a stumbling halt in front of us, tears and fresh blood marking her face; my heart stops: Scales coat my arms as my beast screams at me to act, jaw grinding hard, panting to control the fury at seeing her in this state.

"Miss Whitlock, what the hell is going on? Are you hurt?" The captain is the first to recover; indecision crosses her face as she readies to turn and bolt like a frightened rabbit, eyes wide, heart rate pounding in her chest.

"Elodie," I whisper locking eyes with hers. Instantly her body crumbles, stumbling towards me, reacting instinctively I catch her before she hits the floor and scoop her delicate pale frame into my arms holding her close as if to shield her from prying eyes, I feel the wet tears flow freely soaking my uniform, her body trembling uncontrollably on the verge of hyperventilating.

"Gods, man, what has happened here? Miss Whitlock, are you hurt? Has there been an attack?" Still holding his dagger, he looks for signs of an attacker or danger, but the hallway is quiet.

I begin walking, holding her tight and flush to my body. I need to get her alone and safe. Rage simmers beneath my skin, and I feel my beast crawling for revenge.

Someone has touched what is ours, and they will fucking pay tenfold for that mistake. I feel the residue of magic over her skin, pushing my own power into her to remove the thick, oily remnants. She chokes in a ragged breath, her trembling hands gripping my shoulders.

"Sergeant, what?.... You can't. Where are you taking her? Wait, she needs a medic and to be questioned." Carter stammers, looking to halt me with a hand.

Spinning to face the captain, he sees the fragile restraint I hold onto and pure rage lacing every cell of my body. Stepping back, he raises both hands with a bow of his head, breaking eye contact.

"I will deal with this," I tell him, letting out a low growl, teeth gritted enough to break a normal person's tooth.

"Apologies, of course, we can meet later to continue our discussion." He steps away to give me the space I need to gain control. Breathing deeply, inhaling her terrified scent, I pull her even closer, her arms gripping around me tightly, trembling slightly.

"Do you need supplies brought with your food?" I nod in agreement before purposefully stalking towards my rooms. Taking account of her injuries as I walk, relief flooding in my veins.

CHAPTER 18

Elodie

Relief breaks the last ounce of my strength, and I collapse in the secure arms of my closest friend. His scent of cedar and fresh air tinged now with a smell of burnt sugar. Is he angry? His arms tremble around me, holding me tight. Magic warms my skin, removing the last of her magic, allowing me to suck in a mouthful of air. Memories filter my mind of days when we flirted and joked together, sharing drinks in quiet silence after long nights at Eden, of the easy smiles and lingering touches. How close and safe I often felt in his presence, knowing he would never harm me or demand more than I was willing to offer.

Shame fills me as I catch a glimpse of my reflection in the gilded mirror of the corridor, burying my head in his shoulder and closing my eyes to shut out the world. A feeling of belonging, a homecoming to safety, helps relax and slow my heart rate. Hank carries me to a plain private apartment in neutral colours. Walking to the bathroom, he uses one hand to switch the shower on, holding me tight, steam billowing to fill the room. The warm air soothes the shaking of my limbs. Placing me down gently, Hank takes my chin, forcing me to open my eyes and face his gruff, stern features.

"Don't let them beat you. Wash it away, Starlight," he says with a gentle lingering kiss to my forehead through blood and offal, "Take as long as you need. I'm just outside. You're safe." The promise and sincerity encourage a fresh wave of tears, and with a squeeze, he walks out.

Removing my filthy underwear, I step under the steaming hot shower, watching the red-tinged water. Taking the shower gel, I begin to scrub and cleanse my soul, compartmentalising the events that could have ended up so much worse. My breath catches with a sob. Taking the shampoo, I begin to focus on my hair, feeling the rough short ends on one side and the sting of my already healing scalp.

"Ahhhhhhhhhh!" I roar, gripping handfuls of hair and pressing my forehead to the wet, cool tiles as I scream my frustration and the feeling of worthlessness that overwhelms me. Will I always be at the mercy of others, my fate controlled? Useless anger bunched in my fist. What is the point? I am stuck in this situation for the foreseeable, crying will not solve anything.

Letting the fear, frustration and meaningless tears flow, vowing never to be this worthless, pathetic creature I am now.

Finally, with wrinkled fingers and red raw skin, I switch off the shower and wrap myself in a fluffy white towel, leaving the bathroom with barely enough dignity to face my friend.

Hank is sitting in one of the two armchairs facing an open fire that's gently warming the chill in the air, back straight with tension, a glass of amber liquid in his hand. Without turning around as I approach,

"There are some of my old joggers and tank tops on the counter you can pop on for now. They will be too big, but dress and sit," he commands, leaving no room for a discussion. Stress lines his body, his control barely contained, and he is doing as he said, worried at his reaction.

"Have you been sparing?" he questions as I dress behind him and curl up onto the seat beside him. I wrap myself in the large, warm hoodie, holding together my fragile emotions.

"No," I whisper, shame flooding my cheeks.

"We will start tomorrow morning before your shift. You will not put yourself at the mercy of these fuckers again do you hear me?" His eyes finally look almost fully black to me, with rage, iridescent scales shimmering up his arms, and a pulse in his temple showing his anger.

"Hank," I breathe, "are you okay?" lowering my legs carefully, instinct telling me to run and run quickly, but I know he would never hurt me; quite the opposite, this fury is not directed at me.

"I'm okay. Look at me. I'm okay," I say, crouching in front of him, lifting my fingers, running over his rough, coarse hair lining his jaw, leaving my palm against his cheek as my eyes seek his.

"I just fucking watched you running covered in blood, nearly naked, down the corridor as if fleeing for your life." Standing abruptly, moving from my touch, then running a hand down his face, he tries to take a deep breath as if to calm himself. The fury in his eyes takes my breath away.

"Did they," he pauses, clearing his throat and breathing hard. His hands are clenched to hold the trembling back, as if frightened to ask the question I know is on his lips.

"No, I fought before they took things too far," I tell him, avoiding eye contact. Shame washes through me recalling the two men who had me pinned thriving on the destruction of another lesser Fae.

"Too far? Elodie, look at your hair, the bite mark, the blood that is too far," he says, growling. He refills his glass, downing the contents in a large swallow before hurling the glass against the wall in a fit of rage, electricity crackling through the apartment.

A bang sounds at the apartment door, followed by another, rattling the door in its hinges; in an instant, Hank is there, revealing Pumpkin, who bounds forward, launching into the room, ploughing into my body and knocking me back to the chair.

"Kin flooster," I say, squeezing him tightly. I cuddle into his furry neck a fresh flush of tears escaping my eyes.

"Where the fuck were you, bird brain?" Hank hisses, leaning over the hawk. "You are supposed to protect her. Why else would you follow her around if that's not your fucking job."

Making a move to grab the bird by its neck. I intercept him with a growl of my own.

"Hey, back off, Hank. What do you expect him to do?

Come running in and attack the nobles? They would take him out in a heartbeat." Hank stands, assessing every inch of my body. I sigh.

"Today was the first time she ramped things up_____"

"Who is she?"

"Lady Serena Carter, we had a run-in when I first started. Since then, it's been mainly snide comments, the odd shoulder barge, but nothing major." I shrug. That sort of behaviour, to people like me, is typical, normalised... wrongly, but we worthless individuals have grown up with this sort of thing. I never really paid much attention to it.
"I have avoided her as much as possible, changing shifts, keeping in company so we are never alone."

"What changed today?" His posture resembles that of a calculated man, someone used to analysing threats and dangers and planning solutions.

"the King, I think, jealousy? Probably along with me being in the wrong place at her right time."

"Tell me about the King. Why would she be jealous?" He looked confused, and something else crossed his face. "Are you... you know... with him?"

"God Hank, no! Why does everyone think I'm a fucking whore?" Fury laces my voice, and I stare at one of the men I thought would never see me like a commodity, "You of all," tears try to break free once again, "people." I shake my head. "You know what? Screw this. Why are you even here Hank?"

I lean forward, pointing my figure at him and knock

Pumpkin in the process.

"Did Trixie send you to check on her property? Maybe she wants you to encourage me into the King's bed, hell, maybe even Lord Hanlington's bed?" I stand, agitation firing me up, wanting an outlet for my inadequacy, pacing the small room.

"Does she receive a bigger payout? Do you get a better wage?" I rant, my anger making Pumpkin whimper and click his beak, hiding his huge head between his paws. Hank holds my stare, not flinching from my rage.

He lifts one brow, folding his arms.

"You done?" I stop, fists clenching, jaw grinding, breathing hard.

"Good." Pausing, he grabs another glass and pours a long shot of liquor, and hands it to me, "Now sit the fuck down and tell me everything, including what made whichever high and mighty pissing noble start abusing you?"

I sit and take a long drink, taking a few minutes to calm my raging pulse, before seeing he is not my enemy, defeated. I relay my full sorry tale. A weight lifts from my shoulders as I lay down the events for Hank. Without interrupting, he analyses the facts. Intense concentration lines his features, and twice, he refills our glasses while maintaining his distance. When I finished, his eyes flicked to my injured scalp and hacked off hair.

"You're staying here tonight. I will take the sofa. Tomorrow, we hone your fighting skills, and the magic you do have in your veins needs to be put to use. These vultures will fight dirty." Walking to the small kitchen, he pulls a cheese sandwich together, sliding it across the counter with a large glass of water.

"I have missed my meeting with Lord Hamlington!" I gasped, the sandwich halfway to my mouth.

"I will rearrange it for you. Now eat and get to bed. Tomorrow is a new day." With that, he tosses Pumpkin some sliced meats,

"I'm going to have a shower, see you in the morning," he says, taking a step towards me. A connection radiates between us. For a moment, I think he is going to cross the space to engulf me with his arms and kiss me deeply; holding my breath, I want nothing more than the feel of this man. Running a hand over his face he drops his head and walks away. The sting of rejection stabs at my chest, and the simple act of him walking away reveals a loneliness I had managed to crush many years ago. Vulnerable and defeated I slip into the bedroom between the sheets smelling of him, refusing to allow the new tears to fall, cocooning myself in the soft bed. I fall into an exhausted sleep.

CHAPTER 19

Elodie

Low voices rouse me from my deep sleep. Stretching, I head for the bathroom wearing Hank's clothes from last night. My body aches, faint finger bruises mark my skin, blue and grey bruises cover my cheek, and the chunk of missing hair sticks up at an odd angle. I'm a sorry sight.

Taking care of business, I follow the voices back out towards the kitchen. The smell of coffee and baked goods lingers. Without a word, Hank hands me a coffee with cream (he knows me so well!) and pushes a buttery pastry bursting with chocolate. Smiling, I take both with thanks.

A lean, dark-skinned man dressed in the brightest blue and green fitted satin suit inlaid with golden threads that catch the light as he moves is lounging up against the breakfast bar. Not a black hair is out of place, and bright green glittery eyeshadow flicks up nearly to his brows. The stranger's eyes widen, and he gasps in shock.

"Oh, darling, what have they done to your beautiful hair?" He rushes towards me, taking my face to move my head around to better inspect my hair. "Such a gorgeous profile ruined, absolutely bloody cow bag."

I pull away aggressively, glaring at the over-friendly

face, lifting an eyebrow in question to Hank.

"Elodie, meet Tristan Rousseau. He's the palace stylist. Tristan, this is Elodie Whitlock. As you can see, she is a little bit grumpy until she has had at least two cups of coffee and a potent sugar rush!"

The smile Hank sends me is dazzling. He's in a military uniform, freshly groomed stubble and hair tied in his signature top knot. Smiling, I flick my attention away from the gorgeous man mountain that is my friend, who never smiles as he is a total grump all the time. And back to Tristan,

"Apologies, I'm having a few traumatic days, and I'm a little weary." I extend my hand to shake his, "It's lovely to meet you, Tristan."

"Oh, darling, less of that nonsense," he slaps my hand away. "Come here and give me a proper hug and two cheek kisses." Before I can refuse, I'm whipped into a hug filled with over-the-top air kisses, "Drink up; Hank has only given me an hour!!"

I frown in confusion at Hank as I take a large gulp of coffee and devour my pasty. Tristan begins unpacking a case placing hair accessories, clippers, lotions and potions, muttering to himself as he works.

"What is happening?" I mumble my mouth full of the most delicious buttery chocolate heaven pastry.

"I'm going to make Lady Carter's hack job into the new palace trend! Now, sit still while I work. Better grab another coffee and food now, as your pert butt will not leave that seat for the next hour. You are mine."

With a snap of his wrist and a hip hitch, he raises one eyebrow at me as if waiting for me to follow his instructions, grabbing another pastry and coffee. I smile innocently, plonking my ass down as instructed.

Tristan begins covering my bruises and scratches with a balm while his gentle hands slowly massage the concoction into my skin. Ice cold sensations run over my injuries, making goosebumps rise over my arms, the dull aches reducing.

"Wow, what is that stuff?" The bruise begins to fade before my very eyes as if wiping away the events of yesterday like a stain on a tabletop.

"Darling, I'm not the best in the business for no reason," he empathises best with another flick of his imaginary long hair. "Now sit still, sugar," he points a comb at my burly friend,

"You need to make sure this girl is not required today. Go use your beastly powers."

With that, Hank kisses my temple with affection. Furrowing my brow at his gentle kindness, last night's rejection still stinging, but having him here at the palace with me fills me with gratitude and a family that I have long forgotten yet craved.

"One hour then. Be at the training ground by nine sharp," he states. "I have left sports leggings and a tank top, and Ellie, bring the daggers."

With a wink, he grabs his weapons, exiting the room.

An hour later, I'm dressed. The person looking back at

me from the full-length mirror looks strong and fierce.

"Tristan." words fail me. He stands admiring his work,

"Always turn a negative around darling." His smugness at his creation shone across his face.

The hacked right side of my hair is shaved into a pattern, resembling a starflower opening from my ear into my hairline. The blue in my hair has been enhanced, now having an iridescent green/blue sheen like the wings of a crow, with big curls scooped over to the left interlaced with braids, making me look like a sexy, powerful warrior. The marks that showed my vulnerability have gone, and the thick dark kohl that marks my eyes enhances their bright cosmic blue. Dressed in simple workout attire and, of course, my dagger strapped to my thigh, the overall look screams don't mess with me bitch! And I love it!

My confidence is restored as I vow to make the bitch and her followers pay.

"Thank you, Tristan. How can I ever repay you?"

With raucous laughter, Tristan begins to gather his things, readying to leave,

"Darling, as much of a pleasure this was, as you are the perfect muse, I do nothing for free! That hunk of man meat is footing this bill. You are one lucky lady. I would climb that beast all day long."

Laughing with a mischievous wink he leaves me gaping after him. Blowing a huge kiss, Tristan leaves, and I'm left standing, feeling more confident than before and grateful to Hank for his help; a warmth spreads into my chest, and Hank pays to make me feel empowered again. Is there more to his affection? The palace stylist will not be cheap; does he expect more from me? Or is he here to protect Trixie's assets? Confused, my thoughts run wild, replaying all the evenings at Electric Eden we spent working together, of the comfortable conversations after hours, of the times we would sit watching the world go by in silence together.

Except for that one kiss, he always made it clear we were friends, and we never pursued more. It would be so easy to fall into something more, taking our friendship further, and having a protector like Hank would make life at the palace less challenging. I saw the way Captain Thomas Carter reacted to Hank. And
for him to walk into the palace and take up a role of such importance that he has his own suites?

Hank Dufort is a mystery I need to uncover.

Walking out to the outdoor training area, the sun is bright as it ascends, burning through the early morning frost that glistens under the shade of the trees surrounding the open area. I spy Hank pushing himself through a series of weighted chest and back exercises stripped down to the waist. His chest gleams with perspiration, grunting with the effort to lift the huge barbell. I observe Hank in a new light. He is not just muscular. He has muscles on muscle bigger than any bear shifter, defined with minimal fat, his veins straining along his arms.

"Like what you see, pup?" he teases, knocking me out of my daydream. "Warm up with a jog around the track while I clean up." I don't move, still perplexed over what type of shifter Hank Dufort is. "Now, Elodie," he growls, pushing me into action.

Several minutes later, struggling for breath, we take our positions in the sand arena as Hank takes me through a full hour of hand-to-hand sparring drills. Exhaustion burns through my muscles, and sweat runs down my back. Taking my water, I drink deeply.

"You are rusty and unconditioned, and you still pull your punches."

"I'm not a fighter, Hank," I grind out in frustration, my muscles tired from repeatedly connecting with the wall of muscle that is Hank. "I mean, look at you! Hitting you is like fighting with a bear on steroids," my eyes narrow in suspicion. "What type of shifter are you exactly, Hank? Bear, mammoth, minotaur? God, I would not be surprised if you said a mythical dragon with the size of you."

Pushing a huff through my lips toweling off my body. Deflecting, he rolls his eyes,

"You're just puny. Everyone looks big in comparison to you." He hands me a set of knives, and Hank directs me toward a set of targets set at different distances. The sun's rays heat my skin as I begin to direct my knives. I hit each target dead centre in quick succession, bowing low and flashing a satisfied smile at my instructor.

"At least this skill seems to have been maintained," he says, shooting me a wicked smirk. "By the way, the guard you hit with the butter knife needs several deep stitches."

"Maybe he will think twice before laying his hands on me next time." The comfortable banter stops instantly, Hank going unnaturally still, his jaw ticking in anger. With immense effort, he grinds out,

"That will do for today. I made sure you are not required until evening service." Stepping into his path, He needed answers.

"How?....... You walk into the palace like you own the place, then have the authority to clear my schedule? What are you not telling me, big man?"

My hands have made their way to his chest, the space between us crackling with a hungry need, tensing under my touch, deep brown eyes searching my soul.

"Let's just say I have certain skill sets that are incredibly useful on the battlefield and training recruits. I have an element of power here, but I chose not to live that life anymore."

He is solemn as he speaks, reluctant to answer my probing questions.

"Why come back now?" Uncertainty winds its way into my mind. Has he returned for me? I'm shocked that I want the answer to that question to be a yes. Emotion swirls behind my eyes, and his pupils blacken with so many unsaid words.

"Maybe I'm here because of Griff. That damn bird would not leave me alone moping around my apartment pinning after you. It was easier to just follow you", he jokes as he clears the training area, a wariness and uncertainty in his actions I have never seen before.

"His name is Pumpkin. Not Griff. Why Griff? Do you think he is a Griffin?"

"Something like that or maybe a manticore? Either way, he is probably the only one of his kind and he has chosen you."

Stunned, halfway picking up my daggers, I look at Hank, confusion pulling at my brow.

"Enough talk, go and get some lunch. I have work to do. I will see you back here at the same time tomorrow morning." With that, I'm dismissed with more confusion and questions regarding Hank Dufort than ever!

CHAPTER 20

Elodie

After grabbing some food and freshening up, I find myself at a loose end. The apartment is quiet, so I head out in search of Esta. I know she will be over at the grand library dusting again.

Pushing open the large ornate doors, the smell of paper books fills me with joy. Sitting and reading quietly in one of the comfy reading corners would be epic. Wandering slowly, I read the sections, thinking of Pumpkin and if I could just have a quick study.

Heading to the back of the library, I call out for Esta. Silence follows my summons. It looks like I'm all alone, so I smile to myself. Surely, a little browse will not hurt.

Locating a section on old magic and mythology, I study the spines, selecting a few books of interest before getting comfortable in a secluded corner. I begin to read:

"Seelie magic and its origins"

It is believed that the source of magic is inherently stored within the fabric of the universe, within all living cells, whether animal, plant, Fae, or human, to varying degrees.

It was once believed fae had a natural affinity for magic that connected with the elements, many specialising in one or more elements (water, fire, air and earth)

This magic is deeply connected to the harmonious

relationship between elements and the Fae. Harnessing the power of the Earth is a complex system of nature-based magical practices that reflect the user's kindness and wisdom.

I skim the pages, wanting to learn why magic has lost its impact over the years and why my own is nothing but a trickle in my Veins.

The fracturing of the Unseelie and Seelie courts, along with humankind mixing with fae, is now believed to be one of the reasons so few fae have powerful magic.

Turning to page through the book, I settle into the deep cushions. A second book that looks at mythical creatures grabs my attention more thoroughly. I search for griffons and manticore animals, neither fully fitting my furry companion, leaving me with more questions.

"Erhem," a voice clears, and I start with a small scream. the King stands with a bemused smirk on his face. "You look comfy there, Miss Whitlock!" I scramble to my feet, closing and stacking the books, knocking half to the floor in my haste.

"I came looking for a friend and got carried away. I know we are not supposed to touch them, let alone read them. Sorry," I say, realising I'm rambling. My cheeks heat, and I sink into a clumsy curtsy, failing to meet the King's eyes.

"There is no need to apologise for showing an interest." He looks at the hastily stacked books he reads. "Mythical creatures: fact or fiction, you're interested in magical beasts!"

I shrug, embarrassed. I fall onto my training, forcing my hands behind my back, eyes forward, and standing straight.

"Please, don't do that; speak freely," he waves a hand at my rigid posture.

"I supposed, did they really roam the realm? Will they return?" I state with a smile, finally looking at the King, who stands relaxed and intrigued, so it looks like I'm not getting hauled to the prison just yet.

"It would be amazing to ride on the back of a Dragon Soring to places far and wide or have a pet unicorn with magical powers." I giggle, nerves making me shuffle my feet and begin to tidy my books in want of something to deflect his attention.

"Ah, so you have a romantic view of these beasts?" He takes the book observing the contents "Firstly, a dragon would likely eat you, and the unicorn would turn you into a toad if you ran out of sugar lumps."

Laughing, he sits down into the comfortable oversized cushions, lounging and spreading his legs wide with a big sigh. With a lazy flick of his hand, he motions to me to sit, too.

"Your Majesty? seriously?" I scoff, eyes wide, looking around in case someone, like his general, is watching. "You want to sit with a servant? People already believe I'm fraternising above my station."

I roll my eyes and mimic Lady Carter's voice and stuck-up posture. the King throws his head back and laughs loudly, making me look around the quiet, empty library again.

"Well, you were caught under my Dias, ...intoxicated. I believe on La fee verte. And didn't you also back your ass into my General?"

His laugh turns hysterical. Smiling, I sit next to the King, ensuring not to touch him and be 'inappropriate,' his aura drawing me close.

"Okay, okay, your first impression of me may be a little scandalous I admit" relaxing more into the cushions.

"Really, you don't say, so tell me a little about yourself, Miss Whitlock." Looking ahead, I contemplate what to say. This is the King. I have been taught the art of dance and conversation to seduce, but not court etiquette, as if sensing my unease.

"Pretend I'm not the King. Whatever is said here goes no further... deal?" He holds his large hand hung with gold rings set with diamonds, emeralds, and rubies. I take his hand, pointedly look at the rings, and raise one eyebrow with a smirk!

"Yeah, let's pretend the man next to me draped in enough gold to feed an army, on one hand, is just a normal", I exaggerated the phrase,"person wanting a chat!"

He huffs, placing his fingers on his chin in mock thought, nodding slowly.

"Well, I will start, no court business. What is your favourite dish?"

"Dish?" I frown,

"Your favourite food? What do you like to eat?"

"Oh, erm?" I think, my mind bringing up the basic porridge meals for breakfast or the questionable meat and vegetable stew in watery gravy that was often served on an evening at the dorms. Food has always been a necessity rather than a pleasure.

"Well, up until I came to the palace, food was pretty boring, but," I recall my first evening here,

"Oh! Jenny made this pasta linguine, garlicky, lemon thing with little pink curly fish things in which was" I moan licking my lips as I remember the taste "Devine, I could eat that."

I stop as I see his attention fixed to my mouth, which is so intense it brings warmth to my cheeks. Noticing my pause and his obvious attention, the King clears his throat before continuing,

"A pasta dish!" The raw disbelief in his voice makes me squirm. "Okay, I need to remedy that, Miss Whitlock!" Silence follows, and I'm not sure what to say next.

Taking my hand, whispering softly,

"Explain it to me. It's been a long time since I spoke to people outside the palace nobles. I want to know, to understand," the turmoil coating his ridged shoulders, brows furrowing. "I became king young, in my early 20's to say I'm detached from Joe public is a bit of an understatement."

I feel uneased at exposing myself in such a way I deflect his plead, changing the subject.

"What made you take the throne? My parents died in the war to overthrow the King. I was young, so I ended up in the orphanage. I don't remember before, really, or why the King before was so bad."

"So bad?" He was a tyrant, murdering people on race alone! Outlawing simple trade, enforcing huge taxes making it almost impossible for anyone to live and care for their families." The passion of his words brings a sharper, heated tone, the past indignation and resentment rising once again.

"The old king murdered people like you." he gestures in my general direction, looking up and down my body. "None to little magic, and you would be fair game, not to mention the ridiculous laws and expectations placed on all but the wealthy in his inner circle." He states with agitation running a hand through his golden floppy hair and sighs.

"To be honest, before this escalates," he begins, smirking down at me. He continues, "We rebelled. I was strong with magic and good at commanding people, so I was naturally chosen to lead, then after many years of fighting, we won!"

He wiggles his ring glad fingers and spreads them, sweeping his hand up his torso to indicate himself,

"And now I'm the King!"

"Wow! that easy then? Maybe I should challenge you for the throne."

The King smirks my way, muttering under his breath. My body stiffens, limbs moving without my direction, making me crawl across the floor,

"What the hell?" Internally, I struggle to fight against the possession controlling my limbs, panic and fear sinking deep into my bones.

The King slowly stands, stepping forward, crouching at my side, fingers lifting my fallen hair.

"I could make you do anything. How could you challenge me if you could not move? Look at me, Elodie." Rotating his index fingers, my body turns, and I stand to face him. Annoyed at his display of power, I seek the ember of magic I have and try to bring it to the surface to allow my hand to move, a sharp stabbing pain shoots through me and a cry leaves my lips, instantly the King releases me, jumping up to catch me before I collapse completely to the floor.

Stumbling against his hard body, I right myself, standing fully, breathing hard. The ebbing pain in my head keeps my eyes closed.

"Elodie, are you oky? I'm sorry, I did...."

Rage courses through me, memories of the powerless feelings from yesterday bringing tears of frustration to my eyes. Before he can finish his shitty apologies, I punch him hard in the face, taking him by surprise as he falls back onto the cushions behind him, arms and legs opening to catch his fall; astonishment laces his blue eyes, lips tight as he rubs his jaw.

"Never abuse your power like that again. I don't care who the fuck you are," my voice elevates, and the severity of my actions catches up to my brain, my full eyes beginning to overspill. Flashbacks of the lack of control of yesterday echo, the feeling of worthlessness because of my situation in life, anger that these people think they are my betters.

"I am truly sorry, Elodie. I was out of line. I forgot you are not like the others. Please forgive me." He begins to move slowly, as if approaching a wild animal that's ready to bolt. I take a step back, heart pounding as the residual of his magic still lingers on my skin. "Can we start over?"

My barriers slam back in place. I am becoming too comfortable in this nest of vipers. On a magic and power scale, I am worth nothing. Abusing the staff seems to be the norm. Shame on me for allowing these creatures to lure me in and let my guard down.

"Thank you for the offer, Your Majesty, but I must decline. I have much work to occupy my time." I glare. "Unless that is an order?"

the King regains his composure, adopting a formal stance mimicking my own, placing both hands locked behind his back offering me the same bland shuttered expression he bows,

"Of course, I will let you go about your day, Miss Whitlock. Thank you again for your time." I nod and leave the library, refusing to turn back to him, but I feel his gaze follow me out.

CHAPTER 21
Lord Hamlington

Steepling my fingers with my elbows on my jade green and mahogany desk, I listen to yesterday's events with Lady Carter and Miss Whitlock. My so-called informant has produced little in the last two weeks; nothing but gossip, frustration, and impatience are in the driving seat.

The thought of Miss Whitlock and the scene now playing through my mind has my cock thickening,

"Did they strip her, boy?" Did my little sneaky page, Will, watch the whole escapade from a hidden corner? He blushes a bright red from his neck to his brow,

"Boy," I demand. "Spare no details."

With an audible swallow. Will continues in a small voice.

"Yyyes they tore her uniform off so she was in her… under erm… under…"

"Underwear?" I supply for him, waving my hand with impatience. "Go on."

"Underwear, yes, my Lord, and the guards pinned her. Lady Carter was going to pay for them to have her." He blushes even more, "but she head-butted one and stabbed the other with a butter knife to escape. She was too quick so I could not follow but Lady Carter was livid she hates Miss Whitlock I think said she was going to make her life a living hell."

Pushing my lips into a thin line, this turn of events could become problematic. The girl seems to have attracted the attention of the King, which could be beneficial in the future, but Serena could surely make things a whole lot worse.

"Dismissed." The vision of Estelle de Luzz on that stage at Electric Eden in a leather basque now fighting for her dignity has my hard length straining in my trousers,

"Will," I call before the boy leaves, "summon Miss Whitlock immediately. I want her here in less than thirty minutes?" Afer nodding, he is gone.

Twenty minutes later, Elodie Whitlock stands before me in a fresh, clean uniform and sporting a new hairstyle. The latter brings questions of its own: How does a servant with little to no funds visit the stylist at the palace? I narrow my eyes at her with suspicion. Is Trixie bankrolling her for other means? But for what purpose?

"Miss Whitlock, please take a seat. We have much to discuss." I indicate the seat in front of my desk, set lower so I tower over her petite frame. Her jaw is set stubbornly, her chin tilted in defiance, and her hands clasped in her lap.

"I heard of the unfortunate events of yesterday. Fury blazes in her eyes, making her electric blue eyes darken, her jaw clenching as if she is refraining from speaking her mind. "I had hoped your interaction with the King would generate something useful from you but all I'm getting for my investment is extra trouble,"

Her nostrils flare, eyes blazing, and I know that pouting fuckable mouth of hers will be unleashed, only spurring me to bait her more.

"I have had a very awkward conversation with Lady Carter who you seem to have some sort of conflict with." I pause, giving her an opportunity to respond and respond she does!

"That stuck stuck-up bitch made a beeline for me from day one. I'm working day and night. People like her are drains on our society, and you expect me to gain intel from these vapid creatures?"

She snaps but quickly closes her mouth, realising she fell hook, line, and sinker. I raise an eyebrow, cocking my head in a silent warning, amused. I lean back in my office chair, spreading my legs as I watch her contemplate her next words.

"That mouth of yours has a habit of moving even when it should stay closed. Do you know what happens to open-mouthed servants that fail at their job role?"

The fear that she so often hides behind the fixed mask, flicks her face, rolling her shoulders and holding my stare. She refuses to back down, the challenge heats my chest and I feel my cock stirring.

"Luckily for you, Miss Whitlock, I have use of yours. So you are off the table as it were currently." I pause, my eyes roaming over her tight shirt.

"Another shit show like yesterday will alter that fact, Elodie." I purposely use her first name, my gaze lingers over her body, taking in her curves; it's a shame Trixie never sold her virginity or put her up as a courtesan; I would pay highly for her body and tight pussy.

"As for Serena, she always hates the pretty ones, especially if they gain male attention, and you have the King's. Do I need to remind you to keep away from her and do the job I'm paying you to do?"

Irritated, her feisty mouth continues,

"What is the purpose of this meeting, my Lord? Do you wish to sit all day and threaten me?" With a brazen attitude, leaning on my desk. "You may pay my wages, but that does not give you the right to my body, sir."

The pleasure that runs the length of my body has me leaning towards her, my heart pumping, and my magic swirling to my fingertips. Without a word, I snake my magic up her thigh, caressing her heat. Jumping from the chair, she shoots back, slapping at her thighs, a curse leaving her lips. Laughing, I sit back, waving a hand at her, indicating the chair.

"Oh, Miss Whitlock, you are an angry little kitten. You react like a pure virgin, but your screams from that guard were heard throughout the palace."

The shock across her face confirms the intel the page offered, "Get me something useful and soon."

Ending this game before I am unable to control myself and take that harsh mouth of hers and fill it with something to shut her up. Turning my attention back to the desk and papers in front of me, I hear her stomp to the door throwing it open with force and slamming it behind her, chuckling I grab my engorged cock and relish the day I will sample that mouth when she undoubtedly fails to gain the information I already have.

CHAPTER 22

The Raven

My magic controls the bulbous fly following Elodie down the hallway from Lord Hamlingtons' office. Her hands clench in anger, and the slight shake of her fingers gives away her fear.

Possessing this form, I lose my other senses, other than sight and sound. Why would she be in his office? Why the anger and fear?

My magic falters, Losing temporary control of the fly, my sight tuning back into the apartment, focussing I regain control encouraging the insect to catch up further along the corridor. My mind ponders the woman before me and her actions.

"El.... Elodie,, wait!" A panting familiar guard in casual jeans and a short-sleeved tight white t-shirt runs to catch up, sweeping her up into his arms as he kisses her brazenly on the mouth. Laughing, she pulls away, swatting playfully at the guard. With a pout, he puts her down.

"I have been looking for you! Did you forget we have a date?" He places a hand on one hip as if he is about to tell a naughty child off.

"Date?" Confused, she looks up and places her thumb and index finger on her chin, pretending to think. Is she flirting? Is this her persona? Seducing people to gain favour? Maybe it's a distraction to hide behind another while she plans her assassination? The woman is a mystery with too many secrets buried within to be a normal serving girl.

"It's Sunday! And we missed last weekend. Please don't tell me you forgot?" The guard pouts with a wounded look, a hand placed over his heart.

"Ohhh did we plan something?" She smirks, and my stomach rolls with impatience and something that I will not address. Smoothing back his hair, he continues.

"I must have fucked you into an orgasmic blissful state; my apologies. Of course, you could not think straight after you were Alfied!"

With a straight face, he grabs her hand and begins towing her down the corridor. "Come on, I have a surprise for you." Not wanting to watch these two get intimate, and annoyed at the lack of useful insight, I let my magic go, returning to the King's suites, where I sit by the large roaring marble fireplace in his private drawing room.

Oversized steel grey armchairs flag the fireplace, with pale afternoon light seeping through the lead-lined windows overlooking the King's private gardens. Deep in thought, I stare into the fire, chin resting on my knuckles.

"A sovereign for them," Barrett strides in and plops into the adjacent armchair with a deep sigh, glancing my way, then returning his gaze to the fire.

"Nothing." My tired limbs ache, and a soft pain starts

in my temples. I rub my hand down my face. "I'm just thinking. You know how it is!"

"Yeah," I spent all afternoon with Captain Thomas Carter and the new Sergeant Hank Dufort. Now, he is an odd one. I can't figure him out."

"In what way?" my attention piqued. I turned towards Barrett, assessing him. His posture seemed troubled. With tense shoulders and narrowed eyes, his hand swept to the back of his neck as he rolled his head from left to right.

"Observant, intense like he can read my inner thoughts, or he's assessing me as a challenge, yet his knowledge of battle and strategy is second to none. I just don't get why one of the best commanders and battle warriors in this realm has ever seen is suddenly out of retirement."

the King puzzles as he continues to fidget with his hands, removing his many rings, a telltale sign that something has rattled him.

"He brought up the Old Unseelie King Oberon," he huffs out a laugh. "Are the two courts a thing? I have not heard anything from Oberon in decades."

"Oberon is alive, sitting in his castle on Mount Karayan, but whether or not he is linked to the Shades," my mind whirls. Have I missed such a big, obvious element of this war?

"I will send an informant and see what we can unfold."

Barrett stares off, lost in his own thoughts, concerned for my friend. I give him my full attention.

"What has happened?"

"What, Nothing? Just stressed," he responds absentmindedly.

"I know you, Barrett. We have been friends through thick and thin. Don't lie to me. What is it that has you taking off and putting your rings back on."

Looking at his hands, he laughs without humour.

"Do I abuse my power, Alexander? The power I have grown so used to, the power that comes so easily to me, is a click of my fingers, and I have anything I want. I have one of the strongest magical signatures in the realm. I'm striving for a prosperous world that provides, but do we provide for the many? The weaker amongst us? Do I abuse my power here in this very palace?"

The passion pouring from my friend raises concern. Barrett is rarely so doubtful in his vision for the realm. He is a fair king who tries to stay out of the power-struggling fae drama of the palace.

"The palace provides support to many charities and taxes fairly, especially in comparison to the King before you and his dark reign; people love you; you know this! Who has you doubting yourself?"

Looking flustered, new lines of strain marking his feature. "I overstepped today and was called out for it."

Huffing another agitated laugh, he runs his hand through his hair again. I use my magic to bring the whiskey bottle and two crystal tumblers to the small table between the two armchairs, pouring a generous measure into both. I hand one to Barrett,

"Explain," I growl, concerned growing for my friend.

"I ran into Miss Whitlock."

That fucking name again. Not only is she meeting Lord Hamlington, a guard and now the King is all in knots over this woman. Who is she? Why is she always at the centre of things, mainly trouble? Brows furrowing, I hiss,

"Go on."

"Well, we were just chatting innocently, not even flirting," he pauses, exhaling loudly, resting his head on the back of the armchair. "She made a joke about challenging me for the throne, challenging me; my Lion wanted to show her how strong I was! God, I was a prick, Alex! Using my magic, I made her crawl and then taunted her for her weakness; I think it hurt her on top of that humiliation."

Anger at himself laces his voice, "I bloody hurt her." He punches a fist into soft material, shaking his head vehemently.

"You are the King and a powerful one at that. She forgot her place," he cuts me off abruptly.

"I hurt her, Alexander, she screamed and nearly collapsed," shaking his head, emotion raw in his voice, "She is right. I took her lack of magic for weakness and abused it."

Downing his drink, his gaze finally meets mine. Barrett is not a cruel man; he would never intentionally abuse his power. I know the type of man he is: ruthless when necessary but never cruel.

"It sounds like Miss Whitlock is caught up in many troubles and overreacted. I heard rumours of an altercation between her and Lady Carter." I carefully state, watching Barrett's reaction as his face falls further and he drops his head into his hands.

"Her new hair." Realisation hitting him, "They cut her goddamn hair, then I fucking pushed her over the edge, what do you know?" Wanting to spare him the details, unwilling to foster more concern for Miss Whitlock or to drive her and the King closer

"Only that Miss Whitlock pulled a knife on Lady Carter, your cousin." I give him a pointed look, "for calling her a whore and the two of them have not exactly seen eye to eye since then."

"What about yesterday?" I sense my friend's interest, a dangerous intrigue, as we discuss the dark-haired girl.

"Yes, they cut her hair after a fight broke out. She ran, and it was handled, I believe." I shrug, holding the real details back.

"Fuck, no wonder she reacted in such a way. She probably thinks we are all abusive twats."

CHAPTER 23

Elodie

A lfie rushes me through the Palace outside into the Ethereal Spa gardens.

"Should we be here, Alfie?" My eyes dart around the tranquil and serene gardens filled with large rocks, ponds, streams, and cherry blossom trees. Miniature red bridges connect the pathways over the many water features and ponds.

"Come on this way." Alfie kisses the back of my hand with a little wink, appreciating the distraction from a shit few days I'm happy to follow.

Pink and purple blossoms flutter slowly to the ground, dusting his hair as he moves me through the winding paths. Reaching a tall red brick wall, he moves along behind the rows of shrubs by an ancient-looking gnarly tree with bright red flowers.

Letting go of my hand, he rushes ahead,

"Alfie?"

I follow, laughing, rounding the corner behind the tree to an empty space alongside the wall. Spinning, I call out again. A hand shoots from the red bricks, pulling me through. I cry out in surprise as I stumble into the waiting arms of my date. I gasp, eyes widening at the beautiful garden in front of me. A crystal clear blue waterfall cascades into a calm azure pool with overhanging blossom trees trailing into the water.

"What is this place?" My wide eyes fix on the peaceful pool in wonder.

"I found it by accident. I love to come here and swim my stresses away," he smirks, stripping. He removes his T-shirt over his head with one arm and steps out of his tight jeans. His arrogant, full lips lift to one side before he wades into the cool water, disappearing under with confidence.

A pang of longing flickers in my core. I remove my jeans and pale baby blue jumper, leaving my underwear on, and dip my toes in, a sigh escaping as the warm water sends shivers and goosebumps over my skin. Water caresses my limbs, soothing all of my aches and pains and fading the bruises still present from sparring with Hank earlier.

I let out a low moan as I sank into the lukewarm water, eyes closing as I floated on my back. I felt the anxiety of the days gone by slip away. A feather-light kiss touched my shoulder, bringing a smile to my lips.

"It's amazing, Alfie," I say, uprighting myself. "Thank you" I may not know this man very well, but he seems to want to get to know me. "Do people use this pool?"

"I have never seen anyone else here, and I believe the waters have regenerative qualities."

"Do you bring all your dates here?" I muse, vulnerability showing clearly on my face.

"No." A strange expression flicks across his face. Guilt?

Anger? He steps back, not touching me. I'm unsure what's going on in his head, but he closes it down, his face lighting up with that big, flirty smile once again. Pressing closely to my back, pulling my hair over one shoulder as he gently kisses my shoulder, then up my neck,

"You're the first." A chill spreads low in my gut and I move my head slightly to ward off his attention, confused at my own actions. The need to create barriers around this overly flirty man.

"I hardly know you, Alfie Roberts." I move out of his arms, turning to face him, taking a big breath as I try to use my head and not my hormones, revisiting that strange feeling from moments ago.

"It's a date. Let's just be us with some heavy petting, enjoy this paradise together, relax, and maybe have an orgasm." He wiggles his eyebrows with a cheeky wink, making me huff a laugh.

"Hey, relax, have some fun, and then we will see about the other stuff." With a hard kiss to my mouth, Alfie swims to the shore, kicking water all over me and laughing as he soaks me.

"Hey!" I lunge to grab an ankle, pulling him back and under the water, jumping onto his head to push him roughly under, diving away towards the sandy bank; we fight, dunking each other until finally, I break away.

Reaching the bank, panting, a heavyweight pins me to the cool earth. Hands grab my wrist and waist, flipping me into my back, drawing my wrists above my head; bucking wildly, I try to dislodge his strong thighs, now straddling my slender hips.

"Keep thrusting like that, Elodie, and you will make it too hard for me to stop, pun totally intended!" I feel his length thickening in his boxers, making my own body respond in kind.
Lowering so our heavy lust-filled breaths mingle, Alfie slowly runs his tongue over the seams of my lips, forcing a groan,

"Oh, Alfie," I breathe, fighting my own desire as his solid muscular body heats my skin, the evidence of his arousal flush against my thigh.

His heated stare searches my face, fixing on my pink lips; placing his forehead to mine, he curses softly.

"I can't believe I'm going to do this," I say, sitting up, releasing my wrist.

He runs his hands down his face with a groan. "I have brought us snacks," he announces while jumping up, leaving me wet and wanting on the shore.

"Snacks?" I scoff. "Alfie Roberts, are you trying to impress me and prove you're a good, God's fairing boy?"

He produces a domed glass platter balanced on one hand, droplets of water still travelling down his toned divots. My eyes trace the lines they make. With a flourish and low bow, he presents the fruit platter,

"My Lady, are you hungry?" Taking a strawberry and kneeling beside me, he slowly rubs the juicy ripe berry along my lips, encouraging them to part, pushing it into my mouth, and his eyes never leaving my face. I savour the fruit, moaning as I close my eyes. Any sort of fruit except basic apples and bananas was a rarity in the orphanage.

These are Divine, the sweet, soft flesh sending little parties across my taste buds. Rushing to consume more, I grab another strawberry, only to be denied. A warning growl sounds as I make a second grab at the platter, only for it to be swung out of reach.

"Patience, dear Elodie, these delicate little morsels are not to be ravaged," he takes another juicy red fruit and holds it towards me, "but enjoyed slowly, bit by little bit."

Smirking, he holds the little temptation inches from my face. I lunge and snap the berry into my mouth, nearly taking his fingers, too. Using my momentum, I run him to the ground, pinning his hips between my thighs, grabbing the platter before it hits the ground, ramming several berries into my mouth and devouring like a starved animal.

"Mine!" I mumble, juice oozing down my chin, a wicked grin on my face.

His hand grazing my panties and skimming up my heat stops my feast and a sharp inhale snaps my attention to the male beneath me. Pure lust fills his features, licking his lips as I freeze at the sudden contact with my sex.

"You're wet," he states while taking his fingers and sucking my juices clean from them. With a curse, I'm dragged by strong hands up his torso towards his face, biting my clit through my soaked panties. He inhales deeply, rough fingers pull the fabric to the side, and a strong tongue laps my slick entrance, tasting me before thrusting in and out deeply. I begin to ride his face, forgetting the strawberries as my ecstasy builds. Teeth, lips and tongue nip bite and suck my clit and pussy. My hands grab his hair as my muscles tighten, fingers thrust into my core, making me cry out, muscles tensing with the onslaught of pleasure building and smashing through me.

Alfie continues to devour my essence while my orgasm clenches around his fingers. Panting, I roll to the cool, damp earth, Alfie following, before flipping us and lining his erect cock to slowly slide into the hilt.

"My turn." A dark look I catch over my shoulder is the only warning I get before he slams into me with full force, grabbing my hair roughly without breaking his fast, frantic pace, exposing my neck, he bites down hard, crying out in pain.

"Alfie," my hands try to slow his pace. Hooking my arm and forcing my chest to the floor, my face hitting the sand of the beach. His bite tightens, drawing blood as his fangs elongate, sinking deeper. Panic begins to dissolve any lust, and his thrust deepens.

"Alfie, stop, you're hurting me." I push against his body in an attempt to dislodge him, only to have both hands grabbed in one of his and pinned painfully at my hips.

Picking up his pace, growling like an animal until he finally stills and comes inside me. We still, for several minutes, breathing heavily; removing his teeth from my neck, Alfie withdraws, standing to grab his boxers and then dressing without a word.

"Better than strawberries," he smiles and takes in my prone body, satisfaction shining in his eyes. Twisting onto my back and raising to my elbows, shock and a dash of shame stir an uncomfortable feeling in my stomach; why did something so natural start to feel so wrong? Gently touching the wound to my neck, fingers coming away with my own life force.

"You marked me, Alfie,…….. I asked you to stop."

"In the moment, babe, just jump back in the water. It will heal it." He grabs his clothes and continues to dress, back towards me so I can't see his face.

"I'm on duty tonight, so I have to scoot. You can find your way back, right?" He leans down to ruffle my hair and strides through the wall, leaving me stunned with his seed running down my leg. Shocked, I sit for several minutes, not sure what just happened. The intention was to get to know Alfie, explore this connection … and not sleep with him. Did I recall having much choice there? Bringing my fingers again to my neck, which still trickles blood down, pooling at my collar bone, slowly heading to the water to wash away the mess, sinking deep into the restorative waters, healing the ache at my neck. Finally, with a sigh, I exit using a towel to dry and get dressed. Confused by Alfie's behaviour, I was really beginning to see the cracks- working at Electric Eden for so many years, I have witnessed fake friendships, relationships and intimate acts on a daily basis, how the workers flipped that switch to give the customer a taste of something real, why do I have this sickening feeling Alfie is acting? Those shuttered looks I caught, the aggression during sex, not stopping!

Leaving on both sexual accounts straight after, no lingering cuddles or kisses. Shaking my head at my own stupidity. "Shit," I say, cursing as I realise I am being played, Alfie made a beeline for me from the start. We jumped into a sexual relationship without even knowing who he was and what his role was. How fucking stupid! Ohhh, how people must laugh at the little orphan girl Ellie, who never knew love and who has no friends. Haha, look at the way she soaks up any attention. Of course, Lord Hamlington will have more spies. And what about the other Lords and Ladies?

Feeling useless and ashamed, I always swore I would not be used like a whore. Yet, Is Alfie using me to get information? Does he know more than he lets on? He was right along the corridor from Lord Hamlington's office. He was also the one who delivered me to his office after my first run-in with Lady Carter,

"ahhhhhh" I scream In frustration "what a bloody idiot Elodie" I shout, standing, running my fingers through my damp hair "bigAh!" I screamed in frustration, "What a bloody idiot, Elodie." I shout, standing, running my fingers through my damp hair. "Big mistake Alfie fuckface Roberts." I will not be used.

CHAPTER 24

Alfie

The taste of her lingers on my tongue, and mixed feelings hit my gut; she is a mark, I remind myself, just a fiery hot mark. A fuck, nothing more. Running a hand down my face, I recall the desire to claim her and the rage that followed, knowing the reasons I need to be closer to her but not emotionally involved. The look of confusion and hurt on her face when I left excites me. Elodie sat with a glow about her, my come glistening in her pussy.

There are always some perks to my role at the palace. A snarl curls my lip at the way she laps up my attention like a starved dog. My skin crawls. So much confidence on the outside when, deep down, everything about her is just a trained, polished act. Tasting her today only confirmed that observation, and the loneliness was bitter on my tongue. I still don't understand why she is at the palace. I've seen the interactions with Lord Hamlington but do not fully understand what his interest in her is.

I run my hands through my hair and down my face trying to shake off the mixture of repulsion and lust for her body. Unsure why I wanted to claim her, angry that I want her body when her power is minimal, so my wolf is craving her. She's not a shifter, so is it a dominance thing? She is so desperate, my unique power getting a feel for it. Does Hamilington want her to get close to the King? He certainly reacted to Her presence.

Never before have I felt the King relax with anyone like he did her. Knowing that I'm not the only one, obviously, who is serving that whore, sends another wave of disgust into my gut. I march along the corridor of the old queen's suite, gilded in gold with towering magnificent mirrors distorting my body as I rush to my destination.

I enter through a secret side door behind a panel and slip behind a statue of Aphrodite, the goddess of love, popping out into a large apartment. Roses fill the space, the rich scent quickening my pace and bringing a wicked smirk to my lips.

"Alfie darling," a feminine voice purrs as I enter. "Do pour yourself a glass of wine and join me," her voice calls from the extravagant bathing area. I remove my T-shirt, drop it on the kitchen chairs, and grab some wine before walking towards the marble bathroom. To call it a bathroom is an understatement. The full room is a white and light pink marble with several walk-in shower areas with various jets and seating, rose gold fixtures and fittings display the wealth of this woman, she lies in a deep sunken jacuzzi bath that is placed in front of a floor to ceiling window overlooking the back of the palace and the green fields of the Orion's hunting meadow, her blonde nearly silver locks cascade over the side of the jacuzzi, her head tilted towards the artistic mural on the ceiling, of a cloudy sky with the goddess of love draped in a tunic showing one breast, but she has nothing on the goddess before me.

The keeper of my heart: button nose and plump

lips give her a flawless, gorgeous look, and her ample cleavage peaks above the waters, drawing my attention as she moves to watch me saunter into the bathing chamber. Her blue eyes sparkle as she traces the contours of my hardened body, smirking. I ask.

"My Lady, do you request my services?" I bent down, smashing my mouth hard to hers, forcing my tongue into hers while one hand pinches her nipple, causing her to gasp, her back arching into my touch while her kiss deepens. My dick hardens in my jeans, knowing this woman has the sex drive of an animal. I pull back as her hand connects with my cheek in a hard smack,

"You taste of her," she growls, anger turning her beauty sour, screwing up her nose as she sits up, water rippling down her body,

"I can smell that tramp all over you."

I take a sip of my wine while standing, I observe, choosing my words carefully,

"I'm doing as you asked my lady, getting close to her." She narrows her eyes she mumbles under her breath but holding her retort knowing I'm right.

"Did you fuck her," the demand and anger are the only warnings I need; if I don't get her attention off Elodie, her jealousy will take over, and I will pay the price. I scoff,

"Darling, I wooed her, fed her strawberries. I don't think the poor tramp has ever tried them by the way she gored on them, most unattractive." Placing my glass down, I strip, never leaving her gaze, a wicked smirk on my lips; moving to one of the large walk-in showers, I begin to wash, ensuring to flex and put on a little show; the bite of her lower lip and wide-eyed stare means she is starting to thaw.

"We flirted, kissed, and I made her come, but I did not fuck her. Not sure I could go that far." I pause, looking over my shoulder and shutting off the shower. "She is not you, it feels wrong, dirty"

I strut towards the jacuzzi, stepping in the warm lavender-scented waters. "I did what you asked but nothing more. I'm yours forever," I say, pulling her close. I sit back, taking her smooth thighs on either side of my hips. "I desire only you and you alone" Her eyes darken with heat from my words; I kiss her hard, placing her arms around me, breaking apart.

Her frosty, hard exterior thawing in my embrace. "We need to keep looking at the bigger picture, gorgeous," I purr. "The end goal."

"I know," she sighs into my embrace, kissing my shoulder tenderly. "I know, no one can know we are together, not until we have the power to make a move."

"Elodie has something with Hamlington, and that new sergeant. The huge fella seems very protective, too; there is more to that story that we need to discover." Kissing her plump lips, she begins to move her hips against me. Now I know I have her in the palm of my hand, smiling I deepen our kiss and prepare for a night of pleasure.

CHAPTER 25

Elodie

Dressed and healed from the waters, my brain runs through the day's events, a confused mesh of shock, embarrassment, and anger replaying over and over. Alfie Roberts seems fun and flirtatious one minute, then... What was that? It felt forced, wrong, like a flip of a switch turning the pleasure to anger and frustration.

I just can't put my finger on mine or his feelings, but that bite was not sexual, not a claiming or marking as some shifters enjoy. There was too much rage running through him. The clear dismissal post act left me feeling dirty and used.

Trixie stole my teenage years and childhood innocence, profiting from the suffering of others in the name of entertainment, knowing we were desperate enough to continue in her questionable care. I have seen the detachment and act many of the performers don. Alfie Robert's has that same look, often buried, but it's there. I was just too blind and needy to see it.

Walking back through the tranquil gardens, I feel anything but tranquil. Wanting to explore more, I stroll through the public areas, walking the red-carpeted hallways, observing the artwork lining one side of the vast hallway, portraits of myths and legends of the past.

The other side of the hallway is lined by magnificent arche windows overlooking the Palace gardens, an array of foliage swaying gently in the later summer breeze.

Sunlight warms the space as I slowly take in a canvas of Hera, the queen of the gods. Blue peacock feathers crown her head, spanning down her back. She looks strong and powerful but with a softness about her features that leads you to believe she is loved; the colours of her dress are vibrant oranges, blues, golds and greens that contrast with her pale, almost pearlescent skin. I don't fail to see the resemblance to myself; smiling, I huff a laugh. If only I was the daughter of a goddess! Life surely would be simpler.

Footsteps and voices jolt me from my musing; unsure if I should be here, I slide behind one of the many marble columns, peeking to see who it is.

"Bugger"

The Raven has stop mid stride as if aware of my presence. His hand halts the King.

"Wait," he demands.

Shit, shit, shit. I'm much too flustered and I am not willing to deal with yet another interaction with drama. Maybe I am the daughter of Eris, the goddess of discord and strife. I look for a quick exit. I slide towards the wall, my fingers tingle, and an urge to touch and push a small golden peacock feather set within blue and green gems sits beside the painting of Hera. A soft hiss and brush of air caresses my skin, revealing a hidden doorway; without hesitation, I move out of sight, the door closing silently behind me.

Standing in an old narrow corridor dimly lit by amber gems that seem to direct my way, moving slowly I follow the gems, a strange feeling passing over my skin, as if phantom hands stroke my arms and hair, a whispered breath on a breeze that is not there.

These corridors don't appear to have been accessed in years. Walking, I follow the twists and turns quietly, hoping for an exit. After minutes of endless corridors, passing glimpses of the palace through spy holes, a narrow staircase comes into view, ascending high into the palace. Well, I have come this far.

A strange pull to keep following washes over me again, and my magic within stirs. Hesitating, I feel the lure of strange magic urging me to answer its call, pulling me towards the silver and white saloon double doors, which depict a romantic scene of angels, wings spread wide, and plump cherubs lining the frames.

The whisper of magic brushes my cheeks, and I move without consciousness, opening the doors with ease. The apartment before me is stunning. Soft tones of pink and sage green panels lined and gilded with golds demonstrate a room for someone of importance, with comfortable luxury furnishing set around a white carved marble fireplace that has long since seen any heat.

The lounge has several single white doors with angels carved depicting various scenes of freedom and flight. An impression of peace and calm flows through me. This place is a secluded sanctuary for someone long since deceased and forgotten. The pulse of magic catches my breath, and I grab my chest, bending as if punched. Taking several deep breaths, I straighten,

"Why am I here?" I groan, magic stirring around me, lifting my hair, and an urgency pulls me to another door; a bedroom chamber lies within; a four-poster bed with white drapes sits to one side of the room opposite another marble fireplace, and a vanity desk and armoire are located through a stone archway.

Walking to the vanity, my hands are drawn to a music box in light faded pinks and blues, showing a rolling hillside and pretty sky, angels soaring together, hands entwined. I open the box, and music fills the room. The sweet melody brings a smile to my lips and the small white angel dances.

"Hm, what beautiful music." I feel amazing, magic coating my skin, I could be a princess relaxing and dancing with friends here. "Ha." I smile, dancing and twirling, entranced by the melody, dreaming of what could be.

"Oops!" I bump back into the vanity, halting the music and bringing an end to my daydream. The ancient power leaves a taste in my mouth. Chocolate, Honeyed flavours with a metallic coppery tang cloying at the back of my throat. Disorientated, a headache sharp behind my eyes builds,

"How long have I been here?" Looking at the beautiful box, which appears to be empty, my mind slowly clears. A layer of fine light pink silk coats the inside, running my fingers across the silk to the angel. This must have been a young women's rooms. A place to relax and get away from the court, Nostalgia fills my heart, my soul calling to the room, my magic flaring in a way I have never experienced before, catching my breath. Fine, delicate, priceless jewellery emerges layered carefully within the silk, gasping. I gather up a diamond-studded cluster necklace with a large blue sapphire shaped into a star with small diamonds surrounding it; matching earrings are placed with the necklace. They are gorgeous and fit for a queen.

I replace the items carefully, brushing past a platinum ring with a huge blood-red ruby encrusted in the band, tiny black diamond skulls surrounding the ruby, sapphires and emeralds in place of their eyes.

Pain shoots through my temples behind my eyes. I cry out, dropping to my knees as the ring rolls along the floor. Catching my breath as the pain recedes, I locate the ring. Its deadly beauty pulses with an unnatural light; gently, I lift the ring, placing it onto my right ring finger; power races into my very core, excruciating pain locking my muscles tight. Screaming, I collapse to the floor.

Pain, excruciating pain and darkness dance along my subconscious, my chest tight, unable to draw breath.

"My love, please, we must run. Come... Antheia, if you stay, they will keep us apart forever. They are coming."

"Oberon, I can't run. Please listen to me. I have news— happy news. I think... it's not going to be just us anymore!"

"Pardon? You... we? No, no, not now. How?"

"Ha, I think you know how Obi!! I can't have a baby on the run. The court will understand that we are truly in love and *that we belong together."*

"Don't be so naive, Antheia. The elders want to keep the courts apart, want and will keep us apart, don't... Please don't be sad. My greatest desire is to be with you as a family."

"Then stay!"

"I can't... I can't."

CHAPTER 26

Hank

"When will the new recruits be ready?" Captain Thomas Carter looks my way as we sit around a large table. A map of the realm is in front of us. Figurines of roaring lions are placed where our armies are currently situated. Demons with black curling horns show recent attacks on the northern boundaries. the King and his General listen intently while we discuss the infantry we have at our disposal.

"Weeks, maybe months. They are raw and undisciplined. If you send them into battle too soon, you will lose them all in a matter of days," I state.

"Our forces are spread thin," Carter says grimly, running a hand through his greying hair. "Attacks are becoming more frequent across the borders, reports of goblins."

"Sorry?" the King interrupts, his eyes wide with horror. "Goblins, please explain. I thought these creatures were a thing of the past, mere legends?"

The Captain continues, "It seems not your majesty. There are witness reports of goblin-like warriors using magic to manipulate the elements. Our soldiers are ill-prepared to fight such a foe. We lost eighty seasoned fighters last week, and more will die due to their injuries from one battle."

"Where are these attacks happening? What of your intel from the mountains?" I ask, worried at the thought of the enemy casting magic readily again. The implication of such would be catastrophic. Power surges as my own adrenaline spikes. This last year, my beast has been restless, demanding more action from me. But I'm still unsure of its purpose. "Is the earth's magic restoring?"

"Restoring?" The General's dark, intelligent eyes sweep over me reading every inch of my face.

Holding his stare for several seconds, I inhale. Do I trust this court? These men? the decision that I need to give more information if we are to succeed.

"Mm," I grunt, cagey as usual. "I need the floor, but just you three." I point to the King, his General and Captain Carter.

Narrowing his eyes in suspicion, fixing me in his steady, unwavering gaze for several moments before nodding. Running my hand over my long hair, I gather it up into a top knot, giving me time to choose the information I wish to part with as the room clears. Taking a sip of water as all eyes focus on mine.

"I'm older than I look." I start and the General's eyes narrow even further, subtly positioning himself in front of the King readying for action. Fae typically live longer than humans so age is often hard to gage.

"Calm yourself, little chick," I chuff, watching the raven shifter grow tenser. A snarl directed my way, "I would have you plucked and roasted before you could place a finger on that wicked blade you have poorly concealed!"

"General, if I may defuse the situation, Sergeant Dufort and his father were and are known to my family and well respected. He is invaluable to the war effort," Thomas leans forward, trying to break the standoff between myself and the pompous General.

With a deep breath, I continue.

"My family line are all warriors, protectors if you like, knowledge of the past handed down through generations. We understand magic, myths and legends but not as fiction but facts- goblins were nearly wiped out but not fully."

"You are saying you knew they existed but chose to withhold that information," the General growls.

the King looks at a complete loss. His youth etched on his handsome face, born in a time when magic was fast leaving the world.

"No, the information was not relevant until now," I state, rolling my eyes.

Suspicions tear through the general's expression, his jaw ticking with barely restrained anger.

"If I may continue?" I bait the Raven waiting with a cocky grin, wanting to get a read on his reaction and limits- always understand your competition,

"Please, sergeant, continue; this knowledge will be valuable to our efforts, I'm sure."

"Thank you, Captain; as I was saying, the fae of the

Unseelie court, goblins, demons, trolls, giants, etc. were hit hard after the blood wars between the two courts. Splitting the courts completely was the beginning of the end for magic." taking another sip of water, I pause to pay attention to their expressions. "If the goblins have magic, then the Unseelie have found a way to reconnect with magic and the shadows."

"Reconnect? Most fae don't have magic past their fae forms, let alone enough to use in battle," the King states, rubbing his temple in frustration.

"That is true, but that was not always the case when there was balance. The realm's magic is powerful, flowing and available for those who know how to wield it. Currently, your court has a handful of high fae, including the people in this room, with enough magic to wield, or a select few that can perform minor elemental magics and some I suspect to possess ancient artefacts and conduits that unlock the magic of the past/"

"How do you know all this? Why are you here, Hank?"

Huffing an irritated breath at the General "I'm here because I'm needed. This is my task," I say, snapping and banging my hand on the table.

"So it's nothing to do with Miss Whitlock?" A smirk lifts the general's lips, expecting a reaction from me. Allowing confusion to show across my face, I turn to the captain with a raised eyebrow in question.

"Who?"

"The girls you helped," Thomas stuttered, turning my

attention back to the King and general.

"You mean the poor serving girl that one of your court abused and planned to have raped? If there was a show of misuse of power, that girl witnessed it all!" I allow anger to enter my features, hardening my voice. Thomas fidgets at the tension in the room as if wanting to defend his wife

"Now, wwwwait a-" I glare his way, making him drop his eyes and close his mouth in shame.

"You took her to your rooms, and the hair?"

"Yes, general, I helped her get washed and healed before putting her to bed. Tristan owes me a favour, hence the hair. That girl needed to be able to walk back into your vipers' nest of a Palace with a little confidence and feeling less like a victim.... I helped with that." I jab a finger into my chest before pointing at the Raven, "Unlike others of this court."

Lifting a small smile cocking my head. "Why the sudden interest in a beautiful young serving girl, General? Surely we are still discussing the war? Not the ins and outs of this abusive cesspit of a court."

"Enough," the King says, directing a pulse of magic across the three of us. "Please refrain from calling my court, sergeant. I respect your expertise, but my patience is not always guaranteed."

Savage power challenges my own, and my beast recognises another strong alpha. This is not the time or the place, Hank. I chastise myself, giving a slow nod of respect to the King.

"My apologies, Your Majesty, I am not accustomed to the politics of the court. Let me continue with what I know. While this court has been fighting a dictatorship between themselves to restore peace, the Unseelie court, I predict, has been replenishing. Oberon is a patient man with a brilliant but broken mind; he comprehends the complexity of all forms of magic and has a hatred for the Seelie court."

"What of the demon Prince?" Bewilderd the King begins to pull out a folder labelled with the demon prince's name.

"He is mainly just a pawn, I believe, king Oberon is an ancient being of the old court, his presence has been hidden since the blood wars."

"We do not see ourselves as two courts any longer. We are just fae. Why would he continue this war?"

Standing, King Barrett starts to examine the pieces.

"Look at the people who live here. Do you see many Unsullied types?" I raise an eyebrow as the King stops, clarity filling his eyes. "No. You do not. When you took the throne, the Gods took note. Oberon began the attacks on your borders, challenging your throne which he will want."

"So if our enemy has magic, how do we face such power?" the King's attention is fully on me.

"We learn, we prepare, and we unlock our own power. This is where I come in." I pull a heavy wooden chest from the floor, engraved with a fighting dragon upon its lid, placing my hand and infusing it with my magic, allowing me access to the contents. "This is where we start" Ten antique textbooks lie inside "with knowledge."

"Books, you want to win this war to bring peace, with?" the King collects one large tome from the pile, doubt marring his face. The Elders' Testament," he grabs a second book. "Or The Prophecy of the Divided Kingdoms, really?" He tilts his head, looking me dead in the eye.

"That one in particular has a prophecy in it that is being sent to me through dreams. I took the liberty of marking the page." Taking the book, I flip it open to the page in question:

> *When the final dawn is shrouded in shadow,*
> *Blood will fall to change the Fates.*
> *Before there is peace and power.*
> *From royal veins magic will bloom, in the*
> *hands of Kin, ancient power will ignite.*
> *A princess' gift, passed through the veil,*
> *shall breathe life into the forgotten pearl.*
> *Unseelie and Seelie, divided no more.*
> *Together they will halt the storm.*
> *The price of failure is steep: the very*
> *essence of magic shall forever sleep.*
> *Look to the darker pearl with bonded wings.*

"Does this make any sense to you Hank? Because it sure as hell makes no sense to me" Dropping the book to the table in frustration, "I cannot base all my war plans on this. You are asking us to believe in the restoration of magic in a text neither of us understands."

I cut him off. "In ancient times, we all were more attuned to magic; it was a part of everyday life, and yes, those days have faded, but the magic never left. Those currents are now stirring, and whispers of power long dormant are emerging."

"That may be, but magic on the scale you are suggesting has been absent from the realm for decades. Let us focus on what is real and in front of us now!" Carter moves to look at the texts, a flicker of amusement playing in his eyes. It was the kind of smile reserved for a child with a wild imagination. I growl in frustration, rumbling low in my throat, the dismissive smile gnawing at my patients.

"These texts are more than relics of the past. They are the key to our survival, our future. Without this knowledge, we are blind to the forces awakening. We will be outmatched on the battlefield," I pause, taking a deep breath. I may be built for war, but my passion for magic and history is unparalleled. "With them, we may reclaim the mastery that once belonged to all."

"We will look into this prophecy, but as a backup, but for now let's call it a day we have a look to reflect on."

CHAPTER 27

Elodie

P ain and exhaustion pull me to the surface of my mind, the strange dream fogging at the back of my mind. I wake to prostrate on the floor; a furry, feathery body encircles mine purring softly, the vibrations rippling over my spine, lifting my still-pounding head, my mouth feeling full of sand.

Pumpkin clicks and nudges me in concern "Hey bud…" coughing, dragging my knees under me using his furry body,

"I'm okay." I run my hand over his feathered head, noticing the ring is absent from my finger. Inspecting the floor, there is no sign of the ruby skull ring. "That's odd."

With a spinning head, Pumpkin helps me stand, staying close to keep me steady. Moving to the vanity, I close the music box, staring at my paler-than-usual complexion and dark bags under my eyes in the ancient rusting mirror.

Trixie would be horrified. I'm not fit to perform looking like a drug addict. Movement causes me to gasp, turning to scan the room behind me, but all is still. My heart jumped to a rapid pace, and my eyes widened as I search the room. Analysing the mirror again. A glimmer flickers in an old bookcase back in the receiving room.

"What do you think of all this, Pumpkin? Am I going insane?" His hawk head pushes me towards the bookcase with a click, reassuring me to proceed. His presence gives me confidence.

The shelves of the bookcase contain hundreds of books in different shades of burgundy, greens, navy and black, some large, some small, all ancient looking and gathering a fine layer of dust. Excitement fills me at the possibility of sitting and reading at my leisure; this area could be my little sanctuary, too.

"Do you think the owner would mind me bringing life to this place again, Kin?" Clapping and jumping, the excitement makes me act childish. "Ehhhhh," power flushes over my skin, pebbling my flesh. "Ouch!"

The gems lining the walls flare to life, illuminating the beautiful room, and the fireplace sparks with roaring flames, beginning to warm it. "Ha, I take that as a yes, then. Thank you!"

Exploring the titles on the shelves, one small black leather-bound book falls to the floor, collecting it, my composure begins to slip. The room, the music box, and now this book all seems.. scripted. as if someone is controlling my fate, my heart rate quickens once again bringing a tremble to my fingertips, the book slipping from my hands, landing with a thud, indecision ruling my thoughts, what do the Gods have in store for me? Pumpkin takes the book in his beak and begins to stroll towards the fire, settling down on the dusty damask rug and placing the book on the light green sofa.

"Huh? Are you in cahoots with the ghost of Celestial

Palace?" Gathering the black book fingers tracing the red design of interwoven roses and snakes, then settling onto the sofa tucking my feet under me as I begin to read:

Magic is dying, the two courts have diminished and fae kind looks more and more human, people born unable to access the connection to the earth, to their powers.
My Oberon has left me here amongst the Seelie court... With child, the elders refuse to believe we are stronger together. When there is balance, light and dark, Seelie and Unseelie, we are strong.

My heart is lost, its beat uneven and laborious. The more time we spend apart, the more my magic fades. Why can't they see we are meant to be together?
War is not the answer I have seen!

Instantly, I recall the strange dream. Was it a memory? Is this room somehow connected? Continuing with the diary:

Visions and predictions torment my dreams. The courts will end, many will lose their lives in a bloody end all because our love is denied.

I search for a way to restore life, to gain peace once again. I consult the scrying glass again and again, grabbing snippets of the future and formulating a prophecy, but things are too uncertain.

I write this diary in the hopes of passing on all I know to another. If you're reading this, magic has indeed faded, and you have the level of magic to help restore the future!
And I have failed!

Can Magic be restored? The text continues with daily entries, most a monotonous description of her daily activities, but several pages grab my attention, harsh scribblings and predictions, a prophecy of sorts capturing my attention.

When the final dawn is shrouded in shadow, blood will fall to change the Fates. Before there is peace and power. From royal veins, magic will bloom, and in the hands of Kin, ancient power will ignite. A princess' gift, passed through the veil, shall breathe life into the forgotten pearl.

Unseelie and Seelie, divided no more. Together, they will halt the storm. The price of failure is steep: the very essence of magic shall forever sleep. Look to the darker pearl with bonded wings.

Closing the diary, sitting and contemplating how much truth is in those words, I wonder if something has enhanced my magic. Do I feel any different? Not sure of the time that has passed, I make a move to find my way back to my dorms, Pumpkin jumping up and stretching, yawning deeply before taking the lead. "Can you help me navigate these passages, Kin?"

CHAPTER 28

Elodie

Finally showered and refreshed after an exhausting day running ragged after various members of the court, followed by a trip to my secret retreat and a few hours exploring the mystery diary and rooms.

That place is beautiful and feels like mine, a strange connection and familiarity that eases the feeling of being meaningless in my mediocre life. A message lights up my phone, grabbing my attention. Glancing down, I see an unknown number with a formally written message.

Miss Whitlock,
I hereby invite you to join me privately in my suites tonight at 7 pm.

Kind Regards
King Barrett.

Shocked by a tiny flutter that brought a smile to my face, I re-read the message several times, not taking in the words. Looking at the time: 18.45pm!

"Sugar, I only have fifteen minutes to get across the bloody palace."

My phone pings again… Then again.

Do you accept?

You can't ignore a direct order from your king.

Not wanting to decline the King's order, I rushed from the room. Twenty minutes later, panting from the brisk run, I was just a little bit sweatier than I would have liked to meet privately with the King. Butterflies of nerves had me all jittery, and a goofy smile played about my face in excitement.

Scowling at myself for acting like a teenager in a fairytale when the dickhead abused his power to what? Show me how weak I really am in this palace.

"Can I help you? says the gruff guard manning the entrance to the King's suite enquiries.

"the King is expecting me. Miss Elodie Whitlock," I say as he looks me up and down with a knowing, condescending smirk.

"Wait here," he moves to a side room and speaks through a device. He then nods, turning my way, and beckons me close with a jerk of his chin.

"Place your hand on here and hold still.." I did as instructed, my hand scanning. "Okay, Miss Whitlock, you may enter the receiving room. Stand at the bottom of the stairs as you walk in and wait. Do not move from there until you are collected."

"Yes, Sir." I salute like a soldier and head through the doors. "Gods," I mutter, eyes going wide at the sheer scale of things. If this is just the receiving room, what is the rest like?

Parquet flooring in a herringbone pattern covers the entire space, two sandstone fireplaces sit cold on opposite sides of the room, and the ceiling is covered in artwork of fairy maidens of old, frolicking with males, both beautiful and sexual. Two huge double doors are shut at the end of the room, a polished dark wood throne in between. My mouth gaping up at the intricately painted bodies, many naked. I wait, nerves making me sweat, and my mouth turns dry.

"Miss Whitlock?" Jumping, I look towards the source. King Barrett stands before the left-hand open door dressed in fitted dark blue jeans, bare feet, and a dark figure-hugging polo shirt. His biceps flex as he raises an arm above his head. I stare at the perfect cut of a man standing in front of me, eyes tracing the huge contours of his arms, imagining his strength. Caramel curls flopping into deep soulful eyes I could simply get lost in…

"Ahem!" Remembering he is the bloody King and I'm eye fucking him shamelessly, I stumble into a clumsy bow turn and curtsy, my cheeks heating.

"Please, no bowing, it's just us, come." A shameless smirk pulls at his mouth. He turns and re-enters the room behind the door, rushing to catch up, trying hard not to toggle the shape of his ass.

I enter another open-plan, modern, and comfortable lounge area. Large navy blue chesterfield sofas surround a large burnt orange coffee table in front of the biggest flat-screen TV I have ever seen. Alcoves are lined with shelves and carefully selected items, making the area look like a show home.

After bypassing a pre-set dining area with a crystal chandelier, bi-fold glass doors open to a private courtyard and pool area. The place is stunning, yet homely.

"Please make yourself comfortable near the fire pit. I just need to check on some bits. Can I fetch you a drink?" Standing stiffly with a formal tone. is he nervous, too, or am I going to get a lecture? Stunned and frozen to my spot, remembering our last meeting, I awkwardly shrug and then nod,

"PPPlease, water will do."

"Hm." I can see the smirk on his rugged face from the corner of my eye. He nods and heads back inside, leaving me to get cosy on the grey chairs surrounding an open fire pit. Returning, Barrett hands me a clear glass of water, the ice gently rattling in the glass. Silence follows. Sitting, he takes his beer and relaxes, legs spread wide without a care in the world. Silence permeates the air, my palm going sweaty as I wait, sitting with my back straight as several more minutes pass awkwardly. I finally break, sucking in a deep breath,

"Apologies, your majesty."

"Barrett," he cuts me off. "Please call me Barrett. You are in my home, not the court."

"Sorry, Barrett, why am I here?" He sighs, taking a large gulp of his drink.

"I would like to," he pauses, dropping his eyes and

rubbing the back of his neck. "Well, to apologise for my behaviour the other day, I took my fun too far and abused my power and your trust. I know you declined my offer, but please let me show you I'm not a total prick!" He looks so sincere and vulnerable that I burst out laughing at the kicked puppy look, all big eyes and dimples, a smile playing on his lips.

"What did I say?" He chuckles, looking shy and uncertain.

"The King of the realm that I punched two days ago is apologising to a serving girl. The world's gone mad." We both inhale, smiling. The tension leaves both our postures, and the comfortable connection we seem to have instantly returns.

"I even cooked for you!" he admits sheepishly, tossing a hand through his golden locks and springing to his feet, his cat-like grace evident in his movements. He holds out his hand, "Please this way, My Lady!" Playfully, I rise like a noble woman.

"Certainly, My Lord." Did I imagine the flame in his eyes as he took my hand? We head into the kitchen, where he has prepared multiple small dishes, most of which I have no idea what they are. With a flourish and a low bow, the King announces.

"All my favourite dishes My Lady, plus I have puddings!" Stunned, I look at the array of dishes in front of me. This is a new experience for me. Feeling honoured. A rush of warmth fills my body. To be receiving such kind of treatment is a rarity. Suspicion builds, narrowing my eyes, my cynical brain starts to wonder if his actions have ulterior motives. Wanting to believe the former. I decide to go with the flow and enjoy this evening with Barrett, not the King.

"Wine, let me get wine." Dashing and leaping over a counter, Barrett opens a wine cellar, pulling two bottles out. "White for these dishes, red for these," he gestures, his eyes full of excitement and expectations. Where would you like to start?"

"Ermm, I don't know what half of this is," I giggle, his enthusiasm catching. "The white wine and these seafood dishes?" I guess with a questioning look his way.

"Yes, those are prawns, scallops, and smoked crab," he indicates, "please eat and drink!" His intense eyes sparkle as I begin sampling each dish.

"Ohhhh," I moan loudly, chewing and licking my lips, sucking the garlic-salted prawns into my mouth, all delicate court manners flying out the window. "These are delectable; I try another dish and with a sip of the crisp, dry wine "Ohhh gods what is that?!" Mouth-watering with textures and flavour firing across my taste buds like never before, I moan again, closing my eyes. Have I died and gone to heaven?

My mouth explodes with the new experience, each bite delicious and sending zings to my brain. I almost forget the King is present. Engrossed in the dishes in front of me, Barrett watches, delicately picking at the dishes.

"Clam chowder, it's one of my favourites," he states, chuckling. "Shit, Elodie, you're killing me with those noises." Heat flares between us, his eyes following my tongue as I lick my lips slowly. Unable to acknowledge the intense heat, I fail to respond, dropping my gaze to the food before me and selecting another rich meat dish. Nerves bring a shyness to me. Having never really dated or flirted outside of work and my very small friendship group, I find myself a little lost at how to act.

We continue devouring his food, pairing the dishes with different wines to enhance the taste of each. Sitting close, chatting about each dish, Barrett's arm casually draped over one shoulder does not tear his gaze from my mouth as he observes transfixed, educating me on each dish and what to pair with it. Desire burns hotly through me, and I have to swallow several times to get my voice to work.

"Stop eye fucking me!" I giggle as he seems to come out of his trance, shaking his head and using a whole lot of effort to focus back on my face.

"I like what I see. You have my undivided attention, Miss Whitlock." He raises his fingers to my face gently, capturing my gaze; unmistakable desire fills his face; swiping his thumb over my lower lip, placing it in his own mouth, and sucking the juices. "I think I have found my new favourite way to dine," he comments in a rough lust-filled voice. Slowly, he tucks a stray lock behind my ear, trailing a scorching path down my shoulder and arm, eyes never leaving my face as he intertwines our hands.

Shit! My knickers are soaked from one touch. I'm in trouble. Closing the distance, his lips touching mine, seeking permission to continue; when I don't pull away, the kiss intensifies, a hand knotting in my long hair demanding more, holding me captive. Our tongues clash as shivers of pleasure ripple, wanting more.

My whole body reacts, needing him closer. It would be so fucking easy to just give in to this chemistry to forget he is the King, or the power he holds over me, or the women falling at his feet, lined up to service their king at the drop of a hat. Where would it leave me once he had me? Flashbacks of my time with Alfie send a jolt of realisation of the games people play in this place. I will not be a part of such games.

Panting, I break away, my face flushed with heat, breaking eye contact and clearing my throat, unable to hold his intense flaming stare. I leave our fingers intertwined but relax my hold until just one pinky keeps us softly connected, as if I can't let go just yet.

"Hey, what's wrong?" with a gentle tone, fingers controlling my jaw to make me meet his gaze.

"I want to take things slow. I know I'm just a serving girl, but I'm not... you know, like that... this." I gulp, waiting for my dismissal to leave. I look down to the floor again, feeling the blush begin to colour my cheeks. With a lopsided grin, amusement glinting in his eyes,

"And why do you think I have you here, Wildcat?"

"Wildcat?!" I laugh at the nickname.

Shrugging, he says, "It suits you! So, me kissing you seems to have triggered some negative thoughts?" Giving me space, he sits back slightly, scooping my hand up with that pinky and kissing softly before releasing his touch. Instantly, I miss the contact, not wanting to push him away but to draw him closer.

"Well, I don't want to be another notch on someone's bedpost or picked up for someone's pleasure," I confess,

"And that's what you think I'm doing here?" Embarrassed, my cheeks turn pink. Have I read him all wrong? "From the first moment I laid eyes on you, Wildcat, I have been consumed with thoughts of you. When you're near, I feel this pull to be with you, protect you, and to top it off, I have never felt so comfortable and happy to be in someone's company like I am yours."

"Oh," I can't fully meet the intensity of his gaze, his words bringing a warmth and need long forgotten.

"And for the record, I don't sleep with all the ladies of the court. In fact, you are the first to enter my private suites ever." Leaning forward he tucks a stray piece of hair behind my ear, placing a soft caress up my neck, then finding my lips for a soft heated kiss, sending my heart rate racing again, before sitting back, resting one arm across the chair, giving me a jaw dropping view of the taut muscles of his stomach, T-shirt stretch over his chest, pausing I take a long look at him, a rueful smile to my lips, lifting my gaze, before things become heated!

"Let's get to know one another properly. Take our time. I refuse to deny that we have a connection, Wildcat and I am willing to explore this. If you need to take things slow and learn to trust my intentions, then that is exactly what we will do."

"Thank you." I find myself at a loss for anything more to say. His words spread warm fuzzies to my heart;

wanting to believe him but was still not sure. Seeing my inner turmoil he breaks the tension.

"Now, the best bit. Pudding! Come on!"

CHAPTER 29

Elodie

Snorting my wine, I grab another chocolate biscuit "Nooooo like this!" I place the biscuit chocolate side down on my forehead. "It's all in the facial muscles and getthhing thhhungue to yourth bisscurh." contorting my face, arms pinned behind my back, tongue out. The biscuit falls from my face, leaving a smudge across my cheek and plopping into my wine. "Oppps"

Barrett dives on me and licks the chocolate off my face like a big cat before bursting into laughter once again. I push him away in disgust wiping my face clean of spit, "Stoooop! Erh you are like a big cat."

This side of the King is playful and easy. We have fallen into comfortable, jovial conversation all evening. Breathing hard, his stare intensifies.

"I have never met anyone like you, Elodie. You make me feel like... like I'm not the King Thank you for knocking me on my ass and reminding me I am still just a man." his smile is gentle, not quite reaching his eyes.

The mood quickly descends into a more sullen atmosphere.

"Tell me what it's like, you know, having all this power, having people fear you all the time." I bring my legs underneath me as we sit outside in front of the fire pit once more. Tipsy from the wine and stuffed with multiple dishes, we have fallen close together, often touching softly, both of us seeming to need the contact.

"If people don't fear me, they are plotting against me. It feels lonely." absentmindedly, he trails fingers up and down my arm, sending shivers down my spine and pebbling my skin. In a breathy whisper, I question,

"How did you get all this power?" I snuggle closer, his arm wrapping around my shoulder, pulling me in tight. The fresh pine scent of him enveloping me driving home a feeling of belonging and tenderness, freedom, the desire to stay here in his arms mounting.

"When I defeated the old king, the throne called to me and amplified the magic I already carried tenfold." He scoffs. "Now I just need to hold onto it."

A gust of air blows my hair across my face. His fingers lightly twist in the blue-tinged dark strands, tucking them behind my ear. His eyes flick to my lips as if deciding whether to kiss me or not, catching my lip between my teeth.

"Gods, Wildcat, I really want to kiss you."

I nod, wanting this man closer. Our lips collide, full of passion, the taste of sweet honey erupting as our lips dance together. Strong arms pull me into his lap, my thighs straddling his trim waist, groaning, the thin fabric of my leggings not much of a barrier against our mutual desires.

"You have the fucking assassin in your private quarters with no guards?" a harsh, angry growl breaks the intensity as we draw apart, jumping, creating breathing space as we untangle from one another, looking at the intruder.

Barrett straightens slowly, withdrawing his fingers from my neck, gaze still locked in mine, while responding, anger ticking at his jaw.

"You think I can't fight off Miss Whitlock General?"

"No, I believe Miss Whitlock has you seduced in your quarters, Barrett," the Raven sneers my way, taking in our closeness and several empty bottles of wine. Turning to look at the dark, terrifying fae dressed in black battle leathers, dark wings folded behind him. Rage builds at his disgusted look and ignorance, snarling back.

"Excuse me, Miss Whitlock is right here."

Ignoring me and leaning over the King, towering over the two of us, the General continues. "You do know what she used to do, Barrett, right?" Panic, anger and a touch of embarrassment brings out my sarcasm, I will not let this fae belittle my actions to stay alive.

"Oh, dear Alexander, have you heard, or were you a regular?" I sigh. "You know, with your looks, If you smiled, you would be able to entice one of the fine men of the court to your bed," I gritted my teeth and added "dickhead" under my breath.

Drunkenly, Barrett drapes an arm over my shoulder, hugging me close. "Oh, what did you do, sweet Ellie? Please enlighten me." He kisses my cheek and waits.

I square my shoulder, my attention on the General.

"She was a dancer at Electric Eden.," he says, using quotation marks with his fingers. He curls his lip, and his dark eyes never leave me.

"Fuck you." I try to snarl, but it comes out weak with embarrassment, a breathy whisper, my throat tight.

"A dancer, as in a stripper? Are you any good? "the King's face lights up, not noticing my anguish, trying to lighten the mood.

"Good enough to dance and not have to lie on my back for any man."

"Wildcat, you have to give us a demonstration, please show me! Dance for me. I will get some music, I have never frequented such establishments" launching to my feet, every element of my life coming tumbling down around my new persona, I cut him off.

"No— I will not. You are a friend, and I do not want you to see me like that." I stand, fists clenched at my sides. My shame turning my stomach. A rogue tear slides down my face, and my voice, which I intended to be strong and full of defiance, betrays me, breaking pathetically.

"Ha," the General smirks. "Really, a dancer? I know the clientele of Electric Eden and you're just the right type for that particular line of work, how much do you make per night looking like you do?"

Reacting to the barb, I throw my dagger at the general's head; he moves at the last second, and it embeds into the eye of a majestic unicorn statue behind him. Moving lightning fast, he throws me by the throat up against the glass partition,

"You dare attack the King's general?" He snarls in my face with an outraged expression; I just narrow my eyes, making a grunting noise in acknowledgement like I had no care in the world holding his gaze. There is a wickedly amused glint in his.

Swallowing my frustration and anger, I reply with my own scowl.

"No, I dare to warn the man who has just insulted me by calling me a fucking whore", I scream back, straining my neck in his hold, so close I can taste the fury between us.

"Alex put her the fuck down." the King demands. "That's an order."

"You are blinded by her, Barrett." Corded muscles of his forearm strain, fury only just held back.

"That's enough, Alexander," he bellows. The Raven releases me with a shove, and a hissed curse leaves his throat in warning. Closing my eyes in an attempt to control my own anger. Pushing away from the glass rubbing at my neck, bruising will be evident tomorrow.

"Why do you detest me so much?" scowling at the dark-haired raven shifter, "do you even know what it's like out there for someone like me?"

Pulling my band T straight, my eyes track the two men now standing side by side facing me. "You sit up here with all the power and never having to do without, and yet when I have a rare moment of comfort, you set out, like most of the other nobles, to brand me. Insult me for doing what I have to do, what I have to do to survive. You strut around like it's your god-given right to judge people while giving nothing." I stress the last word, leaning into his space. Despite the height difference, I challenge him, holding his glare.

"Do not judge me, Miss Whitlock. You don't know the first thing about me," he snarls.

"But it's okay for you to judge me," I prod his chest. "And you don't know me!"

Barrett moves to grab a bottle of beer from the ice bucket, popping the top and pointing it at his friend with a smirk. "She has you there, my friend."

"The reason why I don't trust you," he says, pausing to flick his stare to the King. "You have turned up out of nowhere and charmed the King with a dagger strapped to your thigh that you could never afford! And you claim not to be an assassin, and with no magic! Yet you just threw a dagger with the precision of a powerful warrior, knowing exactly how much I would move, Like a warning." He steps closer, his wings springing to life behind him, readying for battle. "Landing a throw like that can only be carried out by someone of magic and skill... trained skill."

Rolling my eyes, I state with sass, "I'm a performer and have a highly skilled friend who thought it would be wise that I could defend myself. If you ever got your head out your own arse and cared to ask," I trail off.

"My job is to protect My King. You threaten that daily! Everything points at a highly trained manipulative honey trap."

The King uses a delicate hand movement to bring the dagger from the wall to his hand, studying first it, the detailed delicate design showing its unique expensive quality, then observing me, mistrust and betrayal burn deep in his sea green eyes. He then furrows his brows in confusion. I see the flicker of hurt as he believes every word from his General. Shutting down his expression, now unreadable, defeat lines my own features, chuffing out a sarcastic laugh. I will always be the mistrustful, worthless serving girl. What are my words but simple lies?

"And there it is, one hurdle, and he retreats." Moving, I take one last deep drink of my wine. "I think I know all that matters now." I will always be untrustworthy, lower, the servant, the dancer, the owned whore in their eyes, nothing I do will change that.

"He's right, though, Elodie." Pausing, suspicion and hurt swim behind the King's, eyes before he turns his back to me. "Let's call it a night, Miss Whitlock."

"That's it? And here I actually thought you would be different," I say, gritting my teeth refusing to show any hurt at his dismissal.

"Thank you for your time, Alex. Please see Miss Whitlock out." He strides from the room without a backward glance. My heart drops; I seem to be attracting assholes, currently, first Alfie, now Barrett. Shaking my head, angry tears forming.

"The reason you are so lonely is because you can't see a friend when they are under your stuck-up nose," I shout at his retreating form.

The General goes to take my arm to escort me out. "Do not lay your fucking hands on me." With that, I turn and leave, the Raven close behind.

CHAPTER 30

The Raven

"Do you know how many actual friends I have, Alexander? No, don't answer. That is fucking pathetic." Barrett strips out of his casual clothes down to his boxers, beer tight in his grip, gulping the remainder before tossing the empty across the room and reaching for another.

"I'm scared to have any interactions romantically, never mind fuck any women in this court, in case they purposely fall pregnant as an easy way to get onto the throne and gain more power. Trap me."

"So, you had the assassin here to get laid?" Walking to his liquor cabinet, I pour two drinks and hand him one, keeping my face neutral as Barrett's attestation mounts. His movements are twitchy, and the majestic beast that lays within is prowling to the surface.

Seeing my friend cut up in this way, the two sides of him at war with one another, I know he's lonely and longing for more meaningful interactions with people he can trust.

That assassin has monopolised on that one weakness, sinking her claws in with promises of a future, of companionship, love, of the hope of more than war and ruling. Her indignant face as she called me out earlier like I was at fault for accusing her or highlighting exactly what she is.

No girl at Electric Eden has that sort of skill with daggers, to top off the magnetic pull she seems to have on people around her. I see the carefully calculated person under that beautiful facade. Everything screams lethal. The way she moves, the way she checks out a room looking for threats and exits.

No serving girl has that sort of perception. And her magic, something felt different today, a raw, unleashed energy simmering beneath the surface, clawing to be liberated. I scoff, sipping my drink, she says she was given a dagger by a friend. Ha! She's highly trained, and the way she challenged me, I'm twice her size!

Most people tremble at the sight of my fury, but not her. A smile twitches at the corner of my mouth. I will not endorse my body's reaction to her; I see the appeal. I want to preen and show her my full self. I could feel the desire to take that smart mouth there and then. That sort of power over anyone is not normal. I'm starting to think she has more power than she has on display. The girl is an enigma.

"Alexander, you ruined one of the best nights of my life. She is funny and sexy as hell but never once actively flirted with the idea of the throne. She is interested in me! She truly wanted to spend time with me, Barrett, not the King." He flops onto his bed, one arm raised over his eyes, hiding the hurt from the world, from me.

Silently sitting in an armchair, I take a slow drink. That woman nearly brought out a full battle shift in me, my control slipping, wanting to take that stubborn set to her mouth and force her into submission. Rolling my neck, I sigh, my thoughts turning to her ice-blue eyes and the harsh set of her lips when she is angry. STOP. I berate myself for allowing these thoughts to deflect back to Barrett.

"You say ruined. I beg to differ. That dagger you're still holding was strapped to her leg the whole time she was in your presence." Pointing to the dagger, Barrett is still inspecting "Did you notice it?" His head snaps up, eyes wide in shock.

"No. I never thought to check," he says, dropping his head back to the pillow "Fuck, is she truly playing me? Alex?"

"Fuck indeed, a black onyx dragon dagger, to be precise; once against the wearer's skin, it disappears; where does an orphan stripper girl get such a dagger?" Hurt fills Barrett's face before he quickly smooths it and dons a blank expression.

"Well, I was truly naive! Thank you, friend. Maybe it's time to back off. I think it's time I got some sleep."

Finishing my drink, I stand uneasy at my friend's obviously unhappy state. "I wish my suspicions were wrong," I said quietly before leaving the King, checking his apartment before I exit.

Outside his chambers, I confront the guards. "Miss Whitlock or any other person is not to enter these apartments ever again. And search everyone even if they are fucking pretty." I press my face to the terrified guard "Do you understand?" He nods, and I raise an eyebrow.

"Yes, sir." He salutes nervously, eyes fixed forward, igniting a smirk. I bite the inside of my cheek and offer a nod before marching down to my apartment.

CHAPTER 31

Elodie

"Hey Ellie, I'm making pancakes if you want some?" Inhaling deeply the aroma of vanilla pancakes and maple syrup surrounds my senses, my mouth watering in anticipation. "If by pancakes you mean that delicious smell wafting my way, then hell yes!"

Sleep did not come easy last night, with accusations and insults running through my head. The most humiliating part of it all is that The Raven is completely just in his distrust. I am here for another's gain. I AM a trained warrior. Untested, yes, but gods, I am trained to seduce, impress, and engage with a mark.

When I checked my phone, I read a message from Lucca. Guilt weighed heavy on my heart at the lack of contact.

> *Lucca:*
> *Girl, I miss you!*
> *How is that sexy guard doing?*
> *I hope he has you walking all kinds of wonky!!*
> *Have you seen Hank?!!*
> *Seems like he has followed you into palace employment.*
> *I want deets, are you banging them both?*
> *Must catch up soon. X*

"What, or should I say, who has you smiling?"

Jenny wiggles her eyebrows while placing syrup-laced pancakes in front of me. Avoiding her question, I concentrate on the food

"Ohh," I moan, gesturing with my folk, "these are good."

"Has Jenny made pancakes?" Esta shouts from her room. "I'm coming now, don't eat them all!"

"Too late, Esta! you snooze, you lose, lady." We chuckle at the thumps coming from her room as she drags and stumbles her way out of bed.

"So, last night? Were you with a certain sexy guard who may or may not be called Alfie?"

"Ha, a lady never divulges such gossip." I mock gasp in horror, "I'm at breakfast service early." I deflect, not wanting to admit Alfie may have been using me. "And Mrs Anderson wants a word first, so I better go."

With a wave, I dash Jenny's voice calling after me. "Stop! Details!"

Laughing, I do not avoid the object that was flung at my head,

"For fuck sake, you bloody psycho twat." Laughing and slamming the door shut, I resume walking towards the palace kitchens, rubbing my head. Pumpkin appears along the hallway, sitting in a regal fashion, head held high.

"Pumpkin, what the hell? You can't be here." I rush toward him, and he simply turns, walking through the wall by an angel statue. I wince as pain shoots up my head, pinching the bridge of my nose. As I open my eyes, a red-tinged shadow materialises across my right ring finger. Examining my fingers, I see the faint outline of the ruby skull ring and heat flares, glowing red, bracing a hand on the wall which Pumpkin walked through. A surge of power pulls from my gut, and another strike of pain follows but subsides quickly.

A door that was not there before now stands ajar. Unnerved, I push through and slide the door closed; the same strange gems light the corridors. Is the palace full of these secret corridors? Pumpkin watches me keenly and begins to pad along with a click of his beak to follow. Power tickles up my arms, coating me in goose flesh. Catching my breath, pausing to absorb the feeling.

This corridor leads behind several state rooms and public areas, twisting and turning with viewing areas into the rooms. At first, panic seized me when I came upon two fae having tea in a parlour, but soon, I realised they could neither see nor hear me.

Pushing through a small plain door, I hear voices. Pausing to listen, I recognise the gruff, stern voice of Captain Thomas Carter. Peering, I see him standing stock still, talking to another out of view.

"The Shades are using magic users and goblins in their ranks now. We are outmatched and have no way to defend successfully. We have sent further recruits to the dark forest and borders, therefore leaving the palace vulnerable." Cater's voice sounds robotic and detached.

"Will the King take the fight directly to Oberon?" A feminine tone questions, but despite the familiarity, I can't place it.

"No—we need the new recruits better trained, and we need time to source magic users ourselves." Still, the captain stands rigidly, eyes wide, staring blankly ahead. The man is usually stoic but is more animated than this? A pulse of power surges through the room. Why am I feeling new frequencies of magic when I never did in the past?

"How does the King hold his power? I need to know his weakness," the seductive voice purrs. My heart begins to pound. Is the Captain a spy passing on information, just like myself? Is the palace in danger?

"The throne holds the magic, amplifying his power. The palace is weak now while we train the new recruits and research how to unlock more power. We are waiting for a fresh rotation to arrive in five days to help patrol the palace." Captain Carter shakes his head as if drunk and confused. Blinking, he looks around and then smiles.

"My dear, forgive me. I seem to have come over a little queer." Stepping forward to greet the person, posture relaxing as he moves out of my sight.

"Let's get you some breakfast, My Lord." A slender hand takes the captain's entwining fingers like a lover. Could that information cause trouble for the King? I presume the knowledge of his power is not commonplace. Whipping out my mobile, I message Hank:

Hey Hank
Just a quickie!
Is it common knowledge how the King gained more power

when he took the throne? Thanks, El x

Hank:
Where are you?
And no. why?
H

Elodie:
Just walking to work I'm late!
Heard a conversation, it was mentioned.
El x

Hank:
See me later,
my room after work.
H x

A flush of heat makes me shudder at his command, his message followed by a kiss. I remind myself that he is older and a friend and certainly does not want me like that, yet I feel this pull towards him. I'm sure I'm not imagining the soft touches, heated looks and gods, he is gorgeous, all rugged alpha male dominance, stomach flipping, and my nipples harden just at the thought of him. Damn, girl get it together first, Alfie dickhead, the bloody king now, Hank? What is going on with me?! Did I boost my sex drive magically in the bloody room?

CHAPTER 32

Lord Hamlington

I grab Miss Whitlock after her serving shift to confirm the rumour that she was indeed in the King's private suites.

"Yes, he wanted to apologise. We talked, but his General put a stop to it and outed me as a stripper, slash spy, or possible assassin—his words, not mine." She waves a hand flippantly, without a care in the world, face devoid of emotion, a complete mask.

The girl is learning to play the game.

"So, he is suspicious of you and your intentions?" Steepling my fingers, watching her closely behind my desk.

"Of course he is. the King asked if I would dance, and I sort of lost my temper and threw a dagger at him."

I stare at the feral beauty before me, the balls on her to take on even the King's general, The Raven. "Tell me everything."

Miss Whitlock relays the events of her evening, including a strange encounter she overheard with the Captain about goblin armies with magic and the court's lack of guards, which led to a huge weakness in our defence. My mind whirls as I compartmentalise this new information.

Someone else is playing for the throne. Why else do they need that information? I need Elodie closer to the King. I want her to use her connection with him to learn of the court's plans. I am Contemplating my next move, taking in the woman in front of me.

"You will perform tonight. What do you need?" I collect a pen and wait expectantly.

"No. I'm not here as a dancer. I will not be the talk of the court." Her expression darkens. Her chin lifts, readying for a fight, rousing the fight in me. She enjoys the way she thinks she has some power when it's just a mask. I will enjoy stripping away that defiance.

"Oh, Miss Whitlock, you misunderstood me." A wicked smile directed her way, she cracked her mask, hands clenched together to prevent her from showing that I had ruffled her feathers. I locked my magic around her, bringing her across the desk violently, slamming her chest flat to the desk, and leaning forward to speak directly into her ear.

"If the King wants you," I slide a finger along her spine, slowly stopping to flatten my palm over her tight ass, "to suck his gods damned cock while dancing, you do as you are ordered. So, Miss Whitlock - get on that stage, perform, grab the King's attention." Taking a breath, leaning back in my chair, and releasing her, watching her jaw flex and grind as she attempts to control her anger, rising and moving back to her chair. "You have no freedom here, girl, at least not until your debt is paid, so I ask again. What do you need?"

CHAPTER 33

Hank

Elodie readies for her performance, and the familiarity of the routine is almost comforting. Wearing a dark silver bra top covered in rhinestones and loose fabric flowing into long silk skirts, she is almost entirely covered, including her face and hair, leaving only her dramatic blue eyes.

Using my broad frame, Blocking the doorway as I watch her, transfixed, the need to protect her escalating, I want to throw caution to the wind and make her mine. I can't deny the attraction between us that has simmered away for years, but now oh, the fucking jealousy. I'm not the only one who has grabbed her attention.

Back at the club, with the punishing routine, she never had the energy or time to consider a romance. Not once did I see her take an interest in any man or woman. I could simply take comfort in being her friend.

Noticing my presence, her face lights up. A smile she rarely displays for others bolsters my beast with pride. Responding in kind, I walk towards the woman who has held my heart for years.

"Hey, Hank, it's just like old times, eh?" She huffs a sarcastic laugh. Her eye roll could win awards; it is so dramatic.

I smile, coming to stand behind her. "How did you end up performing? I thought they wanted to keep your past out of things." Resting my hands on her shoulders, I begin to massage her tight muscles, relishing in the fact that she moves into my touch, relaxing under my fingers with a soft moan, a moan that drives straight to my dick.

"Yeah. Well, Lord Hamlington wishes me to get closer to the King," lowering her head in shame. "I'm not a whore, Hank. I like Barrett, but I don't want to do this." She twists her hands in the fabric of her skirts in a nervous gesture, "I don't want to lie and manipulate to get close to someone; that is not me, Hank."

Fear and embarrassment drive through her body, eyes pleading for help, sending a gutting pain straight to my heart. I scoop her into my warm embrace, lifting and hugging her tightly, twisting so her chest is flush with mine,

"You were right. I can't do this." She sobs, her petite frame trembling, a vulnerability rarely shown as she clings on for support.

"I will not let you become his whore Elodie, I promise. We will run if you need to. The only person that touches your body is the person you want. I will always protect you." I kiss her temple as a rush of love for this spunky woman fills my chest. Lifting her chin with my fingers, I press a gentle kiss to her lips, then place my forehead to hers. "I will always protect you, Elodie. Always." Raw emotion tears at my core, the overwhelming desire to show her exactly how I feel. I hold back, shoulders drooping; she is too young, too vulnerable.

Her gaze bores into mine, a rare moment passing between us. Unable to resist touching her, I kiss her lightly again, my lips lingering; she freezes, eyes widen. Shit, I have read this all wrong. I'm just her friend; she is not interested like that, fuck. She probably sees me as a bloody father or kind uncle sort of figure.

Panicked, I push away, gently spinning her around to face the exit for the stage. Deflection is now my go-to action with Elodie Whitlock.

"Go and knock them on their asses, gorgeous." I breathe deeply, pinching the top of my nose. A building headache is pulsing as Elodie leaves for her performance.

The ballroom is full. Lord Hamlington has built up a performance of a lifetime. The stage is set with strategically placed brass shining concave plates. The room is filled with themed cocktail bars, canapés, and performers working the floor. The atmosphere is electric.

Excitement pulsating with chatter and laughter, many well on their way to getting hammered. Lady Carter sits with an entourage of guards and nobles scowling at the stage, unimpressed not to be the centre of attention, her sly eyes scanning the room; that guard, Alfie, I believe, is stuck to her side, with the lingering touches and whispered words giving them away. Hatred at the sleazy pretty boy guard boiling my blood, how he has played my girl...... "*my girl?*"

The lights dim, breaking my train of thought. The haunting orchestral music begins. She walks slowly, undulating hips slowly swaying her silk skirts, offering a glimpse of pearlescent skin beneath. As the music escalates, she spins in sensual twists and turns, moving around the stage in a voluptuous dance. I notice the King's stare—he is captivated. A low growl escapes me, the man beside me moving ever so slightly, fear spilling from his pores.

She throws a dagger with precision that ricochets off the brass plate, spinning it back like a boomerang, towards the beautiful dancing creature. It narrowly misses her skin to slice away sections of silk, revealing a toned, slender thigh.

The music builds as more daggers are thrown, slowly removing more pieces of silk. Suddenly, glimpses of flesh appear on the ever-moving exotic dancer. My heart pounds.

My breaths become shallower, and holding myself in check becomes harder the more I watch. She is like a graceful warrior contorting into impossible shapes to avoid the strikes of her own daggers, but she is slicing the delicate fabric of her dress, revealing more and more flesh.

Every pair of eyes is locked on the sensual being. Mine included. Finally, her ravishing curves are exposed. Her eyes flick to Lady Carter, who has gone rigid at the beauty on stage, her perverted guards glare with hunger.

The music hits a crescendo, and with one last dagger, she throws it with vigour towards a guard with long warrior braids stationed behind Lady Carter. Embedding the blade into the wall behind him.

Silence fills the room. Every individual transfixed with her performance, her eyes fixed on the burly guard, chest heaving, empathising with her breasts.

"You missed," the guard sniggers full of male arrogance. Elodie cocks her head to one side, a smirk playing at her lips. She stood in her silver bra top and matching knickers, dark hair cascading around her shoulders, the blue catching the lights.

With a perfectly performed and elegant curtsy, she twirls on her heeled sandals and leaves the stage.

The guard turns his head, and his long braid falls with a thud to the floor. I burst out laughing as his face contorts with fury.

"Maybe you will think twice before laying your hands on her again." I bait, clapping loudly. The room erupts with wolf whistles and clapping. I watch the room as the King and his General hiss words to one another, heads close, mouths tight with anger. the King abruptly stands and marches from the room the General fast in his wake. Jumping onto the stage, I rush to the back changing room towards Elodie. Something in my gut tells me to move and move quickly.

CHAPTER 34

Elodie

I throw the rhinestone bra top to the floor and gather my daggers back into their box. I grab a towel and begin to dry the sweat gathered on my body.

A strange reservation overcomes me. Maybe this is who I will always be, using my body to make ends meat, dancing and stripping for the pleasure of others. A strange anger burns through me. Am I only worth what people will pay for my body?

The door bursts open, and with a startled cry, I grab a dagger and spin around. the King stands, nostrils flared, fist clenched, the Raven close behind looking equally pissed off.

"Do you fucking mind?" I pull my towel closer to cover my exposed body.

"You're a… you are a strip… truly a dancer?" the King stammers, eyes glued to my face, as if trying to be respectful and failing miserably. A huge presence closes in, pressing his muscular frame to my back.

"Do we have a problem, gentlemen? Miss Whitlock would like to clean up and retire in private." Hank places a long cotton robe over my shoulders, turning my back to the King to face him. He pulls the robe closed and moves his lips close to my ear.

"Go and have a shower, Starlight. I will handle your visitors. I am thankful for the robe to protect my dignity; it's one thing to 'perform,' but to stand almost naked in front of the bloody king - embarrassment does not cut it.

"Wait," Barrett takes a few paces before Hank's huge body blocks his view. "Please, Elodie," the King pauses, surveying Hank.

Raising one eyebrow at him, I walk from the room towards the bathroom, lingering to observe the three men.

"Careful, Sergeant, you are addressing the King, and she just moved on stage equal to any trained warrior I have witnessed." The General moves into the room, closing the door to keep out prying eyes.

"Of course, she is a trained fighter, people like her need to be fighters. If you don't learn the skill from an early age, you will likely be dead within a month. Defend, learn a skill, and stay alive." Hank's voice raises with anger at the pompous, narrow minds of the two men standing before him. "Do you know what she has had to endure to survive, can you imagine what it is like to live your life as someone's property, having few choices laid out in front of you? They are told what time to get up and go to sleep, their education is dictated, their food and accommodation are basic at best, and then they have to pay it all back! With ridiculous interest that most end up never being able to leave, so forgive me General if I seem a little protective."

The room fills with a potent silence. The three stand

ready to erupt.

"Has she been forced?" the King lowers his voice, concern, and anger lining his features, a growl from his beast making itself known. I have never seen Hank so emotional, fierce, and protective. Warmth spreads through me, deep into my core. He is my rock in a world thrown upside down. Running a hand over his face, he sighs.

"No," he whispers, "she is one of the lucky ones that has enough presence that she can stay on stage to dance and entertain."

"And how, dear Hank do you know all this? If you never knew the girl before you came here? The plot does thicken further." The General moves closer, nose to nose, with my protector.

Shit, I can feel the power crackle between the two, both ready to take the other on, two strong alphas on the verge of war.

"I suggest you back off, feather brain," Hank growls, fist bunching and rising to his full height, violent energy ripe in the air. Black wings unfold behind the General, The Raven in all his glory.

"Maybe sweet little Elodie needs to spend some time below the palace alongside you." A jab to Hank's chest follows the threat and all hell breaks loose. I scream, sprinting from my hiding place. Hank throws a powerful punch, landing squarely on the general's jaw; locked together, punches are hammered into each other until Hank lifts the raven shifter and throws him across the room.

"Stop!" I scream, standing between the two men. Alexander stands, throwing a blast of magic that slams into Hank, sending him flying. Barrett grabs me out of the way at the last second as the Raven races forward to engage once more.

"Let them get it out of their system, love," the King purrs in amusement.

"I can't watch them do this, not over me," I say, pulling from Barrett's grip. The two tussle on the floor, diving forward I land on the Ravens back as his wings flare to draw us both back aiming a savage kick at Hank ribs.

"Stop now!" Power snakes up my arms, starting to build behind my temples, throbbing pain building. Hank rolls, absorbing the impact of Alexander's kick, diving back to his feet as fire erupts from his hands. Catching the Raven's wings, he spins, ignoring my spider monkey form clinging to his back, dislodging me to the floor. Hank follows with a brutal punch to his face, a sickening crunch followed by the gush of hot, wet blood.

I feel Alexander's power surge readying for another attack.

"Stop!" heat and power surge through my body, flying outwards from me, freezing both men in place. Agony proceeds, inhaling sharply electric shocks running up my taught muscles, piercing my head, rendering me useless, eyes rolling to the back of my head as I fall to the floor .....unconscious.

Agonising male screams and fighting sounds, then cut off abruptly. Rounding the corner, a rancid smell fills my nostrils, making me gag and choke; the sound of an animal slurping and sucking a sloppy wet meal makes me pause. Peering through the thick smoke- black hair, long and matted with liquid - a strong hand with a sword - Dad's sword that he keeps on display above the mantelpiece. Delicate hands lift me from the floor, cradling me in her arms. The smell of smoke, blood and vanilla cookies... Mum! Comfort allows me to breathe, burying my face into the familiar warmth of my mother.

"I'm sorry, little one, we love you. Please Remember you are loved."

Excruciating Pain erupts in my chest. Red hot fire burns deep in my heart- it stutters, beating out of rhythm, and I can't draw breath. Darkness, pain, quiet.

Soft covers drape across my shoulders with hushed voices close. The panic from my familiar dream echoes through my mind, unconsciousness trying to pull me under again.

"I suggest, Sergeant, that you speak truly for once."

I slowly regain consciousness, the darkness receding. My head pounding as I open my eyes, squinting against the harsh light of the changing room.

The room is spinning, and my stomach lurches, nausea making me retch and groan. A tender hand strokes my face, and on instinct, I draw closer to the warm touch, mind slogging through thick molasses.

"Shhh, sleep, Wildcat, the nickname drags me from my groggy slumber; concerned emerald eyes watch me.

"Hey, you're awake." A small smile touches his lips but

does not reach his eyes. There is a heap of guilt and sadness. Hank leans over me, too, sporting a huge black swollen eye and split lip.

"Shit," I wince as I try to sit up, taking the three men in the room. Alexander scowls, holding ice to his bruised nose; Hank relaxes with a closed mask in place, then Barrett, the King.

Shying away from the intensity of all three gazes swinging my legs as if to sit up.

"Woah, no, you don't. You took a nasty fall and expended a lot of magic," Barrett states with a questioning look. "A lot of powerful magic."

"What are you talking about? I don't have real magic," but then the memory of that feeling of power that struck Hank and Alexander while they fought, confused. I look at Hank. "How? I can't have magic? I barely have enough to lock my apartment's signature locks."

Alarmed, I lower my head nervously, bunching my fingers in the soft cotton of my blanket, teeth worrying my lower lip.

"I don't know, Ellie. You screamed in pain and then collapsed," he shrugs. "What do you remember from your early years before your parents died?" The matter-of-fact way of his questions still sends a pang of longing for the people I lost so many years ago.

"A dream of that night but nothing else." I shrug. Barrett holds my hand, running his thumb in small circles, allowing Hank to lead. "Has anyone given you anything that may have been a trigger, or has something happened recently?" I shake my head, wincing as another shot of pain pulses, my fingers coming to rub at my temples.

"God, my head hurts." Alexander watches our interactions, analysing our every move like I'm a puzzle he must solve.

"Sergeant, you know magic. Could she be a dormant carrier of sorts?" Barrett hands me a cool glass of water and some pills, watching my mouth as I drink.

"Give her space," Hank growls, throwing a warning look to the King.

"Apologies." Colour warms his cheeks as he rocks back on his heels to stand. He then leans against the vanity table in the dressing room. Alexander still stands, assessing suspicion clearly. That man would have me locked up in a heartbeat. Seeing my fleeting look, a predatory sneer is sent my way.

Panicked at the accusation, realising that everything the Raven suspects is coming to light, is this where I'm locked up and executed? All of a sudden, my chest becomes impossibly tight, my palms sweaty as I fail to get any oxygen into my lungs, and black spots enter my vision.

"Hey Starlight, look at me." Deep brown eyes like melted chocolate meet mine, warm palms cupping my face. "You are safe. I am here now. You okay?"

I nod breathing, his touch calming.

"Lady Carter bit me. She knows I have no magic. She

even made a big deal of it."

"What?" My head snaps to the General, who has gone unnaturally still, mouth tight.

"She did what?" he growls.

"Oh, now you show concern, Raven?" I roll my eyes in exaggeration. "Yes, she bit me, and that was the nicest thing she has done," I huff, ignoring the brooding bird shifter.

Hank stands, turning to face both the King and the Raven, navy and black scales rippling over his arms with clenched fists. Are my eyes tricking me? A growl escapes him,

"Did you see her after the attack?"

The General stands closer to the King, readying to intercept the angry shifter. "What are you?" He questions.

Reaching for his arm, I gently take Hank's hand in mine. "Hey, big man, it's fine, I'm fine. I broke that fucker's nose, remember, and just scalped the other dickhead."

Tilting his head, he gives me a lopsided grin with a huff, "That you did. You must have a fantastic weapons master."

Shivering slightly, unsure if it's from the cold, I'm still pretty much naked in my robe with a smile at Hank.

"Back to that release in power and blinding pain that followed. Is that the first time?" Hank is back on track, his trained mind piecing the bits together.

"Well, I keep getting these intense headaches, usually before something strange happens or when magic is released from another."

"Have they escalated?" Moving closer, Hank hands me his jumper blocking my view of the other two men.

"Thanks, but I'm okay."

"Put it on Ellie," a growl of warning has me reaching for the jumper. I look at him with an unspoken question and half-shrug. "It's cold, Starlight." the familiar nickname brings a shy smile to my lips.

I want to tell them all about the secret rooms, diary, and, of course, the ring, but trust does not come easily, especially with these men. The power surely must be coming from the ring.

"There is something you're not sharing, little assassin. Please don't hold any more secrets from us," Alexander snarls, his contempt for me obvious.

A siren wails through the palace. All three men launch to their feet, taking a moment before rushing into action. "We are under attack. Get her and the King to fucking safety." bellows Hank, scales shooting up his arms.

"No, I'm the damn king. I will fight if I'm needed."

"Get to your apartments and stay there until we figure out what is happening. No arguments, Barrett. Take the girl." With that said, the general sprints from the room, his colossal wings coming to life behind him.

"Hank," I plead

"Stay with the King, grab your daggers and stab first, ask questions later." With a hard kiss to my mouth, he follows the General. When did it become common to kiss me?

CHAPTER 35

Elodie

Inside Barrett's apartment once again, he rushes to the security monitors in a side room, following the carnage of a full attack on the front of the palace.

Muscular dark green goblin warriors clad in metal armour, wielding earth and air magic, have penetrated the palace's outer walls. The devastation behind them is huge. Our Forces rush out to defend the palace, but the attackers outnumber us three to one, and our forces don't seem to have the same powerful magic.

"Barrett, they are using magic! A lot of magic" I grunt a response.

"Get some clothes on." Barrett throws a protective vest over his torso and begins strapping weapons to his back, thighs and chest, checking each gun is loaded, throwing some items my way. I scramble to pull on a pair of large sweatpants and vest top over my sparkly booty shorts. I stand dazed and rooted to the screens playing the bloody carnage approaching the palace.

"Elodie. Elodie!" Barrett grabs me. "Here, take this." He hands me a gun. "Can you use it?" I nod, taking the gun. "Take your daggers too; stay in the apartments. Don't open the door for anyone, ok?" His instructions are rushed as his eyes dart back to the battle below.

"Take me with you. I can fight," I plead, finally recovering from the shock.

"It's too dangerous. You will only be a distraction out there. We need our best magic users if we are to win this."

"I'm not a distraction. I can help!" I strap extra daggers and grab another gun from the table, determined to be of use,

"Wildcat, my beast is drawn to you. I can't remain in control. If you are out there, I will be fucking useless. Shit, I'm sorry, this is for your own good," he says, smashing a quick passionate kiss to my lips before he sprints out of the apartment.

Puzzled at his words, lips tingling from his kiss, I watch him leave. I attempt to follow, but my feet fail to respond.

"Ahhhh, you twat!" His magic surges every time I try to move, locking me in place. I watch as the King's guards engage the enemy, which has breached the palace walls and used the front manicured lawns as their battleground. It's obvious they are well trained, lethal and wielding various elemental magics. The shade soldiers cut down the palace guards like a hot knife through butter. Blood seeps into the earth with a brutality I have never seen. It's clear we are overwhelmed, many dropping quickly dead or injured.

Moving closer, power drives through my muscles, pain spiking at my temples, and inhaling, I realise I can now move again. Horror sickens my stomach at the sight in front of me. I spy Hank armed with a huge broadsword in one arm, expertly felling goblins with what appears to be little effort. Drawing a gun, he shoots an orc between the eyes, but the giant, twisted creature keeps coming, throwing a goblin over his head and knocking two other opponents over. He swings for the orc, taking his head from his huge shoulders.

My heart pounds as the King's magic wears off. I start to pace rotating the dagger Hank gifted me again and again, "I need to be out there. I can help," I say, trying several doors which have been locked. "Fucker," I state, slamming my fist into the door with a growl of frustration burning deep. "Hold on, Ellie, you idiot." Laughing, I grab a few tools from the kitchen and race back to the door- this is a skill that will always be useful.

Pulling some grips from my hair and the knife I grabbed, I pick the locks. A message buzzes in my pocket,

Jenny:
Elodie, where are you?
The Shades are in the fucking palace,
in our block. Help!

Elodie:
Stay put and quiet; hide
I'm making my way to you. I'm armed,
call Pumpkin to you if he's there
El x

Rushing to open the now unlocked door, Pumpkin appears at my side out of nowhere. "Shit!" Heart pounding, I pat him. "Give a girl some warning, Kin."

Sneaking down the long hallways of the Palace, dagger clenched in my palm, we slowly make our way into the public areas. Soldiers run everywhere, and the sound of battle surrounds us. My palms were clammy, and my heart was pounding. I try to control my rapid breathing. Stay focused, I chant to myself.

Memories of that night rush to the surface of my mind, and I dart against a doorway to steady my breath- Pumpkin clicks and nuzzles me before pressing a huge lion paw; he
is definitely getting bigger, onto a painting of a lion shifter chasing down a unicorn.

"Do you know a shortcut, big fella?" He clicks with a roll of his head as if to hurry me into action. "Okay, here goes!" Placing my hand on the lion, the now recognisable tingle of magic and puff of air reveals another doorway. Slipping behind into the belly of the palace, I chase after Pumpkin as he runs to an unknown location, his tails swinging as he ploughs ahead. Pumpkin stops, placing his ear against the plaster wall. A rumble sounds in his throat as he nudges me forward, getting the hint this creature has insight that I don't. I push my hand to the wall, which opens to the residential wings of the palace, my residential wing.

"Handy, this little trick of yours." Gratitude has me hugging the big lion-bird that is fast becoming my saviour. Creeping towards my apartment, dagger and gun drawn, listening for approaching feet, I gasp, stumbling to a halt at the carnage and destruction before me. Doors have been ripped from the hinges, and upheaval is everywhere.

Breathing in shallow pants, my heart galloping like wild horses. Sprinting the corridor to where my door has been blown to nothing, the edges burnt and smouldering. Panic makes my muscles tremble, stumbling over debris, only just managing to catch myself before I fall.

Breathe, calm, Elodie." I close my eyes and inhale deeply to control my racing pulse, falling back on my many years of training.

"Jenny, Esta," I call, creeping low through our apartment, basic furniture has been torn and smashed as a wild storm has passed, leaving nothing untouched. Blood splatters up the walls, and a distinct smeared handprint brings panic to my body, "Jenny? Esta?" Sasha?

Heart pounding, I scream their names again, surveying the room. A mop of bloody brown hair catches my attention. "Esta, gods, Esta." I dive to my knees desperately. I feel for a pulse with shaking hands. Blood pools around her head, so much blood turning black and congealing, seeping into my clothes and the carpet. "Esta, please," I say, holding back tears, holding her wrist, hoping to feel a flicker of life blank, emotionless brown eyes stare back, and her blood covers my hands, and the coppery smell sends terror down my spine.

Biting my lower lip, holding back the sob in my throat, "Oh Esta, please." Grief so potent hits my chest, sobs choking and tears streaming down my face. I need to move, rising covered in my friend's blood.

"Jenny, are you here?" A weak groan sounds behind the door of the bathroom we all shared, borrowing shampoos, lotions, and potions of our simple luxury. Grief-filled tears flow, rendering me immobile, breaths raspy.

Come on Ellie MOVE. Now is not the time for grief or dramatics. Grasping the handle, I shove the door, a heavyweight obstructing the way. Using all my strength, I heave the door open. Jenny is slumped, thick red blood seeping from a stab wound to her stomach. A flicker of fear runs up the length of my body. Frozen, I stare in horror.

"Jenny, please stay with me." Tears run down my cheeks. Blood oozes from a blow to her head, but the steady trickle of vicious bright red blood is life-threatening; a nudge from a beak has me moving.

"It's going to be okay. We will get you to the medics. Then they will stitch you up. A few days in bed, and you will be fine, I promise. I can't lose you too. Just stay, please, stay," I ramble in whispers as I pad the wound to try and stem the bleeding with a clean towel.

"R..run El," a barely audible breath hisses through her lips. Jenny's weak grip holding onto my hand, pain lances through her features, fear shining in the depths of her dark eyes.

Shaking my head, "Run? I'm going to kill whoever did this to you and Esta. They will not get away with hurting innocent people." I refrain from using the word killing to ward off the fate I know deep down is at her feet.

"They were," she stops to take in a ragged breath, her skin becoming paler by the minute, her lips turning a pale blue, "looking for you, Elodie."

"I don't understand. Me? I am no one, just an orphan, servant girl and ex-dancer. What the fuck?"

"Want… The dark p..pearl, the power." blood bubbles at her mouth.

"Look, save your strength. I'm getting you out of here." Real panic knots my stomach as I hold my hands to my friend in a feeble attempt to stop the inevitable, hands trembling and slipping in the dark red liquid, too much liquid.

A gentle pressure squeezes my brain like a headache is building. I breathe deeply, eyes closed, trying to calm my heart rate enough to think, "Think Ellie, come on."

"Enchantress let it flow." Startled, I turn my attention to Pumpkin, regally sitting in the doorframe, his eyes flick with amusement. Am I insane, or did Pumpkin just speak into my head? He inclines his head.

"Hello, enchantress. Yes, and you can save her if you stop staring at me like you have seen a ghost." Astonished, I snap my head to Jenny and then the hawk bird.

"How?" I release the breath I did not realise I was holding. A large cat-like paw gently lands on top of mine, applying pressure to create more contact with Jenny's wound.

"Power, think, push, heal," he purrs, moving to sit behind me, his warmth stirring magic I never thought me capable of. Adrenaline and a flood of pleasure coil around my muscles, absorbing the power throbbing in my veins. I push towards Jenny.

"Heal." I nod, concentrating on the feel of power heating my veins. Agony spasms up my back, muscle tensing, forcing a cry from my lips, but the intense pain of earlier is not there.

"PUSH, HEAL!" Pumpkin clicks his beak.

"It hurts," I cry, but don't stop controlling the power now working its way into Jenny.

"Break the barrier." I don't understand, but terror at losing my friend keeps me pushing, the heat now an inferno at my fingertips, sweat dripping from my brow, panting hard, I begin to shake.

Jenny's head lolls to the side, mouth falling open. A blank stare fixes to the floor, her eyes wide.

"Nooooo!" I push hard against my pain. The scent of vanilla cookies brings the memory back.

"I'm sorry, little one, we love you. Please Remember you are loved" Excruciating Pain erupts in my chest. Red hot fire burns deep in my heart- it stutters, beating out of rhythm, and I can't draw breath.

"They can't find you. Your magic will draw them, so I must encase it."

Screams break my voice, pain then tears run in twin rivers down my face.

"I love you." My mother's face fills with emotion, love and tears brimming in her eyes before she places a blanket over

me, places me in the back seat of our car, and turns without a backward glance, Father's sword in hand.

"Ahhhhhhhh!" Light explodes, pain snapping sharply in my temples. Jenny's back arches from the floor, arms going limp at her side as her head jerks. Tremors ripple through my arms, back and legs. I clench my jaw, almost cracking teeth as I fight the barrier within me; finally, with a sharp stab to my heart, I collapse, panting, heart racing, sweat dripping from my pores.

Rolling, I vomit on the bathroom floor, mixing with Jenny's blood, gasping for breath as my vision begins to clear and the nausea fades.

"Elodie?" A croaked voice enquires, "What was that?" Jenny's voice arouses me from my weakened state. Wiping the saliva and vomit from my mouth, shocked to hear her voice when two minutes ago she was dead! I saw the light fade.

"You're alive," I say, jumping up and pulling her blood-soaked top up. "Shit, it's gone" The skin is raw and red, but there is no longer a stab wound! Jenny's face lights up in confusion, then disbelief etching across her face, eyes flicking to Pumpkin and me.

"Was that you? how?" Her head snaps left and right.

"We need to get someplace safe, Elodie," Jenny coughs, trying to rise. "They are looking for you and a ring?"

"A ring? Shit, can you stand?" I offer my hand and help her up. Rocking on her feet, she braces against me, feet slipping in her spilt life force.

"Come on, I know where we can hide," I say as we

head out of the bathroom, Pumpkin hot on our heels. Coughing, Jenny begins to walk, my arm supporting her weight.

"I need a drink."

Indecision pulls at me, but my own body feels weak. I'm heading for the kitchen. We clean up a little and grab drinks. We both pause by Esta, Jenny letting out a howl full of anguish as she clings to me.

Sliding from the apartment, Jenny unsteady and using me as a crutch, we slowly check each turn for signs of the enemy.

"I smell you, little pearl."

Stopping abruptly, we exchange looks of terror.

What the fuck, Jenny mentioned a pearl? "It's him," Jenny mouths. "The one." She gestures to her now smooth and healed stomach.

"I feeeeeeel you," the male voice moans in pleasure, "tasty...ha yess."

My new magic shutters within me, and I begin to tremble uncontrollably, fear rendering me useless.

"He will be so happy I found you. Please don't make a big ordeal out of this; my hands are full of death already."

Striding around the corner, a black and silver double-edged axe slung over his shoulder casually. A broad, dark-skinned demon clad in black battle leathers with two horns curving from his mid-length black hair appears.

"My, my, you even look like her same eyes." The smile is more sarcastic than warm, calculated excitement burns within his dark eyes. Reacting, I launch Hank's onyx dagger for his heart, sinking it in deep as I grab Jenny and sprint away. Stumbling with a cry, Jenny hits the floor and is dragged back towards the stranger, her fingers struggling for purchase along the smooth floor.

"Now that is not very nice, little pearl, is it?" Hauling Jenny up by her throat, he slams her to the wall, her feet swinging and skimming the ground.

"Let her go or I will-"——-

"You will what?" he cuts me off, one eyebrow raised as he squeezes a gasp from my friend. "I can snap her neck before you can go for another dagger. With a flick of his fingers, he sends Pumpkin flying along the corridor, striking and breaking a statue.

"Pumpkin!" Reaching for my dagger,

"Ah, Ah... Don't." Freezing, anger narrowing my eyes, observing the thing in front of me.

"Let her go!" I yell, but he ignores my words, not concerned that I have already inflicted injury.

"Osiris is the name! or The Destroyer, which some may use— it's like a stage name!" He bows mockingly, a smirk on his lips, and he is conversing as if we are old friends. "Now, when that wee guard said you were here, I thought he was bullshitting, ha! And look," he points his axe in my direction, smiling widely, "you're here, just put your weapons down" he twirls his axe, "Walk over to me, I bind you, we leave, I retreat with the army and leave your friends alive!" Win, win, is it not?"

Cocking his head, he waits, eyebrows raised in question. Distant gunfire fills the air, along with the clash of the enemy sweeping through the palace, innocent screams penetrating the walls. Dread and anxiety build in my chest, indecision warring with common sense. "Tick tock, my little pearl" Osiris conjures up a wicked-looking thin metal blade, sliding it along the ribs of his captive, Jenny hissing at the sting of pain.

"Stop! Okay, okay. Leave the palace and withdraw your army, and I will come willingly," I drop my dagger, raising my hands in defect.

"Oh, sweet pearl," he tuts. "I'm not a trusting person. Swear it on a blood oath, and then we can save your little friend here!"

CHAPTER 36

Hank

Thrusting my sword through a goblin I pirouette to engage my next opponent, I fight back to back with The Raven, falling into the thrill of bloodshed, into the familiar pattern that I was born to.

The shade army is fast, well-trained, and wields elemental magic—a lethal combination. The ruined palace garden is littered with injured or dead fae. Armed with two broadswords, my traditional way of fighting, I slice the head off an Orc without breaking my rhythm, stabbing a troll in the heart and finishing him quickly. Fatigue aches through my shoulders, but to stop is to die.

Suddenly, all approaching enemy forces halt as if listening to an internal command, heads tilted, some among them begin to howl with excitement, and I cast my eyes to the Raven, his gaze meeting mine, apprehension crossing his features, his eyes searching. Locking my gaze, his black feathered wings spread out behind him, "the King" eyes scanning the battlefield. I glance back, rolling my shoulders and readying my weapons, stance widening. This doesn't feel right. I look for the King. He's nowhere in sight. Have they gotten to him? Sensing my thoughts, The Raven shows elements of panic, his body going rigid, wings springing from his back as he turns on his heels, springing into the air and soaring back towards the palace.

The Shade forces in front of me disappear, popping into thin air and leaving the dead behind. The battlefield fills with an eerie, sudden silence. Only sounds of the medics rushing to assist the injured and voices of concern and instructions. There is something I'm missing here. My instincts tell me something is not right. The desire to shift explodes into every pore, the need to find her almost driving me to insanity, exhaustion from the battle long since forgotten as adrenaline surges, forcing me into action, running towards the palace's west wing. Skidding to a halt, I think she was in the King's apartments for safety. Is she still there? My gut says no. That woman will find trouble and is too bloody stubborn to do as she is told, turning to the servant's quarters, connecting to the strength of my beast to propel me forward at speed.

Swords pumping in my fist, I enter through the back of the kitchen. Upheaval and blood splatter are everywhere like a small army has driven through these walls like a tempest storm. Rounding the corners to the residential suites, I see evidence of fighting, people lying prostrate on the floors, and blood everywhere. Panic vibrates through me once again, which I push aside.

The adrenaline springs me into action again, and then I hear it.

"Please let her go. Let everyone go. I promise I will go with you." Elodie's voice is unmistakable. I have craved her presence, every touch for years now, her smell and taste engraved in my senses; outrage at the plea in her trembling voice, clenching my fists, scales rippling over my body as my beast demands action. A darker voice cuts her off, one that sounds vaguely familiar. Creeping forward, I listen. Shit! She can't swear on a blood-blinding oath; he will lace it with hidden agendas and clauses. Elodie knows nothing of magic. She never had to use magic. She's never had magic. If She enters the blood oath with this stranger, she will never break it. Moving around the corner with purpose body coiled, readying for a fight, coming into the view of the tall demon standing, holding Jenny hostage.

"Well, my old friend it's been a seriously long time!" The demon's eyes widen slightly with surprise, shock, or even a touch of fear. He knows of my reputation.

The look is quickly masked, and he lifts his lips in a smug smile. Elodie stands between us. Pulling up to my full height, a deep growl rumbles in my chest.

"Oh, my old scaly friend, time has not served you well, " he dramatically looks up and down me. "You hold a little bit more fat and look decades older! Ha."

The insult slides from his lips, hoping to get a rise. I may be older, but I'm definitely not out of shape. I've trained every day waiting for this moment, waiting to be called to the service of the realm once again. As if knowing the fight is inevitable, the demon throws his prisoner towards Elodie, using her as a distraction.

With a burst of speed, he grabs for Elodie, but she's too well-trained. She's my girl, after all! Twisting from his grasp, hand palming her dagger, driving it into his leg, raising her forearm to slam her elbow across his nose, blood bursting with the impact. With a grunt, Osiris launches, locking his arms around her, twisting her arm behind her back and pulling the dagger free from his leather-clad thigh.

"You will pay for that move, dark one." Focusing on her, I see my opportunity. I cast an air-propelled dagger that embeds into the demon's shoulder. His hold releases, giving Elodie the escape route she needs to slip from his grasp.

Barrelling forward like a bull, taking the demon to the floor on his back, straddling him, my fist flies, and I punch him in the face repeatedly. I hear Elodie move behind me, grabbing her friend.

"RUN! Get Jenny to safety!" I shout, "RUN NOW, get out of here, get to the King, get to the general," I demand as indecision crosses her beautiful face, a stubborn tilt of her chin, and I know she plans to fight, fuck.

Using my hesitation, Osiris throws me across the room and then dives to his feet, trying to get to Elodie once again. Drawing a gun, aiming for his face, letting the bullets fly. They don't do much, but they slow him down just enough for me to try and get her out of here. I feel the adrenaline surge once again as I dash along the corridor, panic making me sloppy, casting air magic around Elodie, pulling her back towards me, Osiris latches onto her ankle: almost like a human, a tug of war, she screams in pain,, that sends a jolt of panic. Letting go of my magic, I instantly allow Osiris to gain purchase as he throws her over his shoulder, driving to his feet quickly, throwing a gust of air magic behind him and sprinting down the corridor.

"NO!" A semi-shift is upon me, eyes turning to reptilian slit, and navy scales coat my neck and arms. Shooting after my prey, a roar of defiance shaking the walls.

"Hank" her wavering voice stirs me quicker. Pumpkin, that faithful familiar, jumps out of nowhere onto the demon, bringing him to his knees, slamming and stumbling across the floor, cries of frustration leaving him, but my girl is on her feet. Instantly, daggers are drawn as she flings one, then another, toward the demon. They take purchase in his shoulder and chest, not deadly shots, but they are enough to stop him In his tracks. Pumpkin attacks, sharp beak tearing like a hot knife through butter, cutting Osiris's face a raw red line down the side of his cheek. Blood flowing, now three against one he knows he is outnumbered. Pumpkin touches Elodie, and the pair disappear with a pop of air only to reappear beside Jenny halfway down the corridor out of reach.

Smokes billows around the demon.

"I know where she is now!" raising both hands. "Can you protect her against me? What you saw today is a fraction of what we can summon," he says, leaning forward, smoke almost covering him entirely. "He always gets what he desires and has waited a very long time for her."

"You will have to go through me." I take Elodie's hand in mine, her power stroking up against my inner beast. She looks at me in wonder, chest heaving, hair loose framing her face.

"We will raze this kingdom to the ground in search of her. She is no longer hidden, Magnus, and we want you, little pearl," he points his axe directly at Elodie. So come willingly and safely. You can save thousands of lives, or we will take back what was stolen," fully engulfed in the smoke. "Your choice, little pearl." Then he is gone.

CHAPTER 37

The Raven

I tap deep into my magic, connecting with the insects of the world, feeling out the tremors of the battle, following, observing, and listening to the Unseelie soldiers. Something is going on, something I have missed. I should've been prepared. I should've seen this coming.

My spies are well placed on both sides of this dispute, and the dark court is closer to home than most realise. I've been too distracted of late, looking out for threats within the palace, to notice the sublet changes within the old court.

Running my fingers through my close-cropped goatee, I intensify my power. In the shadows, I watch through multiple distorted views of the enemy retreating, dissolving into smoke or plunging through windows and shifting to winged Fae to leave the battle. Perplexed, have they gotten what they came for? Is this a feel-out mission, a test of sorts? Rumours of the power to unlock the magic of the realm have long circulated, but how could they be true? Why would they risk a palace invasion? Why strike now?

The trolls, goblins and orcs of the Shade army were excited, leaving not in retreat due to failure but success?"

He's found Her. She is here."

"We have it, we will be rewarded!"

"She is in our grasp at last."

"We will rule and be free!"

Many voice versions of the same delighted phrases, animated body language and camaraderie. Pulling my magic from the insects rolling my neck to shake off the revulsion caused from the act. How did they know we were vulnerable? It just doesn't make sense. I should have this knowledge, but I don't.

Fury coils my muscles tight. Power oscillates over my wings. I dive through the balcony window on the upper parts of the King's apartments, my magical signature breaking through the wards in place. Soft floral perfume tastes in the air, still fucking distracting, destroyer of the King; I see the way people look at her, memories of her performance burn deep, how she had me transfixed, a hot plosives need to rip her off stage and keep her as mine. Gripping tight around my weapon, breathing deeply, scanning the apartment. She's not here. I already knew that she wouldn't stay put. She wouldn't listen. She's too goddamn stubborn to keep herself safe. I saw Barrett on the battlefield briefly. Was she the reason why the King didn't stay on the battlefield? He's looking for her. Frustration raises my blood pressure. These two will be the death of me.

The way he looks at her. He sees something in her, as if she is his brand of pleasure bottled up just for him.

Just earlier tonight, gods, that dance. I shake my

head to rid the vision of her, moving to the monitors. I quickly type a few codes to switch camera feeds in search of the King or Miss Whitlock, aiming to concentrate on my actual job, but my mind wanders back to her, and I find I'm not only looking for the King but her, too.

The way her body moved, her grace as she wheeled her daggers and then the power! That is not a girl without magic; is she the one that they seek? Her power earlier felt ancient, as if taken from another source of old, but I had her tested. The result was low power.

She has no control over her magic. That's obvious, so it must be new. Just thinking of the pale seductress has my cock thickening, pushing against my trousers, my own magic withering in excitement? What the hell is wrong with me?

Commotion outside has me diving for the front door, throwing it open to find the King scuffling with an old goblin, with a familiar red cap on his head. Lashing out, I wield vines to grab the goblin around the neck, pinning him high on the wall. He smirks and laughs.

"Raven, you do still exist," he says with a cocky expression his eyes flick between me and the King. "It's too late." he breaks into hysterics. "Kill me if you like, but she's gone. We have her."

"Who the fuck are you talking about?" I slam my forearm under the red cap's chin, pulling a dagger to plunge it deep under his ribs. He grunts in pain, coughing,

"Your kingdom will fall. We will see it done. You're not

the right ruler." A shuddering breath pushes between his smiling mouth. "We shall rise and take back the throne that is ours, with her power fueling it. It's written in the stars" His tongue darts out to lick his lower lip, coughing and grimacing in pain.

Placing my fingers to his temples, I delve with my magic into his mind, trying to pull as much information from it as I can. He screams back, arching his neck straining, eyes narrowing in pain and anger. Glimmers of a dark court, A huge fae king commanding to find the girl, talk about power being released, talk about Pearl's dark little one? A dark ruby ring with skulls. The red cap fights, his power searing up to meet mine, the pressure building in my mind, pulling images of that dance.

It morphs into Miss Whitlock, now dancing with a demon with two curling horns who bends to whisper in her ear. Those blue gold-flecked enchanting eyes light with an ancient light and flick my way, mischief rife within. Grunting, I throw more power to my own mental shields, and simultaneously, I submerge into his head, gathering information in snippets. Screams of agony fill the room.

Unable to hold out much longer, I pull my power, dropping the gasping goblin to the floor. Blood flowing rapidly, his shallow, ragged breaths edged with pain. the King looks my way, expectations etched on his face.

"Well, what did you find?" he demands. The King stands before me, the caretaker for the Kingdom, concern for the realm evident in every cell of his body. Gone is the carefree blonde lion shifter; in its place is strength, the fae who will bring peace to this world. He will fuse the courts together. That is why I follow him. This is why I relentlessly adhere to my mission to get as much information as possible no matter what it takes.

The goblin wheezes on the floor. He's no longer of use, so I drive my sword through his heart and slice off his head for good measure.

"Let's get cleaned up," I say, smirking and with a laugh. the King eases into a more relaxed posture.

"I could do with a beer," he says, heading back into his apartment with a confident swagger.

"Elodie," he calls. "Sorry about the magic Wildcat!" Placing my hand on his arm, stopping his progress.

"We need to talk about her." I hesitate. "She's not what she seems."

"Well, Alexander, my friend, I could've said that the moment I met her." Taking two beers from the fridge, he hands me one, taking it, I place it down on the kitchen counter without taking a drink,

"There's something special about the girl; she's no orphan. You felt the power she released, it was not normal magic."

Walking through he keeps looking around the room, eyes scouting out each corner. Posture tensing as I challenge his view and interest in Miss Whitlock.

"You're talking like a man after a pretty bit of tail, not a wise king. The look on your face," I say with a shrug. "We need to tread carefully. She's either an assassin with magic or she doesn't realise she's an assassin with magic."

"All the reason to seduce her. If she's in my bed, then she's working with me. Win-win!" Barrett smiles, taking a long draw from his beer.

"Ha, you really think you can control that stubborn girl. It would take me, you, and that big fucking protector of hers to gain an element of control,"

Barretts throws his head back. "Maybe that's what she needs; you up for sharing?" The idea stirs a caveman-like desire in me that I squash under my thumb like a bug, sure it's her magic and not any real attraction.

"I don't share," I snarl, finally taking a drag of beer to avoid his glare.

"Soo you're interested?" he howls with laughter at my expression. "Where is she, anyway?"

"Did you expect her to stay put?" I quirk one eyebrow,

"No, that Wildcat even pushed through my magic," He shrugs, rubbing the back of his neck and downing the remainder of his beer. "We need to get things under control and evaluated from this attack. Call the war council, schedule it in an hour for a debrief," and with that, the King is back.

CHAPTER 38

Elodie

My heart throws an unsteady rhythm through my chest. The adrenaline made my breath ragged, and the last few hours whirled into fast-motion in my mind, looking to Hank the tall, handsome man stands breath in the corridor, eyes of fury locked on mine.

"Why the fuck are you not in the King's apartment?"

"JJJenny," I stammer. "Jenny messaged she was in trouble. I needed to help, Hank, please," I explained, defeat clearly on my face, eyes glassing over, unable to meet his gaze.

The concern breaks through him as he strides towards me and picks me up in his huge embrace, his mouth crashing against mine. Shock at the possessiveness of his hold and kiss, I freeze momentarily before a fire burns hotly in my core. I respond in kind our lips locking as his tongue demands entrance.

I break as years of craving more from this man drive an intense passion through us, the kiss saying more than words. Throwing me against the wall, scooping my legs around his waist as he drives his hips and already thickening length towards my own soaking entrance. My core contracting as I shamelessly wither against his hips, seeking more purchase. I moan his name, earning a deep bestial growl from him. His mouth moves along my jaw to suck, kiss and nip at my neck, arching and tilting my head back to give him access; heat builds my body, aching for more of the outside world and battle forgotten.

Grabbing my hair, pulling my head towards him to deepen the kiss. My hands begin to pull at his shirt exposing hard pecs and muscular shoulders.

"Hank," I breathe, panting heavily. He pauses briefly, deep dark brown eyes almost reptilian slits full of lust,

"Elodie, I can't have you running around risking your life for your friends. I need you to be safe. I can't protect you if I'm worried you are doing stupid shit." he grits the words through clenched teeth as he peppers my jaw with hot, wet kisses.

I pull back, remembering the green scales that coated his arms and the smoke that seemed to pool from him.

"Who is after me? Who am I? Who are you?" My questions running wild, breaking the heat between us and bringing the world crashing back down around us. Searching his face for any hint of an answer, eyes pleading and full of confusion. With a groan and what appears to be a lot of effort, he places me back on my feet. The look he gives me, I can't decipher. It's full of passion, concern, and love. is that love? When had our actions crossed the friendship line? This man who wandered into my life from an early age and who is at least ten years older but feels older, like this is not his first chance at life, is looking at me with such love that it melts my heart. I place my palm to the side of his face no words need to be spoken as he takes my palm in his hand and pushes for more contacts, closing his eyes a deep rumble purrs in his chest.

This powerful connection feels right. There is no awkwardness or shyness. For the first time I want Hank Dufort in a way I thought was impossible.

"What's going on? What do you know?" My eyes are pleading. "Please, I know you know more than you let on. How do you know?"

Shaking his head, lowering his eyes, his face shutting down as if a barrier had come tumbling back into place, he gently lowered my hand and stepped back from me, creating distance between us. His heart sinking, he felt rejected, and sorrow pulled from deep within.

"Another time, Elodie, we need to get you and Jenny somewhere safe and find the King. This is bigger than just you and I-" I cut him off.

"Is there a you and me? " I drop my gaze, embarrassment tinging my cheeks. This may not be the time or the place for such a conversation, but it is a conversation I'm willing and need to have.

Studying my face, he used his large palm to lift my gaze back to his. With a shrug of his shoulder, defeat and hurt flashed across his features.

"I don't know Starlight. I don't know, I'm too old for you, and there is a war." He stops abruptly, straightening, morphing into the old professional bodyguard of our days at Electric Eden. "Please accept my apologies. I care for you and got carried away in the rush of battle." waving a flippant arm my way. "You are a beautiful woman, and we have spent years in one another's company," he takes a breath, running a hand over his top knot, his tell when he is frustrated. "I crossed a line that I should not have. You're my charge."

"Your charge? You mean you're paid to protect me, and that's it?" Rejection does not sit well, and the blush dusting my cheeks deepens. "And here I was thinking we were friends, maybe more! Ha! How wrong was I?" Using both hands I shove his massive frame away from me, firm muscles flexing under my touch. Anger causing me to shout helping me bury the hurt ripping my heart to shreds.

"Elodie, don't make this into a big drama. I was paid to keep all the dancers safe." Anger at his dismissal of our friendship and obvious attraction blooms, and I punch him squarely in the jaw, his knuckles cracking with a shooting pain as something breaks, connecting with his solid face.

"Shit," he curses, "Star-"

"No." Cradling my hand, I shoulder-check him out of the way. "For your information, I can look after myself. You are dismissed, sir. You have done your job." I clap my hands slowly against my leg, one hand obviously broken. "Well done. I will recommend you for a pay rise to Trixie."

"Stop being a brat." He growls, his fury rising, reaching for my arm. Ducking under his reach, I throw another jab into his ribs. A grunt of pain leaves him, but his hand-to-hand combat skills outweigh my own, and he has me restrained in the next moment. I scream in frustration.

"Jenny, get to the infirmary," he glances my friend's way, who nods and makes a quick exit. "You done?" Throwing my head back, I only succeed in hitting his chest. I'm too short to do much damage.

"It was a fucking kiss, not a declaration of our undying love. Do you hold that child guard you keep hooking up with to the same standards?" his lips graze, my ear growling with teeth clenched in annoyance. Mixed feelings ripple down my spine, lust and anger fighting for dominance. He is right. Why has his rejection and underplay of our interaction upset me so much? I feel foolish, and the fact he knows about Alfie turns my stomach.

"There is nothing between Alfie and me. It was a simple unfulfilling hookup." I cock my hip and slip from his embrace, going for sass, no hint of the embarrassment I feel visible now. "A girl has needs, Hank." I assess his body from head to toe, biting my lower lip, allowing a touch of lustrous appreciation fills my ice-blue eyes. "Shame. I bet you know your way around a woman." I sigh with a heap of sarcasm, *"But you have missed that opportunity."* Exhaling heavily, I begin walking towards the King's apartment, looking back over my shoulder. "Is my minder coming?" The pissed-off expression I earn has me chuckling. Two can play this game, my friend, and I will not show my cards so easily.

CHAPTER 39

Demon Prince Osiris

A mixture of fury and excitement travels through my body as the army retreats, heading back to camp. Using a portal, I land in my spacious apartments, throwing my dirty leathers to the floor. I inspect the dagger wound *she* left in my shoulder and chest. Elodie Whitlock is the name she goes by, having no idea of her heritage, which is written all over her skin, her pale, almost pearlescent skin with that unmistakable iridescent sheen just like her grandmother's. Dark hair is the only difference between the two; how she has stayed hidden for so long is a mystery.

I throw my head back and laugh as I inspect the small wounds, fuck she's vicious! A strange respect for her skills despite not accessing that power within her during our fight. If only she knew how to control that. My job would be infinitely harder. For months, we've been searching for the power source that emanated from the central Newgate city, ancient magic stirring the pulse and driving it through the Earth itself.

The Unseelie court has waited decades for this opportunity. We've searched and searched for the person who will unlock magic once again and give us the chance to rise and dominate the realm. A frustrated growl escapes me, throwing a punch against the wall. I came so close that the feel of her magic was palpable through the air. You could taste it. That bitter earthy smell and salty tang, every throw of her dagger laced with that ancient feel, yet she didn't have a clue! Untrained and ripe for the picking.

I sweep across the wounds, healing them with my own magic before diving into the hot tub of my apartment, sinking under the water to wash the blood and sweat from my skin and soak my aching muscles. Now, the adrenaline of battle has left me. Relaxing in the water, I take several deep breaths and rest my head back, arms on either side. Plans ran through my mind, recapping the structure of the palace and the defences they had in place.

A sweet, cinnamon aroma fills the air. Quiet footsteps are barely audible, and the ruffle of fabric ruffles my fabric. Irritation and a healthy dose of trepidation crawl under my skin.

"To what do I owe this pleasure, Delia? I've only just got back. Don't I get five minutes?" I question without opening my eyes. I know who stands before me, entering my bathing chamber without an ounce of embarrassment or sense of privacy. Anger clenches at my fists. I don't yet have the strength to take her out, but I'm a patient man.

the King's advisor, Cordelia, stands clad head to toe in black. Contrasting silver markings of runes and symbols cover her face and arms, pretty much every inch of her skin, and white pupils swirl with another unseen force. She's one of the few ancient sorcerers left within the realm. She holds teachings and prophecies of old and sees the future or what may be.

She swore that the woman who would lift the block on the magic was a woman of royal blood, who was gifted ancient power passed beyond the veil.

"King Oberon requires debriefing. You've returned home without the main prize. That in itself is unacceptable." Her emotionless, unmoving eyes stare in my direction. "I handed that girl on a plate. You attacked the palace at its weakest, what went wrong?"

Her head cocks to the side, pausing, focus set elsewhere, back ramrod straight as electricity cackling through her body, eyes borrow into mine. I know if I continue to ignore the demand in her voice, her power will be used in punishment. I might be the Prince of Demons, holding power that is not matched by many. But Cordelia is not one to be messed with. I will save that fight for another day. Sighing, I rise from the water, letting the droplets run down my dark skin over the ridges of hard muscle. I grab a towel to dry myself, walking past the sorcerer.

Her eyes are distant, fixated on the visions that plague her daily, and her mind is always half-on events that have not happened yet. I grab a pair of tight black jeans, pull them over my slim hips and throw a T-shirt on top with a low bow.

"Lead the way, My Lady. Let me show you what we found." With that, we leave my apartment, heading through the dark corridors of Mount Karayan Castle.

The castle has been built within the mountainside, standing high up amongst the snow-capped peaks, forever chilled thin air, laced with ice and mist. The air is never warm. The cold constantly penetrates the dark walls despite the many roaring fireplaces. Ice lines the windows, showing a view of the dark star-studded sky outside the mountains. The impressive figure of King Oberon sits in a dark, empty room. A huge red and black mosaic lines the floor, and one giant roaring fire is the only light that breaks the dark of the room. He's wrapped in thick animal furs with a glass of red wine in one hand and a large cigar in the other. I stopped behind his chair, facing the fire, bowing in low.

"Your Highness," waiting for a response, the room was silent. My presence was not yet acknowledged. I grinded my jaw to stem the rage brewing, not ready to challenge him yet, reminding myself to bide my time and gather my strength. Cordelia stood, hands clapping in front of her, shoulder straight and pulled back, her white eyes moving, watching the visions only she saw.

Totally unaffected by the quiet room, King Oberon takes a long drink of his wine before flicking his fingers towards the seat beside him.

"Sit," he demands in a gravelly voice, moving to do exactly that, staring into the fire. I wait. "Did you find the Girl?" the King enquires.

"Yes, I had her in my grasp, but we may have a few problems." I delivered my report without emotion, all traces of my anger buried deep.

"Is it her?" Oberon still stares into the fire, unnervingly still.

"I believe so. Her skin, her eyes are unmistakably that of her grandmother. I could taste and feel the power running-"

"Did she wear the Princess's ring? Antheia's ring?" He cuts me off.

"She's wearing it. I could feel the power. It's given her magic a huge boost, but she is clueless," I muse with a small snicker.

"So, you successfully attacked the Palace, you located the girl. Stop me if I'm mistaken. You had the girl in your grasp." Silence fills the space, turning finally to lock his dark eyes onto mine. I know better than to speak. "Please do tell. What exactly are you doing here without said girl? Your mission was..." he pauses, waving his hands. Smoke drifts into the air, and his gaze turns back to the fire. "I believe your mission was to locate the girl, to apprehend the girl alive and bring said girl here. Simple. We have the Intel that gave you the Palace at its weakest..... yet you failed to locate and achieve your mission."

the King states calmly, taking a long drag of his cigar, tilting his head back and narrowing his eyes as he blows out a stream of smoke before his intense stare finally meets mine.

"Magnus Dufort was there," I blurt out, and that is all I need to say in an explanation. "She also has a familiar. It ended up three on one." the King's eyes widened

"Magnus Hansen Dufort? Interesting. I thought that race was extinct. I remember killing his father many years ago! But why would Magnus Hanson be at the palace?" his fingers linked, resting his chin on his hands.

"Get Warwick here. I want answers about that girl, and I want to draw the key players out."

My dismissal is clear, and I rise to leave. "Oh, and Osirius," I pause, annoyed as my steps falter, showing the trickle of ice-cold fear tracing down my spine at his tone. "Fail me again, and you will pay with your life."

CHAPTER 40

The Raven

The noise escalates as many people filter through the receiving room. the King lounges on his throne, banking to one side, fingers drumming rhythmically as he thinks. Captain Thomas Carter stands still, dishevelled from the recent attack at the Palace.

"Let's discuss the casualties and injuries and what was wielded against us," The Captain begins, bringing the Marshalls' attention to the scene.

"The level of magic use is surprising. Here at the palace, we have a handful of wielders. The general and the King are probably our strongest," he gestures our way before continuing. Our infantry is just plain regular soldiers, powerful, deadly, and well-trained, but I've never fought against magic at that level for a very long time."

The fear of what we are up against leaks into his usually unshakable appearance.

"They had elemental magic. Every other goblin, troll, and orc was throwing water, fire fucking earthen vines. How are we supposed to fight against that?" The Captain is shaking, sweat beading his brow, eyes wide with panic, and the smell of his fear is leaking from him in waves.

"Let's stick to the facts, Captain, then we can plan a strategy," I state, raising my eyebrows in a clear signal to calm the fuck down.

"How do we protect the people? We must move quickly. We need to attack before they get more strength. I mean why did they retreat?" He continues to ramble, hysteria edging his words. My attention is swayed as an opposing tall warrior stalks in with purpose, Miss Whitlock fast on his heels. Both were bruised and bloody from the battle. Barrett straightens, attention snapping to the door as she wanders in, holding herself with pride, anger tense on both of their faces, obviously following on from a recent argument. What is going on there? I look between the two of them, trying to assess the threat once again. There is something not right between the two? Often poised like lovers, longing looks then gentle touches and easy friendship that comes with knowing someone for many years, yet uncertainty is lying underneath.

"You didn't fucking stay." the King stands, marching down the stairs across the room to her, irritated, his temper flaring. He grabs her shoulders in both hands, bending her backwards to look at him, worry etched on his face, heart on his sleeve, cards laid out for all to fucking see. She takes in the King, eyes wide and jaw hanging open slightly at a loss for words at his overly passionate display.

"Are you ok?" His forehead pressed against hers, inhaling her scent.

"Barrett," I growl in warning as I move close to the

pair, my feathered wings still out behind me, waiting for a threat. Spanning out to hide the pair from the view in the busy room.

"You didn't say to specifically stay," she huffs, rolling her eyes like a child. "Barrett," she gasps as he stares intently, his eye roaming over her face. "Sorry, I could not sit back while my friends were murdered", pouting electric blue eyes searching his face too. "I left because I needed to help a friend and then we ran into the Demon Prince." Shrugging dropping her eyes as the King of the realm is left speechless.

Hank leans down, eyes still on the room, silencing her with a private warning.

"There's lots we need to discuss, but not here", he glowers at me, straightening, taking Elodie by her arm and drawing her away from the King.

Interesting. Is he worried about us learning about her or the competition? I flick an amused smirk in his direction, which he ignores. Realising we have an audience, the King rolls his shoulders, adopting his regal stance, turning to address the room and pointing at Captain Thomas Carter.

"Get the wounded attended and get the palace locked and secured. I want extra patrols," he pauses, thinking, "find the illusionist too. I want him in front of me in the next hour." He clicks his fingers, trying to recall his name.

"Jade," I supply

"Yes. Get Jade. I want his skills to make it look like we

have more protection. I want soldiers walking around, and I want it maintained twenty-four seven."

The Captain bows low, issuing orders in his wake and vacating the room along with the many other generals. We head to a private chamber in the King's apartments, the monitors showing across the Palace to the right of the room. Without a word, Elodie sits at the table, leaning back, head tilted to the ceiling. Taking a deep breath, the shifter protector stands directly behind, shoulders squared, taking a defensive body position, narrowed eyes locking onto mine.

the King sits across from her, with the outward impression that he is relaxed. I stand in a mirror pose to Hanks, as if I'm the King's protector.

"So?" I begin crossing my arms and drawing my wings back into my body. Her blue gaze met mine, her stubborn mouth pouting like a naughty child, lips quirked up as if goading me, waiting me out. "What the hell happened?" I demand, "How come you left the apartment and ended up with the demon?" I nod my chin in her direction. Distrust at how she could walk away from such a formidable opponent with little more than scratches.

"I am not a woman to sit back while my friends are in danger, General."

"You were given an order by your king!" I all but shout, losing my cool at her petulant response. Before we head down the usual argumentative state, Hank cuts us off.

"The prophecy from the time of two courts, I suspect Elodie is now mixed up in this," Hank states as a matter of fact.

"Let me just stop you there, Sergeant." I lean forward, placing both hands on the table and bringing my face in line with that stubborn pout. "You leave the King's apartment, and all of a sudden, the Shade army retreats?" arching one eyebrow upwards, mocking her earlier taunt, "They are winning, but they retreat after you meet with the demon prince and a word of warning Miss Whitlock, you're on thin ice and in deep trouble. You seem to be at the centre of things, and I'm very suspicious of your activities."

I bring out a pair of magical cuffs, slowly running them through my hands as I straighten. My gaze is locked on hers, and excitement stirs at the prospect of another battle with her. I continue, holding my hand up to ward off other comments.

"Wait. To recap, first, you are a normal low-level magic orphan girl," Hank commits a deep growl in warning of my attitude, mimicking my movements and closing the space between the three of us.

Ignoring his threat, I continue, standing upright and crossing my arms,

"The magic I could taste and feel coming from you earlier is not that of somebody without any magic." I nod my head in her direction. "Care to explain?"

With a huge sigh, her jaw ticked in anger. "I don't know, Alexander, I don't fucking know what is going on with myself, I've always been powerless. I've never had magic. I am a gods damned orphan." She pinches the bridge of her nose, exacerbated by my questions. "My memories of my youth and parents are sketchy at best, I've lived at the commands of others all my life and then I come to this bloody godforsaken place and all shit hits the fan. I have no magic and then I do!" She pants, pitching over the table, trying to stress her innocence.

Her hands reach across the table, taking Barrett's, his face inches from those beautiful soft pouting lips; half of me wants to grab her hair and fuck her over the table, and the other wants to fill her with daggers to reduce the threat to the realm.

Barrett chuckles, "Now look at this, Miss Whitlock. You seem to have created somewhat of a stir within my Palace, and Alexander's threats are a lot more aggressive than my own." He raises an eyebrow in my direction, taking the sting out of his words. "I'm starting to be a little more inclined to see his point of view." He removes his hand, lounging back into his seat, creating distance between the pair.

"You are a beautiful woman. You have skill, you're a good fighter, and now you have ancient magic. Looking back at this video," pointing to the security monitors, he brings up the footage. Showing the residential corridor, you can clearly see the Demon Prince has a huge hard-on for you, Miss Whitlock." The screen shows the dark Demon Prince ignoring the larger threat of the huge shifter and concentrating on apprehending her. Why? The escape is swayed by the support of a blurred creature attacking the prince.

"As you can see by the footage Miss Whitlock–" she cocks her head, a big full smile pulling at her lips, then cuts him off.

"Miss Whitlock, now is it, *Your Majesty*, but when you want to fuck me, it's my shortened names and nicknames?" the King chuckles, enjoying the game the two are playing.

"It seems that way, but let's say, for argument's sake, I don't want to be intimate right now." She chuckles softly, not fully understanding the severity of her situation or how the King can lure people into a false sense of ease with his charm.

Hank blows a small stream of smoke out of his nose. Smoke? What the hell? Anger reigns through his body, and all eyes, including my own, snap towards him. Elodie's eyes widen slightly as Hank's pupils turn to black slits. I've never seen eyes like that. I've never seen a shifter with his power level; with a huge amount of effort, he breathes, and then it's gone.

Steering the conversation back on track, I interject, "So Osiris seems to want you? Why would the Demon Prince want you?" I enquire, scouring up and down her face and body, looking for any hint of deception.

"Well," Elodie flicks her eyes up at the warriors standing beside her, looking over her shoulder. "This protector friend behind me, friend, sorry, not a friend, just someone who's here to protect me, forgot to tell you everything," she says with a sarcastic wave of her hand, causing the massive warrior shifter to flare his nostrils once again anger ruminating within his eyes, growls vibrating up his chest, fist clenched on the verge of losing it, Elodie ignores the dominant display attempting to push his buttons further.

"I was saying he seems to have more secrets than the three of us put together. Hank knows more than he lets on." She leans back, folding her arms in a mirror image of mine, observing the shifter turning in her seat.

Squaring his shoulders with monumental effort, he replies, "Yes, I have a few theories." Breathing deeply with his eyes closed, he regains control and slowly opens his eyes. "Remember I've already informed you, Your Majesty. I'm older than I look. I have knowledge passed down from my race through generations." I cut him off suddenly with a low growl. And what exactly is that?"

"Irrelevant, until we can figure out the prophecy." The growl he permits is animalistic and full of dominance. Barrett responds instantly to the challenge, growing in his seat and fixing the Sergeant with a furious glare. Energy saturates the room, raising the hackles on my neck. We all freeze, the pair locked in a stare of assessing the other.

CHAPTER 41

Elodie

With a big sigh, Hank breaks the King's gaze and rubs his hands on his face, breaking the tension.

"The more pressing question, Elodie, is how your power has developed," he questions, looking down at me, control firmly back in place and that blank emotionless scold making his feature harsh once more.

Feeling three pairs of eyes from three intimidating handsome as fuck men, I suddenly feel like prey. I know my role at the palace is on rocky ground. I know who pays my wage, but I just don't know if I can trust Lord Hamlington. I look to Hank for reassurance before fixing my eyes back on the King.

"Do I have your assurance that I will be protected?" I demand, leaning forward, including The Raven in my glare, monitoring his features, assessing. He folds his arms, leaning back against a wall beside the King, no hint of emotion, expression neutral, giving me nothing.

"Why would you need protection?" Both the King and General have become rigid with that question, brows furrowed and bodies ready for action towards me. My heart pounds ready for action, Hank's words replaying. We could run. Should I just up sticks and run?

"I repeat, do I have your word that I will be protected?

If I'm to bare my soul to you and your faithful Raven," I say sarcastically, fire in my eyes for emphasis; I watch as his jaw grinds with irritation. For some reason, I get under The Raven's olive skin every time I open my mouth. "Do I have your word?" I say a third time. the King takes my hand as he senses the unease deep within.

I assure you, I will protect you against whatever is in your head, whatever you might have seen or done. I will protect you." He looks at Hank. "I'm sure this big fucker would take anyone on when it comes to you." I laugh.

"Him, he's just my bodyguard," I say with a bite from our earlier conversation.

"You know that's not what I meant, Elodie," he huffs a frustrated growl, pacing behind me, momentarily locked in our past conflict.

"Okay, I may or may not have found a secret passage in the corridor, and it led me to some little spy holes within the Palace, and then I may have caught a certain captain spilling some, what I can only presume is top-secret information regarding the strength of your army and the best time in which to strike said army at the Palace." I look down at the table into my lap, knowing that information like this prior to the attack could've prepared us for the attack and saved many lives, including Esta's.

The raw guilt aches in my chest as fresh tears threaten to fall. I whisper, "I was brought here to observe and gather information, too."

In an instant, I'm out of my seat and hauled across

the table, face pinned against the wall, arms roughly secured behind my back. The next breath, I'm spun flush to Alexander's body, dagger to my throat, damn he is fast.

All hell breaks loose. Hank is on his feet, but The Raven uses me as a human shield, dagger against my throat. A hitch to my respiration seems to spark a fury so raw within Hank that his veins are straining in his thick neck. A deep, rumbling snarl pulls at his lips.

"You're a fucking spy, who is employing you?" he growls in my ear. His eyes never move from Hank as he puts distance and the table between Hank and us. "Who are you working for?" Hissing out his demand in a deadly calm voice, "I suggest no more lies past your lips, Miss Whitlock."

My eyes are glued to Hank, the colossal shifter, as power seems to emanate from his every move. Pacing like a caged beast, he has eyes on The Raven.

"Alexander, please, she's not who you think she is," the King says, standing between the two warriors, hands out in an attempt to once again calm these volatile men. "I'm sure," he looks into my eyes, the question written all over his face. Let's just take it down a notch before we end up with a full-blown fight on our hands."

Leaning unconsciously into The Raven's embrace, his magic strokes around mine in the most delicious way, caressing against my own. My heart rate beats heavier in my chest as I try to weigh up my next move. I am utterly distracted by the feel of him, and butterflies flutter in my core.

"Alexander, put her down. She is being honest for once. We are not locking her up," the King demands.

"You are delusional, Barrett, blinded by the beauty of this girl. She's got under your skin; look at the facts. She is a... spy. She needs to be in prison locked up!" Alexander presses the sharp blade, forcing me to lift my chin higher.

Hank's body seems to grow. The reptilian slits are back in his eyes, and navy scales coat his arms, smoke leaving his nostrils as he grunts. "Step the fuck away from her or face the consequences. She's not a spy. You need to trust me on this. She is not what you think."

The situation is spiralling out of control, and Hank's muscles are bunching. Alexander's body keeps me in line with Hank. I feel his anger and the need to protect his King radiating from his pores. I stroke his arm, causing him to flex tight along my throat.

"Alexander," I call in a whisper. "Everything you say I am is ture, and more that I don't even understand. I'm bearing my soul and asking you to trust me. There are people in this palace who are fighting against you. I have been put in here to relay information, but I never..." My heart pounds, but my gut tells me I can trust these three men that I need these three men. "I never meant for the palace to be attacked. I know I'm partly to blame, and if I just trusted you first, we may not be in the position." I exhale, allowing my head to fall backwards to his chest, "if you need to lock me up. If you want to keep me under house arrest until you trust me, then that's fine. I am not the enemy here."

Alexander growls, shaking me roughly in a rare show of emotions, the blade nicking my skin, a hiss escaping me, and a crimson line trickles down, pooling into the crevasse of my collarbone.

The air explodes with energy, and the King is sent flying back. A feathered wing encapsulates me, and Alexander's strong arms cradle my body and head, protecting me as we both fall from the blast of power.

A thundering roar bellows across the room as we turn to face the room, which is now filled with the most amazing armoured beast, long sleek neck rippling with thick scales, sharp, wicked looking horns fanning over its snout, head and neck, electric navy blue swirls and runes in an intricate design coat the scales, radiating power along its body and huge leather wings tucked in, imbedded into the remains of the table.

What a moment ago was Hank now stands a magnificent dragon. Deep, dark reptilian eyes lock onto the sight of Alexander, holding me back with one arm and sword in the other. Growling in warning, the beast's giant head lowers its lips, pulling back in a snarl.

"Barrett, you ok?" Alexander asks, ready to engage, his eyes never leaving the dragon.

"Yep," the King groans, slowly popping his head up from somewhere near the kitchen.

"Move away, DO NOT ENGAGE," The Raven instructs, readying to take down the colossal dragon taking up most of the apartment living area.

"NO! It's Hank. Please let me." I nudge past the Raven,

who tries to grab me with some choice curse words directed at my back.

"Your funeral assassin."

I walk forward, palms raised, looking at the majestic dragon as smoke billows from him, electric power rippling over its body.

"Hey, handsome, now this explains the temper, and you know, the scales and the thingy!" I chuckle, a playful smile pulling at my lips.

"Careful, Elodie," Barrett advises, frozen behind the kitchen island.

"You are stunning. A dragon, eh?" My gaze roaming over the beast in front of me, reaching a palm slowly towards its snout, waiting for him to make contact first. "Can I?" inclining my head in question, Hank's head lowers, a puff of warm smoke curling around my fingers, making me giggle like a child. The dagger size canines were inches from my face now.

The surprising warmth of his solid smooth scales sends a jolt of electricity earning a squeak from me as I pull my hand back, the dragon's lips smirk up with another chuff and plume of smoke, laughing I rub between his nostrils and eyes.

"Wow," I gasp, reaching up with a second hand rubbing along his solid jaw. "Hank, I think you maybe need to, you know..... reduce in size a wee bit. So we can all discuss things like adults?" Giving a pointed look over my shoulder at Alexander. "I'm safe. That big bird brain was just a bit pissed. Alexander put the fucking sword away, will you?"

I roll my eyes in his direction with a side-eyed glance. The room ripples with magic, and a very naked Hank stands in front of me, my hand still on his very naked, smooth inked and chiselled chest, heat scorches up my face, dropping my eyes from my hand on his chest, yes definitely his chest.

"Fuck." I drop my mouth open and stare at his package. A cough sounds, and I snap out of admiration for the warrior before me.

"Like what you see, Starlight?" using my own words back at me from our time at Eden, stirring fond memories of us. With as much bravado as I can muster and with a playful nudge,

"Damn, big fella, if I had known that..." I ran a hand down his muscular chest and rock-hard abs. "This is what you were hiding under all that doom, gloom and grumpiness. I would have jumped your bones years ago!"

Barrett bursts out laughing, springing over the island. "Am I safe to come out?" Grabbing a discarded jacket, he throws it at Hank, who makes no attempt to catch it. The stoic, expressionless mask is firmly back in place.

"Okay, let me grab you something more appropriate to cover yourself." Barrett leaves through a side door, chuckling all the way. Alexander, wings still poised, has yet to respond, simply analysing the man still in front of me. Hank's fingers brush lightly over the small wound to my neck, a growl deep in his chest.

"Touch her again, Alexander Martinez, and I will toast

you and eat you for breakfast."

Hank's eyes never leave my face as he delivers his warning, palm moving to cup my jaw, thumb running along my lower lip. His possessive voice sends a rush of heat to my core, sending the pink back to my cheeks. Alexander simply nods and strides to the kitchen grabbing a few beers.

"We have a lot to discuss. Let's do so in comfort."

CHAPTER 42

Lady Carter

I pace my apartment, anxiety racing through me,

"What news?" I demand, pausing in my walk from the fire to the window; Alfie waits by the window seat, leisurely eating grapes, making each mouthful seem like a seduction, his eyes sparking with mischief and lust.

"The army has retreated. I can't see the girl but that's not to say they did not succeed. I mean, we can't do everything for-"

"Shhhh," I place a finger on his lips, darting to look around the room. Alfie sucks in the finger holding my heated gaze, snatching my hand away as I continue my pacing.

"My husband will no doubt be back again soon. Maybe it's time you stand at your post," I state with too much bite. This man has me hooked, the balance of power tilting well in his favour, and he is just a guard. Irritated, I dismiss him with a flick of my delicate wrist.

"As you wish, My Lady." He stands, offering a low bow before walking to stand behind me, slowly moving my long hair to one shoulder, trailing soft feather light kisses down my neck, allowing him better access. I arch my neck, leaning into his touch. The desire for this arrogant man is palpable. Roughly, he nips my skin, one hand grabbing a breast through the thin material of my shirt, rolling my nipple hard.

Gasping in a mixture of pain and pleasure, before he removes his attention, standing upright.

"Think of me when he's rutting like a desperate animal; it may help," his order is blunt and harsh as he strides from the room, collecting his gun and sword and attaching them before leaving.

Flustered, I take several breaths to compose myself. Ten minutes later, The Captain walks in, utter exhaustion written across his body.

"Serena darling, you are okay? Thank goodness." He leans in to kiss my cheek, stirring no warmth or lust, "I'm just grabbing a quick shower and a change of clothes before I'm needed out there again."

"What happened? Please tell me. I'm so glad you're okay. I was worried sick at the thought of you out there fighting for us all." I lay the drama on thickly, holding tightly onto his arm and kissing the bruised knuckles of his hand. "Let me take care of you, darling, and tell me everything." Command laces my voice, and the captain's eye mists under my compulsion. Then, he begins to relay everything from the battle as I tend his wounds and wash him down.

Once he is newly dressed and I have my information, he leaves our apartment with a brief kiss, confusion marrying his features,

"You're exhausted, my love. Please try to get some

rest," I say with a kiss on his cheek before he leaves for the King's war council. Pouring a glass of wine to steady my nerves. To achieve great power, you must first sow the seeds of chaos, then show the people your value, I remind myself, taking a heavy slug.

Securing the outer doors, I move to the hidden chamber towards the back of my dressing room. Using my magical signature, I unlock the room within the walls. The small room is set with a reading desk stacked with old books and my written notes.

A diagram of the Royal family tree showing me alongside the current reigning King, my cousin Barrett, the bloody fool. The boy who only ever played games and messed around with the serving girls now rules the Kingdom. It's a disgrace! On the other hand, I have studied the old magics and learned and wielded older foreign magic and languages. My father taught me how to 'play' the game and manipulate the field to ensure I ended up on top with the power, Ha and all it took was for my cousin to charm his way onto the throne. I'm not done yet.

Loyalty can be bought and secured through many channels. Applying a touch of gloss to my full lips and pulling out my big blonde curls over my shoulders, allowing my silk dress robe to slide down one shoulder, showing a hint of smooth flesh down to my full cleavage. Smiling at the image I create, I place a rare celestial communication crystal into the mirror surrounding me, chanting the words to activate and focus on the dark, viciously sexy prince.

His face comes into view. Two black and gold twisted

horns protrude among long black hair. His dark skin is smooth, and golden symbols of power glow lightly over his chest and biceps.

"Prince Osiris," I purr, allowing a heavy dose of lust to flood my gaze. "I'm glad to see you are unharmed. I have spoken with the captain, and understand you retreated without her?" I hold his stare as I take a slow sip, his eyes track my mouth, tongue licking his lower lip slowly. "Is she not what you seek?" Tilting my head tracking the contours of his exposed chest.

"You're well informed, My Lady," he tips an imaginary hat. "But you failed to provide all the facts, that she has both a shifter cat friend and Magnus Hansel Defort protecting her pearly ass." His voice escalates, confusion at his words. "As you can imagine, King Oberon is not impressed with today's events. I need to know everything about the girl, what power she has, what strength she has." I cut him off.

"What power? The girl is a worthless whore with little power," I laugh, throwing my head back. "I am baffled you would waste much time on her. Anyway, you don't need to worry about that. I have someone in place who already has an in with the girl; he has her wrapped around his little finger. Seduction can extract all the information you require."

Offering a coy gaze, I trail my fingers over my bare shoulders down the crevasse of the creamy full mounds his purple eyes follow, igniting a potent desire. His raw power and viciousness are on par with my own.

"Things have changed, Serena. Her power is

escalating. We need to draw the King and his army away. We need to draw her out where she's more vulnerable. They have shown their cards and have been found lacking. Tell me about him. What do you know of this protector, Hank? As you know him," his eyes glow with challenge.

"He turned up out of the blue. All I know from the captain is that he is a fierce warrior and that his techniques and strategies are valuable to the war." I shrug, unable to offer up more intel than that currently.

"What do you know of him?" I enquire

"Elusive fucker, we thought him dead along with his father. He has been under the radar for some time, and his race has been long thought of as extinct. The man is indeed an ancient shifter. Magnus, or Hank as he goes by now is an old warrior back from the days when the two courts wielded magic freely before these current wars, before we were diminished and driven to hide away and lick our wounds." a snarl peels to one side as he reflects "Tread carefully with that one he is strong, one sniff of your involvement he will kill you, kings cousin or not!" Glancing over his shoulder, we have talked too long, I must go.

"Well, my handsome devil, I have been doing my research. I'm not just a pretty face. I have a few tricks up my sleeve—something that will quite possibly reduce the protector to nothing! Give me time. I will work it out. Speak soon."

CHAPTER 43

The King

"Okay, so let me get this straight. You're an ancient dragon shifter who believes you have been sent here to protect Miss Whitlock?" I sit wide-eyed, rubbing the back of my neck, the tension not easing with the movement. Hank looks to be slowly weighing his words before speaking.

"No, not- not necessarily sent. Our paths crossed accidentally, and our friendship developed naturally." The sass enters the conversation, making me chuckle.

"Oh, we are friends again now?" Her playful side-eye almost breaks Hank's smile.

"Who employs you? Here at the palace?" My General inquires, not allowing us to get sidetracked. Elodie fidgets a little, obviously a bit uncomfortable, looking to Hank for reassurance before leaning back and taking a sip of her beer.

"Okay, so I'm not sure if you know, but I owe a huge amount of money for my care and education from my childhood. I worked at Electric Eden to pay off said debt. This guy," she thumbed at Hank, "Protects us girls from rowdy, handsy clientele." Looking to Alexander, "You know the type, Alexander, No?" Refusing to respond to her baiting, he point-blank ignores her.

Fidgeting again and running a hand through her long, wavy hair, she lowers her gaze regularly to avoid too much attention. "Hank made sure things ran smoothly. He made sure that we didn't, you know, get into situations we couldn't handle ourselves."

A flush of anger drives me to the edge of my seat, at the bleak picture she is beginning to paint. "How often did these situations occur?" Growling low, my beast is ready to rip anyone who has touched her.

"Whoa, kitty kat chill your beans!" Gently, her fingers trail through my hair down towards my neck, repeating the motion a few times; a bloody purr escapes me, moving into her touch, soothing the lion within.

This girl has my emotions running at an all-time high, and the lion within me is demanding I protect her and make her mine.

"I was one of the lucky ones, remember."

I take her hand and place a soft kiss on her knuckles. This girl has me transfixed, acting like a small adolescent cub.

"I was offered a position at the palace as a serving girl because of my looks, because I'm friendly, and because I communicate well with people. My role is basically to listen to the gossip to find out what people are up to and what people are saying and report back. There's been very, very few words that I've reported bar the conversation I overheard with the captain."

We are interrupted as a clamour from outside causes us to spin and look towards the garden space and the large open bi-folding doors. A mass of fur and wings bundles into the room, crashing onto the floor, wings and paws tumbling over each other.

Adrenaline surges as I spring to my feet, power at the ready. Alexander is in a similar fighting pose, and Elodie, on the other hand, jumps up in excitement. What the hell? I'm not sure my mind can take much more at the moment.

"Pumpkin, oh my goodness, Kin, you've got wings, he's got wings, shit Hank he has wings!" The creature stands on his feet, shaking and ruffling its feathers from head to toe as Elodie runs and dives, wrapping her arms around its thick neck and kissing its face like a beloved pet.

My eyebrows raise, and Alexander looks on as the scene unfolds, eyes widening in Astonishment.

"What the fuck is that?" I managed. Shuffling forward, the laughter and pure joy that radiates on her face could power a whole city. I have never witnessed her like this, relaxed and comfortable, the wide smile softening her features, blue eyes crinkling with happiness.

"I'm not sure! I rescued him when he was tiny," she answers, still looking at the creature. "Look at you!" she accused the creature "Oh, Pumpkin, where have these wings come from? He didn't have wings last week."

Another tight hug and kiss lands on Pumpkin! A pang of jealousy has me wishing I could receive attention on this scale from her lips and body.

"Gods, he didn't have wings this morning." Chuckling,

Hank moves towards the creature to stroke its head, and the beast nuzzles into his hand like a long-lost friend. Interesting, they know one another well, too. The plot thickens!

"Can you please focus and continue?" My General growls.

I give Alexander a look of expiration and a shove, which he ignores, never taking his eyes off the trio; with a deep purr, 'Pumpkin' sits between the two, folds its wings and jerks its hawk head between myself and Alexander, its sharp avian eyes latch onto Alexander, beak clicking in warning. Alexander straightens, locking his jaw before stomping back to the fridge for more beers grumbling under his breath about this shit show and the fucking assassin.

Chuckling, I introduce myself to the bird cross lion creature with a low bow, receiving a nod of acknowledgement and respect from him and a breathtaking smile from my Wildcat, which has me responding with a goofy smile of my own. Fuck.

CHAPTER 44

Elodie

After another twenty minutes of explaining the hidden rooms and corridors throughout the Palace, my new powers, and the role Lord Hamlington has played thus far, Alexander has grown more and more still. Fury lines his body, and his eyes are fixed on me—the biggest threat in the room.

I feel Hank's presence edging closer, sensing the power building around The Raven. Barrett sits, reflecting on my words. He also has yet to voice anything, making me nervous. I have bared my soul. My life is literally in his hands now. On the face of things, I am a spy employed by another to report on the crown. Did I have a choice? Probably yes, I could have refused Trixie's offer and spent the rest of my life repaying my debt in whatever manner she deemed fit.

Finally, the King speaks, his tone formal,

"This is a lot to process," I cut him off.

"Look at me," my voice raising as I see his thought process clearly, fear making me react. "Look at me, Barrett. I have held nothing back. I lost friends today, too."

"If you had adopted that same thought three days ago, we could have saved hundreds of lives today, Elodie.

Now that you have been outed, you come clean. Tell me, how long would you have kept on spying and reporting if there had not been an attack?"

Finally, his eyes meet mine, the accusation clear. The betrayal making his beautiful face harsher, his harsh words and the reality that I could have prevented Esta's death churns, guilt and sorrow crashing through my chest.

"I don't know. I don't know what I would've done. You can be angry at me if you want, but this is bigger than me. I have never asked for this, and I will live with that knowledge and guilt for the rest of my life."

I bow my head, tears glistening, but I refuse to let them fall. Alexander finally speaks in the tone of a commander, both stern and void of warmth.

"She stays under house arrest either in the prison or her rooms, with restraining cuffs."

You could hear a pin drop, the silence defending. I don't even hear or see The Raven move, flicking his magic across my wrist, a pale light ringing both.

"What the- ow!" Magic burns, sending tingles down my fingers and another brutal bolt of lightning pain. I gasp as I clutch my head, hissing against the now familiar pain.

"You stay in your apartment. You are taking on a new role, and I want to know where you are. At all times," he empathises. "I want to know whom you meet, what you fucking eat when you sleep." He closes the distance between us, his face in mine so I could feel his breath mingling with my own. "I want to know when you take a god's damned shit, you will not move without us knowing exactly where and what you are up to."

"She's not a fucking prisoner, Alexander," the King implores.

"No, but the enemy wants her," he responds.

Without a word, I slowly stand, closing the last few inches between us. Now I'm face-to-face with the Raven, hand on his chest. I nod. He inhales, grinding his jaw.

"If that is what you need to feel secure and protected against me," lacing my tone with sarcasm and implication clear he's scared of little old me, "but you need to promise me that I keep my cover, I get nothing for being here. My debt doesn't get paid. Fuck I've got responsibilities outside of this place." pure panic hits me, the Raven and his threats forgotten, chewing a thumbnail. "Shit, Maddison." attention now on Hank.

"I will see to it that she will be fine. I promise you." He strides forward, cupping my cheek with one huge palm, gently removing my thumb before I bite it to the quick, angling me away from Alexander.

"She has no one, Hank. She relies on me to keep in touch, to pop in and check up on her. I can't do that when I'm stuck under Alexander!" I ramble as panic for the sweet little cub rises.

"Who is Madison?" the King speaks up, the anger from before now simmering gently, his eyes lit with interest, inclining his head, observing me.

"Another ward of Trixie's in her first year of education at the moment, Maddison looks up to Elodie like a big sister." Hank embraces me as the events of today finally catch up. My arms circle his huge frame as I bury my head into his chest, my heart constricting my breaths shallow with grief.

"Hey, don't worry. You can stay here tonight. I will send someone to make sure your ward is looked after, and the rest we will work out." Shocked at Barrett's soft kindness, she looked his way while still buried in Hank's arms.

"We are all exhausted, and tomorrow will be carnage trying to plan our move against the Shade army," I nod. Hank squeezes me and nods his head in the direction of the bathroom.

"Shower, then get some sleep, Starlight. I will fetch you some clothes." Grateful for his support, and exhaustion pulling at the seams, I head in the direction indicated.

Alexander walks with me. I scowl at him, "Seriously?"

A cruel smirk is directed at me. "I will show you to a spare room and stand guard for now."

Swallowing my retort, I inhale deep. I paste a sickly, sweet fake smile, holding my cuffed wrists out, looking up at the sharp jaw and violet sliver-flecked eyes.

"Thank you, General for taking such good care of me." I flutter my lashes, reaching up to dust a soft kiss on his cheek. A grunt is his only response.

CHAPTER 45

The King

After yesterday's exhaustion, we all crashed in my apartment, although Hank took off for the barracks and never returned.

Pumpkin is still asleep upside down, legs in the air on the garden sofa, without a care in the world.

Elodie, on the other hand, seemed to withdraw last night, accepting her fate with no fight. The desire to comfort and take away her pain was so strong that I had to move her into the furthest guest room to resist the temptation. What is it about this girl that has me so mesmerized?

The garden bifold doors slide to one side, one pale long leg entering the open plan area followed by another. She enters, a cup of coffee in one hand, a book balanced in the other, engrossed in the text. The oversized men's T-shirt grazes the top of her thighs, drawing my eye. Nimbley, she closes the door with one butt cheek leaving an imprint on the glass. I watch her walking towards the coffee machine in my direction. I ache to run my hands up those legs and grab that shapely ass.

"Hey," I say as I mentally remind myself to stop fantasising over her. Without breaking stride or looking up from the book, she gives a non-committal nod in my general direction, placing her cup once again under the high-tech coffee machine.

I can't deny our obvious attraction to each other, but it is more than that; I want to spend time with this girl. She makes me feel seen and desired in a way no other woman has before; shit, few people engage me enough to warrant my attention for more than the obligatory introductions.

"I'm making pancakes. You want some." Her head snaps up at the mention of food,

"Sorry, I was miles away. Wow, the King is cooking again. Did you say pancakes?" The smile she sends my way stops my heart for a few beats. She is simply stunning without all the fake glitz and glam typical of court nobles.

"Yeah," I laugh, "you want some?"

"Gods yes, please," she says, grabbing her coffee. She moves to the breakfast bar to watch me in action. The lion in me fills with pride at the look on her face; he likes to provide for this woman, and I flex a little under her gaze.

"What's got you so engrossed?" I give a subtle nod to the book, which is still open but now face down on the counter.

"Your library is amazing, do you know that? I couldn't sleep last night, so I explored your collection. This particular book," she points, tapping it lightly with one finger, "is about elemental magic and how to use it; I thought I might as well try to understand how things work.

"You will have to show me this room. The information there may help us understand what the fuck is happening and guide our next steps in the war."

Lighting up like the aurora borealis on a clear night, she exhales, bubbling with excitement,

"Oh, Barrett, the information in that room is amazing. I've never seen anything like it, full of books, a heaven for a reader seeking knowledge."

I chuckle softly at her excitement over a few dusty books, her features soft in a way she never easily portrays to the world. The impulse to reach out and touch her is overwhelming. Without thinking, I take her hand, lacing our fingers together, running my thumb over her smooth skin. Suddenly, I want her close with me at all times, so I can see that stubben smart mouth every waking moment.

"Stay in these apartments with me," her jaw snaps shut, shocked by my request; her mouth opens as if to reply but closes without voicing her thoughts. Her features shutter. Closing down the warmth in her eyes. "You can stay in the guest suite. It's safer. We can research and practice together." I stumble over my own words as she fails to respond, staring wide-eyed. "We can Keep an eye on you; you'll have your room. It's not like you will be sleeping in my bed." With a slow bite of my lip to stop my verbal diarrhoea, cheeks pink as I envisage that exact scenario, "Unless, of course, you want to?"

She dropped her gaze, pink staining her face, but I was unsure if that was anger or embarrassment. I panicked at her lack of response, knowing I was her King and not many people would refuse me.

"I'll say that I've taken a liking to you, and you're entertaining me, but you can-"

"No, I'm no one's whore, and I will not have the palace thinking that is what we are doing." Her posture becomes defensive, her jaw twisting in anger.

"That's not what I mean. I'll say that you're in here helping with admin, that I have you on a research project, and then you can spend time looking through your princesses' books. We can investigate this prophecy; we will investigate your magic."

She begins to relax again, thinking. "I will need to meet with Lord Hamlington and discuss my new role with him." a wicked half smile plays along her lips. "We can feed him some bogus information, watch events unfold, and play double agent."

"You are going to be a bad influence on me, I can see. Now, should we go and have a look at this secret room of yours?" I cock one eyebrow and flip a pancake with expertise, pulling genuine laughter from her, "Food first, of course."

Watching Elodie Whitlock eat has quickly become my favourite pastime. Each mouthful she takes emits a groan verging on sexual. I trace the movement of her tongue as she licks the caramel syrup from her fingers; it's easy to imagine that sexy mouth of hers around my cock; I feel the jump and thickening of said appendage.

A cough brings me out of my daydream, and my

head snaps up. "Sorry, I was miles away," I run a hand through my hair, quirking a small smile.

"What were you thinking of Your Majesty? The look on your face is positively..." she thinks, tilting her chin up to the left and placing a finger to the side of her mouth. "Starving, that's it, like a hungry lion."

I pout, offering her a look that leaves little doubt of my desires. A smirk twitches as I see the same lust mirrored in her gaze.

"Put some clothes on, Miss Whitlock, before my beast wins this battle and takes that scrap of fabric from your body, too." With mischief written across her face, she prowls past me to the dishwasher, pulling the draw open, bending at the waist, the man's shirt she wore to bed rises to give me a peek of the black lace French knickers and that perfect ass, I growl a curse grabbing my cock in a bid to relieve the ache building, dropping into a low squat, the shirt once again covering that ass she slides the draw closed.

"Barrett." I jump, the sharp voice stealing my attention. "If you keep looking at her like that, you will drive yourself into a mating rut like a damn elk shifter." Alexander barks, heading to the coffee machine dressed as if ready for battle in his trademark black leathers.

"Morning, Alexander, " Elodie says sweetly, slowly rising and sashaying out of the kitchen, one hand trailing across his bicep. "Ready for action as always, Raven," she throws a wink my way.

"Give me twenty to get ready, Leo, then I'm all yours." heat rushes to my core, loving the new nickname on her lips.

"We have a fucking war meeting, or did you forget when the blood rushed to your cock," Alexander chastises me.

"Gods, do you have eyes? I'm a red-blooded male." I raise both arms in defeat, sighing heavily. Having that woman under my roof is going to challenge my restraint.

CHAPTER 46

Elodie

Swinging by my apartment, I find Jenny sitting in front of the coffee table, head bowed. Entering, I take a seat beside her and take one hand in, my own squeezing.

The apartment is too clean, no sign of the murder that took place, no sign of our friend. Silence replaces the early morning chatter and food prep we had comfortably fallen into together.

"I could not save her. I didn't know how," I whisper. My heart constricts as tears fill my eyes. Slowly, her head turns to face me.

"You did not kill her. She was trying to give me time to run" Jenny's voice is broken, barely audible as a sob chokes in her throat. I hold her hand tighter. We lean together, soaking up one another's strength.

"I will find that demon prick and make sure he suffers for ending such an innocent, beautiful soul."

The vow rings true in the air, a tingle of magic pulsing through our connected hands. Her eyes widened in surprise, taking me in. She leaned back to get a better look at me.

"You saved me last night with magic. How?" Her wide, bloodshot eyes filled with moisture. "One minute, I was failing, I'm sure. Then, that rush. Then, I'm alive. How?" Shrugging I drop my gaze to our locked hands.

"Hank believes I have always had magic but was blocked somehow. Coming here has triggered the release. Pumpkin pushed me to connect with you."

A tear spills down my cheek, gut-wrenching grief churning. "I nearly lost you too, Jen. God, I don't know what's happening, but I feel like I'm involved somehow. I feel my magic growing."

"That black-horned monster prick kept saying he could smell you and asking where you were," Jenny scoffs, a sneer pulling at her lips.

I nod, already knowing that I or the power unleashed from the ring—the ring I have yet to mention—was his target.

"I fear he will be back," a new crippling fear for my friend turns my stomach. "Can you fight Jenny?"

"What me? fight with swords and daggers a gun?" She shakes her head in disbelief. "I'm a serving girl. My fighting stems from my childhood in the school playground, where I pulled a girl's hair once for taking my doll."

We chuckle at the memory she holds, but worry courses through me, knowing she will be targeted to get to me now.

"I want you to start learning, just the basics, so you can start to defend yourself better. He will know your worth to me and will target you to get at me."

Emotion burns my eyes, tears pooling again, and anguish makes our limbs heavy as we sink into each other. I never asked for any of this, and now I find myself at the centre of a brewing war I know little about. I heave a sigh, giving Jenny a squeeze.

"I need to grab some more clothes and bits. I am going to be staying near the King's suites, and he wants me to do some research."

"Pardon?" A hand grabs my arm and forces my attention. "You're staying with the King? As in THE FUCKING KING!"

Jumping to her feet, she drags me to her feet, towing me along the corridor to my room. "Girl, you need to plan what you're taking, not just grab a few things." She mocks my voice. "You need to keep his attention and show him what Miss Whitlock has underneath."

Laughing, I grab a bag from my wardrobe. "I'm pretty sure that performance showed him what I have underneath. Anyway, I do not want anything from anyone. Life is complicated enough."

Throwing a few items into the bag, Jenny gasps.

"Gods, no! At least put these little short silky Pj's in, not the onesie."

As quickly as I fill the bag, she refills it with more appropriate items. The normality of her actions tugs at the grief still raw within my soul.

"Jen, I'm no whore," I say, giggling with excitement that I don't want to acknowledge. the King is hot and seductive. The way he watches me sends shivers up my spine, but can I seriously engage in anything with him? Talk about drawing attention!

"Elodie? Jenny?" A voice calls as Alfie walks in. "Oh, thank god you're okay." Striding over, he scoops me in a crushing embrace. "I heard about Esta. I'm so sorry." He reaches to pull Jenny into the hug. I stiffen at the essence of him; he feels wrong. His touch that once flooded my knickers, now churns in my stomach. His wide smile fails to reach his eyes; rather than looking relaxed, concerned and friendly, he just looks fake. He pulls back, looking from me to Jenny and then back at me,

"Were you ladies hurt?" Forcing a smile I know is flat, I can't help remembering our last time together and his abrupt departure and the way he bit me. Confusion keeps me quiet. Jenny's eyes flick to me, and then she quickly looks to Alfie.

"We are fine, Alfie, we had a run in-"

"With a few enemy soldiers, but Hank got us to safety." I interrupted, not wanting to give Alfie too much information. He watched me, eyes narrowed and locked onto mine, but just as quickly, a brilliant smile filled his face.

"Thank the stars for Hank, the saviour," he laughs to lessen the salty comment. "What's the bag for?" Indicting the bag with his chin, his smile still in place, that wrong feeling spreads. My magic stirs as if reading for a fight.

"Oh, I'm required to relocate temporarily for a work project," I say vaguely. "So, were you involved in the fighting?" I deflect.

Noticing my deflection but going with it, he shrugs, rubbing one hand through his hair and flexing his arms. The action that once had me eye fucking him now only sends revulsion down my spine.

"Not directly, I had protective duties of the nobles," he says, waving his hand in dismissal. What project?" he inquires, trying to steer the conversation back, a flicker of annoyance entering his gaze.

Picking up my things, I give Jenny a big hug. "Be careful, Jen. I will message you about the training, okay?" I speak quietly into her ear and then turn to leave. See you later, Alfie. Thanks for checking in." With a casual wave, I'm out of the door.

"Wait, El, please." Alfie dashes after me, blocking the exit and halting my progress. "Are we okay? You seem a little off."

Squaring my shoulders, I drop the friendly mask. "I just lost a friend, Alfie, and frankly, I have a lot on my mind at the moment. You are not one of them, I'm afraid."

Reaching out, he tries to stroke my arms, twisting I avoid his touch, leaving his hand hovering in mid-air, clenching his fist and pursing his lips into a tight grimace.

"Can we get together soon? Just us." Folding his arms, he flashes that sexy smile of his, but the effect it now has on me sends a wave of disgust.

"I'm not sure what you think we have here, Alfie," I

indicate between up. "Yes, we hooked up, but that is all. I'm not looking for anything. " Stepping back from him, I look pointedly behind him, lifting the shoulder strap of my large bag.

"I know you're hurting, Elodie, but don't push me away. I'm here for you." He steps back into my personal space, gently capturing my chin to look into my eyes. I see his intent, his signature moves, where he will brush his lips over mine, murmuring sweet nothings. Gently pushing him back, creating distance a second time, a flash of anger crosses his face but is quickly switched to that false-ass smile once again.

Was I that blind before not to see the power play for what it is? Was I so deprived of love and attention that I looked at the man with rose-tinted glasses and ignored the obvious rot underneath?

"Thank you, Alfie. You have been a friend, but I really need to get going. I have work to do." He finally nods, his eyes still assessing me as I leave him standing at the entrance of my old apartment. I refuse to look back, but my shoulders prick with unease. Alfie Roberts is a wolf in sheep's clothing, and I need to keep my distance.

CHAPTER 47

Hank

Alexander leans back, not saying a word, eyes fixed on Elodie, watching every move she makes. My dragon bristles in agitation, having not forgiven The Raven for cutting our girl. On the other hand, Elodie pointedly ignores him, listening to the room and taking notes as requested by the King. He wants her to appear like a personal assistant while keeping her close and hopefully safe. Our losses were high. Our recruits were unable to adjust to the use of magic against them.

The Captain and I discussed new training strategies late into the evening and this morning, but the simple fact is that we will be overpowered if we don't have more magic users.

"We need to try and get as much Intel on the Demon Prince and what the Shade forces are capable of. What we saw yesterday is just a fraction of the power they have been harnessing." Holding the floor, several sombre faces stare back at me.

"If magic is truly awakening within the two courts again, we are going to be at a disadvantage. Captain, how many magic users do we have in our ranks?" Despite his panicked meltdown yesterday, Captain Thomas Carter holds his head high, the strong warrior back in place.

"Around seventy-eight active users that can cause harm or make some difference, twenty-four shifters that have low-level magic but nothing of great use, so in all, one hundred and two."

My heart sinks. No amount of training will be able to defend against the Shade army of yesterday with those numbers. Keeping my face neutral, there was no evidence of my turmoil within. "

What of the enemy forces, what are the predictions?" This question identifies the unease within the room. We all experienced the battle against the goblins and fought hard to stay alive.

The Captain exhales heavily, pinching the bridge of his nose.

"Of the estimated six hundred troops, which split into quadrants, at least thirty per cent of each quadrant held useable elemental magic of varying strengths."

"Fuck." the King cuts the Captain short. "I presume you two have a plan?" He looks between The Captain and I.

Clenching my jaw, I nod. "Honestly, there are a few techniques and elixirs that may shield against some types of magic use, especially coercion. I have units working on these already. We can train the recruits differently." The room is deadly silent. It's not enough, but it's what we have currently."

"Can we unlock more magic?" Her first words broke the tension in the room, and several people at the table snigger. Her jaw ticks as pink coats her cheeks.

"It's a fair question, Miss Whitlock. I'm putting together a team. I want to research and look into an old prophecy." I survey the room, glaring at the men who sniggered; unable to hold my glare, they squirm and drop their heads.

"The Shades have waited a long time for this, letting us battle amongst ourselves while they have unlocked their magic, so we know it's possible. We just need the knowledge on how to achieve it." I pause, observing the maps and stats pinned around the room, sharing a knowing look with the King himself.

"We are building our hopes on unleashing magic to win this war." Sergeant Williams, an older wolf shifter, grunts. A wicked scar racking down one side of his face is healing slowly.

"No, this is one area we are investigating with a team of non-soldiers. We already have a lead and a small team working on how the Shades held onto their magic. We have not," I growl in warning, sensing his alpha nature rising, allowing a small shift, scales shimmering up my neck and power pulsing, making the old shifter sit up and take a good old sniff, hackles rising. Cocking my head, readying to assert my dominance. Suddenly, the King stands with a withering look my way; the table mirrors him, standing.

"Well, we have a lot of work to do. I expect daily updates. I will not allow these faes to destroy everything we have built in the last decade. I want patrols doubled, and appropriate training increased."

Elodie pushes forward, leaning forward to peer up at

the King. "May I make a suggestion?" Without waiting for permission, she continues, "Get all staff and people within the Palace to go to self-defensive training. Most of our losses are people without any combat skills."

"We cannot start training staff. Do you know how long it would take to get a basic semi-trained person who would be useless in real combat?" Williams sniggers, once again dismissing her ideas. Glaring, she fully turns to face the alpha wolf. I smirk with pride at her ballsy attitude, waiting to see how this will pan out.

"Do you know how many people we lost that had no combat or self-defence skills?" she fires back, folding her arms across her chest. "When it comes down to sheer numbers, trained staff or people may be able to get themselves to safety, rather than be slaughtered like animals?"

"Miss Whitlock, I appreciate your passion for keeping people safe, but Sergeant Williams is right; we don't have the manpower to train new people from scratch. I'm sorry." Remorse floods the King's features at Captain Carter's announcement.

"Let me teach them then," she demands, throwing up her hands. "I know the basics and can train people in the morning." I can feel her desperation to help her friends and prevent what happened to Esta. The grief and guilt are displayed for all to read.

the King's eyes light up with her display, roaming over her body. He is enjoying seeing her at his table.

Envious of his open regard for Elodie, I struggle to watch the interaction as she smiles warmly back at him.

I sigh, knowing what I'm about to do will be mainly a waste of time and energy, but I can't bear the disparity in her features.

"I can spare an hour each day to train those who want to learn if the King will allow." I indicate the King with a questioning look. "Elodie, you can support and hone your skills, too." She reaches out to place her hand on my forearm. The gratitude she offers me in one glance brings a tight-lipped smile as I look into her eyes.

"I shall help too," the gruff growl of The General carries across the room from his place in the corner. Elodie's head snaps his way, grinding her jaw in a scowl that would make most people back away. He appears not to notice her at all, instead looking directly at the King; the slightest movement of his eyes and bite of his cheek is his only tell that he is enjoying riling her up. With a clap of his hand, the King nods and dismisses the room.

"Come, Miss Whitlock. We have much to discuss." I watch as she walks behind the King, a snarl directed at The Raven as she shoulder-checks him. He simply follows her and barrages out of the room, trailing her every movement.

I watch as the trio vacate. A feeling of loss burns in my chest. I can see how both men look at her; they will fall in love with her easily, and I will forever be on the sidelines watching and protecting. My destiny, my sacrifice. Running a hand over the back of my neck, I leave all thoughts of Elodie Whitlock behind and head to the barracks.

CHAPTER 48

Elodie

The princess chamber is as I left it. Moving to the bookcase, I search the books, grabbing a selection to take to the reading table opposite. I feel content, a sense of peace relaxing my shoulders as my mind wanders over all the information I have gathered so far, much of which I believed to be myth and legend, but as it turns out, was always built on truth.

"So you just happened to stumble on this little secret room and the labyrinth of interconnection spy tunnels?" the King's voice is playful as he strolls around the room. I offer up a smile as I begin to sort the books into subjects.

Alexander, on the other hand, has gone completely unnaturally still, his attention solely focused on my movements, his face closed, not betraying his true feelings. I am annoyed at his moping, angry gaze and sniping comments that follow me everywhere I go—and I mean everywhere.

"I want you to see what you can find regarding the unlocking of magic. You have obviously been offered a gift. Have you practised wielding your gift yet since the cuffs came off?" Barrett casually drapes one arm over my shoulder as he peers at the book I have opened, his thumb tracing lazy circles on my arm. The action sends little shivers over my body, and the heat drops lower.

"I'm a little nervous, to be honest," I admit, feeling my cheeks warming under the King's attention. "The few times I have accessed this new power have been under stress or times of high emotion. I can't feel anything different. Maybe my magic does not work normally?" Shrugging my shoulders, I turn the page, dust flittering from the large book on the two courts and their history.

"You just need to practice. Alexander will help you." The only evidence that Alexander is unhappy with the King's words is a small tension in his jaw. "That's an order, by the way. I have a few things I need to sort, I am the King after all." He laughs, running his hand through his golden hair and offering the most dazzling smile, clapping Alexander on the shoulder.

"Look after our prophecy, and please don't kill each other." With a booming laugh, he cupped my face to place a hard kiss on my lips. His eyes heating, he bit his lip in restraint. Gods, you are a beautiful woman. See you later, Wildcat." With that, he left me standing in shock at his boldness. He left the room whistling down the corridor. Eyeing my minder briefly, I began to read.

Several hours must have passed as I read book after book, all discussing the laws of the Unseelie and Seelie courts, the magics available, and the different species of Fae often seen in each court. I sigh in frustration, finding nothing of much use for modern times or unlocking magic.

Leaning back, I stretch. Movement in the corner makes me jump, forgetting in my research that

Alexander is still here. Molten purple and silver eyes glaring my way.

"Gods, you're like a statue. I totally lost track of time." I stand to move towards the vanity desk, shivering at the reduced temperature in the room, the fireplace sparks to life with only a thought.

"Did you do that?" His gruff voice almost sounds accusatory, rough from disuse.

"No, the room seems to respond to my needs. Well, it did this last time, too, when I became cold and thought of heat."

A grunt is the only response I'm offered as he stalks towards the desk, picking up the journal and flicking through the pages, brow furrowing as he flips the book back and forth.

"They are all empty," he says, flicking his wrist to plant the journal back on the desk, I frown back at him in confusion.

"No, it's not?" Collecting the book, I read the first page out loud. "*Monday, May 22nd, I saw him with his father! Tall and broad like a warrior, with dark brown, almost black hair braided to show his status, and intense eyes that take everything in. I sense his magic brush against mine in a soft caress, bringing a sigh to my lips. Outwardly his attention is fully on the King and Queen, my parents, but that touch. Patricia nudges me, eyes widening in warning, hissing at me to look away and concentrate! I am The Princess! Forcing my face into a neutral, bland expression, I push my magic into him with such power and love I see him straighten slightly, flicking his eyes to mine with a twitch of his lips."*

I pause. "It's her diary," I explain, looking at The Raven, leaning in to peer over my shoulder, shaking his head.

"I see nothing… just blank pages."

"Huh, so you can't read it? Interesting, maybe you're too weak to read it," I muse, walking towards the fire to sit amongst the deep rugs. Pumpkin obviously takes that as an invite and shows up out of thin air and snuggles beside me. Huffing, I glare at Alexander.

"Why don't you grab us some snacks and make yourself useful rather than standing around thinking no one has things harder than you!"

"I don't just stand around, Miss Whitlock. I watch, and I learn." He looms over me, his face inches from mine. "Others may fall for your act, but I will not let my guard down. I will take you down if need be."

Pumpkin gives a low hiss in warning. Holding his glare, he inches forward, closing the space between us further.

"Is that a promise, Raven?" I allow a soft purr to coat my words, "It's been a while since someone of your prowess took me down." Biting my lower lip, I exaggerate a long look up the length of his body. My magic responds, brushing up against his, stealing my own breath away in the process.

"You're insufferable." Abruptly standing, Alexander takes a book from the case and flings it to land in front of me. "Learn," he growls. "Unlocking your power."

I read the title, lifting the book with a shrug. "You need to understand how to use your magic and practice. That should help you," pointing to the book. "Read. I'm getting us food."

"What, you trust me enough to leave me unattended?" I mock gasp. The arrogant smirk he offers is the only warning I get before rope-like vines shackle around my ankles and wrists, securing me to the huge desk.

"Hey! You can't do that!"

"If you're not too weak," he mocks, "undo the magic." A pulse of magic is in the air, and he fully transforms into a black raven and is gone.

Ripping at the vines only succeeds in rubbing my skin raw. Even Pumpkin's beak cannot break them. After letting out a few choice curse words and a childish strop, I finally, I settle back down and pick up the book. The book is laid out into sections that appear to be elements, with each page filled with symbols, incantations, and simple hand and finger placements to control different magics.

Locating what looks like a basic spell to summon water, I begin practising the words.

"To summon water, the user simply curves the ring and little finger of the left hand while curving the wrist in a scooping motion. Visualise the water pooling in your hand in a sphere shape. To support the word "aqua" can be used."

Kneeling, I practice the hand movement several times, feeling foolish at my lack of... well, anything.

"Here goes, Pumpkin." Visualising water in my left hand, I flick my wrist. Mothing, nada nitch.

Wrinkling my nose in frustration, I try again, repeating movement along with the chant. Still, nothing. Frustration burns within. Huffing a sigh, I reread the text, making sure I have everything correct, my patience wearing thin.

"What am I doing wrong, Pumpkin?" Absentmindedly, I stroke him, continuing to flick my left wrist.

"Feel the energy inside and around you, Enchantress."

Pausing my movements, I look at the familiar beside me. I definitely heard that in my head. Speaking aloud.

"Did you speak into my head, big lad?"

"You need to let the magic surface that has been buried for years, and yes, it's me." With a laugh, I kiss his big head. Feeling for that warm trickle of power, a dull pain throbs behind my temples again.

"Feel the magic push past the barrier." Delving deeper, I sense a pool of power sealed in ice, the cracks oozing power. Following the trickle of power to the large pool within, I push, unconsciously still moving my left hand.

The cracks increase power flowing thick and fast. I'm panting hard, and my heart rate is picking up. Is this my power? Can I unlock it?

"Push through, release the magic," Pumpkin encourages. My excitement surges, and I clearly feel the barrier in my mind, my power striving to be unleashed.

The pressure builds as I slump forward, bracing against the new wave of pain, but I can't pull back. The ice is shattering, power racing towards the surface. With an earth-shattering scream, a tidal wave of water erupts from my hand, driving furniture across the room before forming a giant sphere which builds. Magic pours from me, feeding the creation in front of me. Unable to catch my breath, I pitch forward, water continuing to fill the room, and magic flows through me, a never-ending tsunami.

"Elodie," I hear a distant shout. Shut it down, close your fist, and cut off the power." The voice bellows as the water bubble encases the room. "Elodie, shut it off," Alexander's panicked voice muffles under the rush of water and power.

Adrenaline courses through me, my heart rate increasing as panic starts to set in, all logical thoughts leaving me. Sweat beading my brow breaths now, just shallow pants. Suddenly, the water engulfs me, the power controlling me, and I am unable to pull it back. Feeling myself floating upwards, panic begins to take hold, thrashing against the vines still holding me. My eyes widen as I see Alexander in the corridor, and my lungs burn, screaming for help. The water rushes in, filling my lungs, my vision filling with black spots, thrashing hard, sucking in another lungful of water, and the world darkens as I finally lose consciousness and slam to the floor.

"Fuck wake up! Elodie, come on," the feel of strong arms cradling me and the hard press of lips to mine, exhaling air into my saturated lungs. A spasm of coughs brings water from my mouth as my eyes open to dark violet eyes and the chiselled face of The Raven. Seeing me awake.

"What the hell were you thinking? you nearly killed yourself." His hands grip my shoulders tightly, hiding the tremble I desperately try to ignore. Pushing into a seated position, I pulled my wet hair from my face.

"You said to practice." Embarrassment at my lack of control making anger lace my tone.

"That was you trying to commit suicide, not bloody practise - for a girl that shows such control and precision with a dagger, I expected a little more control than that."

"Girl? Huh?" Tutting, crossing my arms to stop the shaking, "I had never done this before, Alexander. Maybe if I was not angry with you for tying me up like a common prisoner, I might have been in more control."

The look of utter disgust and hatred he throws my way has me backing up from the intimidating warrior. For the first time, I truly see the man he is. Lethal. A trained, powerful, controlled killer. Scrambling to my feet, I turn away in an attempt to hide my fear.

"I need to get dry. Can we head back?" I chance a look over my shoulder, fear and adrenaline saturating my muscles. The Raven nods and turns for the door, not even checking to see if I'm following. Arrogant pig head alpha twat.

CHAPTER 49

Elodie

By the time we make it to the King's apartment, tremors have set in. Folding my arms across my body, I stand feeling shattered. The raw magic that coursed through my body has left me feeling like I have sparred with Hank all day.

A hunger so potent rumbles loudly in my stomach, and I can barely keep my lids from closing.

"Get a hot shower. I will make you some new food. Magic expenditure on that scale will take its toll." The shock at his soft, almost caring words leaves me frozen in place. Alexander looks at me, letting out a defeated sigh,

"Elodie, you're dead on your feet. Please get in the shower and get changed."

I nod, stumbling towards the en-suite in my room, turning the shower on and stripping out of my wet clothes with trembling fingers.

A wave of dizziness washes over me, and nausea has me aiming for the toilet and bringing up the contents of my earlier breakfast. A few minutes pass as the steam fills the room. Taking big, deep breaths through my nose, I attempt to stand, grabbing towards the shower and hot running water.

The water soothes my aching muscles, exhaling heavily. I close my eyes and attempt to ward off the new wave of dizziness. The room spins as I try to grab anything to steady myself. Slipping and crashing to the floor, my head banging against the wall, I feel the hot wetness of blood, my eyes roll as oblivion tries to steal my consciousness for the second time in one day. A loud knock sounds at the bathroom door. I groan, vision blurring.

"Elodie? Elodie, are you ok?" I groan, fighting to stay awake; steam billows out the now open door as Alexander storms to my side; without a word, he lifts me against his chest, cradling me tight. Carefully, he wraps a towel around my body to protect my modesty; shutting off the water, he walks me to the large bedroom.

Neither of us speaks as he gently dries my body before sitting me on the bed, wobbling as he holds me until I'm steady. Nodding, he stands, gathering the large T-shirt I sleep in, covering my body before softly examining the wound to my head. His hands hold my face as he strokes down the side of my cheek, the caress tender.

Our magic collides gently, rubbing over each other. I study his features. The beauty of his face, strong jaw, straight nose, and dark violet eyes tinged with flecks of silver that look to mine. My lips part. He is so near we could easily kiss. The heat warms, causing a light gasp as I inhale. My body wants to close the last few inches between us, our magic seeking. Pulling back, removing his hands.

"Get some rest. The wound will heal, but you will have

a bruise." I nod as he rises to his full height, his mask firmly back in place.

"I will grab that food, then you need rest." I'm once again left in a state of confusion.

I am attracted to Hank and flirting with Barrett, the King, and now I'm having a moment with the bloody Raven. Since this magic awoke in me, my body seems to have gone into heat. Sighing, I lean back into the pillows, stretching my long legs out across the bed. Alexander returns with a tray of sandwiches, hot chocolate and several chocolate biscuits.

"Eat and rest." I don't miss the heated look he scans down my legs, but it's gone in a second, making me question if it was really there.

"Alexander-" he stops me by handing me the tray of food.

"Eat," he commands, sending waves of pleasure at the sound of his demand; his nostrils flare, and quickly, he steps back to the wall, taking up his signature stance, leaning back against the wall, arms folded, watching.

"Thank you." I groaned with my first bite. The food in the palace, even a basic melted cheese sandwich is delicious.

"Next time we start smaller, maybe in an open area?" A smile pulls at his lips.

"Yeah, that's probably a good idea. But at least I know I can access my magic. I felt the barrier break. The rush felt powerful." After finishing the sandwich and then grabbing the hot sweet liquid and biscuits, I began to devour them, too. The hunger left from my magical fuck up has me finishing the packet in record time. Alexander watches in that stoic way of his, not saying a word.

"Hey gorgeous, where are you?" Barrett calls from the living area; I try to answer with my mouth full, spraying crumbs over the bed. Alexander tuts, shaking his head before calling out.

"In here."

"What have I missed?" Barrett walks straight to the bed, flopping down onto his side to face me on my bed. He pops his head with one hand, his expression a mixture of concern and mischief. "You look…" Frowning, he flicks the crumbs from my bare legs. "I want to say just post-sex exhausted, but… that's not right. I can't smell that sort of satisfaction on you." he looks at The Raven with raised eyebrows, "Or you, you still have that stick up your ass and scary 'I'm going to murder you, Miss Whitlock' expression."

I burst out laughing as Alexander flips him off, biting his cheek to stop a smile gracing his lips.

"Miss Whitlock decided to practice her magic and ended up nearly drowning the both of us."

"Ah, hence this," he gestures at me, his teasing smile reaching his eyes. His trailing fingers up my arm send goosebumps over my flesh. What is wrong with me?

the King scans the bathroom, noting my clothes tossed across the floor and the blood on my head.

"And this?" he questions, inspecting my wound.

I wince, "I fell in the shower."

"Alexander you sly, clever Raven." the King chuckles, kissing my head gently letting the heat of his magic flow, stroking my body. "Did you get a good view?"

Sighing, the ache in my head soothes, my muscles relaxing with his healing magic travelling through me, my own magic rushing to meet his.

"Are you jealous, Barrett?" The brooding male taunts, "Maybe you should keep your distance from such a powerful, unstable female. Your judgment is off if that is your train of thought." snarling in disgust. "I'm not interested in her in the slightest, desolate orphans don't do it for me."

Before I can snap back at that insult, he storms from the room.

"Well, I do believe he protests too much!" Barrett kisses my cheek one last time, moving to lie on his back next to me. He folds his arms behind his head, sighing an exhausted exhale. Taking one arm, he pulls me in close, so my head rests on his chest, feeling his steady heartbeat beneath. A feeling of comfort and safety has me closing my eyes to soak up the warmth of this man.

"So tell me everything that happened Wildcat and let's see if we can help gain some finesse."

CHAPTER 50

Oberon

*H*er smile lights up as I enter the throne room. Her long golden hair simmers against her pale skin, and her blue eyes sparkle as she finally runs into my embrace.

"You came" Her soft lips brush against mine, igniting a potent desire, pulling her closer so our bodies are flush I deepen the kiss, tasting the vanilla of her essence, threading my hands into her silky hair, tilting her head back to places kisses over her jaw and neck moving lower as a hand roams over her breast pinching her nipple through her dress, a needy moan escapes her.

"My love, I have missed you so much, but we need to be careful." Her hands move to halt my exploration. Her words are like ice over a fire, making me pause as we both breathe heavily through our combined love and lust for one another.

How can our love be forbidden when it feels so right? Our magic connects whenever we are close, making us both powerful.

"I have missed you too, sweetheart," I declare. "We need to run, just be us. We can survive. I will provide for us." I plead with her. These brief encounters and secret letters are not enough for me anymore. I want us to be together forever, where we can touch and make love every day without the fear of being found.

"Oberon, I have news" Her eyes soften, full of love. "It's not going to be just us anymore." Her smile lights up as she takes my hand and places it over her stomach. Lowering my head, I stare in shock at our hands locked over her smooth belly.

"Are you pregnant?" My tone is less than soft, panic and anger causing me to lash out, how can I provide for a family when I can't openly be with the women I love?
Laughing up at me "Are you not pleased?" Her beautiful face falls with my lack of response. Her eyes instantly fill.

"How can this be? What a disaster," I begin to pace in front of her, my mind going a million miles per hour like a herd of galloping horses.

The sound of a maid entering my chambers to deliver my breakfast knocks me out of the past. Guilt sours my mood further, growling.

"What are you doing girl?" The girl stumbles placing the tray down on the small table by the window,

"Y y-your b-breakfast, My Lord," she says, staring with a deep bow, the girl looks terrified.

"Get out," I hiss, not in any sort of mood to be in company, my memories of her surfacing much too frequently at the moment, ever since I felt her power awaken, lying each night sleep evades me, dreams plagued by visions of a long-ago past. Could I have done something different? Guilt and sorrow burn deep within my soul, quickly replaced by a rage so visceral my power rises to the surface, flames dancing over my hands easy to action.

Clenching both fists to stop the rush of magic, inhaling to steady my nerves, I must find this power. If I can access her magic and merge, the options are endless. The Seelie court will kneel before us and pay for their past crimes against me and mine.

Too long has the Unseelie court been left in the shadows while the others bicker and fight for the scraps of power that have been left to dwindle over the centuries. That power will allow me to restore the natural balance of things, the Earth's power calls to me daily and I have waited long enough, willing or not my kin will ensure my success. The power I felt just yesterday awakened something within my soul. I must make it a priority to find her. Sending out a pulse of power, summoning the Demon Prince, he's failed once already, I will not tolerate another.

A knock at my chamber door indicates his arrival. He walks in, shoulders back, head held high. The challenge in his eyes clear. I know he strives for my power, my position but he's not yet strong enough. Noting the coiled tension with a clenched jaw.

"Care, Osiris. If I accept your challenge now, you will lose." I sneer at the dark-horned demon, lowering his eyes with a bow much too shallow, masking his features to show the required respect. "That girl's power is becoming stronger each day. If she gains control, she'll be a force that neither you know nor I will be able to control, do your job and get the girl."

The demand is met with irritation that lines his face. "I'm working on it, My Lord."

"Well, you need to work harder, I suggest you use this." I hand a box to him. This will hunt her down, making sure you cannot fail."

"What... What am I dealing with here?" He narrows his eyes, inspecting the box.

"It's a Gollum, probably the last available. Give it the scent; blood is best, but hair will suffice. I presume you can use your contacts to retrieve what is required?"

"I can," he nods, taking the box from my hands, a cruel smile sits on his face. "Can you defeat something like this?" The balls on the man bring a rare emotion to the surface, smiling.

"Ha, nice try, Osiris. You will need to be a little more cunning than this to get my throne! It was created for my use, so it can't be used against me; it's nearly impossible to kill. It can go through doors, windows and most wards."

The man before me pauses, thinking about the elements of his plan, setting a wicked grin on his dark, harsh face.

"I will have the girl before the end of the month, that I promise you, alive as dictated."

"Good, the rest is collateral damage. Just ensure she is unharmed." Gritting the last words out, I fix a vicious glare at him. The bow he presents is a bordering insult, with a sneer to match; I know I should reprimand such behaviours; maybe a round in the pits will knock the schemes out of him. Although I see the ruthlessness of youth, the desire for power and dominance, not dissimilar to myself at that age before... stopping that train of thought. "I will hold you to that, and Osiris there will be consequences if you fail again, that I can promise you" Turning my back, insulting his presence, to enjoy my breakfast, the itch of his glare that is sent my way stirs some unease. Still, he is yet to gain the required power to challenge me directly. Once I have my little dark one, the power balance will shift further in my favour.

CHAPTER 51

Elodie

My control is poor to non-existent. I set fire to everything and grew a borderline useless plant. Then, to top it off, I exhausted myself so much that I had to be carried to bed again. Exhaustion however is only one word to describe how I'm feeling. I only seem to be able to connect with my magic when a certain dark birdman is about. I mean, there is just something about that man that makes my blood boil and causes explosions of uncontrolled powerful magic from me. When he's not there, it's like spitting dust. I mean useless, one blade of grass!!! Nothing, no vines, no thorns, no fire or winds! Nothing. Nada.

Gulping the last of my coffee, sitting at the kitchen table, I'm hoping a good session with Hank will make the difference. Dressed in black leggings and a matching tank, I grab the last slice of toast. I've not seen much of Barrett.

He's busy with the war effort, and each night, he comes in exhausted, the tension in his shoulders, the beautiful lion shifter smile slowly becoming less and less by the day. Twice now, he has climbed into my bed snuggling in close, neither of us saying a word, only embracing one another and falling into a blissful deep sleep. Each morning, he is gone, only a rapidly cooling space where his hot body once was.

To say I'm confused with this turn-in event is an understatement. Not once did Barrett move things along sexually, leaving me a little highly strung and frustrated. Sighing, finishing my toast, noting The Raven is not hovering. Alexander is always there in the background watching. I swear he still thinks I'm an assassin. Let's rephrase that, he knows I'm a spy, just not a very good one. But he suspects that I bear ill will towards the Kingdom and his King.

One good thing to come out of this whole situation, though. the King himself managed to get Madison into the palace. She has a training role where she'll be educated and live within the Palace grounds with people her age, allowing her to choose which area she would like to work in and follow her interests and agenda. Everything is being paid for, and she'll be looked after. Barrett promised me that she'll never have to rely on the likes of Beatrix.

My phone beeps, and I look down to see a message from Lord Hamlington. The last few days with these men in the King's Apartments have led me into a false sense of security. I had almost forgotten about this man. The plan is to still have him believe that I'm working for him and feed him false information. I look down at the text.

Report
My office
4 pm

H

I'll have to come up with some good information to be able to feed it to him. Rushing out the doors and heading towards the training grounds, I will see Jenny there today, too. She's training each morning, with more and more staff members turning up to learn the basics of how to defend themselves. Smiling to myself, lost in thought, I round the corridor, pausing as two imposing figures walk the corridor in my direction. Alfie Roberts and Lady Carter, shit.

"Look what the cat has dragged in." Her cruel voice travels down the corridor. Alfie flicks a quick glance before dismissing me to give his attention back to Lady Carter. That feeling of distrust stirs as I look at him, lowering my gaze as is correct of my station. I stand aside, not wanting any drama. I've got enough of that in my life.

Giving a deep courtesy, then looking ahead, encouraging her to move on.

"The dog has learnt some manners. Can you see that, Alfie? All dogs can be taught." with a sneer, turning her beautiful face into an ugly contorted cow, Alfie's eyes don't quite meet mine, falling short as his chin drops, embarrassed by his actions, as he should be. One moment we are friendly and fucking, the next he is a bullying lap dog.

"I can see that, My Lady, but do take care. These feral types often revert."

Angered by his words and not really giving a fuck, I look up with an exhausted dramatic sigh, "No, Lady

Carter, I just don't have time for the likes of you, and I'd rather get on with my day than have to deal with the drama that you create to give meaning to your boring as shit life."

In a split second, Alfie has me pinned by my throat, his forearm under my jaw, pinning me against the wall; frustration crosses his face before he shuts it down, offering me a sneer of his own. Refusing to show my fear, I glare. My body betrays me as a slight tremor of fear and unease, biting down on that fear and allowing hatred to burn in my narrowed glare,

"Do you like this?" I Whisper, "Do you want me submissive so you can assert your masculine dominance?"

Alfie fails to meet my glare, dropping his gaze without a response and driving his arm tighter against me, looking to his mistress for guidance.

"To be anything in this world? You need to have the right sort of power, people that have your back, you might be playing at the King's whore, but that doesn't mean you're protected. You need to be a lot more cunning, Miss Whitlock."

Moving into the small space crowding me, she takes a small, thin blade and drives it into my neck, bringing blood to the surface of my neck. I flinch giving a small hiss, cursing. "I just require a little bit of you." With that, she takes a little piece of my hair and then walks away. Alfie releases me, dropping my feet back to the floor; with a fleeting glance back at me, he turns to follow his mistress.

Bright sunshine is beating down on the training yard. Jenny is already warmed up, standing and watching Hank as he instructs the new line of people. Radiating authority and confidence, he demands respect as he moves between individuals, correcting techniques, making sure the group is just perfect, fixing mistakes and offering advice. My full attention is on the movement of his hands and the way he repositioned people. Adjusting positions of feet and hips with sublet gentle movements that remind me of the way those hands feel on my skin. Damn, I want those arms around me again! I

It's been too long, and Hank seems to be keeping his distance, which is frustrating.

"Miss Whitlock."

Jumping out of my skin with a little squeak of surprise, his deep, commanding tone carries across the open space. I hear Jenny snickering and send her a scowl.

"Stop drooling and warm up. You're my demo dummy," he flicks his head towards him. "No special treatment for me."

Rolling my shoulders to warm up and loosen my tight muscles, I use the practice sword to run through the drills I have been taught. The movements are second nature after so many years. Hank's demonstration begins, showing different attack positions. Slowly, we work through set pieces.

"Always keep the person in front of you." He circles me like a cat around a mouse, and I move with him.

We have done this many times. I know his fighting style like I know my own. "Your weapon is between you and them. If your attacker gets under your sword, then you're dead."

He dives to grapple my sword arm, but I pivot and stab forward. He deflects, increasing his pace from demo to full spar, spinning. I hold the swords between us before attacking again. I know with Hank, I need to move quickly. His strength overpowers mine, hands down, so speed is my power. We dance around one another before Hank blocks and parries my attack, disarming me and effectively killing me.

"Yield?" I whip a dagger from my ankle, driving it under his throat,

"You're dead too!" I chuckle.

Standing, Hank offers his arm to help me up. "Even wounded, you can take out your opponent as Miss Whitlock cleverly demonstrated."

His praise and heated look sends my stomach muscles clenching, and my thighs following suit. After the demonstration, we split off and paired up. Starting to practice with the beginners, I worked with Jenny and helped her develop her skills.

"Girl, the sexual tension between you two," she wiggles her eyebrows. "Are you and him a thing yet?"

Shaking my head, "Concentrate. We are just friends," I state, looking at the god in question.

"No way, no one is that ultra-focused on a person if there is no D involved."

"Jenny! Stop!... I'll have you know I'm a lady, and I have never seen his D." colour flushes my cheek as I realise my mistake, flashes of Hank stood stark naked in the King's apartments all pumped up with rippling sharp cut muscles, Jenny laughs at my obvious lie and discomfort,

"What of the King? Are you two making progress in that department?" her easy demeanour has me relaxing and laughing.

I shake my head. Jenny, you are encouragable. I'm just helping with a project, you know, with me having new magic." I stage whisper the last bit. Now will you concentrate, please?"

With the sun rising high, heat beats down on my already sweaty body. That's when I feel him. I know it's him as soon as he enters my general space, my magic stirs, calling to him. I hate the response he brings out in me, distracted. I turn to look behind. His wings are out, making him look like a dark, avenging angel. Fuck my life.

The distraction costs me. Jenny swings her sword, catching my hip in a hard attack.

"Sorry, sorry, sorry, sorry. Oh, my goodness, have I hurt you?"

Chuckling, I say, "Sorry, I was distracted, and it cost me! You would've hurt me If you had a proper sword. Well done!"

She giggles. "I hope I didn't hurt you. Was it the dark angel eyeballing you across the yard?" Fidgeting I pick up my sword.

"No," I feel his nearness. He moves so silently that I jump when he speaks.

"I see you're easily distracted, Miss Whitlock. Why don't you spar with me, and I can show these people how to win?" His lazy drawl and cocky, arrogant stance irritate me, and I shoot him a glare.

"Bring it on, bird boy/" Confident that I can hold my own, we move to a clearing on the training grounds, attracting several pairs of eyes.

His attacks are fast and brutal, getting under my defences and landing blows to my thighs and abdomen. Panting, I struggle to keep him at bay, all my pent-up hate and aggression pouring into my attacks, making me sloppy and predictable.

The Raven, in all his glory, is breathing deeply, his expression calm and calculated. With a small lip curl, he lands a hit to my ribs, knocking the wind from me, forcing a spin and retreating a step. Clenching my teeth, I attack, knowing my anger is beginning to cloud my movements and decisions.

His next thrust disarms me, my sword skirting across the yard, without thinking as panic starts to grip me. I fling a powerful blast of air, sending him stumbling backwards. A look of pure hatred scowling back at me, "shit." His huge frame slams into me taking, me down to the ground hard. Realising he plans to continue the fight, I slam a punch into his kidneys. This is no longer a sparring match, gaining the upper hand, his weight pinning me, securing my hands,

"So full of hate you can't focus, Assassin." the cruel amusement in his gaze causes me to pause, hands pin mine as he straddles me immobilising me completely.

"You're dead, Miss Whitlock." Anger burns through me, and I want him to hurt. Slaming my forehead toward his with a scream of frustration, catching his cheek as he moved, sniggering, he leaned down towards my ear, "You may have Barrett wrapped around your little finger, but know this, I will crush you."

We struggle, our bodies rubbing against one another, magic sparks between us, butterflies clenching at my core at the sight and feel of him hovering over my sweaty body, suddenly realising the position we have found ourselves in, Alexander slams my hands to the floor in frustration.

Before I can retort with a snarky response, Hank intervenes. "Enough you have made your point, Alexander. Now get the fuck off her."

The possessive warning lacing Hank's voice warms my soul, my anger quickly dissipating, Hank's tone and The Raven's magic flirting around my own. Arousal hits me hard, causing a very sexual gasp to spill from my lips. With a growl, Alexander pushes off me, not offering a hand to help me up, storming from the training yard and taking flight, those magnificent wings sending him soaring in two powerful beats. Leaving me sprawled on the ground, starting after him in confusion.

What is it about pricks that have me turned on? I'm blaming the magic. Hank, ever the gentleman, however, takes my hand, bringing me to my feet,

"You okay? Starlight, you seem to have gotten under The Raven's feathers." His concerned look searches my face, and the use of my nickname stirs my arousal further, as we both look at the distant black general flying away.

"Yeah, tell me something I don't know, but I held my own pretty much," I smile up at Hank, running his hand over the back of his neck, and a small half smile lighting up his face.

"Shit, Elodie, you sure know how to pick a fight. Come on, let's get cleaned up."

He dismisses the class, and I bid goodbye to Jenny, who insists on stirring the pot further with several innuendos and suggestive looks at Hank. Threading his arm around my waist, Hank places a soft kiss on my bare shoulder. I stiffen slightly at the closeness he instigates, my core tightening in anticipation, then relaxing into his warm, solid body. The feelings I try to hide from myself rush to the surface.

"I have hardly seen you recently … I miss you" I whisper, pushing past the fear of opening up to him "Can we catch up … tonight?" His fingers tighten on my waist pulling me closer, a deep sigh leaves him" I whisper, pushing past the fear of opening up to him. Can we catch up tonight?" His fingers tighten on my waist, pulling me closer. A deep sigh leaves him, and then he releases me.

"I have a lot on Starlight," Hurt crushes through me, feeling the rejection once again, as he shuts down, pulling away.

I shrug. "Sure. Yeah, of course, in the middle of a war and stuff," I fake a laugh, wrapping my arms across my body and trying to hold back my emotions. "Cool, I'm going to grab a shower and should probably hit the books." I almost run away.

"Elodie," his fingers wrap around my wrist, halting my escape. I'm embarrassed, so I look to my feet. "It's not because I don't want to. God's El, you have no idea how much I would love to escape the world and just be us, but it's just not possible."

All my insecurities surface. The majority of my life has been being on my own, with no family and short-lived friends. Hank was, no, is my rock, the only constant element. I can't hide the hurt that crosses my face as I draw my hand from his grip.

"I'm sorry, kid."

The use of that word. *Kid,* like I'm some child with a crush on her mentor, sends my gut plummeting, fuck did I read our relationship completely wrong? That heated kiss full of passion and possessive energy? Surely not?

Whatever he is feeling is locked down tight, kept behind his careful mask. His muscles twitch as he folds his arms, trying to act like everything is okay.

"God ha! Hank, you're only what? Eight years older than me? And we are friends," stepping back and looking up towards the palace. Unable to look at the man my heart is straining towards. "Yeah, so no big deal." I fidget awkwardly, spinning to head away from him, making a total twat of myself, the threat of tears rising like bile, my cheeks burning.

Hank just lost his last chance with me. He can sit in the background, watching me live my life with the biggest blue ball known to man. I can't keep offering up little pieces of my heart for him to take a taste and hand them back, for them to rot.

CHAPTER 52

Elodie

Back at the apartments, I grab some food and set about pouring a large glass of water before settling down in the lounge area to read the diary and try to unlock and understand how to access my power.

Raise voices from down in the kitchen grab my attention, and curiosity overtakes me. As I pad barefoot towards the kitchen, the three gorgeous men who have stolen my focus over the last few weeks stand huddled close. Hank and Alexander glare at one another, tension radiating between all three.

"These attacks require action, and you're fucking focused on teaching her some sort of lesson. Why the hell were you even there?" Hank hisses, using his huge frame to square up to Alexander.

"He's right, Alexander, we need to act now, sitting here at the palace screams that we are weak. The new attacks are escalating." The king runs a frustrated hand through his floppy blonde hair. "I can't just sit here behind these walls waiting for The Demon Prince and the Shades to wipe out our army. We need to attack head-on with me at the forefront. I'm a fighter, and this vendetta against Miss Whitlock needs to stop."

I have never seen Barratt confront his friend in this manner. Alexander clenches his fist, his eyes darkening with suppressed anger, and a vein pulses in his temple.

"You are fucking blindsided by her. You see a bit of tight pussy, and you're all over it. What are you two gonna do, share?" He sneers, glaring at both men.

The visual he sends my way is way too sexual for me to handle, and my power stirs within me.

"She walks in the room, and you are desperate for any snippet of attention like a pet dog. She is not The Key. She can barely summon her magic." his voice has risen, taking on a cruel note, sneering through clenched teeth.

"I'm sensing a bit of jealousy there, Alexander," the king scoffs, looking at his friend. "Or was your cock not hard against her back when you had her pinned over the table?" With a small, humourless chuckle, he moves from my view, creating space between the three.

I shuffle, trying to get a little bit closer. Three sets of intense eyes snap towards mine, immobilising me. Heat flushes up my cheeks as I back away from the heat and anger in their mixed gazes.

"Wildcat," Barrett calls, breaking away from the two and heading toward me in a relaxed, casual gait. Alexander, however, scowls in my direction, running his hand through his short-cropped hair with a frustrated string of curses, muttering under his breath, storming towards the kitchen.

Choosing to ignore the big prick, I look at the two towering men in turn, mixed emotions flooding through my system.

"Everything okay? I get the impression that I have

caused a little bit of trouble between you three."

Barrett wraps me in a bear hug before planting a lingering kiss on my lips. I sink into his embrace, excitement and a hot dose of desire running through my core. With the foot he holds over me, I tilt my head up to look at him, knowing this interaction will truly piss Alexander off. I allow heat to enter my gaze, arching my back as the king growls, crushing his lips back to mine in a passionate, open-mouthed kiss, the pent-up touching over the last few weeks driving us together.

I lace my arms around his neck, fist clutching his soft hair, holding him to me as he swallows my low moans, his hands roaming my body under my tank, one thumb brushing over my erect bud. Gasping, I drive my hips onto his hard length, hooking one leg over his waist. The world around forgotten as we sink into the depths of our combined longing.

Someone clears their throat, pulling both of our attention back to the room. Barrett runs a thumb over my swollen lower lip.

"Should we save this for later?" Gently pressing a feather-light kiss in response, I look over his shoulder without releasing my hold to make eye contact with Alexander.

"Don't you, like, have a war to try and win? Rather than bitching me out, Alexander?" irritation and anger flashes through his ice-cold violet eyes, biting his tongue and his lip as if trying to hold back his anger and harsh words.

"Despite what you might think of yourself, Miss

Whitlock, you're not the focus of everyone's attention. We do have other things to discuss. You are a distraction at best."

Peeling my arms away from Barrett's neck, I keep Hank and Alexander in my sights. Hank's gaze held mine captive for a long minute. The hurt from his rejection earlier still burned brightly, and I avoided the question in his own eyes after my display with the King.

Focusing on the only smile in the room, I lean into Barrett's loose arm around my shoulder, reading the room, he pulls me close.

"Don't worry, Wildcat. I still like you, probably more than I like you." He chuckles, giving me a kiss on the cheek, bringing a smug smile to my lips. "These two fuckers are just too stubborn to admit their desire to themselves."

"You do know she is sleeping with others, too. You are not special, Barrett." Amusement flashes across The Raven's face as he leans back, crossing his arms in his signature brooding stance, a smug, cruel smile donning his face.

"Correction, I slept with one other in the heat of the moment to scratch an itch. You know Alexander, a girl has needs, and calling me out in front of the king," I glare, pausing, "is simply low even for you."

Allowing disgust to fill my gaze as I look him up and down before heading towards the coffee machine and switching it on, power whirls through my muscles. The only time I seem to get any response from my magic is when this dickhead reels me up. Clenching my jaw in an attempt to prevent the rise of power, my eyes flick towards Alexander, unconsciously tracking his movements and response, and his eyes burn with irritation.

"You should maybe start asking for payment. At least then, you can start paying your own way." The barb is said with such venom and cruelty that it hits far too close to home. Without thought, power slams through my body, spinning, ice forms in my hand, and I fling a perfect lethal ice dagger towards his smug face. Taken by surprise, he only just manages to avoid major injury, the sharp edge of the dagger slicing a deep crimson gash over his right cheek.

His power retaliates, slamming against mine, making me inhale sharply. My own power engulfs his, reacting to the volley of insults, a strange sort of foreplay sending ripples of pleasure through us. Alexander sucks in a deep breath through his clenched jaw as his eyes heat with hatred and lust striding forward, only just stopping inches from my face. Body trembling, it takes all my effort not to close the distance between us and climb him like a tree, my treacherous body reacting to his magic, but my brain reminding me he is a prick that I do not like.

"What the hell is going on?" Barrett has edged closer, placing a restraining hand on his friend. Feeling and seeming to fear the potent magic storming between us,

"El. Wildcat darling, just stop looking at him and breathe... Come on, look at me before you explode or something." He chuckles, stepping closer, nudging the panting Alexander out of the way, into my line of sight, blocking my view of the mountain of energy and dark violet eyes.

The break does the trick, allowing me to switch my brain back on slightly. The lust throbbing through me needs more contact, hands snaking around the King's neck I pull him in for another bruising kiss, power unleashing around us, siding his hands down my waist, groaning and grabbing my ass in both hands, encouraging my legs to wrap around him, his hard cock pushing against my core.

While I'm focused on the warmth of Barrett's mouth on mine, a crash sounds, halting our passion, turning as The Raven's fist slams into the plasterboard wall again before a string of curses leaves his mouth while he storms from the room.

"Shit," the king whispers, placing my legs back down and clearing his throat. My body is strung up and thrumming with energy.

"Do not stop, Barrett," I demand, pulling him closer once again. Barrett's entire body stiffens, fingers digging into my ass. "I need you, Barrett, now" My magic is an inferno of pent-up unused power and sexual tension threatening to explode, as shivers of pleasure travel down my spine.

He wavers for a moment, shifting back, creating inches of space between our bodies, too much space. Casting a glance Hank's way.

"Are you watching Drake?" I purr, following Barrett's eyes to the big dragon warrior. Failing to respond, he only stares, jaw clenched, and a bloom of smoke puffing upwards.

"My room or yours?" I whisper, latching his mouth over my erect nipple, Barrett strides from the room.

"Give us half an hour Sergeant." Our mouths collide, hands frantic to rid the barriers on our bodies, clothes are torn, stripped and tossed to the ground. Barrett's teeth nip and bite across my breast, heating my skin.

"Take me now, Barrett, I need you inside me." Already, I am soaked, my clit swollen with need. My magic surges through my body, seeking an outlet.

"Wildcat, I want to taste you," with a hard push, I'm thrown to the bed, bouncing slightly. "Spread your legs."

I do as he demands, feeling his desire. In the next breath, The King, My King, is before me, sliding the pad of his tongue slowly up the full length of my slit, sucking my clit hard. Waves shudder up my entire body, the pleasure too much as I gasp, pant, and wither, needing more, needing the release. Large, calloused hands grip and pin my hips so he can drive his tongue inside me, licking, sucking until I'm tittering on the edge.

"Barrett, please," I beg for release so close, my core clenching, muscles tight. With a smooth movement, Barrett stands growling,

"Fuck you are amazing, Wildcat." With that, he grabs my legs, pulling me along the bed and thrusting into me, stretching my soaked, ready cunt.

"Shit, Shit, Barrett. More." With a roar, his abs flex, hips driving a hard and fast pace. My orgasm builds, and I wrap my legs around him, moaning as he fills me up, hitting a depth I have never experienced. Barrett leans forward, taking my erect buds into his mouth and biting hard before sucking softly. The combination of pleasure and pain makes me cry out, sending me crashing in the most intense orgasm. Electricity dances across my body, every cell fizzing with heat and pleasure; my pussy pulses around The King's hard length feeling him swell further, his mouth swallowing my pants as he thrusts, stills and comes inside me with a deep, satisfied growl.

We collapse together, softly kissing each other's bodies. "Wildcat, you are beautiful. No one has ever made me feel this way" he plants a hard kiss on my lips, then simply stares at my face. "I want to watch you fall apart every single day."

He takes my hand, helping me stand on still, unsteady legs, wraps me in a tight embrace, and kisses my forehead.

"Let's shower and get back to the dragon," he says. At the mention of Hank, a slither of guilt stirs. Barrett notices my expression, taking my chin and lifting it so I have to look into his green eyes,

"We have done nothing wrong. You needed an outlet for your magic; I'm just lucky you chose me." He winks, linking our fingers and kissing the knuckles before leading me into the ensuite.

Feeling more controlled after another shattering orgasm and a hot shower. This time, taking time to explore one another's bodies, caressing and teasing, prolonging the pleasure we both crave.

We're back in the kitchen, relaxed, and making our way through a homemade meat feast pizza Hank made. The dragon warrior is brooding.

Hank looks at the King. "She needs help. That raw power is going to backfire. We need someone to help her access and harness that power."

Looking at me, heat enters his gaze while a half smile touches his lips. "Gotta say, though, Starlight, I was going to teach the big-headed prick a few manners. You seem to have it handled with your ice dagger!" he chuckles, easing the guilt and tension I have been feeling after my display with Barrett.

"That was pretty cool if I do say so myself" I laugh and mimic the hand action like a mean ass-kicking warrior with sound effects, "Yah, pow. Although the power thing is a little strange."

I drop my gaze, turning back to the coffee machine to hide my rapidly pinking cheeks. The humour leaves Hank's face as he takes a seat at the breakfast bar, and a pensive look crosses his face.

"I don't know what is happening, but your parents must have blocked your power for some reason. You had to have some level of power to acquire more magic, and I believe this is what happened to you. They blocked you to hide you. I am starting to believe you may be at the centre of this prophecy."

Barrett's hip checks me out of the way as I fumble with the espresso machine and start pressing beans and pulling together cups of coffee. He bumps his hip again to mine, moving me out of the way, and then nods thoughtfully.

"What do you suggest? Do you have something in mind to help?" Placing cups in front of us, I gather the hot nectar offered by Barrett, taking a deep gulp, holding the steaming cup with both hands. I watch the king as he slides onto a stool next to me, gently placing one hand over my thigh.

The simple touch sent shock waves through me, fuck, get a grip, lady. Growling deeply, Hank rubs a hand down his face before shooting me a warning glare to listen and focus. Clearing my throat, I shuffle away from Barrett in an attempt to think of anything but the feel of his hard cock so close to where I want it again.

"I suggest you combine two birds with one stone, travel to the front to organise tropes and swing by the witches. They know magic and held onto theirs after the rest of us have lost most of our power."

"Hold up, witches?" Mouth gaping open, I lean towards my mentor. "As in the scary ass women who do not mix with others at all," I stress the last words.

Hank nods, smiling at me. "The very same. My contacts should be able to help you with control and see which elements you hold." He pauses to check my response before he continues, "And at the same time, I need to assess the front lines and these new rumours of strange creatures killing without leaving a trace."

Frowning as a thread of anxiety bubbles in my gut, I have never left the city or travelled until coming to the palace, and now he wants me to travel across half the realm.

"Hold up, you're expecting me." I point to my chest, eyebrows skyrocketing up, "to travel with you across the realm past active fighting to a closed-off secretive group of fae witches known to be highly volatile?" Shaking my head laughing. "Can you not just bring a witch to me? That makes more sense, than I can still pretend to be under Lord Hamilton's employment!"

"I don't want that man anywhere near you." The possessiveness in the king's voice gives me whiplash, and I snap my head towards him.

"Sorry," I raise both eyebrows, waiting for an explanation. Meeting my glare, the King holds mine, deep green eyes burrowing into my very soul, claiming me. A beautiful smile lifts his face.

"I've already informed him that you'll be working for me. He's well aware that he will no longer use your services." Shocked at the revelation, my mind played back to the scene with Trixie and the enormous debt she holds over me. Without an income, it will only be a few weeks before I'm back at the club dancing, angry at the situation he has forced me into. Placing my coffee cup down on the counter with a slam, I rise, both hands planted on the counter and glare. Barrett's smile falters.

"And what? He just accepted that deal?" I enquire between gritted teeth. "You never thought to consult me on this? Or how this may affect me?" Sucking my tongue across my teeth, tension and anger crossing my ridged back and shoulders.

Barrett shifts uncomfortably, his gaze flicking to Hank fleetingly before looking at me and clearing his throat, oblivious to why I'm angry.

"I, eh, well, I only wanted to protect you. He has been paid. He has already threatened you, and you were attacked by the demon Prince. It's evident that they all want you for your new power." I cut him off with a growl

"What, so I'm now yours to command?"

"You can't even defend yourself, Elodie, Fuck… so it is up to us to keep you safe." His fury begins to rise as he adopts a defensive stance, crossing his arms and leaning back in his stool.

"I have managed to keep myself safe and cared for without any help from anybody my whole life. What makes you think I need a spoon-fed lion cub to take care of my business now?" The blow is low, but I stand my ground, allowing the events of the last few weeks to fuel my anger.

"That's not strictly true now, is it, Elodie?" The King gives me a smug look. "Your whole life? You've been a servant to Beatrix; she paid for your education. She paid for your food. She paid for your keep."

Embarrassed at his new knowledge, I send a glare towards Hank, who has the grace to avoid my wrath. The king has bought me. To what? Use is my power? Get me in his bed? It is no secret that he is attracted to me.

"And until now, I never felt like an object." With a sarcastic huff, fixing the king with a glare that could melt the skin off his bones. "So your true feelings have finally shown through that fake smile and easy going king facade."

Hurt drives a dagger through my lungs as I try to draw a deep breath. Being here leads me to believe I could be someone other than a possession, like I could have a chance to choose my own path! With a bitter smile, I dip into low, mocking curtsy eyes locking onto those emerald green ones opposite.

"Go and fuck yourself, Your Majesty," I say, rising to leave with my head held high. However, a gruff, calm voice halts me in my tracks.

"The King bought your debt from Trixie and provided for Madison, Starlight. He is not the bad guy here." Hank sighs. "Come on, just listen and do as he says, please." That one phrase, *'do as he says,'* sends my fury spiralling at the lack of control in my own life once again.

I lash my words at both men, violently hissing. "I am no one's fucking puppet. You can't just decide my fate without discussing things with me. Anger contorts my face, and I feel moisture welling, distorting my vision, "Buying my debt does not mean you own me. I will not be your whore, Barrett."

Standing shaking with the effort of holding myself together. Deep down, I know this is a good thing for me and Maddison, but my anger is too raw. I really thought I had something with Barrett, but now? Am I just a consort, a glorified whore? Our sex earlier now feels tainted.

Barrett's face flushes red with intense anger, but it is gone as soon as it rises, smoothing his features into an expressionless mask. The King is back in play.

"Yes, I do own you, Miss Whitlock, so you will do as I say. If I have to make you, then so be it." My eyes burn hot with unshed tears. With my fist clenched, I try to control the new surge of power, closing my eyes and taking several deep breaths.

"Will that include fucking you?" huffing a harsh laugh to hide the fact that my worse fears seemed to be happening with the people I was beginning to trust.

"Ha, you would like that, wouldn't you?" Licking his lower lip, he relaxes, all traces of anger gone. "But no, darling, I do not fuck unwilling women. That will be your choice."

Unwilling? Ha! Moments ago, we could taste one another, a desire so potent I fucked him there and then. I am unable to control the situation and need to get some space before I do or say anything more damaging.

"May I retire to my cell, sorry- My room now Master?" Tilting my head, a sneer curling my lips. "Is that the correct term? or maybe just My Lord?" I shrug. "As you are aware, I have always been under someone's rule, so let me know. Your demands"

I can't help the hurt, anger, and sass flooding my tone. The sarcastic question throws him off. He drops his eyes, a strong hand lifting to rub the back of his neck, offering a small nod in answer.

"This was for your own safety, Elodie. Please don't hate me." His defeat was evident in his posture, and his soft eyes pleaded with me to understand. I left without a backward glance at my two prison guards. I needed

WORTHLESS

the space to calm down and reevaluate my situation.

CHAPTER 53

Elodie

I wake with a start, the reminiscence of a nightmare fogging my brain. Outside, dark storm clouds move across a waning moon, stars flickering bright. After the recent revelation I simply crashed out buried deep in my bed covers, tears flowing free as years of pent-up rage, frustration and loneliness soaked my pillow, finally falling into a disturbed sleep.

Groaning, I throw back the covers and go in search of coffee and cake, knowing sleep will evade me. In nothing but my panties and an oversized T-shirt, I head to the kitchen, padding along the cool floor on bare feet.

The apartment is quiet as I set about making coffee, and the aroma helped ground me. One thing we always had at Electric Eden was decent coffee! I suppose Trixie wanted her workers awake and functioning without the addiction to hard-core drugs.

"A late night snack, Starlight?"

I scream, startled, spinning around, sparks springing over my fingertips, almost dropping the cream cake I found under a dome on the bench. Hank is lying on his back on the sofa in the open plan living area, his long hair unbound, his eyes closed, and a blanket draped half across his naked chest, one huge, inked bicep flung over the side of the cushions. My eyes track the contours of his arm and shoulder towards his face. Pain at his early rejection and collaboration with Barrett has left me feeling hollow; I have relied on Hank for many years without even noticing the friendship we were forced into through Trixie had developed into something stronger. What I felt was more, but maybe I read things wrong, and I was just a job to him. Turning my attention back to my coffee and sugar fix in a clear brush-off, I'm unwilling to answer those questions.

The sound of movement and soft feet across the floor indicate his approach. Refusing to acknowledge his presence, I collect my snack to vacate the kitchen area, only to find my way blocked by a strong chest, arms crossing over the naked ink, brown intense eyes captivating and holding my gaze. Neither of us speaks as confused emotions churn in my stomach. Inches separate us, but I can feel the heat from his body, a large, calloused hand cups my cheek, dragging his thumb over my lower lip before popping it into his mouth and sucking some cream from it. My eyes follow the movement. My body reacts despite my hurt and anger, swallowing as I press my lips together.

The look he gives me is pure sex, closing the distance by pulling my waist into his own body. With a monumental effort, I push back, trying to break free.

"Absolutely not, Hank Dufort. You can't keep pushing me away and then expect me to fall into your arms at the drop of a hat." pausing to look at him directly, the hurt flooding my gaze. "Typically, when we are alone." I huff, looking away, but he pulls me closer again.

"I know, but I can't seem to stay away from you,

Starlight, and I especially can't bear to stand and watch others take your heart."

Placing my cup onto the island, I fold my arms across my chest, lifting my boobs; his eyes flick to admire the asset, still clad in a baggy shirt.

"You done?" I ask with a mocking smile, and his gaze snapped back up to mine.

Using both hands and pushing him back a few steps, he respects me enough to give me the illusion of creating space. The hard planes of his chest do not go unnoticed! My fingertips linger longer than strictly necessary.

"Sorry Hank, I can't do this right now. You allowed them to take away all my freedom and said nothing."

"Elodie, this is in your best interest. Do you think we're fucking around in this war? Someone is coming for you, and I won't lose you! Osiris is a mean bastard, El. He is not out to kill you. He will use your power. Use you." He growls, moving back into my space. "Hate me all you like, but I will not lose you, and I'll do anything in my power to keep you safe, and if that means I spend the rest of my life making things up to you, so be it. As long as that life is a happy life, I'll take it."

I search his face and saw such warmth and sincerity fixed on my face, swallowing hard to ease my own intense emotions. I'm not stupid. I know my life is more dangerous each day, especially since the ring embedded onto my finger giving me this ridiculous power, but I can't keep up with these moods that swing in roundabouts; one minute, I'm a job! The next minute, he looked at me like I was his whole world.

"You know you're giving me whiplash. I don't know what you want from me." I sigh heavily, exhausted emotionally.

"I want all of you, Starlight." Stroking my face, gently committing my face to memory, "but I don't deserve you. I'm too old for you."

With that, he steps closer into my personal space, placing strong hands on my hips as he lifts me and deposits me onto the island, the cold marble biting into my bare ass. I stare, tongue wetting my lower lip.

"Fuck it." His lips crush against mine, a demanding, passionate kiss. I hesitate for only a moment before my body responds, his Hands sliding up my back to fist into my hair, demanding more. My back arches into him, nipples hardening against his chest as my breath becomes shallow. He pulls my hips closer to him, forcing my legs to wrap around his lean waist. The make-out session has me soaked in seconds, my gasps encouraging more.

"I don't want to pretend anymore. I need you," he demands as he breaks our kiss. "Just give me tonight," he pleads, "and then you can go back to hating me tomorrow."

His mouth drops back to mine as his tongue drives between my lips. There is no finesse or tender gentle kisses. This is all consuming possession, the clashing of two souls, trailing kisses down my neck, sucking and biting, leaving his mark. My chest gains his attention next, stripping me of my T-shirt and exposing my hard nipples, his mouth playfully teasing the erect bud as one hand massages the other. I claw at his muscular shoulders as a loud moan escapes me, pleasure rippling through my body, my head falling backward, his fingers tightening on my ass hard enough to leave bruises, veins popping along his arms, one hand sweeping towards my panties tracing along my slick entrance.

"Gods, you're so ready, baby girl," his growl showed me how close his beast is to the surface. Moving down my body, one strong palm forcing me back onto my elbow before he buries his mouth in my cunt, devouring me like a starving man, my body pulses and ripples with pleasure burning through me.

"Hank, please!" I moan in a breathy whisper, my muscles beginning to shake. His strong hands grab my legs, forcing them up onto the counter, exposing me fully to him. The cool air brushed over my swollen bud. He sucks, nips, and bites my clit; thrusting my hips, I shamelessly ride his face encouraging him to give me everything he has.

I gasp, breaths becoming shallower and my body pulsing with the first hints of an orgasm, Hank drives two fingers into my core hard, making me scream out,

"Please, Hank, stop toying with me." With a chuckle, he increases his pace, adding a third finger and stretching my walls as his mouth and tongue continue their assault on my clit. Pleasure builds as I tip my head back, an Earth-shattering orgasm pushing me over the edge, muscle spasming, crying out as my heat shudders through my body.

"You are mine," he says, biting into my neck, he

growls, applying sucking kisses down my body once more.

Unable to move as my muscles continue to contract, Hank slowly rises, his gaze burning into mine.

"Gods, you're so beautiful." His lips find mine once again before taking my hips to spin me onto my front, dragging me until my feet hit the floor. With one hand, he frees his cock, lining himself up with my slick pussy, teasing his tip over my juices before slowly pushing into me; my muscles still tight, gasping I grip the marble island pushing back onto his hard length.

"Fuck," he groans as he palms my ass holding my hips still before he slams all the way to the hilt; my knees almost buckle, if it was not for the strong hands holding me up, hands likely to leave his fingerprints. He glides slowly back, eyes fixed on his cock covered in my arousal.

"Hold fucking tight, I have dreamt of this for far too long." With that he slams into me setting a punishing pace, already I feel the build of a second orgasm, a string of shallow curses leaving my mouth as he fucks me senseless.

Movement to my left catches my eye. Barrett is frozen in the living area, and green eyes are fixed on my face. A crack to my ass and a bite of pain switches my attention back on Hank.

"Come for me, Starlight. I want to feel you coming on my cock" A hand pushes me flat to the island as the other circles my hips to apply pressure to my swollen bud sending me into another crashing orgasm.

Hank does not slow his pace, driving through my clenching muscles as he follows me with his own climax, crying out, pulling me up by my dark hair, flush to his chest, kissing my neck softly.

"Mine."

Turning my head, I kiss his mouth, the passion cooling, complex emotions waking. I catch the heated gaze of Barrett, the lust-burning holes in my skin. With a playful laugh, he breaks the spell,

"So you two seem to have kissed and made up. Can I apologise too and join in?" Barrett watches as Hank kisses my neck, following with a nip, before rearranging himself and collecting my discarded T-shirt. Excitement at the new visual entering my mind involving the two gorgeous men has me pulling away from Hank, grabbing my coffee and cake before turning to leave. Two sets of burning eyes follow me.

Hanks cum sliding down my thighs. "One fuck does not excuse the choice you two have taken from me," smothering the heat, allowing my anger to rise once again.

Sighing pulling one hand through his loose hair, He lets me leave, calling out before making it ten steps.

"Be ready to leave by eight tomorrow, wrap up warm, and pack what you want to bring with you for at least a week." Turning, I look at Hank and Barrett, who gives a small nod. My new life is accepted.

CHAPTER 54

Elodie

Unsure what was in store for me, I packed a bag, grabbing the diary and a few other texts that may help. My daggers are strapped to my body with a gun to make sure I'm protected.

After the mind-blowing sex with Hank last night, I unsurprisingly slept like a log until a gruff voice announced I had two hours before we hit the road.

I sent a quick message to Jenny and Maddison, saying I would be away for a few weeks. The former insisted she come and say goodbye. A knock followed by Jenny's red pixie cut popping around my door frame, a wide mischievous smile on her face halted my packing.

"Hey girl, are you going to let me know what's going on?" Walking to my bed, she flops down dramatically. "I swear things in this place have become strange very quickly."

Exhaling, I flop down next to her on the soft mattress, a dagger digging into my waist, making me flinch.

"Are you expecting trouble?" she raised one eyebrow, dropping a look at the many weapons. Come on, Ellie, what's going on?" Sitting up, she looked at me with concern, her playful smile gone, as she grabbed my hands in hers. "Are you okay?"

Okay? The question is loaded. My automatic response is yes, I'm fine, but am I really? My whole world has been turned upside down and inside out. I have magic now that my parents probably blocked for an unknown reason. The Shade army wants me. And the king now owns my ass! I want to scream at the lack of control but instead, I sigh and nod.

"The King is insisting I travel to find someone to help me with my magic. He needs to be at the front, so I'm tagging along." I shrug, down playing the situation.

"You bloody kidding me? You are traveling across the kingdom into the war zones? Are you crazy?" Grabbing my shoulders, she pulls me up to look at her, worries etched across her face, "Elodie, you have to refuse. People don't come back from the front easily." Huffing a small laugh,

"I don't have a choice, Jen. It's the king's demand, and Hank is supporting his decision, not to mention their attack bird Alexander, who hates me enough to have me killed out there, I'm sure." Turning I continue loading my bag with clothes avoiding the concern from my friend who throws her head back and howls with laughter.

"Ha hates you? God, Ellie, you're blind if you don't see the way those three watch your every move; I have never seen grown-ass men obsess over the same woman before; it's almost like a wolf's mating bond gone haywire!"

Shifting, I pull a disgusted face while my cheeks

heat, shaking my head in denial, memories of last night fucking Hank while Barrett watched, eyes full of undeniable lust.

"It makes no difference. They are taking me."

"Taking you? What alllllll at the same time?" she winks and wiggles her eyebrows while nudging me with her elbow "Pllllease tell me you are hitting at least one of them, I mean please tell me you are hitting at least one of them. I mean, how can you stand the heat?" She pauses, fanning her face as I squirm, avoiding eye contact. Her eyes widen, jumping onto her knees. "Oh my- Tell me everything. Was it the King? Or Hank? yeah, it's got to be him." Looking to the ceiling, her fingers gripping her chin. "No. Hank's too noble. He would wait! It was Barrett? Come on, girl spill."

I shake my head, laughing. "It was Hank," I confess, giving her a snippet of the gossip she craves, as she squeals, jumping and grabbing my shoulders. "Was it fucking hot, God, those arms," draping an arm over her face and collapsing onto my bed. "Shit, girl, I could cum just thinking of that shifter and those chocolate brown eyes," moaning dramatically.

"Jenny, stop!" I throw a pillow her way. "Please, it was just a heated argument that turned into more." Standing, I start gathering the rest of my things. "Can we change the subject, please?"

"Sure, sure, I mean smoking hot sex with your protector while two other hot men are chomping at the bit for a bite of your ass is not a good topic to discuss."

Pushing her off the bed with a big shove and a laugh of

my own,

"Please, those three are controlling alphaholes, and I will not be partaking in any hot three-way sex."

"So it was hot?" she sobers, standing to walk around the bed back to me. "They are obviously trying to protect you, girl. You understand that, don't you?"

"They have stripped everything from me, Jen. Barrett bought my debt. I'm nothing more than a power source they hope to mold and control." Taking a deep breath to control the rise of familiar anger and hurt, looking at the imprint of the skull ring on my finger. "It's made what Barrett and I had into something more seedy. I feel like his whore, the talk of the Palace! Ha, Lady Carter was right in that regard."

"That demon Prince nearly took you and nearly killed me, Ellie. If this trip helps you protect yourself," she shrugs "they will keep you safe until you can do that yourself. Sitting here with fuck wits like Lady Carter and Alfie playing school bullies will just get you killed," embracing me in a tight hug, "And I for one would like to keep you as a friend Okay." I hug her back, with a huff.

"I knew you would take their side, But I suppose there is some merit in your words of wisdom." Barrett moves in my open doorway, knocking, then leaning to one side, not entering my room but watching as Jenny and I part from our embrace.

"You catching Jen up on the hot sex on the kitchen island last night?" He smirks, letting everyone know he was there front row seat to witness said episode, his gaze heating as he takes in my body strapped with weapons. Jenny's jaw almost hits the floor as she looks between the two of us, her eyes popping out of her head as she fixes a shocked mocking glare at me.

"If you guys have a three-way, I want full deets. Fuck, just record it for me, please." With that she kisses me on the cheek leaving the room, stopping in front of the god damned King, one pointed finger prodding his hard chest with every word.

"You-keep-my-girl-safe and stop with the alpha shit, you hear?" The shocked look on his face has me chuckling as we both watch her leave with a backward wave and sassy as fuck walk.

I grab my bag and coat and look at Barrett. "I just want to grab some food, and then I'm ready."

"What? that's it?" Barrett blocks the doorway, weariness making him fidget as he searches my face for what? I'm unsure. Shrugging one shoulder.

"I don't have a choice and lack the energy to fight you on this, Barrett. Who am I to go against my owner and The King." Fury and hurt lace my tone as I push past him, ignoring the look of hurt. What is that? Sorrow? Shit holding onto this anger when he looks like a kicked puppy is bloody hard, but he chose without me. Ahhhh, I growl in frustration, pushing all other emotions aside in search of coffee and sustenance, the lion shifter stalking behind.

"Wildcat..."

"No," I cut him off before he could use nicknames and charm to win me over. "I understand you are trying to help me on some level, Barrett, but you took my freedom," I say, gritting my teeth, counting to five before I continue. "For that, I'm not sure I can forgive you," the last sentence is said in a whisper, keeping my head low and using my back as a shield to avoid looking at the raw emotions I know I will see.

"I know. And I apologise. I never intended to treat you as a commodity or take away your choice, but if it means you're kept safe with me, then I will do the same every time." Still facing the coffee machine, I distract myself from his words by making an espresso.

The silence stretches as I breathe slowly to calm my racing heart. "Make another to take away, Elodie. We are late—there are pastries left by the cook, too." Gripping my bag, he heads towards the door.

Military trucks and armoured vehicles line the courtyard. The sheer number of soldiers preparing to move out brings reality crashing down around me. I never envisioned travelling, but with so many people all heading to fight, a tendril of fear worms its way into my mind: We are heading to the frontlines against the Shade army.

A rough hand grabs my upper arm. Even though I know who the culprit is by the way my magic stirs like a cat being stroked, yet I still jump slightly.

"Do you mind?" I growl, trying to pull my arm away. Ignoring my struggles, Alexander directs me to three large, protected, and armed to-the-teeth army vehicles.

"You will travel with myself and the King in the middle truck; the others are our armed guards. Get in and buckle up. It will be a long time before you sleep in comfort, assassin. " His mouth twitches at the idea of causing me discomfort.

"Great," I reply with an eye roll. "This is going to be such fun with your amazing personality!" I lay on the sarcasm as I climb the steps into the back of the truck. The Raven slams my door, moving around to the front into the driver's seat. Checking various buttons and screens within the truck, he's not wearing his usual warrior leathers but black combat trousers, a black shirt, and a black ballistic vest. Multiple guns are strapped to his body. Just observing him has my magic coursing through me in excitement; his nostrils flare, and turning, he fixes me with a look of pure hatred.

"Get a fucking grip on your magic, assassin." Rocking back from his intense glare I grit my teeth, hissing back at him.

"Likewise, Raven, I can feel you too, you know?" I'm aware that I sound like a child, but this man brings the petulance out of me. The door opens, knocking us from our standoff, as Barrett climbs in the passenger seat, leaving me in the back alone.

"Safety checks are complete. Hank is behind with the guards." Green eyes flick to the rearview mirror, locking onto mine for a brief movement, catching my reactions to the dragon shifter's name.

A loud bang on the roof sends both men springing into action, drawing weapons; the Raven is halfway out of the truck when he pauses with a string of curses and a glare sent my way. Understanding dawns as Pumpkin prowls down the front of the truck and sits to look through the windscreen at me, sorrowful eyes boring into my soul. Feeling the brush of his consciousness in my mind, I open up to communicate with him,

"Hey bud, what's up?" I speak into his mind

"I come?" It's a question that is given with a tilt of his head.

"It's going to get pretty dangerous, Pumpkin. I don't want you getting hurt." In the blink of an eye, the huge bird-cat-wolf-griffon familiar disappears and materialises in the back of the truck with his big head flopping into my lap.

"I protect so I come" With that he curls up beside me and I reach for the spot over his neck, I know he loves to be scratched: two sets of eyes look my way.

"He's coming with us."

It takes several hours to leave the city behind via the guarded gates. Our Convoy of three trucks branched off away from the army trucks full of soldiers heading to the front lines.

The three of us and Pumpkin sit in a strange sort of thick silence, emerald green eyes regularly flick to his mirror, checking. His mouth opens then closes with a clenched jaw, I meet his gaze but offer nothing, turning my attention to the view outside the truck.

The landscape is green, with various crops and big areas of mature trees. I have never seen such vibrant colours and so much space. The odd lone farmhouse dot the countryside, seemingly unravished by the war.

"Have you ever left the city?" Barrett's voice breaks my daydreams, shaking my head slightly,

"I barely left my dorm or Electric Eden," I huffed humorlessly. "The first time I travelled was to come to the palace."

"This must feel pretty daunting for you. The world is beautiful but fraught with danger at this time." He stumbles at my failure to respond to his attempt at conversation, shifting around fully in his seat to take me in, "We will travel through several areas before we get to the witches; that's many hours together in a truck, Wildcat...."

"Don't call me that," I cut him off. "Friends shorten friend's names or give them nicknames, not owners."

"Okay, then, I order you to have a conversation with me, Miss Whitlock. I will not spend days with you stropping in the back." A smirk pulls at his lips at the indignant look on my face. "Tell me something real about yourself."

"What the hell? Something real? Haha, you're the bloody King. Nothing you portray is real. You tell me something real". I add with quotation marks and an exaggerated eye roll "First"

"Okay. I never wanted to be king. I enjoy the pace of being a soldier, living life in the moment, never knowing what tomorrow will bring. The adrenaline is addictive." I see the truth in his words. Alexander keeps his concentration on the road, knuckles flexing, turning white at the death grip on the wheel. He does not like us conversing, casting a mischievous grin.

"I love to dance. The freedom to express emotions and capture an audience is intoxicating! Although I would prefer to wear more clothes, it kept me off my back and forced me to spread my legs to pay my way" I remove my jumper, stripping down to a strappy vest top, leaning forward through the middle of the truck. He keeps his eyes firmly on my face to give the king his due. Alexander, however, I did not miss the jerk of his head back to the road and his knuckles turning even whiter.

"You are an exquisite dancer." Barrett nods, leaning one shoulder into the seat and angling his body towards mine. "I hate wine," he declares, pulling a face. "And every fucking noble loves the stuff. It's overrated. Give me ale every day. yum" Exaggerating he licks his lips, tilting his head back in an impression of a common drunk.

Laughing, I allow myself to relax, the easy banter flowed. "I once collected swamp fairy snot and put it into Trixie's cocktails for a full week because she put me on troll service."

"What's troll service?" he laughs.

"Exactly what I say. We had to look after the needs of the trolls, and they stink, are always oozing snot and get very handsy! Luckily, I never had to service their sexual needs." I shudder my mind in the past.

"Shit, that is just plain nasty. Was she ill?" Chuckling, he runs his hand over his face, shaking his head in mock disgust.

"Oh yes, she had the shits all week. But it was nothing compared to entertaining that hideous letch." I shudder, closing my eyes tightly against the flashback of the slimy warty male who always tried to take things further. "Thank god for Hank." I smile softly.

"I'm guessing he protected you even back then." Too much pity enters his gaze, taking away the fun of our conversation. I give a one-shoulder shrug, push back into my seat, and turn to face out the window once more.

"I don't want those looks of pity, Barrett. I have had it better than most, pity gets me nowhere fast."

"It's not pity you see, Elodie. I admire you, your bravery and strength. Most in your situation would have crumbled or blamed the world for their lot, but you rise to the challenge."

"Stop," I cut him off with a sharp demand, turning to face him. "You know nothing, Barrett, nothing of how my life has been. You do not," I emphasised with a pointed finger, "get to butter me up with your charming words. I'm not some stupid whore."

"I never implied you were." His calm, rational reply stokes my anger. I find myself falling into this easy, comfortable camaraderie and flirtation every time we are together. The attraction on both sides is palpable, but I can't forget he bought me. My feelings were not discussed or considered like a cow at the market, even if Jenny was right. He is no better than Trixie. Turning and breathing deeply, I stroke Pumpkin, who begins to purr at my attention. He sighs deeply, leaving the heated subject and changing it.

"My mother still sends me a knitted jumper every holiday. A themed jumper, too, and I secretly love them." He laughs at the fond memory. However, it only emphasises the difference between our upbringing more.

"I have never even had a birthday gift." I aimed for a playful tone, but it came across as forced and sad.

"What, never?" Barrett turns fully in the seat again, giving me the full force of his attention. "What about holidays like solstice? the equinox?" I shake my head with a grimace.

"I'm sure when my parents were alive? But not that I can recall. Much of before, it was just a blur of jumbled, hazy memories."

We are quiet for a time. Barrett takes in my face, and I hold his gaze.

"I have never been in love," the statement comes out of the blue, shocking us both. Panic enters his eyes, running a hand over his hair. "Ha shit, sorry, that went deep pretty fast!"

Nervously, with his cheeks pinking slightly, he looks at Alexander briefly, remembering we are not the only two in the truck. "I do feel like it may be possible that love could be right in front of me." heat enters his gaze as he looks at me, raw emotions playing across his face, at a loss for what to say, knowing it should be a cutting remark something bitchy to show I'm way out of his league, but I just stare heart pounding, clearing my throat, I deflect,

"How long until we stop next? Did you bring snacks?" Accepting my change of subject, Barrett turns back to the road, looking to Alexander.

"We have to travel along the Western road to skirt around the silver marshes, avoiding the majority of the fighting." This time, the king is back; in fact, the amusement is gone. "Then we should travel into Northfield. The Witches are said to live in the forest before the Void and the Karayan mountain pass."

I picked up a map on a handheld computer and handed it back to show me the intended route. "We will stop a few times at local establishments. Nothing like the Palace, as we are trying to fly under the radar here, so be prepared to rough it."

"As long as I don't have to share with grumps over there" I nod in Alexander's direction " I will be happy with anything."

"Ha, you two would either hate fuck each other's brains out or explode and bring down the building." Barrett burst into hysterics as fury erupts over Alexander's face.

"Don't worry, assassin, your precious pussy is safe from my attention; I would rather sleep in a barn with farting trolls", he growls, struggling to control his temper, magical lightning dancing over his taught arms, smiling to myself at his reaction, I taunt further enjoying this aggressive sparring match he brings on himself.

"I always pegged you as a man of strange fetishes," I nod slowly in thought, fingers to my chin. I know some good contacts for people with your particular tastes. Can I hook you up?"

"Fuck you."

"Oh," I gasp in horror while Barrett struggles to hold his laughter, Alexander throwing him a warning angry look. "Darling, it's nothing to be embarrassed about. We love who we love. You don't need my boring plain old fae pussy to prove your worth to the world, No judgement here!"

Slamming on the breaks with a screech of tyres and a blare of horns behind the truck behind, "I don't fuck trolls," he snaps, turning furious silver-tinged eyes that spark as he loses control of his power too, panting hard, teeth cracking as he grinds his jaw.

The radio crackles. "What's going on? Report Raven." Hank command fills the truck. Alexander takes several calming breaths, as I burst into laughter throwing my head back. Barrett throws some snacks my way, chuckling before answering Hank.

"Nothing to report, Sergeant. Just Miss Whitlock testing the general's composure."

Waking with a jolt, the sky outside has darkened with the last rosy hints of the sunset painting the horizon. Wiping the drool from my chin to see where we are to find the truck empty. Sitting up stretching my aching limbs with a yawn. The trucks are parked outside a grey brick three-story hotel, the windows lined with the same dirty nets and pasty green curtains. Spying Hank outside with several security guards, I exit the truck.

"Hey," I offer a little shyly, after the session on the kitchen island last night we have not had a chance to talk.

"Elodie you're awake," he smiles broadly. "Finally. Barrett said to leave you." he begins to fidget, running his strong fingers over his top knot to grip the back of his neck. Since when did Hank fidget? or bloody smile?

"I need to introduce you to a few people travelling with us," he says, guiding me closer with one protective arm, an awkwardness creeps up my spine at Hank's friendly, unusually chatty 'new' personality. "This is Sergeant Zane Sampson."

An older, stocky soldier with a buzz cut nods in my direction holding his hand out for me to shake. "It's a pleasure, ma'am."

"Elodie, please," I smile taking his strong palm into mine.

Hank clears his throat,

"And this here is Lieutenant Helena Koshkin." A stunning, athletic female feline shifter swings her hips and embraces me in an overly friendly hug, purring a hello in a thickly accented voice.

"Hank tells me you are wicked with a dagger. You will have to teach me I rely too heavily on my own claws," with a suggestive wink over my shoulder to Hank, who scrubs his neck, avoiding all eyes around him.

"Ha! Yes, well, these two will be your main security during this trip. We all have rooms here for the night but will hit the road early tomorrow. Maybe grab a shower, then meet downstairs for food?" Hank nods, looking like he wants to be anywhere else but here, in my presence.

"Come, Elodie, let's find our rooms." Helena takes my hand, trailing the other over Hank's muscular arms.

CHAPTER 55

Elodie

The next few days were much the same: travelling by day and staying with Helena in small hotels by night. Barrett and I talked about anything but the fact that he owns me. Alexander avoided speaking, looking, and touching me each day.

Helena and Zane trailed me everywhere but provided plenty of entertainment with their stories of things that go on outside the Palace. By day four, we entered the town of Northfield. It's a bustling, beautiful town with sandstone houses set in rows alongside smooth roads, people and fae of all sorts mingling and going about their day.

Barrett turns in his seat to look at me (a regular occurrence these last few days), excitement etched onto his face. He watches me carefully for my own reaction.

"Welcome to Northfield," he said, beaming a smile with a flourish of his arm. "Once through this slow traffic, we will spend the rest of today and tomorrow here to replenish supplies and rest."

"Sampson and Koshkin will be with you, so don't get any ideas." Scowling back at me via the rearview mirror, Alexander ruins the mood once again. That man is a mood hoover.

"The first words you chose to say to me in days, and

it's a threat. It must be difficult maintaining this level of assholeness."

"I don't trust you," he shrugs, "I will not make things easy for you, simple."

"How did you become a general? Did you sleep your way to the top?" I ask, throwing a heap of sass behind the question. Barrett looks between the two of us, waiting to see what insults are thrown. He just needs the popcorn. He is so engrossed, with a smirk across his face.

"I mean, aside from the weird kinks."

"You seem awfully interested in my kinks again Miss Whitlock" I roll my eyes not taking the bait.

"You just seem a bit dense for The King's general." I indicate the view outside the truck. "I'm a million miles from anything and anyone I know." I inch forward, dripping venom. "And you three dragged me out here not the other way round. What could I possibly be trying to achieve?" I pause, locking my gaze with his as he turns to face me, arching my eyebrows. I wait for his response.

"You're a whore. I'm sure you are resourceful." Bang. My fist slams into his nose with a sickening crunch, blood runs down his face instantly. Before he can retaliate, Barrett jumps in.

"Woah, woah, stop it, you two," he glares at his friend. "You fucking deserved that, Alexander." he threw a few napkins his way to stem the bleeding. "Elodie is right; we brought her here. Engage your brain and get over this anger before you do irreparable damage" Barrett is almost shouting the anger at his friend.

To my surprise, Alexander nods, turning back to the road and muffling a quiet reply. "Nice punch."

My head snaps in astonishment to look at the dark, angry face sitting rigid; a small tug at his mouth shows he is fighting a smile. A smile directed at me. The rush of magic shocks the breath from me, and that twitch in Alexander's soft, full lips moves again. Slamming my shoulders back against the seat, Pumpkin grunts in annoyance at being disturbed, folding my arms to look out the window again, willing my heart, breathing and magic to still.

"Call me a whore again, Raven, and I will remove your feathers one by one before taking your balls. Am I clear?"

"Crystal," he grunts.....Probably the best apology I will ever get from the dark bastard.

We drive for another hour in silence before pulling up to a huge fancy hotel set in a semicircle of white stone Northfield Spa Hotel in silver swirling letters that sits elegantly over the pillars leading up steps to double glass doors.

"This looks fancy." Nerves coil in my chest. I have heard about these swanky hotels in which you are expected to conduct yourself in a certain manner and use the correct utensils and attire.

"Follow me, Wildcat." Barrett opens my door, holding out a hand for me to take, smiling at his infectious delight, "Did you pack a swimsuit?" He whispers in my ear and waggles his eyebrows at me. I frown in confusion.

"Of course not. Why? I don't swim." I begin to realise that this hotel will be much different from the others we have stayed at.

"Don't worry. I can't wait for you to have the full works and relax, have some fun, get pampered. I want to make sure you really enjoy yourself." He cuts his own rushed string of words off, ruffing up his curls and exhaling. He places an arm across the doorway to slow my progress as Alexander continues into the hotel, leaning down so his lips brush my ear, sending an involuntary shiver down my spine.

"You and I have things that need to be said." I turn my head to look up into those now bright sea-green eyes. You can predict Barrett's moods by the shade of those eyes. The space between our mouths was so close I could almost taste him, gently lifting his fingers to my face, running a thumb across my jaw, and taking the back of my neck.

"Sorry, look, can we-"

"Barrett, let's move before we are recognised." Alexander's sharp tone has us both moving off the street into the hotel lobby, nervous flutters spreading up my body and constricting my chest. This lion shifter has a way of charming the pants off me and making me forget all the pain and anger he has caused.

Barrett's suite has several bedrooms, a lounge, bathrooms, and its own bar. And holy shit, room service. My room has a super-sized bed that could easily sleep three or four people. Yes, my dirty as fuck new magic mind goes there, and I can't help picturing three broody, sexy men sharing that bed with me.

"Here, Wildcat," Barrett hands me a strip of fabric on a hanger, eyeing the material with suspicion.

"What is this?" I take the garment, the tiny black bikini. Raising my eyebrows watching the cheeky smirk pull at his lips.

"It's the only one they had," Barrett shrugs. "Look I wanted to apologise" he huffs a long sigh massaging the back of his neck giving himself time to formulate his words "I did not consider you or your feelings, I saw a problem and bustled ahead without assessing the full picture. I'm a total twat!" His green eyes lock onto mine, and I see the truth in his words. "I want us to start over. Let me make it up to you, starting with a full day of pampering." He spreads his arms wide, an almost shy, vulnerable expression so at odds with the confident, powerful King who is usually at the forefront. Maybe I need to let my guard down a little, too. He seems to actually care about me, and his methods may be a lot to be desired currently with the whole purchasing my debt yada, yada.

Staying quiet, I look between Barrett and the tiny piece of fabric in his hand, cocking and placing one arm on my hip, I raise one eyebrow, tilting my head as I observe the strong, handsome man in front of me, pursing my mouth in disapproval of the skimpy garment. He stammers,

"You know I don't have to be there with you. It can

just be you having a spa.... I have got lots of things to do anyway, you know, being king and all." Laughing, I relax my posture, taking the little black bikini.

"I've never had a spa day. I would love to relax a bit. You know, Barrett, I can't remember a day when I had nothing to do and no orders to follow, so this will be a treat. Thank you." I smile, landing a light kiss on his cheek.

The broad smile that lights up his face is breathtaking. I've never seen Barrett so playful, so childlike. Everyone sees the jovial king, the joyful, playful person, but never this spontaneous, impish man. How me agreeing to a simple day of relaxation has made his whole fucking day! Striding forward, wrapping me in his strong arms, swinging me around, kissing my cheek and then the other cheek.

"I promise I will be better and never make you regret trusting me, Elodie.

After several hours of my skin and muscles being kneaded, oiled, and rubbed, I can safely say I have never been so relaxed. My skin hums and glows, and the smell is delightful. Placing the well-worn book down, I move into the empty salt sauna, lying back on the bamboo benches, closing my eyes and inhaling deeply. Gentle music plays softly in the background as my mind envisions spending some time getting to know Barrett a little more on this journey, without the pressure of Lord Hamlington or Lady Carter being all-round twats.

Beads of sweat glisten on my skin as the temperature rises. A smile tugs at my lips as I think of how it would feel to explore Barrett's naked body if he was indeed accompanying me in this very sauna. How the droplets would travel over the ridges of his chest down his taut abs to the sharply cut V I have seen peeking under his shirt on several occasions. I feel my nipples harden at my daydreams and curse myself for allowing such a fantasy when, only days ago, I wanted to kill him with a rusty spoon.

A cool brush of air peppers my skin as the door to the sauna is opened. Alexander walks in with Barrett hot on his heels. They are deep in conversation and don't notice me at first. Barrett's muscular frame was fully on show in just pale blue swim shorts, hugging his strong thighs. Entering the room fully, they pause as they finally see who already occupies the sauna. Both sets of eyes drink me in, neither man saying a dam word. I stare with wide eyes, lifting up slightly on my elbows.

Barrett licks his lower lip, inhaling deeply, a hunger so potent I feel the heat rocket between us. Suddenly, I feel exposed, his gaze stripping me to my very soul, and his nostrils flare as my excitement rises.

"Wildcat," he almost purrs while skimming over my body and the tiny bikini. I feel the usual draw of Alexander's magic stroking up against my body in a gentle touch, pulling a soft moan from my lips, stealing my attention from the dark, chiselled body. The rush of arousal makes my pussy clench at the sight of his silver-rimmed violet eyes scorching lines of fire over my flesh. My pulse begins to race. Alexander is leaner but no less defined than Barrett, and the dark tattoos appear to swirl and move across his chest; my eyes track the contours of his body following the dark artwork, my own magic heightening, reaching out to discover the raw energy surrounding him.

The growl he emits is all sex and lust, which drives a flood of wetness between my thighs. My eyes travel the length of Alexander, evidence of his own desire, thick in his tight swim shorts. Our power collides, sending waves of pleasure rippling all over my skin. Tilting my head back, I emit another soft moan, my body taking over as my hand caresses down my stomach needing the release from the pent-up sexual tension his magic stirs in me. Alexander burns with desire as he steps forward towards me, muscles strained as he fights the desire to take me there and then. In one long stride, we are face to face, electricity crackling between us as he places a hand on either side of my hips body, towering over me.

"Control yourself," he hisses, sending shivers directly to my hardened nipples, the rush of desire tilting my face to his. Our lips barely brushing as another moan escapes me. That moan is his undoing. Unable to hold back, his lips crash roughly against mine as he drives my back down into the sauna's bench. Our tongues fight for dominance as I groan into his mouth, my mind short circuits, my body taking control, legs wrapping around his waist dry (or not so dry!) humping his thick cock that strains against the thin fabric of his swim shorts. Soft curses leave me as my body drives towards an orgasm, My magic sparking across my skin, adding to the sensual pleasure. His large hand roughly palms my breast, pinching one erect bud hard, gasping all control lost as my magic thrives against his, needing this release.

"Wildcat," Barrett groans. "You need to pull this magic back or you're gonna have two men devouring your body." Barrett's words only spark the electrical pull towards them both. I clamp my thighs around Alexander's waist, creating more friction as I try in vain to regain control of my desires.

"Control your fucking magic, Assassin." Alexander pulls my lower lip between his teeth, biting down hard with a growl. Barrett grabs him by the arm, halting his movements, muscles popping as he forces himself to stay in one place. Hovering over my panting form,

"I need more," I whisper on a breath as my hand cups my breast squeezing my nipple hard.

"Gods," Barrett curses and, with what seems like a monumental effort, dives from the room, coming back with an arm full of crushed ice, throwing the ice over me and Alexander, shocking our bodies. I let out a scream as my magic slams back into me.

"Barrett, what the hell?" I yell, trying to catch my breath as I glare at the men standing before me.

Alexander still hasn't moved. His glare hardening but still fixed on mine, hissing several curses as he turned and stormed out of the sauna leaving me in an aroused frustrated state. My body coiled tightly.

"Gods, do not leave me like this."

"Wildcat, gods, I really can't believe I'm doing this." he pauses, pinching the bridge of his nose and inhaling. "Shit... I would love nothing more than to sort that frustration out, Wildcat, but not fueled by magic after

Alexander has you wound up."

Coming to my senses slightly, the hot burn of arousal ebbing as my magic settled.

"What just happened?" I pant, giggling as my cheeks turn pink. I can't believe I've just fondled myself in front of the king while dry-humping his fucking general after he watched me sleep with another man on his kitchen island. He must think I'm a complete whore.

CHAPTER 56

The King

I stand staring at the raw, fiery beauty before me, the tug between us too hard to ignore. Her very essence calls to me in a way I thought I would never experience. I believed my life would be a series of consorts and random hook-ups, never being able to fully be oneself with anyone... until now.

The tension in the sauna is palpable, my Wildcat dropping her eyes, the pink glow still dusting her cheeks, clearing my throat.

"Are you okay?" She finally flicks those striking eyes on me, her smile quirking up at the corners, and nods. She sits up and subtly rearranges her bikini top. The silence deepens, trying to suffocate me.

"I was a prick to not consider you," I admit, slowly moving to sit beside her. My entire body aware of the heat and power radiating from her pearlescent skin. Resting my head back, my heart still pounding and breathing a little unevenly, focusing anywhere but the temptress next to me, trying to stop the throb in my cock. "When I'm around you, a possessive need surges," I sigh, trying to be honest with how I feel, "alongside a healthy dose of desire to make you mine that tends to affect my rational thinking."

"Oh," she stiffens, fixing her gaze on the wall of the

salt room, avoiding eye contact, a soft vulnerability coating her actions. I never meant to take things so far with this woman. It's just something about her, but seeing that flicker of hesitation, she pulls back, slamming the door, and locking away pieces of herself. I thought after the way we connected, the way she responded to me, that maybe, just maybe, she was ready to let me in, but now I am not so sure.

"I got a little deep there, didn't I? Sorry," the silence stretched, thick and unspoken. I want to tell her everything would be okay. That we can figure things out, take it slow, that this went deeper than just sex. Swallowing, trying to regain composure and slow the rush of emotions rising in my chest.

"Anyway, I think your magic is attracted to Alexander's and you both like what you see." I change the subject with a shrug. Rearrange my still-hard cock, which jumps as I notice the attention she gives it before looking away again. "Even if you don't like each other, It's a potent mix and a hard emotion to ignore."

"Sorry" she whispers, "I'm not usually this promiscuous," she sighs, leaning back again. "Ever since my magic awoke, my control has slipped, and my sexual desires have magnified." She closes her eyes, inhaling deeply, her still erect nipples rising and falling with her breaths, not helping the very hard cock still fighting to be let loose. Rolling my head, easing out the tightness in my neck and barking a laugh.

"You can say that again. Why don't you relax a little longer? We have dinner booked for seven with the rest of the convoy," I say, sitting forward. "I need a long, cold shower after all this." I direct my hand in her general direction, reminding myself that I need to build on the fragile trust we have begun to mould the last few days with this stunning creature and do things in a better way.

"I will do everything in my power to help you, Elodie," I declare, turning and capturing her hands in mine. Snapping her head up, she nods, holding my gaze captive, distrust swimming in her eyes still.

An uneasy feeling spreads in my gut for putting it there. Dropping to my knees in front of her, the urge to make her mine riding me hard, placing my forehead into our clasped hands.

"I know I'm the one that put that look in your eyes, Wildcat, and I don't expect anything from you. You have your freedom. I will not hold you to me."

Unable to look directly at her, knowing I could lose her if she decided to walk away, the primal hunger to devote my very being to her body, mind and soul, so alien but screaming at me not to give her the option to put distance between us but to keep her close.

"You can choose your path, Wildcat."

"Barrett," my name whispers on an exhale from her lips, sending a pang to my heart as I wait to hear that she hates me and that she wants as much space between us as possible. I swear my whole body and heart pause, chest tightening, unable to take a breath in anticipation.

"Look at me," her delicate fingers, so lethal with a dagger yet soft and warm against my skin, lift my chin, electric blue eyes peering into my very soul. "Thank you."

She places a small kiss to my lips, resting her forehead on mine before pulling back. With a small nod, I rise to my feet, towering over her small frame, noting the way she has filled out from the lean serving girl I first laid eyes on. Holding my stare, her lips close, with no further information on her plans, wishes, or thoughts.

Her face is a careful mask, not giving away anything. My lion growls and paces with frustration, demanding I make her mine. Holding that side of me back is becoming increasingly difficult the more time I spend with this woman. With a sigh, I nod again, my heart picking up its pace as my beast demands I take action to secure her attention, mark her as mine, protect her, and not walk away.

Pinching the bridge of my nose, I force myself to leave,

"See you tonight, Your Majesty"

Your majesty? Not Barrett? My hand freezes on the handle, my heart skipping a beat, sinking.

"Enjoy the peace Miss Whitlock," I reply formally without looking back, determined to give her this space and time to reflect. My beast is going wild in frustration within my chest. I may have just walked away from the one soul that makes me want to be a better person, my true mate.

CHAPTER 57

Elodie

We spent another day travelling, conversations stilted, and one angry-looking raven shifter sat at the wheel once again. His jaw-clenching gaze fixed on the road in front like it could somehow erase my presence from his mind.

He refused to say more than one word at a time to me, the heated kiss in the sauna burning in the back of my memory.

Heat and magic still dance alongside each other whenever we are close. I feel his essence burning at the edges of my consciousness, impossible to ignore. Now Alexander seems to have locked down his tightly.

How did I let things get this far with both these men? I need to create more distance between us and stop jumping into bed and giving in to our desires.

Today is worse. These men are creeping under my skin. Every day, we are together, close, with soft touches, lingering looks, Hank's protectiveness, Barrett's soft, green eyes connecting with easy smiles, his kisses, and my mind believing that whatever this was, could mean something! But what with two men? Three? I am a fool!

I've spent hours replaying the declaration from

Barrett. His offer of freedom and his assistance to help me control my magic simply let me choose my path. His words, not mine; after paying off my debt, he could clearly demand I stay with him, work for him, shit even become his consort. But what do I want my path to be? I've never been offered the option of a choice, the option to do something for myself. There are so many questions and possibilities. How would I make my own money? What do I want to be? What would I want to do? My mind tumbles with opportunities. I'm not sure where my talents lie because my talents were always driven for a purpose.

I know I'm good at dancing. I know I'm good with a blade, but where does that lead me career wise?

Sighing heavily and fidgeting in my seat, Pumpkin grumbles beside me, placing one large paw across my lap to keep me still. I need air and space.

Barrett's eyes snapped to mine. "Is something wrong?"

Wrong? How can he sit there so calm, so collected when I am emotionally spiralling out of control?

"No," I say, closing my eyes trying to avoid the feel of him watching me, his eyes burning across my skin, stirring something primal and dangerous inside me.

By night, we should be at the borders of the witches' territory. Hank has already briefed the others on the dangers of this area. I will get my space.

The witches are notoriously neutral when it comes to conflict, keeping themselves to themselves and holding onto their little nugget of power.

Nerves flutter in my gut as I snuggle into Pumpkin,

stroking his fur as he omits a rhythmical purr, lulling me to sleep. After dozing for several hours in the back, the murmurs of soft hissed voices between Barrett and Alexander grab my attention. Keeping my eyes closed and my breathing steady, I try to listen to their conversation.

"You were quiet last night. Is it the guilt, or do you realise your obsession is just that, Barrett?"

The king huffs at his friend's harsh words. Are they discussing me? I stay quiet, waiting for his response, but Barrett is quiet. The ruffle of fabric is the only indication of acknowledgement of Alexander's words.

"Did you fuck her?" Alexander hisses low, Just a hint of jealousy and anger. Confusion spins my thoughts around my mind once again at the back-and-forth moods from him, the passion of that wild kiss still fresh in my mind.

"Are you jealous, Alexander?" Amusement colours Barrett's voice before he sighs heavily. "But no. Quite the opposite, actually."

"Meaning?" Alexander growls, and I can imagine his knuckles gripping the wheel tightly.

"I gave her the option to be free of us. Once we have the answers and control she needs, it will be her choice."

"Choice to do what, Barrett? Run back to her employer, sneak in and kill you? Share her power with the enemy?"

"I will not cage a woman like her for my own selfish needs whether I want her to be mine or not."

I can almost hear Alexander's jaw grinding as he aims for control. "What happened to keeping her close in your bed to help you control her?" Raven's control slips, his magic pulsing from his body to lash out against my magic. "It's clear that you like the woman."

"I can say the same to you, Alexander. That kiss." A fake, exaggerated groan spills from the king's lips, ignoring his general's obvious outburst. "If I had not stopped you, it would've escalated, and I may have joined in."

"It's her fucking magic," he almost shouts slamming his fist in agitation on the steering wheel. "The pull drives me crazy whenever she is near," he growls. "When she lets go of that control, it's almost as if my magic wants to merge with hers. I've never felt anything like this before."

A growl escapes Barrett, more lion than human.

"You do not fucking touch her. Nobody touches her. Do you hear me?" The possessive demand makes me realise not only has the King offered me my freedom but he has done so against his basic instincts. He wants me enough to warn his friend not to pursue me.

"No need to worry, your pretty little mane, brother. I intend to keep my distance."

I gasp at his words, and the car goes silent, knowing I've probably been rumbled. I stretch against the seat, rubbing a hand over my eyes, my intense blue eyes connecting with violet ones lined with silver, sparks of electricity running through me. Holding my breath, we stare at one another before he turns back to the road, dismissing me.

"Hey, sleepyhead, how are you feeling?" Barrett's jovial tone completely contrasts the words he just spoke to his friend.

"Sorry, I dozed off," I laugh, shifting in my seat, my gaze moving between Barrett's and Alexander's. "I don't know how I'm so tired. I did nothing but sleep and relax yesterday. I don't think I've slept so much in my life!"

"We have another hour or so before we stop on the borders. From there, we will split as planned to enter the witches' territory." He twists in his seat, taking me in fully "Hopefully, Hank can work his magic and get us what we need?"

"Hopefully I can learn a few things. Or at least some control." The awkwardness and tension within the car escalate. Alexander refuses to even acknowledge me. I feel like I need to smooth things over between the three of us, now that I have relative freedom or at least the choice of freedom. What does that mean? Especially For the suspicious general.

"You must be tired, Alexander. Doing all the driving. You know I've never learned to drive," I chuckle, looking his way. "It was not one of the skill sets required for a money-making dancer or potential assassin." I joke a false lightness to my tone as I sit up and rearrange myself in the seat.

Dark purple, almost black eyes flick to the mirror, taking me in before dismissing me once again, focusing back on the road. Grinding my teeth and rolling my lip, the fact that he's unwilling to even attempt a conversation with me quickly sends my happy mood into anger and indignation.

"Alexander, I asked if you were tired." The command was clear in my voice, leaning forward against my seatbelt to glare at the dark, fixed mask of his face. A fake wide smile that does not reach his eyes appears,

"Sorry, I did not hear you." The smile drops, a sneer replacing it. "Or at least... Why would you be interested in whether I'm tired? We are not friends or even colleagues."

Fury heats my blood. I can feel my magic stirring once again. He feels it against his own because that's what my power does. It seeks him out and flirts with him whenever I get angry. Is he intentionally baiting me? Does he like it? I take a deep breath, trying to get my power and emotions under control, growling out my next words through gritted teeth.

"I'm just making conversation, you know." I cock my head, lips pursed in a small smirk, raising my eyebrow in question. "After you ravished my lips yesterday and then stormed out, it leaves a girl well and truly frustrated and a little confused with your intentions, Alexander."

Ha, you fucker take that. My self-satisfied smile widens while Alexander tries to turn the steering wheel into dust; straightening in his seat, his jaw clenches hard enough to break a tooth.

The chuckle from Barrett steals my focus as he leans back and looks at me with a playful smile on his face.

"Seems to be a lot of sexual tension flying around yesterday" Barrett takes in a thoughtful look, using his thumb and forefinger to stroke his chin. "I distinctly remember Alexander finding things particularly hard! before he left the sauna."

Barking a laugh, his emerald green eyes filled with mischief lock with mine,

"Yes, very hard and large indeed." I mock gasp, bringing a hand to my chest.

"Screw you," Alexander growls, pointedly engrossed on the road ahead.

"Oh, Alexander, language please, ladies are present," I school in a mimic of my old boarding house teacher. "I'm merely questioning your intentions towards me."

The truck lurches to the side of the road, its brakes slamming to an abrupt stop, and my shoulder hits the seatbelt hard.

"What do you need? payment?" vehement laces his tone as he swings back, immobilising me with his full scrutiny. "If it wasn't for your fucking magic, I wouldn't come anywhere near you." he spits. "Least of all kissing you. I don't even want to touch you, never mind fuck you, I scrubbed my skin red raw in the shower yesterday and can't bear to look at you—"

"Alexander," Barrett tries to reason but is cut off by a vicious glare from his friend.

"No. She is here at your request," he says, pointing a finger at me as he holds Barrett's outrageous glare. "You have paid a small fortune for some pussy that is sleeping with several members of your court."

Shaking his head in denial. "I know about Hank, Alexander, and it changes nothing."

"What about Alfie Roberts?" he shouts, then clarifies at Barrett's furrowed brow. "Lady Carter's known informant, a little bit of a coincidence, don't you think?" The sarcastic, cruel laugh sends a ripple of fear through me, my cheeks warming, and my heart begins to race at the impact of his words. "Lord Hamlington hired her, but is that all he bought? She seems to have no hang-ups sexually."

His words sting. My actions from the outside looked questionable, unseemly. *shit,* I look like a fucking spy! How could I be so stupid?

To them, to Alexander, I'm trained to seduce. Paid to enter the Palace and gather information, then connected with another informant, hanging my head in shame.

"Alfie? The arrogant, pretty boy, guard?" I hear the hurt and disbelief in his voice "You are sleeping with him too? I thought Alexander was just trying to get a rise."

My chest tightens at the mistrust in his voice, the man who has asked for nothing but offered me so much more than any other living person, hurt burning deep and tears welling behind my eyes, inhaling I refuse to allow my humiliating past mistakes be portrayed as shameful.

"It was a mistake. He was kind to me," I offer in a small

voice, lifting my head to look at Barrett. "I knew no one at the palace," I say, biting my lip to stop the tears.

I fold my hands in my lap, his green eyes darkening, his face turning it into a mask and shutting me out. I have no idea what he thinks of me. A hint of disgust pulls at his lips, causing my chest to tighten. That one look is like a dagger to my chest.

"Now you see why I have never trusted her?" Alexander slams the truck back into gear, no longer acknowledging my presence as the King turns his back to me, facing forward without another word. "Hopefully, once this is all over, we won't have to see each other ever again, Miss Whitlock and now everyone sees you for the worthless whore you are." Too shocked to respond, the tears finally breaking free to paint tracks down my cheeks.

The king says nothing to defend me, my lack of reaction shows my guilt. I feel sick to my stomach, just moments before I was thinking of my future, of walking away from Barrett and my past. Now, my stomach rolls and curdles at the thought of never being a part of his life. A sickening silence follows.

Pulling up to an old-fashioned bar hotel with a thatched roof and white-washed walls, Alexander and Barrett vacate the truck without a look in my direction, stumbling to catch up as people mill about organising our luggage and equipment.

"Barrett, please wait," I run to grab his arm. "Barrett."

Turning his face a mask of rage, jade green eyes cutting straight to my gut, towering over me with a growl.

"Remember your place, Miss Whitlock. I am your king!" He snatches his arm from my grip, dusting his sleeve with a look of disgust before storming away, leaving me frozen in place and shaken to my core. His judgement and distrust run through my very core, trembling as I try to hold myself together, my power driving through my veins and sending shocks to my heart.

Frozen in place, Helena moves close to my side, nudging one shoulder to mine.

"That was a dickhead move." She looks me dead in the eyes, a brave determination shining through. "Don't let them see your pain."

She strides away into the farmhouse tavern, leaving me standing. Her words awaken my reserve, taking several breaths, anger starts to replace the pain. How dare they judge me. Sleeping with three people in months makes me what? A whore? One of which is a long-term friend. How fucking dare they.

Fury rages, elevating my pulse, my power thrumming in every cell of my body. Squaring my shoulders, I follow after Helena. All my life after my parents' death, it's been me. Yes, I've had friends, and Hank was always in the background, but it was me! I have built a barrier around my heart and soul to protect me from the likes of this hurt. In the last few weeks, I fell into the idealism of a different free life where I could choose and make my own friends and love.

The King, I refuse to use his name, is no different to

anyone else; he latched onto the idea of saving me and having me close, to what we could be. Then, in the next moment, with a glimpse of my past, he can't handle it.

Treating me just like every other serving girl, like something lower than him. My mind is now made up. Once I have control, I'll find my own fresh start. Barrett, Alexander, and even Hank will just be distant memories. I will carve a path of my very own where the control is in my hands.

CHAPTER 58

Elodie

I don't see the king or The Raven for the rest of the evening. The bar area is full of our convoy milling about, quiet conversations, and the smell of food as we all relax after a long day of travel.

I sit with Helena in companionable silence. Hank has been at another table in the depths of strategies, his gaze meeting mine on several occasions. Finally, with a nod to a large soldier, Hank rises, bidding the table farewell and pacing towards me.

"Star—Elodie?" He questions seeing more than I hoped he would. Hank has a knack for reading me, even when I am at my most guarded.

"Hey," I respond, unable to muster much more enthusiasm. I know that whatever path I take, this dragon shifter will need to be left behind. If I'm to do this, I need a clean break from all who know me.

"Koshkin, you are relieved," he inclines his head away from our table. Helena rises with a good night and a quick squeeze to my shoulder, ignoring her superior.

"You okay with that, Elodie?"

I nod, giving her a weak smile, taking her hand in mine. "Thank you."

Hank's frame dominates the space between us, emotions locked down tightly, his face unreadable as he searches my own for hints, unable to hold his gaze, the embarrassment and hurt too raw to hide, the people working the floor become riveting as I turn to look anywhere but at Hank.

"Look at me." The command is low but leaves no room for rebellion.

Don't let them see your pain. Helena's words run through my mind. Forcing myself to meet his gaze, lifting my chin, setting my face in my stubborn mask, and mirroring his. A brief softness warms Hank's face, but it's gone in a heartbeat,

"Come," he says, inclining his head to the restaurant exit before heading in that direction, not stopping to check if I'm following, which, of course, I am.

A life of following orders and not having a choice is hard to reverse. We head down a corridor in silence, passing door after door, before stopping at 201. Withdrawing a key, Hank opens it and gestures for me to enter. The room has two basic single beds, a table and chairs by the window, and an ensuite bathroom. My luggage is set by one bed. Tiredness creases my eyes, which begin to well with more tears. My heart sits heavy in my chest.

"Sit.," he practically barks the command, obvious anger lacing his tone, the mask slipping as scales ripple over his bare forearm. I choose the chair by the window rather than the bed, which feels far too intimate in the small space.

"Can I ask why I'm here, Hank?" I ask, leaning back in the chair, folding my arms to a defensive position, watching as his hands clenched by his side in an attempt to control his dragon.

"Did you know there's been attacks on groups of soldiers? Every group that has females with them being targeted?" He turns to face me, his eyes ablaze with fury. "You're squabbling with the king in public, and now he's hidden away with his general when we are in danger. What is going on? You may as well paint a big neon sign saying 'come and get me' on your back, Elodie."

"What attacks?" I say, leaning forward and ignoring the dig about Barrett. With a sigh, he strides across the room and takes the seat next to me, rubbing his hands down his face as he leans on the small table between us.

"Starlight, if Oberon wants you, he will stop at nothing to get his hands on you. Think of the prophecy. Do you believe it a coincidence that you find a secret room, gain power and unlock some sort of innate magic from within yourself and the Shade army attacking the palace, looking for you." his eyes bore into mine. "You have to stay focused. You and only you are my priority. What happened in the car?"

His face softens, defeat pulling through his shoulders as he bows his head towards the table. I sigh and tilt my head back against the chair, looking up at the ceiling. My cheeks warm as I remember my humiliation at the hands of the king.

"Barrett seems to have a pretty idea of me, one where he rescues the poor little orphan girl, and they fall in love, and they live happily ever after, but we're not in a fairytale, Hank." Swallowing hard, I take a movement to collect my thoughts. "Alexander laid down a few home truths, or facts as he recalls them, least of all that I happened to have slept with another man in the palace, and he couldn't handle it."

I can't quite hide the wobble of my voice as I take a big, deep breath, the rejection stinging. Hank barks a laugh, leaning back and spreading his legs wide.

"He's a fool, Starlight. If only he realised a creature like you cannot be tamed by one man" A bright smile lights up his face, changing the stern dark features to something even more stunning, biceps flexing as he runs his hands through his top knot, undoing it so his hair falls free around his shoulders, chuckling to himself as he looks at me.

"Starlight. The King is jealous. You do know he watched us the other night?" The laughter erupts at one look at my shocked face. Hank knew he was there, too, but said nothing. "Let me tell you a little something, Starlight, dragons are a little bit like wolves. They find their queen, and she's so precious that one man is not enough to protect her. Typically, one queen would have at least two protectors, but I have seen more."

This revelation sends a mixture of shock and desire running through my body. The thought of not having to pick between Hank and Barrett sends a strange mix of emotions running straight to my toes, and by toes, I mean my pussy! my magic expanding, filling every cell.

But then my head reminds me of Barrett and how he

reacts. Controlling my racing libido, I begin to shake my head as I look at Hank.

"Hank, I'm not sure what you're suggesting right now, but I can assure you now that I have the option of freedom, away from all this," kicking off my shoes and stretching, "I will not be taking any protectors. I want to find my own place in this world, and if I can be as far away from the King and his General as possible, I think that will be for the best."

"Elodie, don't be foolish. I know your pride is hurt-" I cut him off sharply.

"No, Hank, Barrett, the king will never change. I can't stand around while his mood swings give me whiplash, never fully knowing if he's gonna take back my freedom." I pause, breathing hard, a new fear spreading through me. "Once I gain control of my power and I can defend myself, I will leave the palace." Hank takes my hands across the small table, calloused skin rubbing across my smooth hands. His fingers take my jaw, demanding I meet his gaze.

"Then hear this, Miss Whitlock. You have captured my very essence. I don't think I've ever said this out loud, but I am yours. I belong to you, every part of me. My thoughts, my heart, my soul they have all been yours from the moment I met you and will always be yours. You hold more power over me than anyone else, and that is not something I can control anymore. Where you go, I will always follow." The possessive need in his body radiates, rushing against my power, which purrs in response. His dragon is so close to the surface that I see the scales rippling across his arms, his eyes morphing into reptilian slits.

My eyes widen in shock, staring at him, my breath catching in my throat. Those carefully constructed walls crack piece by little piece. The raw honesty in his words, not said in the throws of sex or the heat of the moment. He truly meant every single word. I swallowed, whispering his name on a breathy exhale, which seemed to be the undoing of his control.

In a heartbeat, he has me across the table in his lap, my thighs straddling him as his lips crash to mine. Large hands grasping a fist full of hair, demanding and possessive. This close, I can feel the heat between us, intensity coming to the surface; I want nothing more than to toss all my reservations away and give in to that feeling once again. Our kiss deepens as I begin to roll my hips over his hardened cock, a potent lust causing me to pant for more.

"I am yours," he growls, kissing my neck and then sinking his teeth into the flesh, marking me. Gasping at the mix of pain and pleasure, driving my core against his hard length, his hands seized my ass, pulling me closer, the beast housing his body unchained, determined to claim me.

His hand grabs the side of my leggings, pulling them down over my ass, stretching my knickers aside, exposing my soaking wet pussy. His fingers quickly find my clit, pressing down hard, drawing a loud moan which he swallows with his hot open mouth, his short beard tickling my jaw and neck. His tongue licks over my pulse point, sending it skyrocketing. Moaning and arching into his touch, my skin alight. A hot hunger for this man leaving me breathless. I already feel the familiar build of tension as my muscles ripple with pleasure. Two fingers are suddenly thrust deep into my wet core fucking me hard, his thumb continuing to circle my clit, his mouth consuming every sound I make. I ride his hand shamelessly, pleasure building, the muscles of my cunt twitching around his thick digits. Hank rips my vest top off, yanking down my bra to suck and bite my nipples while his thumb expertly rolls over my clit, sending a wave of pure ecstasy pulsing through my body. I cry out, arching my back and driving my pussy onto his hand as I ride out the waves of my climax.

"Holy shit, Hank," I collapse forward, panting, body going limp as I twitch, riding out the end of my climax and kissing the grove between his shoulder and neck softly. Pulling back, I don't miss the satisfied smirk, which is absolute on Hank's face, as he sucks my cum from his fingers while holding my gaze.

"Beautiful," he sighs, "I want you coming on my cock next, Starlight, now strip." His strong hands lift me and deposit me on weak, shaky legs in front of him, a challenge laid down; his intense stare fills with heat as he takes in my rumpled just fucked state. I have never personally stripped for anyone. I'm used to being nearly naked and dancing on a stage, but that is not intimate or as raw as standing before a man who has just watched you come all over his hand!! Who has declared that he is yours? I find I can't look away. I watch the want on his face as I begin to slowly lower the straps of my bra, unclipping it and taking it all the way off to finish what he already started. Heat burns hotly as he grasps the base of his erect cock into his hand, firmly pumping. I begin to move seductively as the bra disappears, hands grabbing my hard nipples as my body aches for more stimulation, his lust burning a path straight between my legs, forcing myself to move agonisingly slowly, my leggings follow my bra to the floor, standing only in my lace knickers.

"Touch yourself," the command is guttural, animalistic, and sends a flood of desire. His demand causes my pussy to throb and pulse with need, my breaths shallow as I feel a second orgasm building just from the need in his stare. Driving a hand slowly down my stomach between my thighs, I pinch my clit, gasping at the contact. My eyes lock on the man in front of me as I bite my lower lip in anticipation of what's to come. A growl leaves his throat as he launches forward, capturing me by the hips and slamming to his knees in front of me. His mouth connects with my sex, feasting like a starved beast, his beard adding to the sensation, my legs buckle, but Hank holds me to him, supporting my weight as he fucks me with his tongue, teeth scraping over my swollen bud.

"Fuck Hank. Don't stop!" my hands grab at his shoulders, nails digging in deep, drawing crescents of blood. He picks up the pace driving his tongue deeper, sucking and biting my clit until I'm coming again, screaming his name so loud I'm sure the full building can hear me. Not allowing me to come down from my high, he stands, picking me up and throwing me onto the bed before stepping out of his trousers. He crawls between my thighs, my juices coating his face, a hunger for my body blazing in his eyes. Holding the base of his thick cock, coating the tip in my wetness before thrusting in hard, pain lined with pleasure drives a gasp from me as Hank's mouth devours my own once again. He begins to fuck me like the beast he is. I can only hold on as he drives his large, thick shaft at a furious pace, grabbing my hips to angle them for an impossibly deeper thrust. I feel another climax building, Hank's cock swelling, close to his own release.

"Mine," he growls as he takes my nipples in his mouth, biting and sucking hard pushing me over the edge. The pleasure becomes too much as my orgasm pulses around his cock his hands holding my hip, prolonging my climax, muscles tight around Hank's dick.

"Fuck." With a curse, he follows me with his orgasm, cursing and biting the nape of my neck hard, his dick twitching as his hips continue to pump slowly as his cum fills me up.

We still, catching our breaths, heart rates sky high as we collapse, slowly kissing as we come down from our combined orgasms.

"I am yours," he declares, eyes burrowing into my soul. I swear my heart stops at the conviction in his voice. My magic swoons swirling with Hank's power, at his sincerity and adoration, but my brain has other ideas. The part of me that wants to be free! to choose a new path. Hank is my past and present, but do I really want to take him to my future?

I tried to convince myself that our relationship was that of friends, that I did not need Hank in my life, but I cannot keep pretending that what we share does not have meaning that I am truly his creature, too.

The fear of rejection stops me from embracing his love that is being offered. This is a moment of trust and surrendering to our innermost primal instincts of acknowledging the risk and taking that step. A step I'm not sure I can or want to take.

A building panic at the thought of not having Hank, of starting out alone accelerates. He sees the indecision drawing up onto one elbow, one hand trailing fingers gently up my arm.

"I will be whatever you need me to be, Elodie, in whatever capacity you offer. Don't overthink things you can't control just yet." Holding a long kiss to my tummy, inhaling my skin, he stands, taking me with him to the bathroom, his mouth not leaving my skin.

"Hank," I laugh, wrapping my legs around his waist. "What are you doing?"

He turns the shower on with one hand, adjusting the temperature before he steps under the warm water. He lowers me slowly, our chests pushed up against each other, gently without a word, he washes my body, rubbing a soapy sponge over my collarbone down towards my breast, and ripples of desire trickle up my muscles. His expert hands roam over my stomach, heading between my legs, and my clit pulses in expectation.

"Hank, shit," I clench my thighs together over his hand, reaching for his hard cock, trailing my thumb over the tip, circling his pre cum. "Let me take care of you for once." I breathe, licking my lips, wanting to taste him, to bring him to his knees, to give him the same pleasure he has given me. Sinking to my knees, I run the pad of my tongue along his thick shaft.

"Gods Starlight, do that again." His eyes are fixed on me with raw lust. Repeating the move before I take him in my mouth, one hand stroking his shaft while the other tugs gently at his balls. Winding his hand in my wet hair, Hank begins to thrust into my mouth slowly at first. I pull away with a loud pop, fire setting every cell in my body alight. I need this. I need him.

"Fuck my mouth, Hank, don't hold back. I need to taste you." With a guttural moan, Hank thrusts hard and deep, making me gag, saliva coating my chin. Taking my hand, I press hard circles to my swollen clit, my cunt clenching, causing moans to vibrate over Hank's thrusting cock. Hank growls at me as he slams into me one last time, spilling his seed to the back of my throat. I swallow every last drop. My own climax follows quickly as I cry out around Hank's still-twitching dick.

CHAPTER 59

The King

Choosing a room adjacent to Elodie's was a mistake. The sounds of her moans and his name screamed in ecstasy drove me to a new level of torture. Unable to comprehend the monumental fuck up of my actions, cock straining to break free of my trousers, I stormed for a cold shower and several furious hand-released self-care. Followed by a few snatched hours of restless sleep filled with seductive dreams of a certain fae temptress. I can't explain the sheer jealousy that drove me to act like a complete dick head, letting out an involuntary groan. I don't want to share her with anyone, even her past. The lion in me wants to eradicate everyone that has ever touched her so it is just us. Angry at myself for judging her, my knuckles bruised and sore after the punch I sent Alexander's way for allowing him to speak to my mate with such derogatory language. Mate? Yes, mate! I truly believe that is who she is to me, I just need to prove to her that I can be worthy of her. The phone at my side blares to life. Grabbing the receiver, Alexander's voice is straight to the point.

"We are under attack, Shade forces, escape manoeuvres as planned, understood?"

"Understood.." Hanging up, I hurry to get ready for battle. Slipping into this side of the King is easy, second nature. I was born to fight. My lion form is huge, with deadly teeth, claws, and strength. Adrenaline rattles through my muscles, readying me for battle. Her face pops into my mind, and for the first time in my life, I feel panic. I must protect her. Elodie Whitlock has never seen war, never seen bloodshed on a huge scale.

***

Several minutes later, I stand outside room 201, knocking and waiting. I roll my shoulders, fingers gripping and releasing, heart pounding, and the need to protect rife.

The door pulls open Hank's semi-naked frame, filling the doorway with the smell of sex pungent on the air. My head snaps to the bed to the dark-haired beauty clutching the bed covers to her naked chest; the churn of jealousy sickens me like a punch to my stomach.

"Your Majesty?" Hank moves to block my view, jolting me from the turmoil of seeing her in another's bed; the urge to kill the dragon shifter is so overwhelming that I want to shift and tear his throat out, a low warning growl escaping me.

"Barrett, snap out of it," Hank straightens. Gritting my teeth, I growl, moving closer to the glare in his face.

"We are under attack. The thing has caught up to us, ready for battle and evasive manoeuvres." Instantly, Hank is all business, throwing the door wide as he marches into the room.

"Elodie get ready, strap your daggers on." Moving into

the room, I watch, mesmerised as she drops the bed sheet, revealing pale, smooth skin and small bruises marking her hips, breasts and neck as evidence of his claim. Without even acknowledging my presence walking past me on the way to the bathroom, my eyes follow her every move. Finally, our eyes connect through the en-suite mirror, a knowing smirk playing at her lips before slamming the door shut. My heart sank, and a bitter taste filled my mouth.

"How many? What are we dealing with?" Hank is focused, easily slipping into his military role, oblivious to my gut-wrenching jealous thoughts as he checks and lays out weapons, strapping several to his body.

"Unsure. Alexander is out front. We need to get outside quickly." He nods as Elodie emerges, quickly striding to the weapons laid out by Hank, who begins helping her secure them to her body; the familiarity between the two is one borne of many years in each other's company; they are comfortable with each other's touch. Hank runs his hands over her in soothing, gentle caresses, the odd squeeze, a thumb ran up her neck, light kisses to her head, forehead, and shoulder, almost carrying out the movements without noticing the contact.

The look in her vibrant eyes is so pure and captivating that I find myself unable to look away from them. The look was so different from the hurt I placed in her eyes yesterday, the visual replaying vividly of me destroying her trust once again. The heart-stopping awareness that this woman is not mine, that my actions have pushed her further away into the arms of another more worthy protector.

In the car, I felt foolish. Everything Alexander said made sense. How she instantly caught my attention. Within weeks, I had her in my rooms and my every waking thought on her. People have tried to play me since I became King, manipulating and conniving their way into my inner circle. I'm never sure of people's intentions, leaving me anxious and insecure. The moment I saw the guilt and shame on her face, all those self-doubts rushed to the forefront. I could not deny how things looked, even now, while my body screams for me to embrace the wild creature who stole my heart and reassure her that I care and want her and only her! I don't care about her past or what brought her to the palace.

Hank drops his forehead to hers, gripping her narrow, delicate shoulders.

"Remember your training and stay close to one of us. They are here for you. Don't give them an easy target, Starlight. You own my heart; do not break it being a hero. Run if you have to." With a brief kiss, he ushers her towards me out the door, nodding a command for me to get moving. He matches my stride as we head out of the hotel.

"If I can't protect her," Hank grunts in a low whisper, "promise me you will sort your shit out and step up, Barrett." I don't need to question who he is talking about. Our eyes fixed on the woman confidently heading towards the battle ahead of us.

"I will keep her safe and alive, but that's all I can give right now, Hank." He nods.

"I don't know her whole past, but the view Alexander paints is way off. I know she feels something for you, and there are only so many times you can knock her down before she walks away for good. Hell, she may already be there."

"I can't ignore the facts, Hank. I am the king, and you're so close to her. Who's to say you're not a plant as well?" Rubbing the back of my neck. "You clearly care for her too, Hank. Gods, you're sleeping with her." I laugh at the absurdity of the situation. "I heard it all last night. Yet you're encouraging me to what? ...Pursue her?"

"Dragons want their queen protected. I feel the way her magic pulls towards you. Will you deny your own feelings over pride?" he shrugs, watching Elodie as she stops looking back at us, raising one eyebrow in question, cocking her hip.

"She is fucking special, Barrett, I feel her power; I know your beast calls to her too." he locks eyes with me, intense power glaring from him, eyes wide, but his features softening, taking on a faraway look under some sort of mystic power. His voice changes becoming softer as he states:

"Protect her, fail, and we all fall, and we will be no more."

"Hey, are you two coming to fight or stay here and share your feelings?" Her voice snaps Hank out of the strange trance. A deep furrow lines his brow as he rolls his shoulders, purposely walking to Elodie's side, one hand placed on her lower back. A strange sense of foreboding anxiety claws at my chest. Was that a warning from some strange sort of prophecy or magical being, fate?

There's something about her that doesn't fit. Is she the key? Are we all just chess pieces on a big board being manipulated by a bigger force? We near the front entrance of the hotel, and sounds of screams and carnage erupt, filling the air with the stench of fear and panic.

A roar rocks the foundations as people begin to flee in panic. Drawing a gun, I summon my magic we begin to sprint. Gunfire sounds outside the hotel as we exit, taking cover behind a military truck. The military entourage we arrive with is engaged in various fighting with Shade forces, and a truck tumbles through the air, crashing into the side of the hotel. Following the destruction, an inhuman clay giant appears across the car park, laying waste to several people with one swoop of its huge forearm. A group of soldiers try to take it down.

Bullets don't have any impact, simply absorbing into its flesh, not slowing it down at all. Alexander is there in his semi-shifted form, colossal black wings out behind him, fire coating his arms with a giant broadsword expertly twisting and turning, trying to take out limbs with double-handed strokes of his sword. The creature seems to hold no pain, swatting at The Raven like a fly and sending him to crash to the ground between parked cars. The creature's huge foot crushes down over a car. The Raven narrowly avoids the impact, rolling and jumping up to take another hack at the tree trunk legs.

"What the fuck is that thing?" I looked to Hank for answers. Eyes wide as I take in the carnage.

"A Gollum," he curses. I haven't seen one for hundreds of years. You need serious magic to create one and a shed load of power."

"What does it want? Hank looks at Elodie and then to me, his mouth tense, lips pulled tight.

"I can only suspect it is you. You take a piece of your enemy's blood or hair, then send it after said person." He pauses, breathing rapidly as anger bubbles to the surface, a semi-shift appearing across his body. "And that thing will not rest until it has the owner of the substance in its grips."

"Shit" she gasps looking at me, Lady Carter. She pricked me the other day, drawing blood, and she hacked off my hair." She punches the car we are seeking refuge behind growling out curses. "The fucking bitch!"

I rise, peeking over the car. My own cousin is working against me. She was always power-hungry, but the betrayal hurt all the same. I will deal with her later. "How do you stop it?"

"We can hack it into pieces, which will buy us some time. It will take a couple of days to recover. The only true way to kill it would be to kill its maker."

"Fuck."

"Barrett, get Elodie to safety. I will help Alexander take this fucker down" Hank draws his sword from its scabbards while grabbing a rocket launcher from the back of the military truck. Elodie halts his movements,

"Hank... I want to fight." Growling, the dragon locks its reptilian eyes to mine.

"Get to safety, Starlight. Don't argue, Barrett." He nods, placing a kiss on her forehead before striding purposefully into battle. Knowing I need to get her away from this fighting to the awaiting trucks, as per our escape plans. I take her hand. If the Shades are truly seeking her out, then she must be important, and this conflict is about to escalate.

"Come on," I say, pulling her closer I place a hand around her waist. "Let's take out as many of these fuckers as we can, Wildcat."

CHAPTER 60

Elodie

Sparring daily with Hank has conditioned me. It made me strong and fit, but fighting in a battle is exhausting. Barrett is a marvel to watch, fiercely moving with a dancer's grace with lethal accuracy. Keeping me slightly behind him as he engages the Shade army, disposing of the fae in front of us easily. Throwing my daggers, I disarmed soldiers trying to advance and take Barrett unawares. He is yet to shift, choosing to fight close to me, protecting me.

"Thanks," he grunts, grabbing my upper arm as we sprint around the back of the tavern towards the rear staff car park. We slide to a halt as a mass of soldiers blocks our path, forcing us to draw apart and breathe hard. I see the indecision on Barrett's face. He will be more effective as a primal lion. Looking my way, I nod.

"We fight."

Barrett draws a wicked sword from his back, lunging forward and swinging it in an arc. He clashes steel against steel, sparks flying as their blades meet. Twisting, he brings his sword around with a practised, confident thrust, impaling the orc. Slicing upwards, he swings, moving to the next man in his sight.

Taking my gun, I aim and shoot a tall, dark elf several times, blood spraying from his wounds as he falls to the ground dead. The shots echo in my head as I stare at my kill, his eyes glassy, blood oozing from the holes I created. Retching and stumbling, I turned to vomit, panting in shallow breaths, I had taken a life, my first kill.

"Elodie move!" The roar of the King snaps me to attention. He is fighting two grotesque horned creatures down to only one sword. He sidesteps, bringing his sword up to block the force knocking him to one knee.

"Barrett!" I scream as he rolls to avoid the attack, springing to his feet with an agile backflip. A growl behind me has me diving out of the way of an attack from a goblin. A powerful air blast sends me tumbling into a tree, knocking the wind from my lungs, my head cracking hard into its surface, my vision blackening with spots. I see Barrett burst into a huge lion, ripping the head off his last opponent, roaring, golden fur and muscles galloping towards me. The goblin spins, throwing wooden spears Barrett's way, screaming. My power erupts, fire and air mixing to create an inferno of molten heat, sending the deadly blast to engulf the goblin, who explodes into piles of ash.

Before Barrett can reach me, a troll the size of a bus crashes through the trees, hurling a wicked swing at the lion shifter. Barrett leaps to the side, rolling before spring and engaging the giant monster. Huge paws slam into the troll's chest, flames coating the tips of sharp claws, tearing and burning into flesh. Scrambling backwards with a cry of pain, the troll throws jabs into Barrett's ribs. Huge jaws tear chunks into its colossal shoulders, latching teeth over the troll's neck. Barrett's lion form holds firm.

Taking my last two daggers, movement catches my eye. Low, deep growls rumble from the shadows. I freeze my eyes, scanning my surroundings. Snarling two dark hell hounds, red eyes fixed on me, spring, teeth bared, their powerful bodies primed to attack, lunge for me. My magic flares with the increase in adrenaline, infusing my daggers with a molten hot power, reacting on instinct, throwing my first dagger. The sickening sound of the sharp metal sinking into the eye of the first hellhound, stopping it dead in its tracks, fire spreading over its face and body, turning it to ashes before my eyes. I spin, barely having time to raise my next dagger before the dark, massive hound crashes into me, jaws clamping down on my shoulder, sharp pain shooting as its teeth pierce my flesh. I scream out in pain. Its superior weight pins me to the ground as we roll, arms shaking my power heating my hands. I punch and stab furiously; an excruciating howl leaves the hound, and saliva and blood pour from its mouth, collapsing on top of me: my third kill.

Crawling from the beast, my vision darkening, my head pounding as I open my eyes, the trees spinning around me, stomach lurching as my magic stutters inside me. I try to stagger up from under the collapsed hellhound, nausea making me retch and vomit the remaining contents of my stomach onto the floor. Wiping my mouth, I scan the area for Barrett; evidence of his struggle with the troll spills all over, but there is no sign of them. Pumpkin is fighting in the distance his winged form battling to get close to me.

My left shoulder bleeding and hanging dislocated,

pain throbs with every movement, and my breaths were shallow.

"Get to the truck, Elodie," I prompt myself, staggering to the nearest tree to catch my breath, summoning every last ounce of strength. Rounding the corner, I see the trucks waiting. With a surge of hope, I move quickly towards the vehicles, making it. I pull the door, whispering for Barrett, head spinning, vision blurring further.

A dark laugh sounds. "Wow, you're her double," A grunting, ugly goblin rounds the truck, swinging a black spiked bullwhip, blood and gore sticking to the ends. "And all alone! Ripe for the taking."

Pulling my gun with trembling, weak hands, I fire, but nothing happens.

"Oh dear. All out. How unlucky." he gloats. "You are mine now." A harsh laugh bellows. He moves quickly, the whip connecting and wrapping around my arm, digging in tight blood and wheeling up with the multiple wounds. Pain burns up my arm, my vision blurring again as I fight to stay conscious, and poison floods my veins from the whip wrapped around me as he pulls me closer.

In one instance, I'm in front of the goblin, rancid breath adding to my nausea. Swinging blindly, knuckles cracking against his ribs weakly. I am yanked forward, and a punch I do not see coming connects to my temple. Shock waves ricochet through my jaw. Pulling in the dregs of my power, I force an air blast his way, making him stumble to his knees with a grunt.

"Elodie, down!" the voice of the Raven bellows as I drop to my knees on instinct. His sword swings and impales the goblin straight through his chest. Pushing the body from his sword, the goblin goes limp before me. Skidding to his knees in front of me, the Raven releases me from the poisoned barbs, gently helping me to my unsteady feet. Strong hand cradling me, supporting my weight. "Hold on" his stunning face looks full of panic, lifting me carefully and placing me into the truck. Gasping in pain and fighting for consciousness, as the poison courses through my veins, head rolling. "Shit, shit, just hold on, okay?"

"Alexander," I breathe, relaxing slightly knowing, hoping I'm safe. My vision darkens again, stars flickering and pain radiating up my arms, spreading into my chest as it becomes difficult to breathe.

A high-pitched scream echoes around the car, taking several moments to realise I'm making the noise. Vaguely, I hear the truck doors open and a foul liquid forced under my nose. Drink, or you will die, Elodie. The smell turns my stomach as I turn my head away, gagging.

"Drink." My nose is pinched, making me gasp before the liquid is poured down my throat. Coughing, I struggle against the hold of Alexander, completely exhausted, head spinning; I swallow. "Don't worry, I will get you out of here." He places a blanket over me and secures my seat belt. I watch with a fuzzy head, the pain already clearing, my body starting to relax, and my arms going limp.

I cling to consciousness as Alexander jumps into the driver's seat, starting the truck. "Han...k, Bar... the others?" I croak, looking into the dark blue eyes of the Raven. A smirk looks back at me.

"Don't worry. They will be fine now that you're safe." A jolt of fear and confusion pulls at my subconscious before my head lolls and sleep overtakes my body.

CHAPTER 61

Hank

Roaring, my dragon form finally pulls the head from the clay Gollum, rendering it broken into enough pieces to immobilise it. The car park and surrounding area are in total chaos. The ground trembles beneath my feet as I descend, folding my wings. Turning, I spy the king, majestic in his lion form, taking on several Shade soldiers, blood flowing from wounds inflicted during the battle. I soar down to aid him, looking for my light, scanning the area for the one woman who holds my heart. I unleash a torrent of flames, incinerating two soldiers, turning them into chard corpses, screams echoing all around me as people flee.

Attention back to the fight, a group of goblins surge forward, flanking me, aiming ice spears foamed with magic, trying to locate weak spots in my navy-armoured scales. Swinging my spiked tail, I send them flying like toy soldiers, spinning to attack another dark fae, clamping my jaws around him, lifting and flinging him aside, broken.

Barrett and I fight side by side, taking out the enemy quickly as a team. Looking for my next enemy, we notice a lull in the fighting, and soldiers retreat. Panting, I shift back into my bipedal form, blood and sweat coating my massive frame. Barrett changes, grabbing a discarded sword and gun from the dead soldiers at his feet.

"Where is she?" I growl, frantically checking through the piles of dead bodies. The stench of blood fills the air. I inhale trying to pick up her scent. Spinning wildly, my heart hammering in my chest, grabbing Barretts dirty, blood-stained shirt. "Barrett, where is Elodie?"

"We were ambushed and outnumbered. She was right here with me fighting," he grabs his hair with both hands, scanning the battlefield.

"No, no, no, I saw her take out two hellhounds and make for the car park."

"Elodie!" I scream her name, voice cracking with panic. I can't lose her. Not now, please, not now. A flash of dark hair, a female sprawled face down, has my heart leaping into my throat, pushing closer, I grab her, cradling the body in my arms.

The dead, vacant, brown-eyed stare of a wolf shifter was not hers. Relief allowed me to take a breath, steadying my thoughts.

"Hank the staff car park, she may be there." Barrett takes off at a fast pace, the battlefield now quiet only the odd distant sound of any fighting still under way.

"The Raven?" I ask, as the bird shifter had left, letting me finish the Gollum and engage in more fighting. The king grunts with a shrug. "Never saw him after we left you." Entering the car park, our trucks have gone, and something doesn't feel right. A wheezing goblin lies in a pool of blood, holding on to consciousness half dead. I lift him in one hand, his face full of lethal fury.

"Where is she?"

The beast coughs a blood-filled smile. "She is her double, is she not?" coughing again, spraying blood onto my chest and face.

"Where is she?" I punch him in the face, causing his head to roll and breathe out a wet, bloody rasp.

"Ha, he has her now. My sacrifice will be celebrated." Fury at his words burns bright. Taking my hands, I rip his head clean off his shoulders, roaring to the heavens, exploding into my dragon form, taking and to the sky, the forest north of the Silver Marshes rushing below me. Exhaustion pulls at my muscles, but I have one thought: Elodie, I must get to her.

Mile after mile, I fly, searching for any sign or pull of her essence. The dragon within me was growing increasingly frustrated with the lack of evidence, refusing to give in to the exhaustion, wings beating hard, head moving left and right, scanning the ground below. Roaring, causing the trees to shudder and the ground to tremble below, my magic churning, looking for a threat, readying for a battle. The need to destroy whoever has touched what is ours pounding in my chest.

My magic warms, sensing her. Alive she is alive. Hope surges as I follow the pull, her magic calling for mine. Roaring, I dive towards the tree line. Pain explodes in my chest as my wings falter, breath ragged in my lungs. Crying out, wet splatters of blood coat my body and face, vision blurring as I call out again. So close, she is so close.

Another shot of pain tears through my wings, and I feel my bones shattering. My breath catches as my wings finally fail, spiralling down. The ground rushes to meet me with the full awareness that I have been hit. I crash to the Earth. Dirt and gravel exploding on impact. Before I black out where I lie, my last thought of the dark-haired beauty is that I have failed.

The End.

AFTERWORD

Curious to find out what lies ahead for Elodie, now that she has fallen into the hands of the enemy? Wondering what fate has in store for the men who hold her heart - will they survive the trails that await?

Follow the tangled web of loyalty and deceptions in the Raven's betrayal, and uncover what the future holds for them all.

The journey continues.... Coming 2025

                    Follow:

Grace Williams Author

grace_williamsauthor

ACKNOWLEDGEMENT

First and foremost, I owe a huge thank you to John for getting me started on this journey. Without his initial nudge, this book might have remained an idea. My deepest gratitude to my incredible husband and children - thank you for your patience, humor, and for putting up with my endless book talk: I couldn't have done this without you , and I'm beyond gratefull to have you by my side. To my family, thank you for understanding the late nights and the distracted conversations - I owe so much to your support.

Andy, your advice and encouraging words gave me the confidence to keep pushing forward; thank you for being in my corner.

Rebecca, your honesty and unmatched grammar skills saved me more times than I can count.

Catherine, every full stop you suggested was a needed reminder of the power of precision - thank you.

And Lucy, your enthusiasm and praise kept me motivated when I needed it most.

Finally; To everyone who took the time to read, encourage, and support me; I'm deeply grateful. This book is a testament to each of you.

ABOUT THE AUTHOR

Grace Williams

I was born in a British military hospital, and spent my childhood located wherever the army needed my father, until settling back in the North East of England, where I now spend most of my time.

With a love of animals, especially my failed foster animals and horses, my ginger mare certainly adds a different type of spice to my life!

To sum me up plain and simple: I wear my heart and emotions on my sleeve. I love and protect those I deem friends and family, fiercely, and I swear and cross social boundaries far too much for polite society.

Writing turned from a reading obsession to a hobby and then all of a sudden I wrote a book! I'm inspired by many, encouraged by a few and fuelled by a boatload of coffee and dark chocolate to keep me functioning daily.

Like the lady I am!

I like to read and write porn... Think romance with a little bit of spice, that will keep your bed sheets warm and Love Honey in business!

Printed in Great Britain
by Amazon